From Whence They Came

The Harbingers Cycle
Book I

Natalie Horn

Disclaimer: The resemblance of the following situations and characters to any real-life situations or characters may or may not be entirely coincidental. A lot of research went in to writing this book. Though it is true that nothing is based *entirely* on one person or thing.

This book is dedicated to my mum, for the "What if?" and the sweet tea; to my dad, for saying he would read it just from hearing a paragraph or two, despite not being an avid reader; to Julia, for making sure her written counterpart did her justice and warming me up to the nickname "babes"; and to British English, for letting itself be gratuitously used in all my writing, as it is the proper way of things.

Part One:

In Which We Dive Into Liquid Poison

NATALIE HORN

Gearheads at War

October 9th
Los Angeles, California

Aiden Kinsey

I don't know where I am, but this pile of bin bags makes for a lousy bed.

No, not *bean bags*. Bin bags. *Bags* that go in *bins*. Got it?

The thready beat of the music from the stereo echoes through my ears. Someone needs to turn that shit down; can't they see that people are trying to sleep? Unconsciousness is close, but avoiding me, like that guy at the party who can't decide whether he wants to keep drinking or try out his mediocre flirting techniques on the nearest girl. Six shots and a beer will do a lot to someone's self-confidence. Make it disappear in the madness, along with his hat and his wallet, and possibly his cell phone. And his shirt.

I'm that guy tonight.

Just — double the amount of shots and beer. No, let's get more specific: twelve shots of cheap vodka, plus tequila that tasted more like paint thinner, and two beers. (I'm not counting what I drank before even setting foot inside this house.) The party ended an hour ago, yet no one's bothered to turn off the damn music. Is it really that hard to crank a knob to the left? Is it *really* that hard? Probably, considering I haven't risen from these bags and done it myself. I blame it on the drugs. Not the alcohol—the drugs. I can't remember how much of those I've done, either. It's been one of *those* nights.

You know why it ended up this way? Because *I* wanted it to. No other reason besides that. If I'm taken to court, they can't make a plea for insanity; I'm not out of my mind. (That didn't happen until right after I dropped acid.) Other than that perilous twenty minutes or however long it lasted, I've made my own choices. There's been no outside persuasion or influence. Yes, at one point, making these terrible decisions would've been a huge deal and really messed things up for my future. But my time for such a thing has come and gone — and stayed gone. I'm twenty-three and part of the extensive, yet highly welcoming, deadbeat community of Hollywood Boulevard. That's the way it's going to be. No more "future" for me; besides, I live in the present. Which is basically all this stuff. All night, every night. Same shit, different day. So it doesn't matter.

However, there's some good news: unlike half the people in this room, I actually have a house of my own. (Is it pathetic that I consider this to be *good news?*) I live in a big blue monster with my adopted sister and, you guessed it, *no parents.* What happened to them? Don't have the capacity to give a damn anymore.

I decide that I don't really want to fall asleep on some person's random crappy bin bags. If I'm going to go comatose, let it be under the weight of a hand-woven quilt with a pillow tucked beneath my head. The same head that is swimming in protest, screeching at me about just how much I've managed to put in my body over the course of a few hours. As punishment, my limbs refuse to work. I find I am face down, one hand flailing aimlessly on the surface of another bag, while the other's crushed under my hipbone. I'm obviously getting really far in life.

"Come *on*, you stupid son of a *bitch*," I grumble. My lips grind against the rubbery bin bag and the clashing textures shock me into propelling myself quickly backwards. So quickly that my knees buckle, unable to let the weight shift happen smoothly, causing me to crash onto my ass and blink up at the ceiling like some sort of toddler who just lost tug-of-war. And of course, the ceiling just so happens to be super interesting to me.

Not many of the ceilings in California houses I've been in have those patterns that make it look like someone shot a paintball gun at it. The splatters remind me of another place I used to call "home"; I shake my head rapidly to get rid of those nasty little thoughts. Otherwise, I'll be stuck here, letting my imagination happen on that white ceiling and never getting back to the heartless place I now live in. It takes me long enough to do shit without being distracted. And the music coming from the other room, the stereo system that someone left at *almost full volume,* is distracting enough.

The steady pulsing of the beat has me bobbing my head up and down, one hand reaching for the edge of the nearest table to assist in me standing up. I'm still high as hell — *so* high, in fact, that this track makes me feel like even standing up is the climax of a fantasy novel. A crackling noise comes from my left; someone's cellphone rings off the hook, emitting that stupid Nokia tune that's been around for ages. A mom calling, worried about her daughter; a girlfriend, wondering why her boyfriend isn't home; an uncle, confused as to why his nephew quit on their habitual game night and still hasn't come back from that supposed study session right down the street. Bunch of lying bastards, these street urchins. They should appreciate what they have and be honest with the people that love them.

(Like I should talk. Aiden Kinsey, preaching honesty. Now there's a crime.)

All I've ever been is some sort of confusing paradox walking blindly through the night, telling lies about a self I didn't know and still don't. All I know is that right now, the self has tattoos and kohl-rimmed eyes and dyed-black hair. That's it. Might be able to know more later on, when the table I grasp isn't made up of coloured fractals and jagged flashes of light. There had to be something more than acid in that tab. That stupid tab with the Kool-Aid man stamped on it. Ironic, right? My childhood haunts me even through the drugs I take. Just proves to me no matter how much I try to escape, I never can.

I need to get out of here. This cookie-cutter box of a house isn't doing me any good. I'm already low enough without this atmosphere of desolation weighing down on me. I push myself from the table and stumble over someone's haphazard legs sprawled several inches apart, landing against the wall. Someone decorated said wall with scarlet and indigo paint, which of course hasn't dried; it sticks to my fingertips, my palms, and my entire left side, making me even more of a chaotic mess. The flashing neon strobe lights in the living room, in in time with the stereo, render the colourful strokes into little more than bloodied slashes.

You are a dead man. You are a hollow man.

No, dammit. The hallucinations can't start until I get home. Maybe those bin bags wouldn't have been so bad after all, but it's too late to go back to them. I find my shirt slung over the arm of a love seat and cling to it, wadding it, wrinkling it in one hand. My wallet's underneath the table holding the stereo; the bass rattles my skull when I bend over, trip, fall onto one knee, and force myself to get back up. My cellphone — *shit*, it had been the one ringing! And it isn't the Nokia tone; it's just the standard issue Apple ring, whatever that's called. (Probably something lame like *Default*.) The light blinds me when I click the home button, and numbers flash across the screen for a couple of seconds, an imprint of them floating in front of my eyes, even after the backlight goes dark.

02:14. Two in the morning. It's *two* in the morning. *Two* in the *morning*. (How many times should I repeat that? Shut up,

Aiden.) What the *hell?* I have *no* sense of time.

> *You are a dead man.*

No. *Stop it.* I'm not having any of this right now.

> *H o l l o w   m a n.*

I wince through gritted teeth when my hand, still holding the phone with six percent battery, gropes for the knob of the front door. Hearing voices isn't a normal thing for me; it's only happening 'cause I'm all drugged up and tried to drink myself back down. You'd think after a few years of trying this method to no avail, I'd give up; alas, I'm one of the dogs that goes back to its own vomit. I'm the classification of insanity: doing the same things over and over, thinking one of these times, they're going to work for me, when they never have and aren't going to start. Living through a veil of delusions. But that's the reason everyone lives out here — to cover themselves in the glitter of the superficial and ignore the festering wounds of this hellhole. To tourists especially, there are no flaws about the Boulevard. If only they bothered to stop and smell the pollution! Unfortunately, it's easier for people to just clamp a clothespin over their nostrils and continue on.

Hypocritical sons of bitches, the lot of them. These same people judge me for having sleeves of tattoos on my arms. For having gauges in my ears. Having the long, black, shaggy hair with the blood-red tips. The kohl-lined eyes. (Eyes everyone says are amber.) *Whatever.* What the hell ever, that's what I say.

I pound a fist against the door in my stupor, feeling satisfied that I managed to come to this conclusion. Someone stirs at my feet - a girl who, in her miniskirt and out of her blouse, package of cigarettes half-opened, groans and attempts to get comfortable, dark hair splayed out on the prickly doormat. I stare down at her, and her face becomes someone else's. Someone's that is bathed in moonlight and caressed by the stars.

Oh, *come on*. I want to go home already. (But, with this new development, I realise I don't want to get home *that* badly. I can make sure that she's comfortable.) Vision blurred, I glance back at the couch, which is empty other than a seesawing pizza box and a half-broken empty beer bottle doing the tango. Shaking my head briefly from side to side to clear the double vision, I bend at the knees and scoop her upward. Poor kid. Can't be older than eighteen. What's she doing out here, letting her life be ruined? This isn't for her. Oh, God. I want to wait around until she wakes up so I can tell her to *stop*. I don't want her to be like me. I don't want her to end up like this. Her makeup, other than being slightly smudged, is flawless. If she did that herself, she could be one of those makeup artist people for the movies. Or Broadway. Yeah, Broadway. Then she wouldn't have to stay here.

"Go to New York." The words tumble out and dance in front of my eyes. Breathing turns shallower as I slip her onto the love seat, lose the weight of her in my arms, watch as she turns restlessly, pressing one cheekbone into the cushion. *"New York."* She has to hear me at some point. Right? Even dead people continue to hear. It's the last sense to go. Blinking, I stare at my own shirt, thinking about how I almost didn't find it. For a minute, I think of giving it to her – just to preserve her modesty.

But I don't know how she lost her bra and her shirt. Don't *want* to know. (Doesn't really matter; it isn't my problem.) But at least she'll wake up, at whatever time, and realise that someone gave enough of a shit about her to move her from the floor.

Or maybe I'm just being really stupid and fooling myself.

H o l l o w.

I need to get home. The cookie-cutter house is three blocks from the blue monster I live in. I can make it. (I *need* to make it.) There's part of me that makes me think I can't. But I really shouldn't be thinking like that. Otherwise, I'll stay in the deadbeat community. Come on, Aiden. You've dropped more acid than this. There's more than acid in the tab. *Doesn't matter, you moron, just keep walking.* This trip is going to turn bad. I'm going to be one of those news stories that you hear at the top of the hour.

BODY FOUND IN LOCAL ALLEYWAY. BODY DISCOVERED IN OPEN GUTTER.

BODY FOUND—

BODY FOUND—

BODY FOUND.

No, I'm *not* going to be one of those people. That's *not* going to be my photo flashing across the screen. I'm going to make it. I have to.

The coolness of the autumn air makes goosebumps appear on my bare flesh. I shiver, rubbing my arms instinctively for friction, and I refuse to look at the streetlights, because they refuse to stand still; I refuse to look at the headlights, because they turn into screaming entities with fangs bared. I just stare at the sidewalk, watch as the white toes of my sneakers slap against the concrete, propel me forward. My mind doesn't need to be involved in this journey. I've found my way home from worse places, from worse parts of town. This is tame. *This is tame.*

No, this is just pathetic. Twenty-three-year-old man. Someone who's supposed to be finishing up college, having it all together, finding his way. I'm not doing any of it. There was no *college experience* for me, unless you count the extensive amount of attended house parties. I'm staggering home from one, and I must look like a sight and a half. When you're on a bunch of crap like I am, the roads become a maze and thoughts become a swamp. A screech in my ear, and all I can think is, *they got me.*

I've been in the back of the fuzz's car before, with that

metal woven chain between me and their judgmental eyes. Red and blue lights whirling, a flip of the switch and that yawning scream of the siren warming up. The smell of uniforms, one freshly ironed by a wife back home and another with a coffee stain on the right pant leg. My shoulders hunched over, ribcage curved and bent, glowering out the rain-splattered window, wrists chafing against the cold steel of the cuffs. Fourteen and on my way to a record so long, it trailed behind me on my way out of the station - where I did *not* use my one phone call. Not until the third time around, when air caught in my throat, when the weed on my breath was stronger than the lies I weaved, and when my ballooning pride had deflated. Only then did I ask for the one phone call. Only after I'd run myself through the muck. You'd think after all these times, I'd learn. But I just don't want to learn.

This place, this state of existence — it's comfortable. I know how to handle whatever gets thrown my way. It's the devil I know very, very well. It's a habit, and a bad one.

The disguised car doesn't stop for me, but continues on its way and speeds around a corner, tires squealing as it takes the turn too sharply. Looks like they're in pursuit of someone. As long as it's not me, I can't be bothered. I just need to get home, and the inner compass malfunctions, needle skewing this way and that, footsteps following in its wake, making me reach into the right back pocket of my jeans and pull out a carton of Marlboros. The last thing I need on my tongue is the taste of nicotine, but maybe the acrid dust will wake me up a little bit. I'll take what I can get.

I fumble to extract one of the slender white sticks, and it's even more of a chore to get it to my mouth. I blink several times at it, forgetting what it is as it bends and melts, but then it turns solid, and I remember. My parted lips quiver as I clench what's hopefully the filtered side between my teeth, tongue pressing against the cylindrical opening. The lighter's worse. Five flicks and nothing more than a spark. Hand that can't get a grip. (Aiden Kinsey needs to get a grip.) On the eighth try, I get a small yellow flame, and I wave it on the end of the cigarette, pulling air into my lungs with such force, it makes my insides curdle and ache. Desperation fills me. But the cigarette lights, ending my misery and panic. The smallest, stupidest things can make for a bad trip. Once I get home, I'm going to sit and let this simmer down—

"Get off the road!" Someone honks their horn, a loud blast in a major key that sounds much happier than it should. Sounds like music. I jerk forward, almost leaving behind my skin, and turn around to stare at the headlights. When did I get in the middle of the road? Shaking my head back and forth, I wobble to the side of the road, toe of my sneaker catching in the opening of a metal grate. Twenty-three-year-old man. *Pathetic.* I can hear the driver grumbling to himself as the motor whirs and the light blue car speeds past. I can hear him mumbling, *"That guy's asking for it."*

I'm asking for it? I feel that degradation all the way into my bones. No, *really*? It's not like I don't know that I am the scapegoat of society. I suck on the cigarette and yank it out of my mouth to expel the smoke. This is turning into one hell of a night. Why did I even go to that party in the first place? Did someone invite me? *No.* I'd legitimately been walking down the sidewalk, coming home from my first shift of work - I have three part-time jobs, which might come as a surprise, might not - and I saw the lights flitting into patterns on the front lawn, and I asked myself: Why not? *Why not?*

What a stupid question. Never ask yourself that when you're depressed, when you've sunk so low into the well that you can't see the light of day above you even if it's there. Don't ever ask yourself that question when you're like this. You'll end up doing things that push your face more profoundly into the stone and grind your bones into the dirt. Never ask yourself, *Why not?*

D e a d.

D e a d m a n.

That's why, and that's why not. I'm a terrible person. I'm a dead man. Or rather, to be politically correct, a man who *should* be dead. I'm that guy you look at and ask yourself, "Why was it my innocent cousin who ended up dying of cancer instead of that moron who puts his life at risk?" or "Why was it my wife who died in a car wreck and not him?" (As proved by the guy in the car.) Man, I'm useless. I'm just wasting space and air on the ruptured cesspool named planet Earth. I'm disposable as hell. I'm just a dead man, a hollowed man.

And I'm not going to make it home.

No one can say that I didn't try. I'm not back at that house, collapsed with the rest of them, the rest of the limp bodies that don't know whether they're unconscious or dead. I'm going to be discovered the next morning, and some random people will cluck their tongues against the roof of their mouths as they watch my tragic story unfold. Do I have my wallet on me? I should throw it away. That'll make it even better. *Nameless young man dies in alley.* John Doe. I'd be a John Doe. I am going to be one hell of a dead man.

Knees turn into pudding for the last time. Calves scrape against the unforgiving sidewalk curb through the holes in my jeans. Hipbone jars against the metal grate, left arm attempting to hold up the majority of my body weight. But all my efforts are for naught. I end up in nothing more than a crumpled heap. Thrown-out rubbish. Not even a damned bag to sleep on. Just the metal and the concrete. Just my own heavy, liquefied bones.

Breathe in and out. In through the nostrils, out through the mouth. Control the rate. But nothing's being controlled.

Bodily functions are spiralling out of it. There are lyrics to an old folk song being screamed out into the street; a couple scurries past the man lying on the ground with his arms flailing this way and that, back of the head rolling in place. He's a poor wayfaring stranger, travelling through this world of woe. He is me.

That's me. I'm legitimately disconnected and staring down at myself.

I hope to God (and I am not a praying man) that it isn't me down there.

Oh, but it is. *It is.* There's crimson slowly dripping from the nostrils. I can hear a heartbeat quicken until it echoes into the alleyway behind the head. I think it's going to stop. I don't think there's going to be a heartbeat at all.

Dead man. D e a d   m a n.

D e a d.

Thud. — Thud. — Thud. — Thud.

Does anybody deserve a fate like this? Does anybody deserve to die alone and shirtless in the streets? Does anybody deserve such a thing, even if others think they're asking for it?

H o l l o w.

— T h u d.

The dreams begin. Without fail, whether I'm alive or dead, they remain with me. Always in the same order, never faltering or changing from their beginnings to their ends.

I float on my back alongside a transparent river current. No flesh or sinew burdens me or causes me to sink to the murky bottom. I sense the water rushing over my arms, wrapping about my waist, guiding me someplace else, but when I turn my head to the left or shift my eyes to the right, I see no water at all. I've become the dead man, the hollow man, and I'm more than content to allow this "river" to transfer my bodiless mass elsewhere.

The gaseous feet solidify when their soles breach the edge of a riverbank. Sand erupts in-between pairs of toes as I am shoved upright, forced to stagger forward. It's a linear path, leading straight on through a small patch of woods. On the left side, the briars are thick, brambles entwined around tree trunks, and any visible flower blossoms are the colour of dried leaves. On the right, all is well with the hues of the bushes and the odours from the lilacs. But these two patches sink down into a dust bowl, six inches of sand and a carved-out, whitewashed road. My bare feet pad against it, grit pounding into the dilated pores. The greyish-brown substance sticks to my arms and lodges itself in my hair. The barren pathway leads me past white cookie-cutter houses, much like the one where the house party went down. These houses line the road, one right after the other, all the same. The front windows, one on either side of the door, completely uniform, remain empty.

But moments after I pass the first house, the windows fill with faceless beings created from writhing shadows and eyeless hoods, pulsating and moving just as human organs would. One of them dissipates through the front door, floating down the sidewalk towards me, and before I can meander past it, it presses something into the palm of my hand. The handle of a knife, with a serrated edge to the blade. In the real world, I would scoff and toss it back at the figure, cuss him out, tell him to quit handing that shit out. Obviously, this isn't the real world.

I turn the knife so that the serration faces my skin, and without further ado, I drag it downward, tearing through the skin and the veins at the underside of my left wrist. The ripping noise fills me not with pain, but with a sickened sense of satisfaction. As though doing this has started the process of completion and fulfilment that I seek in all the wrong places outside of this realm.

18

But it's *not enough*. I need to continue; the urge is too strong to resist. I rake it down the length of the forearm, following the blue lines underneath the flesh. Rivulets of crimson appear at the seams and spill out, dripping black acid onto the ground. The dehydrated dirt hisses, displeased at being disturbed. It doesn't matter what the dirt says; I'm doing what needs to be done. I turn the blade inward and punch it into my abdomen - not once, not twice, but eight times, each in a different place; tearing through a tattered, sack-like shirt; shredding through the contracting, spasming muscles underneath. It doesn't hurt; none of these pulsating, bleeding wounds do.

There's still no pain when I cut the knife, downward and diagonal, across my jugular — because all of this *needs* to happen. All of the terrible things I've done, manifesting into the black of the blood, need to spill out onto the ground and be absorbed. This is the deadness and the hollowness which will overtake me. From ashes into ashes, and from dust back to dust. (I haven't touched a Bible in a long time, but I know those verses to be true. Seen too many dead and hollowed out bodies for it *not* to be.)

As the faceless beings watch in agonising silence, I continue on.

At the end of the dirt pathway, I step off into what seems to be an endless cavern. For a moment, it's as though I've misplaced my foot in walking down stairs, and I'm briefly claimed by a nausea that makes my throat constrict, my gut twist. Soon, the cavern materialises into asphalt underneath the sole of my sneaker. A road with faded painted lines stretches out now in front of me, and no longer do cookie cutter houses line the sides, but broken sidewalks, detached car bumpers, wrecked trucks, disjointed houses fissured in several places, snapped in halves and fourths. Unidentifiable odours burn my nostrils, cause the hairs inside to stand on edge. My wounds have healed and I'm dressed as I normally would be if I was at home: sweatpants hanging low on my hips, sweatshirt pulled over and hood thrown up over my hair. Remnants of kohl smeared down my cheekbones. A great heat sweeps toward me on a harsh breeze, and the acrid smells become clearer when I next inhale. Putrid smoke, belching from the opening in the side of a brick building. The pungency of the inevitable sweat from both desperation and overheating. That crackling, licking noise of flames devouring sheets of paper and slabs of mortar.

The city burns in front of me. Hollywood has allowed hell to rise up from underneath the glitter and take hold of it. Fires consume its streets and attractions, beacons illuminating the black expanse of flat sky in a lighthouse of warning. *Stay away*, it says. *You are damning yourself if you come here.*

My sister rushes up from behind and yanks on one of my hands, attempting to pull me backwards. One shoe follows, then the other, but ultimately, I stay rooted to the spot, and try to move forward, taking her with me. Then (as always) she screeches at me. Her words reverberate in my ears, reminding me of a thousand fights I witnessed before my dad finally caved and signed himself out of our lives. As unfortunate as it is, Cheyenne gained our mother's scream. A scream that could be heard six houses down and called in as domestic abuse.

In Cheyenne's defence, she *has* to scream right now. Otherwise, I wouldn't be able to hear her, not over the sirens of ambulances and fire trucks battling her voice for dominance. The blues and reds whirl against the dilapidated, falling buildings; someone screams for help, they're trapped, they can't get out. Now she competes with a hundred or more rising voices, each saying separate things, all trying to get my attention. I block them all out, though, including her; I have to touch the fire. That's my goal. That's the intention. I want to be near it. I want to put my hand in it and let the element take my skin, take as much as it needs. Self-punishment, self-inflicted injury.

"Aiden, come on, we have to go!"

No. I want to stay here. I want to watch this city burn.

"A i d e n !"

I jolt out of the dreams, choking on my own spit, blinded by a cool cloth on my eyes, an even cooler hand on my hot forehead. But I don't stand a chance. Before I can see where I am, I'm pulled right back into them.

-

The hellfire is replaced with the nastiest nightclub I've ever seen (and that's saying something.) I'm standing outside underneath a flickering streetlight, staring hard at the numbers hanging sideways above the door. My head's canted so I can read them in somewhat of a straight line. I'm checking the address. Once, twice, three times. And though the numbers match the ones scribbled on the sweat-dampened piece of paper in my palm, this can't be the right place. Mom said she was going over to a friend's house; said these were the numbers. She told me to write them down, then grabbed her pursed and disappeared without so much as a wave behind her shoulder.

(I knew what was in her purse, by the way. A wallet. Her cellphone. A bag of heroin. After the divorce settled in, it's all she needed to survive. She certainly didn't need her kids. She left us mostly on our own.)

So I had gone down the street to a friend's house. Left my kid sister napping in her bedroom; I'd be back before she woke up. Once she's fast asleep, she's out for good until the morning; not even an earthquake can snap her out of it. My friend had already packed weed into separate bowls, and he distributed them out to the five guests he'd invited over for this intimate party. Music played in the background, not unlike the beats filtering out from behind the closed, thin door of the nightclub. We laughed about shit that wouldn't make sense once we were sober, revelled in the kinship we discovered that had been unknown until lighting up. We ate too many slices of fresh and leftover pizza and rolled around on the beds and onto the floor, and it was, in its own strange way, nothing more than innocent fun.

But the hours had fluttered by, and when I finally emerged from that house, baked out of my mind, it was much later than I'd anticipated. Alarmed, I'd stumbled up the front porch steps; relieved to find Cheyenne was still sleeping, I checked the clock and scowled at it. 2:36 am. I will always remember that time for as long as I live.

2:36 am.

Mom, despite her lifestyle changes, always made sure that she was home by two in the morning. Didn't matter if she came home alone or not - her footsteps and the jangling of her keys, and sometimes the murmuring grumble of her current fling, could be heard on the front porch, stepping over the threshold at that time. Never failed.

It was the first inclination that something was wrong. And so I went to the piece of paper, and I followed the trail. I know Hollywood like the back of my hand; I know where the buildings are located, how they're numbered in the different sections. What I didn't know was that this friend's house wasn't actually a house, but a nightclub. And now, she was inside of it.

So here I am, in this current moment, a path in front of me and a path behind. Looking back, I wonder: what if I had chosen to turn back and wait Mom out while sprawled on a comfortable bed, awakening to a throbbing migraine at my temples and birds chirping on the dry branch of the dead tree outside my bedroom window. How long would it have taken for me to figure out something had happened? Would it have been when I trudged downstairs and didn't see her half-asleep in the living room, mumbling to herself in her stupour? Would it have been when I pushed open Cheyenne's door and noticed she hadn't been awakened by Mom screaming at her from down below? That's one thing that wakes her up, I guess. Mom's screaming. Probably why she's so good at mimicking it; she's heard it a dozen times.

I guess this retrospective shit doesn't matter. As the dream refuses to deviate from true events.

No bouncer stands at the door, so I don't have to worry about flashing my fake identification cards. Seventeen and living large on a love seat. I think I had two marks on my record at this point in my life. I'm not sure, though. I'm never really sure about numbers.

I pull open the door and slip inside. It's small and crowded. Almost immediately, I trip over my own shoe and am shoved against the nearest wall, which has been covered recently in spray paint. So recently, in fact, that the paint's still wet. (Didn't this happen to me somewhere else? Amazing how the past repeats itself.) When I manage to peel myself off, my entire left side's been slashed in yellows and red. My shirt now sticks to my body and will have to be cut away with a pocketknife by the night's end. Being coloured like a page with a box of crayons isn't my concern, though. I want to know why my mom came here with her wallet and her bag of heroin. I want to know what the point was to all this.

(I have to keep telling myself it's just a dream, it isn't happening to me again. It's the dream that makes me realise just what occurred. Just what I witnessed. One that I don't want to haunt me, and yet it's still there, creeping around whether I consciously think about it or not. It's a shard of the past digging into my scalp, a second skin seeping through the first.)

The pot wears on me, and my vision blurs as I tuck my arms hard against my sides, wanting to ensure that I'm as small as possible. It's difficult, considering back then, I was already my peak height — six feet tall, plus an unnecessary two inches — and not exactly an attention avoider. Whether I wanted people to or not, still they stared me down. My gaze never rests on anyone in particular; I make eye contact with someone, accept that he or she isn't who I'm looking for, and I move on. Looks like these are interpreted as mysterious and intriguing; no one's sober enough to realise I'm just some lost kid looking for someone. Looking for his mom.

Strange to think about it. I hadn't wanted to even be around her in a long time. And it feels childish of me to admit that I just needed something stupid from her like a hug. Because if she's hugging me, then she's not doing whatever out in this half-constructed piece of shit. If she's hugging me, she's home, and Dad's back in the picture, and our dysfunctional life isn't so bad because at least it isn't *this*. It isn't taking one day at a time and carpe diem and not giving a general shit about its quality. It's relishing in the fact that we're alive and tasting that black cherry Kool-Aid on my tongue; it's not the bitter supposed tastelessness of acid or the burn of nicotine or the remnants of someone's flavoured lip balm.

I just want my mom.

I'm not here to pick up some beautiful girl with a charming smile. I'm here on an actual mission. An actual purpose. I didn't know I could have one now that all of my dreams and aspirations had been killed. Slaughtered mercilessly when I wasn't looking.

And I find her after some time. I push against a girl

holding her half-consumed bottle up in the air as she flings her hair, platinum and silver in the strobe lights, moving her out of the way. I break up a dancing group of five in order to make my way to the sectioned off sitting area in the back. The futons and cushions of the seats have stuffing falling out of them, rips and tears made from pocketknives and sharp fingernails. Writhing shadows take up residency on most of them, faceless images like the ones in the windows of the white houses. This dream is half memories. It lets me see what it wants me to remember. Torments me on purpose. And all I'm allowed to see in colour vision are two particular figures.

One is male; the other, female. The shirtless man leans forward, sprawled across the futon, mouth widened in a grotesque laugh. A purse is nestled in-between them, but the small bag doesn't do much in the way of keeping them separated. A bag filled with white powder gaps open on the flat of his thigh, almost toppling over and spilling onto the ground as his motions toward the woman become more animated. He snuffs it right off his own forearm, and she watches him, enraptured with his talent. No, wait a minute, it isn't *his* arm that's extended outward, but *hers*, with an orange elastic band tied around her bicep, the vein protruding in the crook of her elbow.

Despite the remnants of powder around her nose, still she needed to shoot up. At the time, this didn't make sense to me. But now that I'm six years older, I can sadly realise suicidal when I see it. (Cocaine and heroin. Deadly when separate; stupidly so when combined.) I can see now when someone stops giving a damn about their own life and about what little amount of good things will be left behind. And this much older, much more weathered self, who has seen this expression and this limp-limbed attempt at staying upright in his bathroom mirror, watches, frozen in a seventeen-year-old body.

Not that stepping toward her and taking her by the arm and pulling her from off the couch and shaking her until she snapped out of it would help. The reality passed onward; it's buried in an eroding grave. This is a dream, a reminder and torture. A spark and a trigger toward the niggling instinct that I should've done something, despite knowing that it wouldn't have worked, despite knowing that she'd already sealed her fate when the man wielded a syringe like a weapon, the silver of its needle clouded from a previous use. Inwardly, my two selves, one past and one present, scream when he inserts it into the vein at an angle; even from here, we can see the blue cylinder rolling sideways beneath her flesh.

I've never been one for shit with needles, even when it comes to getting blood drawn. And the amplified detail on her arm as the vein rolls makes me bend at the abdomen, feeling as though I'd been stabbed by that serrated knife and am just now getting around to knowing how deep it went. Something's caught in the back of my throat, a hard bauble of air. Before I can control it, my oesophagus constricts, my lungs tighten, my chest heaves and my stomach twists into knots — and I vomit, right there, all over the shiny dance floor.

Throat burning and eyes searing, I inhale tremendously as I slowly push myself upright again. Eyes go from the trail of vomit to the base of the futon, up the legs of its two occupants, right into one's eyes. Right into my *mother's* eyes. Her ash blonde hair flows in rivulets around her face, tearing itself from the braid she'd done before heading out. A braid that had once been neat, with all hairs tucked into place and sprayed down until they grew stiff. *The stiffer, the better.* One of her innuendos. When I was *really* young, hearing that come out of her mouth was like shocking to me. I would stare at her and shake my head and run off to my bedroom. When I was a teenager, I'd snicker behind two hands plastered on my mouth. The week before the moment this dream's replaying, I'd rolled my eyes and said, "Whatever" without a hint of a smile.

I'd give anything to hear those words again. She might've gotten cross after Dad left, whirled down the drain, but it didn't matter. She's still Mom. She's still the woman who raised us and who was there for so many years *before* the downfall. Still Laura Kinsey

And she looks right through me. Her eyes pierce mine, *a strange moss green that remind me of another pair of eyes from far away in the past.* The pupils dilate, growing large enough that they swallow me whole, take me into their depths. I'm no longer standing in the nightclub, cursed by neon lights following me around like unwanted suitors. I'm horizontal and vulnerable in the black splotches on backdrops looking right through me.

(She didn't see me. Her eyes gazed at where I stood, but she didn't realise who I was. She didn't know that it was her son, trying to find her, seventeen, isolated, and scared out of his right mind. Either she didn't know, or she had stopped caring, had stopped being able to give out any sort of blind affection even to someone she gave birth to.) With this, her face turning away from me, features sagging as the high, the one to doom her, overtook her - I knew it was the end. It settled into me, this knowledge, a cold weight in my bones, shards of ice in my blood. Still palpable after all this time. Within seconds, it's over.

And that part of the sequence ends as well. (You'd think that'd be the worst of it, but it isn't. No, they save the worst for last.) The murkiness sinks into my pores, clogs my nostrils, but still I continue to breathe. Slowly, as though someone's sedated me and I'm half-unconscious. My eyes work underneath closed lids, moving back and forth, this way and that, diagonal and sideways. My ears strain so hard to hear through the driving silence that after some time, they begin to ring. Heartbeats echo against the four walls that cage me, but none of the pulses belong to the organ in *my* chest.

I feel her approach. Her, the girl with the pair of moss green eyes from a long time ago. From a time when I still had dreams and aspirations, when I didn't want to be part of the deadbeat community, when I knew I'd make a name for myself. From a time when the summers stretched longer than they should've and the smells of the mildewing pond wafted alongside blackbirds' fluttering wings on the slight breeze. Long hair brushes against my bare arm, and then - there it is: the warmth of her palm against my forehead. My forehead, which stays the temperature of cold glass, smooth and slick with fever. After a pause, she whispers to me. Nothing special. Just my name. My name, over and over again.

Aiden.

She says it so softly. It makes no sense to me. It's like she still cares.

Aiden...

Could've fooled me. I hand-wrote letters to her and sent them each week for *three years* after the last time we saw one another. And she never responded to a single one of them. So much for caring.

Aiden...

You'd think I wouldn't mind this bit, since I get to hear her and all. But that's exactly why it's the worst. It reminds me of what I'll never have.

Aiden...

A hand that won't ever really touch my skin.

Wake up.

A mouth that will never cause mine to be set aflame.

-

"Aiden."

The person whispering my name isn't feminine in *any* sense of the word. Hard calluses perched on worn fingers dig into the skin of my shoulders, shake me hard. The majority of my senses remain numbed to this outside world, but I manage to deduct that I'm lying down on something kinda comfortable, but not really - either a lumpy mattress or an old cot. Someone's at least had the courtesy to put my head on a pillow - and from what I gather with my right nostril pressed into the pillowcase, it's clean. It smells like the musty remnants of aftershave, but at least the case itself doesn't have that roughened feeling to the cotton. I'm also not as cold as I once was; someone bothered to put my shirt back on for me.

The hands release my shoulders with a tremendous sigh, and I hear the creaking of a chair as the person leans back in it. A pair of scuffling footsteps rings through my painfully sensitive ears, then stops next to the creaking chair. These two people stand there, observing me with cautious regard. (I'm just guessing here; I have no idea, honestly, considering my *eyes are closed*.)

"Any change?" The higher tenor voice of the newcomer cuts through the moment of hesitance and piercing silence. "It's nine o'clock. He's been out for almost eighteen hours."

"— Has it really been that long?" Now that the owner of the whispering voice speaks at a normal volume, it becomes starkly apparent how exhausted he is. How long he must've been staying up to sit next to my comatose figure. Ah, so I *haven't* been kidnapped by avaricious drug lords or hellions bent on exacting revenge on whatever poor souls they reap from the street. Sounds like the people above me at least give a shit about my well-being. And if I was a betting man, I'd say that the guy in the chair's been there for the entire eighteen hours that I've been out. *Eighteen hours?*

And here I thought I was a dead man. I felt myself die in the street, for God's sake. I looked down at my body, and I saw blood streaming out of my nostrils. There wasn't any doubt, as I floated through the dreams, that I wouldn't wake up from them. That I had been given a thousand retries and yet hadn't used a single one of them to my advantage. Just let them rot, let them be shoved to the bottom of the bin, forgotten about, oily and cold and slick with sickness. Here, I thought all the people who hated me for surviving — when their kids, who deserved to, didn't — would be able to sigh in relief and move on.

It seems like either the joke's on them - or it's on *me*.

"He stopped vomiting about three hours ago. He's just been lying there ever since. Completely unresponsive. I don't know what the hell to think, Gearteeth."

Gearteeth. That sparks recognition in my memories. It's one of the nicknames of the four guys I work with. One of the four guys on my repo team. I haven't been rescued by dealers or kindhearted strangers - I've been snatched up from the muck by the boys I've grown up with through middle school, been arrested with, gotten good jobs with, gotten into amateur (illegal) repo with. These stupid bastards who deserve to have their photographs plastered in the dictionary next to the definition of *comrade-in-arms.*

"He'll come out of it," Gearteeth replies, confident in things no one else is or can be. "I mean — he's *Flame.* No matter what he does or what happens to him, he comes out of it. Bounces back like some weird-ass trampoline. Or that pink rabbit."

"The Energizer Bunny—?"

"That's it." A clap on the other guy's shoulder resounds out. I still can't place the voice of the man in the chair, though I have an educated guess as to who it could be. "So just keep staring at him; when he opens his eyes, it'll creep him out and we'll all laugh."

The radio's on, and though the music's turned down relatively low, all things considering (I'm used to it blasting out of the warehouse and attracting an entire squad of patrolling cops to this little shop of horrors) it causes a pulsing to start at my temples. I want to pipe up, yell for someone to turn that shit off, but my mouth's coated in molasses and my limbs are made of steel. I can't even shift in place. Maybe if I give myself a few more minutes, then I'll be able to yell like I used to.

Or maybe I'm actually dead, and my hearing hasn't shut off yet. Does shit like that happen? Knowing my luck, even if it hadn't, it would to me. And then people would groan about how not even death could take the deadbeat. No dead deadbeat today. Just a paralysed, zombified one. Not sure what's worse.

Gearteeth shuffles away, and the seated guy lifts himself up in order to pull the chair closer to the side of the cot I'm on. I'm settling on it being a cot; if I'm surrounded by people I know, then it means I'm definitely in our designated "storage and repairs" warehouse. And if I'm in there, then I *know* I'm on a cot; we keep one tucked in the corner next to the door that sections off our boss's office from the rest of the open architecture. Just in case one of us needs a catnap. And to think I've been here for eighteen hours. That's one hell of a catnap.

You overdosed, you idiot.

Brain, you're about as helpful as the guy who drove past me and insulted me earlier. It's not like I *don't know*.

"Wake *up*, Flame." Oh, I know that low growl. The guy in the chair is Greaser. "Come on. You stopped vomiting. You stopped dry heaving." And now he's doing that murmur to himself, talking to me, but also comforting himself. He's more than likely rocking back and forth, elbows resting against kneecaps, staring me down as Gearteeth suggested. Though he's the eldest of us all at twenty-six, all that maturity and calmness gets thrown out the damned window when it comes to someone he loves being threatened, whether it's due to their own choices or beyond their control. You think I'm bad? You think I went over the deep end? Should've seen him. So out of all these guys, he'll have the most sympathy when it comes to self-medicating or wanting to get so reckless that you "accidentally" kill yourself.

"This is nothing, man. This is *nothing* compared what we've been through. To what could've happened. Just *wake up*."

Huh. Honestly, I didn't think I'd have anyone pleading over my deathbed. Sounds depressing, but it's true. I mean, don't get me wrong, I know that these guys are my friends, and they say sometimes, when we're all equally wasted after a job well (or awfully) done, doesn't matter, that they'd die for me, or one another; that we're a brotherhood, not just friends; that we're united because of what we've gone through and managed to get each other through. Despite this, I couldn't ever really imagine someone being laid down or prone on a cot, with everyone else gathered around them, staring at them, begging them to wake up. It just seemed like some story to me. Some sort of event everyone loves to talk about, fantasises about, yet never would it come to fruition. Deaths in general are cruel in the deadbeat community. Most of the time, no one even notices if it happens.

"W a k e u p."

I don't want to. I think it'd be much better if I just shoved myself back under and allowed myself to fade away into nothing. But the end of his words breaks. It crackles, as though it's made of a light bulb with the fuse burned out. As though the bulb has been thrown against the tiled flooring. As though it's just — shattered completely.

When my mother collapsed from the futon onto the

dance floor, and no one picked her up, I'd stepped forward. I'd made myself known to the man on the couch who had killed her. I'd picked her up and brought her into my lap, and I'd looked down at her, and I remember whispering the same way. She didn't hear me; she was already fading. The music had been too loud anyways. But her eyes had glistened as she looked up at me, attempted to read my mouth as it murmured her name over and over again, as my sweaty palm combed back the tangle of hair — as though she was the child and I the parent. And there was nothing I could do.

In the last moment - my voice broke. I had felt it in the back of my throat: that current, that zap signifying something had gone wrong with the cords. And now, I hear it. The gurgle. I hear how horrible it would've sounded in noiselessness.

I can't just — well, no, I *could.* I could still fade out. But I won't. I refuse to make that decision. I'm not going to do to these guys what my mother did to me.

I don't know how I'm going to do this. Slowly? I think that's all I can do, because for real, I'm not sure what's part of my actual body and what's melted into the cot. All the saliva in my mouth has dried out, and when I attempt to swallow, I get nothing more than a bob of the Adam's apple and a glob of phlegm in my throat. No talking for me yet. So I settle for opening my eyes, sliding the lids upward though they seem to weigh a good tonne or more. Vision blurred, I can't see much of anything. I just see shadows and lights. That's all I can distinguish: shadows and lights.

"Flame?" Greaser's noticed. "...*Flame?*"

He keeps his voice at a whisper to not attract the attention of the others, just in case this is a false alarm. I must've done this before, opened my eyes briefly before closing them. But I'm not going to be closing them again. Whatever I've done in my stupour, it's erased.

He leans forward, very close to me; I didn't realise how close he was until now. He presses something damp and cool against the corners of my mouth, then my eyes, almost forcing the lids shut. In response to losing my regained sight, I grunt at him. It's a guttural sound, something that belongs in a horror movie and not real life. But it gets his attention again. It makes him realise that this time's different from all the others.

"You're awake." A heavy sigh. Greaser doesn't believe it at first. I blink a couple of more times to get the blurriness out of the way, and finally, the smoke clears. I stare down his face, one that's extremely familiar to me, all the way down to the tongue flicking out nervously to touch the two rings piercing the bottom right corner of his mouth. Bright red hair around the roots, orange in the spiked body, platinum blond bangs sideways across his sweating forehead. Green eyes that make me think I'm looking at the human embodiment of a cat.

But then I make the mistake of looking at his bare arms, the skin of which has been transformed into a demented mural of rotting zombies and dripping skulls. I really shouldn't have looked at that. Immediately, my stomach clenches, gives a tremendous heave—

Thankfully, he has quick enough reflexes to reach over and snatch up the bin, just in time to hold it underneath my crunched-up face. Nothing comes out of my stomach, which has already been emptied by the apparent fits of vomiting I've had for the past eighteen hours since they've found me. But the convulsions seizing my abdomen at least help in relieving the nausea spreading through me at the sight of his tattoos. I make sure not to look at them as I come back up, collapsing against the cot, panting through parted lips like a dog. Despite what his tattoos might say about him to people who don't know him, he's twenty-six and has his life together - and he plans on marrying his girlfriend of five years next spring.

"Flame. *Breathe*. You're *fine*. Everything's out. Just—"

"*Jesus*," I spit out, the single word crackling on the back of my tongue. "*Jesus, God, Mary, Joseph*."

"Is he talking?" Someone else calls out from across the warehouse. His voice sounds tinny, as though his head's trapped in a metal can. "Is he *actually* awake this time?"

I hear the clattering of a wrench hitting the ground, the soft collapse of a greasy towel next to it. Another pair of feet - or maybe it belongs to the same person - makes its way over to the sink at the back, sneaker soles slapping against the concrete before skidding to a stop. The shriek of the faucet as the tap water emerges makes me wince. I want to burrow my face into that smell-good pillow and never come back out. Maybe waking up wasn't such a good idea after all. Is it too late to pretend like this never happened?

"Guys. *Guys*." The new voice, over by the sink, which makes them the same person, grows excited. "He's awake! He's *really* awake this time!"

I reach my hand up to pinch the bridge of my nose between my forefingers and thumb. An almost innocent, child-like voice, but it belongs to one of the lankiest kids I've ever seen: Jam. Only half an inch shorter than my six-foot-two-inches, with a shock of tie-dyed hair - today, from what I can see as he rushes over from the sink, balancing something in the palm of his blackened hand, it's a ridiculous indigo, chestnut, and bright pink mix - and also no shirt. But I don't have to worry about any violent tattoos with him, just the carved out head of a roaring dragon on the inside of his right forearm and a titanium barbell stabbing through the arch of his left brow. The last thing I see is the dark of his eyes before I'm forced to stare at the ceiling.

Throbbing begins at the nape of my neck, just at the two pressure points where the thick column connects to the back of my head. The migraine wants to seep up and manifest at the centre of my forehead.

"Here, Flame, drink this."

A shuddering cup presses against my mouth, and one weakened hand comes up to grasp at it, shoving it closer as though that'll help with things. Half the water in the cup spills onto my face, trailing down onto my neck and bare chest. But the other half makes it into my mouth, and I swish it around into the dried cracks and the canker sore starting near my bottom teeth, hissing before swallowing hard. My mouth now feels like it's on fire.

The water did, however, soothe the aching dryness on my tongue and in the back of my throat.

"Don't vomit again," I hear someone say drolly, the same guy who spoke earlier with Greaser when I was still down and out. Good old Gearteeth - one of the only ones in our ragtag group who looks like he sounds. He's sturdier and stockier than the rest of us, and he's also the youngest at twenty-one. His voice sounds like he's been chewing on a mouthful of gravel as he paces over to me, rotating and flexing out the muscles in his shoulders. His tribal tattoos are much easier to look at, black slashes across his biceps and waist and back. He stares at Jam for about thirty seconds before snatching the small plastic cup out of his hand and trudging back over to the sink himself.

"Jesus, God, Mary, *Joseph,*" I spit out again, just to fill the strange silence that overcomes us all. Besides, I need to get my mouth back into the habit of moving. I don't think I'll be able to survive for long without being able to jack my jaw however much I need to.

"None of those people are here," says the fourth and

final voice, completing the rat pack. "Wait — well, I dunno, can God be classified as a person?"

I do nothing but groan. That philosophical, airy tone combined with the blaring of the boom box from underneath the nearest work table has me wanting to pull my hair out. Clunker, as he's known in the group, meanders around the foot of the cot and perches himself on the edge, slapping his hands against his knees as he turns his head to stare at me, one brown eye clear, the other slightly opaque from blindness. Ash-blond bangs fall out from underneath the bill of his torn baseball cap, and the brightness of his cerulean sweatshirt hurts my eyes. I hate being so visually sensitive that I can't even look at anyone right now, but it can't be helped, I guess. He has the cord of his earbuds draped around his neck; with him and Greaser sitting so close, I find that I bask in the body heat emanating off of them. (Is it freezing in this stupid warehouse or is it just me?)

"Nah." Gearteeth is the one who answers as he shuffles back over from the sink. "He's some diamond in the sky."

"No, that's a reference to The Beatles."

"It's actually a reference to an acid trip coined *by* The Beatles."

Acid trip. My skin turns colder at even the brief mention of *acid trip*. I don't have to be told where they're going to steer the conversation. It's not like these guys haven't been around drugs before. They'd know - and if I'd talked in my stupour, or screamed while I vomited, who knows what I'd inadvertently told them? I feel my pulse slow, my heart hesitate before each beat, and it reminds me too strongly of what I experienced in the street, cradled against a metal drain, waiting to die.

Just waiting to die.

"S p e a k i n g of acid trip," Clunker says, rather cheerfully all things considering, "Some undeniable train of thought tells me our friend here on the cot had a long, hard night."

"Shut up," I manage to croak out, throwing an arm over my eyes. Not even the whiteness of the ceiling - or the *attempt* at whiteness, as it's covered in cobwebs and splatters of dirt and a coating of dust, and probably asbestos - fends off the migraine now. "Damn it, all I want is some peace and quiet."

"You had eighteen hours of that." Gearteeth tut-tuts his disapproval at me. "What you actually want is some more water."

I peek out from underneath my forearm and eye the little plastic cup of water, which he waggles back and forth at me with a shit-eating grin. Gearteeth might be smiling, but I can tell you that Greaser isn't, and if he isn't, then nothing's funny, no matter who you are. Out of them all, he's going to be the one to make sure the conversation pinpoints all the nasty shit I'd rather avoid before the nights over. Or the morning.

"Nah, what I *actually* want is to know what time it is." I cling to the edges of the cot and work on pulling myself back upright. My stomach heaves again, and my chest tightens, but once I clear that awkward angled stage, and am at a regular ninety degree angle, the nausea disappears. The migraine doesn't. It decides that it's a prime time to spread around my head and meet at the bridge of my nose. It doesn't just trickle outward like slow rain, though; no, it explodes and moves at an immeasurable pace. I tuck my trembling knees up toward my face and shove my forehead against the kneecaps, pressing as hard as I can, so hard that I'm sure the material will form lines in my skin. "— You sure it hasn't been eighteen *years*? It sure feels like it."

"If you overheard that, then you *also* heard me say it's nine o'clock," comes the retort. "But I guess I'll clarify: it's nighttime."

Jam reaches up and touches the hair at his temples,

scrunching up his face. "If it's been eighteen years, then I'm probably making like my father and greying like a banshee."

"Took less than six of those hours for Dollar to decide he needed to go out and start looking for a replacement."

The harsh words come from Clunker, who drops them like boulders onto the floor and lets them lay there, becoming white elephants in the room. I raise a brow incredulously. Dollar, our boss, out looking for *my* replacement? How many times had the damned rat said I'm irreplaceable? Or, better yet, said there's no one in the world who can get away with half the shit I have. A little bit less of a compliment, but I take what I can get. I finally manage to remove my face from my knees so the four guys can see my bewildered expression. Head still swims viciously, like someone's filled it up with water and inserted sharks into it to swim and devour whatever brain cells float toward them. And everyone still blurs at the edges. But it's a hell of a lot better than being unconscious. "Wait, *what?*"

"I don't think you realise how bad you looked," Greaser says grimly. I swallow and reach forward to take the cup of water from Gearteeth. "How bad you *still* look. Like – dude, you look like *shit.*"

"Thanks." My voice is just as toneless.

"Death warmed over."

"—Thanks."

"Like a walking—"

"*I said, t h a n k s.*" I shoot a glare towards him over the rim of the cup. The water sloshes into my mouth and cools down the wretched heat from it being closed for too long. It makes my body wrack when it splashes against my aching gums, but soon, the pain begins to subside into a dull throbbing, one rivalling the pounding in my head. (My senses are returning to me full-force and too rapidly to compute.) "Could've just stopped with the *you look like shit.*"

"Well, shit comes in many different shapes and forms," Clunker comments, taking on that philosophical, sage-like tone. As though he's the shit connoisseur. (He might be; I'm ninety percent sure there are things I don't know about him still.) "But *death warmed over* generally has the same aesthetic. Probably a little bit paler—"

"—I got it," I say, voice growing tight. These guys are *too* good of friends sometimes; they'll needle at me until someone finally manages to push one of my many buttons. The last thing I need to do right now on top of all these obnoxious physical ailments is lose my temper. "I look like shit and death warmed over and a walking corpse. Great, thanks for the input."

"You won't *actually* get it until you look in a mirror," comes the remark back. "But more power to you."

That's the last thing I want to do right now: head to the bathroom and stare down my reflection in the mirror. I can't remember the last time I took a good, long look at myself. Has it been months? Years? Time blurs together with each blink and doesn't seem to be passing any slower. We're all hourglasses turned upside down, with our sand trickling into the bottom, never stopping until it's all filled up. And we don't get turned back around again. Once the sand's done, it's done, and so are you.

What's that one song? Life isn't a Nintendo game?

"No thanks," I say, trying to lightening my tone and the mood. "I'll just stick to your guys' word. But, okay, seriously, what's up with this replacement thing?"

"Well, like I said," Greaser continued, picking up where he left off, "you don't really know how bad you looked. You were throwing up all over the place and screaming—"

Just what I thought.

"—and he just sort of stared when we laid you on the cot, started doing that stupid head shake thing that he does. Commenting about how *nobody who looks that bad makes it.*"

Someone else promising my impending demise, or hoping for it, who's gonna end up sorely disappointed. "Sucks for him. Guess I'm alive and well."

"Alive, sure. *Well?* Not even close." To my surprise and chagrin, it's not Greaser who pinpoints me, but the ever-sagely Clunker. His voice and expression sour quickly, like milk left out too long in the heat. "You missed one of the jobs. Dollar called us in the middle of the night because some dude bailed on an appointment — apparently this one was to *discuss* why he missed his *other* appointments or some shit. And y'know Dollar. He wants us to head out, take the guy's stuff that was supposed to be taken a couple nights ago, and if he gives us shit, to teach him a lesson."

This is probably the most I've ever heard him speak in a single sitting. I don't know how to react to this except to blink a couple of times and try to keep my breathing as controlled as I can. The quicker I breathe, the quicker my anger rises.

"And what ends up happening? You don't answer your phone." He isn't used to speaking this much, either. His hands start shaking; he quickly swipes them on the stomach of his sweatshirt, as though that'll rid them of sweat. "And you *always* answer your phone. Whether you're higher than shit, drunker than shit, with one girl or three - doesn't matter, you always at *least* shoot back a text. But n o t h i n g. Started out as nothing for thirty seconds. Then nothing for a minute. Then, five minutes. Ten. *Twenty.* Next thing we know, it's an hour. And you still haven't said a thing. Not one letter."

"Don't think even an hour would've been enough time to scribe a letter and mail it," I mumble, half-attempting at a joke.

He ignores it. "So here we are, at a loss, with Dollar getting irritated and you off doing *God knows what*, and we have no idea where you are, or where to even start looking for you. So we do the next best thing and split up. Because hell, we'll cover more ground. We only have, I dunno, the *entire span of Hollywood* to comb through. Not just the streets, either. And here we'd thought you'd just be conked out at your house. Nah, of *course* not. That'd be *too easy*."

I had the choice before me, with his pause to catch his breath, to stand up and let myself go. I could clean up the mess afterwards, storm into the restroom, not come out until I'm ready, and if I never got ready, then I'd never come out. (Simple.) Instead, I choose to let him continue talking. To get out the rant. Because God also knows, whether He exists or not, these guys have let me ramble on and on, both drunk and sober, when I most needed it. The least I can do is return the favour. Even if he's rambling on about me.

Gearteeth wordlessly rises from the foot of the cot and returns to the sink. I can tell by the hesitance in his movements that he isn't sure whether I want more water or not, but that's what he's going to do. Because he doesn't like confrontations. He gets uneasy, starts twiddling his thumbs, glancing this way and that. He ends up being the mediator most days (as does Jam), but regardless, despite being able to calm them down, it doesn't mean he likes them. And when Clunker decides to talk - no, to *rant*, which has only happened twice in the twelve years I've known him - no one can mediate. We either have to overthrow his argument or wait for him to bluster himself out.

"As luck would have it, we found you in the alleyway two streets down from your house. Lying in a puddle of this nasty ass water with blood running out of your nose."

Now we're getting to the shit I remember.

"What were you *thinking?* Were you trying to get yourself killed?"

I almost yank the cup out of Gearteeth's hand this time around and push it against my mouth. The million dollar question of the night. *Were you trying to get yourself killed?* It has a simple answer, but these guys aren't going to want simple. That's not how we work. (Plus they already know the simple answer; now, they want reasons.) We push, and we push, and we push to get the answers we want. If I wanted the simple way out, I should've made like a bouncer, stood up with a hulking glare, and stalked out, leaving behind this life and these people and doing - something. Probably just going out and trying to kill myself again, knowing me. In my rage, I'd start a fight with the wrong people. And this time, these guys might not get there in time - or might not come after me at all.

Another hand comes out of nowhere from the corner of my vision, smacks the cup out of my hand, knocking the precious water onto the floor, right next to the rubbish bin. I stare at the discarded cup, then slide my eyes slowly upward toward Greaser's taut features, his nostrils flaring, the hand clenching into a fist, his pointer finger still extended towards me. I'm a kid being chastised by the overbearingly concerned parent.

"You're not doing this." Whenever he's overwhelmed, he gets that low note to his voice. Like at any moment, he could start rumbling like an earthquake. I've never seen him pushed beyond the limit of that, but I've no doubt if he really gets going, he could make the earth turn upside down. "You're not shoving your damn face into a cup and not talking. You're gonna talk. You're not getting out of this bullshit. We have a right. We have a *right,* Aiden. We've known you over half our lives. We've gone through enough *shit* together."

I take in a deep breath and hold it. But my techniques

aren't working anymore.

"You can't just do this. You *can't*. You lost all rights to that after a year. After all the stupid skinned knees and first heartbreaks and whatever else we've gone through. All this shit. This is shit. *This is shit.*"

I knew he'd be the one to push me over the edge. He probably knew it, too. Which is why he bothered to step forward, push the cup out of my hand. Yeah, *push me over the edge.*

"You're right, this is shit. *Shit.*" I stand up from the cot so quickly my head spins. "Couldn't have said it better myself, Greaser. Oh, and — thanks for the updates, Clunker. Thanks for the play-by-play of my last hours. I was *dying* to know what happened while I was writhing on the ground like a fish." He winces at my emphasis and prior description, but manages to salute me nonetheless. "Was I trying to get myself killed? Nah. *Nah,* not at all. Not at *all.*" I want to pace, but there's no room with how they've managed to cage me in, the four of them, and so instead, I turn in little circles, alternating at whom I stare, at whom I jab a finger, at whom I clench and bare my teeth. The true incarnation of the trapped animal. "Guess what, guys. We all hit rock bottom. Every single one of us."

"You —" A finger at Greaser, who stares me down — "and you —" A finger at Jam, who averts his eyes — "and everyone *else* in the world!"

"Point that finger one more time, and I'll break it." I whirl around, but Greaser locks his hand around my wrist, twisting slightly, just to show he's serious. "I *mean it,* Flame. We're not the ones who need to be taught lessons. You think we don't understand hitting the bottom of the well? You think out of all the people in the world, we don't get it?"

"If we don't get it," Jam slowly adds, each word like a slow-falling drop of water from a leaking faucet, "then no one does. We've been through it all with you, man."

"That doesn't matter and you know it. I remember when you tried to off yourself with your dad's old pistol and you didn't tell us about it for a damn month. Hell, none of us would've even known it if it'd happened!"

He stiffens, back going straight as a board. I've crossed the line with him, bringing that up. Because his family had thrown him out on his face when they discovered he's gay. And so he'd found his father's new child - the pistol. And he'd decided to wipe his life clean with it. But something made him not. And that something was Gearteeth. But you know what, they're striking below the belt like cobras with me; it's only necessary I return the favour. They're making me feel the pain; that's fine, they can feel it, too. They can suffer and turn over in the nasty graves of their past right along with me.

"This isn't about me," is his tight-lipped response. His face goes whiter than a sheet. "This is about you, Flame, and your chaotic grip on life. I've dealt with my shit. Now it's time to deal with yours. And if you don't want to do it on your own - then we'll make you, and we'll do it for you."

I knew that's what this was about.

"I don't need intervention," I spit.

"Yeah, you *do*." Clunker crosses his arms. Greaser stands up out of the chair. The four of them are about to corner me further. I just know it. I don't know what they're going to do. I really don't. Shit's never gotten this real before. Sure, there've been jabs here and there about my rapidly deteriorating lifestyle. But there's a conjoined determination in their eyes. It dilates their pupils and make them look like they're the ones with the ultimate high. There's not going to be any backing down now. Things probably are gonna get violent. So much for keeping the terrifying temper reined in, in check.

"All right, *fine*. Since we're being technical. How's this: I don't *want* intervention."

Greaser just half-smiles at this. "Too bad."

By the look on Gearteeth's face, I can tell he's still uncomfortable. I stare him down, hoping to win an ally, someone to tell these bastards they need to step off right now. But he doesn't say anything. Instead, he averts his gaze and lets his shoulders droop forward.

It's the last straw. Maybe I do need to go to the bathroom after all, despite my initial desire against it. I'm a violent guy, but regardless of how mad I am, I really don't want to punch any of my best friends' lights out. Plus I'm *really* tired. Like — standing is a huge burden on my legs, a burden I didn't expect. Already I can feel all the stamina just draining out of me, like someone cut me open and I'm bleeding out. Bleeding out like I did in the street. But this time, it's not from my nose; it's from my calves. The music in the background, however soft it's been turned down to be, doesn't help in any of this, either. It just fuels me. Stokes the fire. As annoying as it is otherwise.

I go to step towards the bathroom; we walled off an area near one of the two large offloading doors and changed it into a closed-off unisex restroom. Open toilet, haphazard sink, crooked mirror, and shower head with a drain in the opposite corner — just in case. It's basically our second home, this stupid warehouse. Now, with this, it's been transformed into a war zone.

Greaser's there to meet me, hand grasping my wrist.

"*M o v e.*"

The single word rings out.

"**N o.**"

His is an echo back.

"Let go of me," I snarl. "And *get out of my way.*"

I push against him, and he pushes back. The bone in my

wrist screams for release. I need to drink more milk or something; it feels brittle, like one wrong turn and it'll break, cleave itself in half. I grit my teeth together and push harder. He stumbles backward a couple of paces, heaving a tremendous, frustrated sigh - but still doesn't let go.

"And what are you gonna do if I just let you walk away? Run from your problems again?" He shoves me backward, and in the half-stupour, I let him. "Run like you *a l w a y s* do?"

"Greaser—" Gearteeth becomes even more uneasy.

"Time to man up and face them down. Stare them right in the eyes." One hand comes up and grasps my chin. He's entirely too close for my comfort. Breathing down my neck. Red lines apparent in his bloodshot eyes. "So look me in the face. *Look at me.* And tell me you wanted to kill yourself. Say it. *Say it to my face.*"

Hold the phone, I can't do this. I don't want to do this. I thought I wanted to get angry after all, but it's becoming painstakingly clear that I have no idea what I want. Except this anger. This boiling anger. This urge to strike again, again, again.

"*Say it.*"

But he's asking for it. Dear god, he's asking for it.

"*For the love of Christ, Aiden —*"

Then, he uses my real name. Not the repo-man moniker; the real deal. It reminds me, painfully, that he knows me. These aren't strangers. I'd been glad for this at first, but now, I resent it. I resent not waking up in the back of someone's truck, tied up and gagged. I resent not waking up still alone in the middle of the street. Though when it boils down to it, when all of the meat slides off the bone, when the muscle tissue rips open and leaves nothing but scarring behind, when all the sand in the hourglass runs out and leaves an empty bowl on top— I resent waking up at all.

"Yeah, *I wanted to kill myself.*" The sentence explodes outward from me and smacks him in the face. I don't know if he expected me to refute this claim, to push at him and demand he'd turned stupid with age, ripened with it, his brain frying in his skull from too much weed or some shit like that. But I don't deny it. There's nothing to deny, and everyone in this room - and the man outside of it, Dollar; and my kid sister back at home doing god knows what; and my parents; and damned strangers in the streets - knows it. Everyone and their mother, brother, uncle, cousin twice removed knows it. "Are you *happy* now, Greaser? I said it once, but I'll say it again. I hit rock bottom and I didn't want to come back out of it *ever again—*"

"Now tell me *why*, Aiden." He almost cuts me off from finishing my sentence. His fingers curl around my shoulders, and he shakes me. He shakes me hard, violently, almost picking me up off the ground, because I've lost too much weight, because he's suddenly stronger than I am. And to think I used to be unbreakable. Aiden Kinsey's lost his way. Aiden Kinsey's a hollow man. "*W H Y?*"

"What do you mean, *why?*" I bark out a crazy laugh. "You say you've been around since the beginning. If that's the case, then you'll already *know* why. Can't you see? Everything is shit. My *life* is shit. My life and everything in it. Down the drain, gurgle, gurgle, into nothing but a *pile* of *shit.*"

"Come off it." One of his hands flexes, as though he wants to take it from my shoulder and wrap it around my neck instead. Strangle the life out of me and give me exactly what I've vocalised wanting. "Come *off* it. You can't say that to us. You *can't.* Because all of that is bullshit. Life's hard, you idiot; it kills us, after all. We can only take so much until we crack, so just *admit* you cracked, and talk about it, and stop dancing around the issue! Our lives are shit and we've hit the bottom, too. We did. I'll say *that* again, and again, and again until you start remembering we're all the same here. We've *all* been down this road. But don't you look me in the eyes and tell me that everything in your life is shit."

I feel a seizure surround my heart, the cloying grip of guilt. It only lasts for a moment. I know where this'll go.

"Because that includes us—"

Hook —

"And your sister—"

Line —

"And whoever the *she* is that you were muttering about in your stupour."

— And sinker.

If only he hadn't brought *her* up. Then, I might've been on board. Sure, mentioning Cheyenne didn't do much good, because I don't consider her to be a sibling – not anymore. Not since I had learned the truth just hours before the party. They try to emphasise that you choose your family, that it isn't blood, but when it comes down to it, blood ties are stronger. Blood ties make you feel as though you have an obligation to the ones who share it with you, to put out their fires and solve their problems. There's no obligations when it comes to friends and those not related to you. You don't *have* to do a damned thing for them. And that's how I view Cheyenne now. Someone who lives in my house, but whom I don't have to do a damned thing for. And a good thing, too - she makes enough of her own problems without me walking around with a vacuum trying to clean up.

But that's not what gets to me. It's the nameless *her*. No one's allowed to talk about *her*. No one's allowed to *know*. There are some things not even the best of friends can be told. I don't think they'd understand, because frankly — I don't. Can't even begin to put into words what she is, what she could've been and isn't. They're talking about the girl who never answered my handwritten letters. Each week, for three years, futile attempts. If I really wanted to, I could *blame* her for being the reason behind my life going to shit!

Regardless, I thought I was finished with this conversation before. Now, I'm *beyond* done with it. I reach forward and grasp fistfuls of Greaser's muscle shirt. Ironically, hearing her mentioned, even though it's not by name, strengthens me. It gives me the shot of energy I need. "You can't talk about *her*. Don't even bring *her* up."

"*Greaser*—" Gearteeth tries to get his attention again, but it's to no avail. His next words emerge in a tight whisper, "Just let him go."

"Yeah, Greaser." I sneer at him, pressing ever closer, because nearness intimidates, and the closer you get, the more uncomfortable the other person feels. I'd probably have to kiss him at this point to make him the *most* unnerved. But it's doing something. The crazed glaze in my eye or the gravelly roll of my voice. "*Let me go* — to the bathroom in peace."

"Come *off* of it." He pushes at me. "I'm not letting you run from the issues at hand."

"Let me go to the bathroom in peace," I repeat, lower, more evenly. "Or else you're going to be pushed into the wall face first."

There's a moment where the force of his shove sends me reeling, and a scuffle ensues, fingers grabbing, knuckles whitening, teeth clenching and sounds of disgusted frustration emerging from the both of us. But then — Gearteeth comes forward, and for a split second, I think he's going to restrain me, pull me back, put me on the cot, tell me to sit in the corner and think about what I did. Instead, he puts both of his hands in-between us, one on each of our chests, splaying his fingers out to push us apart. I can feel the vibrations of his trembling against my sternum; he's nervous as all hell getting into the middle of this. Jam and Clunker neither make a move nor relax; they seem to be ready for the scuffle to turn into a full-out brawl.

But then, Greaser surprises me. With the interruption, he releases my shoulders and turns away from me; he admits defeat, surrenders, but manages to do so without legitimately stepping back from the issue at hand. In other circumstances, this would make me reach out for him; the last thing I want is to alienate him. But I'm too stupidly mad about this entire thing. I'm mad and I'm wanting to be left completely alone. And all I can think at the time is that I'm finally going to be alone, like I want. Never mind the realisation that being surrounded by a bunch of people at that party still made me feel alone. Never mind that these guys slapped me in the face tonight to try and wake me up. Still I wanted to wallow in the guilt and the nastiness and the shallow parts of me. Twenty-three and a deadbeat and king of the streets and whatnot. Nothing acceptable. Nothing good.

My steps turn into staggers as I make my way to the bathroom. When I reach the door, I twist the knob and shove it open, slamming it behind me. Not that I think anyone's going to follow, but I want the point to be made. *I want to be alone.*

Something inhuman emerges from me, something low from my throat I've been holding in since this entire thing began, almost akin to a scream, but deeper, more guttural, a monster being released, a beast unfastening its shackles, no longer imprisoned, no longer prohibited from roaring. With it, I lunge forward, and the fist I want to push into my friends' mouths, into the side of my own head, into Dollar's gut, into my father for leaving, into my mother for loving heroin over us, I plunge into the mirror hanging above the sink. Knuckles deep in glass, the dirtied slivers shatter, cracking and falling down into the sink, against the side, smashing into halves and quarters and clattering onto the floor. Blood pours out from a multitude of shallow cuts now in my flesh, and when I yank my fist out, I'm more than glad to see pieces stuck in the deeper wounds. I'm *glad* for it. I want to feel the *pain*.

The released endorphins leave my brain swimming in a bowl of water once more, and I slap my palms against either side of the basin, leaning against it, more mirror shards cutting into the calluses on my palm. If I don't hold on to it, I'll melt into a puddle. The migraine racks through my entire head now, no strings attached, blasting me over and over until my stomach twists into a tight knot, wanting me to retch again. Nothing's in there, though, and all I end up doing is dry-heaving into the metal drain. Blood skirts down my hands and to the indents of my bent wrists, dripping and staining the already dirtied white sink. Those same grotesque hands now twist up and over my head, as though I want to tear out my hair, but I refrain.

Drip.

Drip.

Drip.

In here, nothing reaches me. I can't hear the talking outside. I can't hear the low drone of the radio pounding into my ears, though I still hear the echo from the previous tune. It'll fade at some point — and then, maybe thirty seconds after I consciously think this, it does. It fades into a multitude of whispers instead, ones that repeat the words of my friends and the things heard in the dreams. Images run in front of my eyes, regurgitating like the vomit in the rubbish bin, and it makes me dig my blood-covered fingers into the roots of my hair to rip at them. A drop of blood rolls onto my scalp and down the side of my neck. I can barely breathe.

And I don't want to feel the cool hand attempting to calm

me. It's not going to work this time. Damn her. Damn her and everyone else. I'll see them in hell.

I shoot upright, hands tearing away from my hair and curling into monsters in front of me. I stare into the fissures remaining of the mirror, seeing through the cracks, or attempting to. And what I do manage to see - I don't recognise. I don't recognise a single bit of that reflection. My hands slam back down on either side of the basin, grinding into the remnants of glass, which turn to splinters and disintegrate into my callused palms. Because as I continue to stare, it grows harder to keep my knees from buckling. My elbows quake just as violently, holding up the majority of my body weight now that my legs have started to give out.

Who *is* that peering back at me? I don't know him. He has a sickly pallor to his skin, the pallid flesh stretching taut against bone, enhancing the hollows of his cheeks and around the curve of his chin. Shirtless, it's apparent his ribcage isn't filled out, and despite his wiry build, he has a certain fragility to him. As though if the right person knocked him over, he wouldn't get back up. How many drugs has this guy eaten? How much booze has he drunk in one night? How many times has he preferred white powder up his nose to salt on actual food? His eyes sit back, deep in the skull, dark pools of amber melting the black liner on his lids. His hair, the colour of pitch, sticks straight out from his scalp, and with the dye job, the strands look more like spears dipped in the blood of defeated enemies. Two metal baubles, snakebites, underneath his bottom lip, which parts from his top one as he continues to gasp; the previously uninterrupted plane of his features is streaked with crimson lines. He clenches his jaw to a point where all the tendons in his neck extend out.

What a mess. That's what I think to myself. What a *mess*. I don't know that person.

Oh, wait, but I do. It's me. Well, now, that's unfortunate, isn't it?

I stare down at the bruised, sliced-up knuckles, almost willing the cuts away with my gaze. If only it were that simple. What the hell has happened to me? When was the last time I bothered to *really* look in the mirror? It's not like I apply my eyeliner by feeling around my eyelid and hoping it turns out somewhat presentable. Why haven't I noticed any of this before?

Because the guys are right. Because I've been wanting to die. So me looking like death warmed over in the microwave wasn't a bad thing. It's what I've wanted.

Without much thought put into the movements, I switch on the sink, waiting until the dirty faucet cleans itself out. I swipe shards out of the basin and onto the floor before shoving my ruined knuckles underneath the warming stream of water. The wave of discomfort permits a gasp and a shiver of goosebumps trailing up my arms. It's nothing compared to the pulse of life bleeding out, literally, from my nostrils, though. It's nothing. And I think this is the point in time where I start to ask myself, again, *what is my life?*

"I don't know." My voice rolls over like a man in his grave. "I don't know."

I once read somewhere, probably in a high school textbook, or maybe I overheard someone's conversation on the matter, that once you start talking to yourself, you've crossed the line over sanity and finally lost your marbles. Going insane isn't some wild idea; not in the Kinsey household. Even Cheyenne, who isn't technically related to me or my parents by blood, went off her rocker by just being around us. Our influence runs deep, it seems. The promise of a terrible lifestyle seeps through our blood, formed by woven strands of DNA. And now I know why I personally have sworn to stop the lineage. I'm not having kids.

I'm not carrying this name and this downfall into other generations. The world has enough bullshit as it is muddling around in it. The last thing we need is another family of it. Another family like this one.

I focus on the knuckle wounds and nothing else. (I just need to block out my thoughts for a minute. Then, maybe things will get clearer.) I study their patterns, their lengths and their depths, the jagged edges, the smooth, the shards still stuck in there, protruding out like stalactites and reflecting back the monster I already saw. I also need to get those out. I need to do a lot of shit—I'll just focus on this task for right now. It's not monumental; it's not necessarily life-changing. I already diddled around with something like that when I overdosed. Yeah, okay, I'm saying it now. I'm saying I overdosed. Sue me.

I position the pads of my forefinger and thumb on the two sides of the first shard.

Plink. The minute it's released from the skin, blood flow starts anew. I keep the water running, though I turn down the pressure, and wince just a little bit before setting my teeth. This pain is nothing. *Nothing.* ("This is *nothing* compared to what we've been through.")

Plink.   —   *Plink.*   —   *Plink.*

I died, you know.

Plink.

No pain's greater than that.

Plink.

The departure of air from the lungs, the sudden seizures in the fingers.

— *Plink.*

I'm not one to remember things like that.

Plink.

But I can't let myself forget.

Plink.

Dying isn't nice. It's not quick like you'd think. It's slow. It's agonising. It's wheezing until the body realises - it's shutting itself down. Until the heart stops completely.

P l i n k.

The various slivers of glass clog the drain, forcing the medium-pressure water spilling out from the faucet to spin them around in order to get where it needs to go. I stare at them, knuckles going numb from the repeated pounding, hand a different temperature from the rest of me. Ire slips out of me and follows the water -

down,

down,

down,

leaving me feeling nothing, absolutely nothing, not even the dull throbbing from the multiple slices, not even the racing of my heart as it tries to regulate itself, the tightness of my lungs as they remember they aren't permanently deflated. I've been put in front of a crossroads; I've been rendered into the trope of the guy who should've died, again, and didn't.

How many lives do you need to be given before you understand?

This voice doesn't belong to her, nor is it my sister's. It isn't coming from the guys outside of the restroom, calling in here and interrupting me, but it also doesn't come from me, not my actual voice box nor the one inside my head. It's disembodied; it floats towards me from an unseen source. I don't understand it. My head whips up, ignoring the reflection in the shards, the mishap in the glass, searching for it. Searching for who spoke to me.

Yet there's no one. I've never been more alone in my life.

But I heard it. Clear as a cathedral's bell. Clear as the bad music on storefronts which is meant to attract the attentions of tourists. Clear as my own beating heart. The heart which shouldn't be beating.

What the hell just happened?

And then, it comes again. Repeating itself.

How many lives do you need to be given before you understand?

"Understand." I repeat the last word, clenching my teeth together, shoving the faucet handles off, shutting the stream of water out, about ready to drive my hand back into the mirror. "*What* am I needing to understand?"

My own words echo back at me, and no answer accompanies them. What's the point of listening to something if it's not going to respond?

"That's fine," I say, trying to be easy going. "That's fine."

If it doesn't want to talk besides dropping the same line twice, then I'm not going to push it. God knows I don't want to be pushed into talking when I don't want to. And then, a wild thought strikes me. *God knows*. Oh, but that's impossible. That's bullshit.

There's no way I'm hearing God talk to me. God, who doesn't exist. God, who walks away when the going gets tough. Who didn't stay around much longer than my real father. No way am I going to walk out of this restroom having turned religious or something. Gone through a conversion over a cheap sink and cut knuckles. What a story. And yet - I can't help but shake that something beyond my reckoning just happened.

Because if I didn't talk, if none of the guys talked - then who did?

"The angel Gabriel," is my sour remark, which I make out loud with a scant laugh. "Or maybe what's his name. Michael. You guys are dicks for standing behind me, invisible."

Aiden.

I freeze up again. It's still not her voice. It's the tranquil one that unsettles me.

Aiden.

"Stop that." I remove several sheets of paper towels from the rack hanging on the wall, draining it, rendering the roll unusable. "When I want to listen, you don't talk. And now I don't want to listen—and you're talking. Make up your mind."

I stare down at my arms, realising there's going to need to be a bit more work done than I originally thought. Huffing out a breath, I wet down one of the towels and wad it up, proceeding to scrub at the crimson trails left by the blood. It's practically coated my left arm, concealing the sleeve of coloured flames stretching from knuckle to elbow, and my right's no better. Some of the cuts start oozing again without the water pressure to keep them at bay, but I pay them no attention. I need to get myself cleaned up. *How many lives do I have to be given before I understand?* Not another damn life. I think I understand now, whether it's a little cricket or the angel Gabriel or God himself or no one at all talking to me, what it means.

Clean up your act. And the voice that says it is my own. Though if that requires me suddenly becoming some cookie-cutter member of society who follows the rules and loves his family unconditionally, then everyone's just gonna have to lower their standards. Don't know if I'll ever get to that point of acceptance, but if I do, it's not going to be overnight.

I do need to start eating again, though. Something other than cocaine and shit.

Not the literal shit, but y'know.

"Oh, well, look what the cat drug in."

Now *that's* not a disconnected voice. I glance around, but I'm still alone in this bathroom. The words come from the main area of the warehouse; screeching pulleys tattle someone's opened one of the large doors, followed by the rumbling of a motor. A chuckle cuts through the silence after the engine's shut off, and my blood runs cold in my veins. The guy speaking before had been Greaser, but the one chuckling is none other than, you guessed it, the dread boss, Dollar. *Just what I need right now. Son of a bitch.*

"Glad to see me, boys?"

"Sure, sure," Greaser says, trying to be amiable. I can just see him gritting his teeth, crossing his arms, straightening ever so slightly to make up for the otherwise untraceable height difference. Dollar's a big dude in more ways than one, and bald as a newborn egg. I swear to God, whenever I talk to him, I get distracted by the way the fluorescent lights shine off that dome of a head. I've also wondered what'll spill out if I was to crack it open with a chisel and hammer. Candy? Nah, he's not pleasant enough for that. If any candy came out, it'd be stale or half-rotted in the wrappers. Honestly, I'd just get a waterfall of worms. Or AIDs. Or possibly chlamydia. (Safer to assume all of the above.) Right, his head needs to remain intact; I don't need to be touching his corrupted brain matter, or what's left of it after all the meth he boils up his nostrils.

"Since our main man was out of commission, I took this little errand onto my own shoulders. Sharing the load with the rest of you." It's all I can do to keep from bursting out laughing; I nearly stuff the bloodied paper towel into my mouth. *Sharing the load.* Does he not realise that we *know* he's a freeloader, a gold digger, just a flat-out moron? Don't think I don't notice the subtle threat in there, though. *"Since our main man was out of commission - and if he still is, I'm going to put a bullet in his skull and end this. My secrets will die with him."*

"How nice of you." Greaser's commentary isn't helping the matter of me keeping silent. It's so apparent how done he is with the entire night — and then, the pang fills me, because I know I've contributed towards that. "Well, since you seem to be so entirely concerned with the *well-being* of our *main man*, I'll go ahead and give you the update. Don't want you to ask the question and get choked up about it. Don't need you crying."

"You mean I *don't* have to go back out and look for a replacement? I'm *so relieved*, I'm getting choked up already."

The smugness irks me, pricks at me right in the open wounds already formed. He so very obviously had wanted me to be dead, had wanted to come back and discover I hadn't made it. Of course, I knew this. But having it be confirmed is something else entirely different from just assuming it. Assumptions, until proven right, aren't.

And I shove myself off the bathroom sink, moving towards the door, pushing through it with a shoulder, swiping at the blood on my arms. My hair's probably covered in it, sticky and destroyed, but I can't be bothered. If Dollar hadn't made some unannounced appearance, I would've showered and gone in my boxers for the rest of the night. Now, I'm going to go through with my first plan of action to clean up my act - sans the shower.

Whenever I've stopped procrastinating, that's how you know shit's about to get serious.

"He's —

Greaser's about to answer the unsaid question, but the restroom door swinging open on elaborately noisy hinges changes his mind. With a little bit of a head shake, he steps aside, revealing Dollar in all of his bald-headed glory. I'm already on the verge of losing it (in laughter this time.) I can't take him seriously; I never have been able to, and after this, I never will. There's no chance, there's no way in hell. I can't look someone dead in the face who looks like an oversized Easter egg. Doesn't matter if he's twice my width and eye-level with me. He's not intimidating to me. He's just squishy. Squishy and dumb.

"The man of the hour." The greeting holds no warmth. Dollar stands at the front bumper of the car he's taken from some unsuspecting neighbour. I quirk my brows up at both the faux endearment and the vehicle - someone's custom-restored Ford Galaxie. Repossession my ass. We all know this is a cover for a thieving ring. We don't even have licences to do this shit. I don't know if there are licences out there, but if there's driving ones and building ones and teaching ones, then there's bound to be repo ones. Nevertheless, they aren't in our possession. So we're just a bunch of illegal delinquents pulling off heists. Before my weird-ass revelation in the restroom, this wouldn't bother me. Now, it took on an entirely different meaning. We were stealing other people's stuff, and for God knows why; Dollar always hinted about achieving his contracts from someone else, but we never saw this supposed person. Of course, not seeing someone forces me to question their existence, their tangibility, their reliability. What if all this time it's been Dollar orchestrating this? Milking us from our money? I know he doesn't pay us what he should. I know. And there's always the chance of it having gone deeper.

God, I've been caught up in a bunch of scams and frauds and whatever other shit you can think of to bog someone down. What the hell have I been doing with myself? Waiting to die, man, waiting to die and wreaking havoc the entire time. Going out with a bang. Living life once and to the fullest. Refusing to back down. Whatever other clever mantra you can think of to be stamped across the forehead like some irrevocable inked brand. And it's just come time for me to be done, I think. Just time for me to be done with it all. Gonna have to quit cold turkey, just sort of throw myself off the edge of the cliff.

"Yeah," comes the belated answer. Everyone's been

waiting in silence for me to react. "I'm the man of the hour. More like man of the night."

I can't muster up more sass than that. I'm far too tired of playing this game. This stupid cat-and-mouse game which used to entice me so.

"So it'd seem," Dollar returns, reaching forward and grasping my shoulder. I don't know if that's some sorry excuse for a slap on the back or what. "Glad you're all right, Flame."

"— R i g h t." His fingers clench, a silent threat for me to muster up more enthusiasm. I don't comply. "Of course you are."

A moment of hesitation occurs, where no one knows what exactly they should be doing. Gearteeth scuffs his shoes against the concrete. Clunker reaches for his ball cap, which he must've taken off, and shoves it back on his head. Greaser starts cracking his knuckles one at a time. Jam takes a step forward, wanting to turn in a circle or another formation, but decides it's better to stand still, and instead returns to his previous position, fidgeting. I just stare hotly at Dollar's hand before moving my gaze meaningfully up that beefy length of an arm, into the beady dilated pupils. He returns the glare with more vigour than I've ever seen. I think I might be frying his brain more than the meth ever did.

"Of course I am," he repeats in order to put an end to this senseless debate. I'm too stubborn to back down, and he's too bewildered to do much about it. The gears in his head will start churning soon enough; he's capable of nothing but malice, that son of a bitch. "As I was saying, when I *didn't* know you were alive, I shared the load with you all tonight. Went out and got this beauty. She's gonna sell for a pretty penny, I can tell you that much. Completely redone on the inside."

Gearteeth, who's in charge of interior design when it

comes to cars - if the ones we take need to be worked on, that is - provides the expected low whistle as he pretends to be impressed. As though Dollar doing one heist in the however many years of this business is something to be applauded and fawned over.

"You're welcome for running intervention for you."

Intervention. There's that lame word again. Wonder if the invisible angel Gabriel's trying to tell me something. *Something, something, something,* turns into *nothing.* I hate this.

Clunker inhales so deeply, it resembles a jet's engine preparing for take-off. "Who'd this belong to? Who was the client?"

"Someone high up and well-known on the market," is the vague explanation. I refrain from rolling my eyes. Too much acting out, and he'll get suspicious. I don't want him to figure out my plan to quit on him. I can only hope the other guys follow suit; I don't see why they won't, but stranger things have happened. For all I know, the fates could've solidified me walking out of here by myself. Fickle shits. "He'll be missing her dearly, but — that's what happens when people refuse to pay their debts. The rich think they're exempt from it; we're here to prove them wrong. They're no better than the rest of us. In fact - they're *worse.*"

It's the one point on which I agree with Dollar wholeheartedly. And what a blow to my ego and pride it is to admit I'm in accordance with anything at *all* when it comes to him. Soon enough, the smoke clears, and I view the statement through the necessary lenses: it's nothing more than the repeating of the pretty speech which captivated our attentions and made us sign off our souls to him, made us become his little puppet lackey bitches. I'm not going to be fooled again. I've died too many times in alleyways and unknown houses and beds of women who have no names for me to believe in this petty bullshit anymore.

My friends nod along with him, but I don't know if they're just play-acting or if they still agree with him. Either way, I can't back down.

"You know what."

My statement does what I want it to. It's dropped quietly, it doesn't demand attention, but because I've opened my mouth, flicked my tongue against my chapped bottom lip, swiped at the trickling sensation near my right temple and smeared the blood remaining in my hair halfway back down my face, everyone turns to me. Well, as best they can. The four cohorts face me, while Dollar digs his stubby fingers and thick palms into me, as though that's going to shut me up. The only way I'll shut up now is by getting a gun in my face - and probably not even then.

No one asks for me to clarify. They know I'm going to continue.

"I think I'm done."

It takes a minute for that to sink in. Done with what? They all ask. Is he done with this conversation? This car? This night? Skittering glances and an awkwardly tense silence set in, and Dollar's fingers can't decide whether they want to dislocate my joint or remove themselves entirely. When it does, Greaser looks like some proud mother seeing his kid off to school for the first time. His smile isn't even borderline smug; it's all the way there. Clunker glares a silent inquiry at him; the mystery clears up when Greaser leans back on his heels, almost rocking, crossing his arms. An undercurrent of comprehension rattles through them. They're all on the same page as I am.

"Done?" He blackmails me with the gentle words and the feigned stupidity. "What exactly are you *done* with, Flame?"

"This." I shrug his hand off my shoulder and back away from him, one pace, then two, before spreading my arms out wide to encompass the warehouse in its entire being. "This whole shit-storm. That's what I'm done with. I'm done. I'm done answering to you - and to you" — I include the guys in this, unfortunately, because although they're my friends, I'm not having their words or their thoughts dictate my life; you understand? I just want some freedom here — "or to any of you. I'm done. I *quit*. I'm l e a v i n g. I want no part in this. Dead. Over. Gone. However you want to phrase it, all of it ends the same. With me walking out that damn door and not looking back."

The silence isn't awkward this time around. There's tension stretching across it, covering it, preparing to snap in half like a rubber band extended too far. If I'd been thinking at the time, I would've attempted a different approach. Maybe I would've walked out without saying a damn thing to anyone, and hoped the other guys understood what I was going on about. I think it could've worked out like that; they'd been with me longer than him, and I know we've been through enough things *like* this to have some sort of code established. We communicate without words mostly. Words can be dangerous. Like that isn't obvious. Actions are worse, but words perpetuate. Words exaggerate, or remove, or stimulate, or ruin.

Maybe a pin will be dropped to break it. Or a nut. Or bolt. Doesn't matter what's used, as long as this gets broken. Time to move things along. We've been putzing around for long enough. But no one says anything. It's like they expect me to continue the conversation. I don't know what else there is to add. Like, do I need to expound on my reasons for leaving?

"All right." I look back and forth between them all, throw my hands into the air, fingers stretching towards the ceiling, a gesture of surrender, of giving up. "All right."

Phone. Wallet. Grab my shirt. Time to go.

I back away from them, vision blurring as I turn.

"Where do you think you're going?"

"What the *hell* did I just say, Dollar?" I don't bother even sparing a glance over my shoulder. "I said I'm done. So where the *hell* do you think I'm going if I'm done? I'm going home. That's where I'm going."

C — L — I — C — K.

My veins turn to ice. I hear someone gasp before an electrifying uneasiness spreads throughout the warehouse.

"You're not going anywhere."

"Dollar." Greaser's voice rings out. "Put the gun down."

D e a d   m a n. The words mock me now.

"You're not going anywhere." He takes a step forward with each word, shuffling his feet so that I can hear them. My hands go back to where they'd been when I'd admitted defeat and asked for surrender - right at the level of my eyes - as I slowly meander back around to see him. And there he is, approaching me like a skittish rabbit, and the confidence has seeped right out of him, replaced with a wild-eyed look and a respectable attempt at keeping his hand as straight as it can be. But the gun trembles. Ever so slightly, yet I notice it. I've had a lot of guns pointed at me. This isn't getting shoved in my face, almost into my eye socket or up my right nostril. This is in the hand of a man who hasn't quite decided what he wants to do with it. The idea, though, cultivates itself as he stares me down. "Didn't you hear *me*, Flame?"

"Yeah," is my slow response. My toe lifts, preparing to take another step, to take flight, to dodge bullets, but his fisted hand propels forward, the black barrel of the pistol leaping at me, and instead, I wince in place. "I heard you, Dollar. I heard you."

"*Dollar.*" Greaser follows close behind. The four of them could overpower him, and he knows it. The other three stand at attention, keeping at his hip and his back, unsure of what to expect from this as an outcome. "Put the gun down *now*. Don't be stupid."

"I'm not the one being stupid, Greaser." The egghead regains control of the situation; he visibly relaxes into his stance, the pistol one inch away from the centre of my forehead. "He is. Seems like he's fallen prey to the same plague that's got the rich kids all hyped up on their cash and their coke and their *fake lives*. Yeah? Looks like he's no better than the rest of them. Walking out of here like he's some God-given talent to the rest of the world. Like he knows everything."

"I *do* know everything." Courage borders on idiotic. It's a line too easily crossed. I can readily admit I'm just using words to perpetuate the situation. Flat out being a shit-head. But it feels great. Like I've set myself free from an eternal prison. Like the gates of the underworld have yawned wide open for me to exit. "I know everything about this little son of a bitch you run."

I now take a step forward, a single, menacing step, right into the barrel of the pistol, forcing him to move back. "You lying sack of *shit*. You think you could keep this shit-hole open without someone eventually finding out how you do it?" I slowly shake my head. "Well, congratulations, *Dollar*, the guy who never makes a mistake; you just made a big one. You hired us on and expected us to not find out you keep half our salaries for yourself. We aren't *stupid*. We know when the wool's being pulled over our eyes."

It's like I'm tripping again. The world turns multicoloured and strange, and noises are heightened to an almost painful extent. I seem to lack common sense, as well as logic, and run purely off the adrenalised emotions which pump through me like fuel injections in a blower. Never have I caved completely to the flood of heat arriving with each rush of anger, that addictive flush of hot to cold, being submerged in the frozen ocean waters only to resurface in a desert. I've always kept it under control, let my temper be lost to the point where I could control it. I have such a nasty one. Such a nasty temper. And if I let it rip without supervision, it goes wild.

"You think you're just so smart, don't you, Flame?"

"I don't think it. I know it."

Things will be forced to speed up now. I'm still taking steps forward. Still intimidating him. Still bringing forth empowerment I didn't have previously.

"Since you don't seem to get it, I'll say it again. I'm done with this business. And I'm done with *you*."

As his trembling increases, his finger rests on the trigger. The shaking becomes so violent, it seems to transfer into my own body, through the ground, as though it's making it split in half under my feet.

"And you think I'm just going to let you walk away? Like I said. No better than the rest of them. You know shit? All right. Fine." His voice, turning deceptively calm, pitches up a couple of notches. "I believe you. But if that's the case, then — I *can't* let you leave, Flame. Because if you leave - all that information goes with you. And I just - I can't chance that getting leaked out."

— Shouldn't have opened my damn mouth. Should've just walked out without a single word. But even so - wouldn't he have pulled the gun anyways? (I'll never know, will I?)

"You understand." He shrugs one shoulder and his mouth twitches forward into a small bow. "It's just good business."

"Holy shit, l o o k *o u t ! ! !*"

At first I think he's pulled the trigger, lodged a bullet in my brain. Then, it becomes apparent the problem's much bigger than him. I wasn't exaggerating when I said it felt like the floor beneath my feet moved; it's because it *is* moving. Earthquake.

Earthquake.

"Flame, *get out of the way!*"

A pair of hands shoots out and shoves me backwards, and on the unstable ground, I easily lose my footing. I hit the concrete just as a shot rings out, ricocheting against the wall - but not the wall, a metal beam from the ceiling. The back of my head collides with the lip where two individual slabs meet, and for a moment, all I see is a blackness crawling at my vision, a strange harrowing sensation, as though I'm sinking into myself, and a quick flush of the skin from cold to warm before settling back into clamminess again. No, no, no. Seriously. *Seriously?* I cannot have met my demise from smacking my damned head into the ground. If that's the case, I —

BOOM!

A great crash which resembles a rockslide barrels towards me, and then a terrible screech, someone dying, yelling to the sky for someone to help them, but the sentence is cut off in the middle of it and I don't get to hear what else the person thinks. Someone's *dead.* The egghead. Dollar. Dead because of an earthquake, right before he's about to shoot me. But it isn't the only danger. The world spins itself around on its axis, and a rampant heat attaches itself to my left arm, wrapping around the skin like a glove. It clings to me, refusing to let go, and another inhuman sound rips out of me. This is too much. Too much like what happened this evening. I can't stand it. I can't stand dying *again.*

This is a joke, Archangel Michael. Gabriel. Whoever's up there laughing at me. (Maybe even God himself.) I swear this is just some sort of sick joke. All this time, I'm taunted about not realising why I'm being given a thousand and one second chances, and the minute, the *minute* I decide I want one, it's like, *"Oh, sorry, time's run out, you're gonna die now."* Or, "sorry, but *you're going to be heavily wishing you're dead by the time we get through with you."*

"You're all right, dude. You're all right. Get up. *Get up."*

"Put that shit *out* before it burns his arm off!"

"Get it off of me! Get it off! Get. it. off!" That's my distorted voice. Cloth smacks against my left arm numerous times in a row, beginning at the wrist and not ending until the crook of the elbow. Some places get harder slaps than others, and the person doing the slapping, probably Greaser, if I know him, curses as loudly as I'm screaming.

"Shut *up*, Flame! You're on fire!"

"Flame's on fire. Flame's on fire." Jam repeats this several times. "Flame's on fire."

"This is *bullshit."*

The dust clears from my eyes, and the disoriented ringing continues in my ears, and I blink several times as I take in a deep breath, let it out, lungs feeling as though they're on the verge of collapse. A strange ripping, tingling sensation runs along the areas smacked with the cloth, which Gearteeth throws over his shoulder before pulling my arm away from my waist. I cradle it like an infant child, though my mind hasn't registered what's just happened. I'm too concerned with other things. Like the burning pile of debris in front of me, and the strong odour of gasoline searing my nostril hairs off, and the roiling heat covering me, the roiling heat which I craved but now, I'm sweating, sweating beyond belief, it's pouring off my temples, into my hair, matting with the blood from my knuckles, which throb, throb with my pulse.

"Flame. Talk to me. *Flame."*

Gearteeth grips my chin and stares me down. Is that water in his eyes? The earth still quivers, rocks back and forth. This is no gentle tempo of a lullaby. This is a ravenous cavern being opened from the gates of hell. This is the world being tilted on its side and thrown through the outer reaches of space. This is a thousand stars colliding with the grass and making it explode, making things fall, making things be set on fire.

"What — the *hell* — just happened?" Throat coated in charcoal and ash. I can barely speak. "What *just happened?*"

"Earthquake." Clunker grimly comes out of nowhere, swiping crimson off his forehead, where I see a distinct gash down the centre. There's another similar cut on his right cheekbone. "Place is burning. Maybe even the city. We gotta go."

Time's slowed down for me. I don't realise how fast things are going. Still my ears ring. Still I can't comprehend. what. just. happened.

"We gotta go." Gearteeth steers me toward the Galaxie.

"Wait a minute. Just - *wait* a minute." They've wrapped my arm in the same rag which was used to put out the fire. I couldn't have been imagining what just happened. I needed to see it. I needed to see it for myself. "I want to — see."

"You can look later, you whiney child!"

I snap out of it. Come on, guys, I'm not acting like a child. I'm in shock or something like that. Give me a break. "I'm *not* a child. Wait - where's Greaser?"

I scan the burning warehouse, and I don't see him, I don't see that hair the same colour as the flames. I see the rags around my arm, I see the shock of turquoise hair, I see glistening eyes, I see tall forms, but I don't see Greaser. I don't see Dollar, either - death of the egghead, Humpty Dumpty had a great metal beam and shards of wood fall on top of him. They can't be in the same place, though. Greaser's hands had been the ones to reach out and push me down; he'd been the one shouting at me.

"*Flame, get out of the way!*"

It still echoes, you know. I still hear him saying it. He's just ducked out of the picture. I'm sure he's going to be back. But we can't leave without him. We have to wait.

"Where *is* he?" My head whipping accelerates, turning frantic. I see nothing but walls of fire bearing down on us. Pairs of hands grip my arms and tug me towards the car Dollar lifted from that one guy whose name we never discovered. "*Where is he?*"

"He's not coming." Clunker drops this matter-of-factly. But there's a trembling emotion in his voice which rivals the intensity of the earthquake. "Greaser's — not coming."

"We gotta get *going,* people." Jam wails.

"Don't let him drive!" Gearteeth yells at Clunker. "Just get him in the car!"

Another steel beam, with a great yawning shriek, dislodges itself from the roof and topples downward. A hand on the back of my head thrusts me forward, the four of us stumbling away from the scorching hot metal. The door to the Galaxie opens and Jam clamours into the backseat just as Gearteeth starts the ignition.

More screams (not from us) permeating the air, and when it's all said and done, the chaos contained, I find myself seated between Clunker and Gearteeth; the latter's the one behind the wheel.

"Don't let *anyone* drive off yet!" I feel like I'm shouting against the shrinking walls of an already narrow maze. "Where the *hell is he?*"

"He's *dead,* for the love of *Christ!*"

I can only stare.

"He's *dead,* Flame." Jam's normally high treble of a voice goes flat. "He pushed you out of the way of that debris and —"

— No.

Out of all the people in the world that could've been taken.

—No, I refuse to believe in this shit.

I refuse to believe in *karma*.

One dies so that another might live. Bullshit. *Bullshit.* No. Not Greaser. It's not been someone I know before; always strangers. Out of all the people in the world, why did it have to be him? He was going to get married. He had his *life together,* for God's sake, and look at me! *Look at me,* a mess, and still I'm breathing, staring at Jam as though he's speaking another language, lips parted, tongue darting out to touch my snakebites. To reassure myself of something tangible. Unchanging.

He died so that you might live.

Real hilarious, archangels. Get the hell out of my life after this. I don't *need* you. I don't want you. And I don't need a cruel God who speaks to me without showing himself and *kills off my best friend.*

"Move."

I spit out this single word to Gearteeth. Turn my attention from Jam. This isn't happening. This isn't real.

"Do you really think you should —?"

"Guess I wasn't clear enough. How's this: if you don't move out of that seat, you're gonna find a fist in your mouth and your ass on the floor."

If I can't do something anymore - there's only one option left.

Autopilot: engaged.

Untold Stories of Infected Glitter

October 9th

Los Angeles, California

Cheyenne Kinsey

I sit at the bar, having found an empty stool, forehead resting on the counter and arms akimbo over my head, shielding my eyes from the bouncing disco lights and neon flashes accosting the nightclub walls. I try to keep my breathing steady, in and out, biting down so hard on my lip, I have long since scraped away my maroon lipstick and replaced it with an open wound. My jaws clench together. My fingers flex, one hand digging into my scalp, yanking at the hair while the other grasps at air.

That's what I feel like I'm doing, you know. Grasping at air, walking through life, searching for something that's never there. I mean, here I am, at one of the hottest nightclubs on the Boulevard, where I work, where I'm supposed to be doing my job and behaving raucously out on the dance floor, getting the people excited to be there and using it to manipulate them into staying until closing. Instead, I've collapsed in an unmanageable heap at the bar, trying my damnedest to not start screaming out nonsense and obscenities at everybody.

You wanna know why? I'm sure it'll come as some super surprise. It's not like my brother doesn't have a reputation or anything. Except now, it's been taken to an entirely new level. He's gone missing. Not for a few hours, not even for eight hours. I glance at the clock behind the bar. *9:30 pm*. It's been almost a full day since he left. No word from him. Just gone. No drunk, sloppy-as-shit texts. Just silence.

The whining synths in the beat of the current song grate

74

on my nerves. I'm about to go up the wall. But then, I hear a clink, a glass being set down in front of me. I sigh in relief; if the music wasn't so loud, you probably would have heard it, I was so loud about it. Because obviously Miguel, both the main bartender and a long-time friend, has come around and decided to let me have some booze, to calm my frazzled nerves. I raise my head, a smile of gratitude already in place, but immediately my expression fades back into its previous scowl.

That isn't whiskey. That isn't tequila. That isn't anything with alcohol in it. It's a fizzy, all-too-familiar red drink called the Shirley Temple. Also known as - ginger ale and grenadine on ice.

"What the hell is this?"

Miguel doesn't even turn away from the wine glass he's polishing. "You know."

"Yeah, okay, smart-ass," I say dryly, "but I asked for whiskey."

"When are you gonna learn it doesn't matter what you ask for?" Miguel snaps. "You're underage, so you're not getting it; especially not from me."

I gape openly at his back. Damn, getting married has certainly changed him. He's only been hitched for a couple of years, and already he's turned into some sort of "responsible adult". It wasn't that long ago that he used to be just like me and Aiden. But I let all my hot air blow between my cracked lips and don't bother complaining to him further. He isn't going to listen. He thinks that by keeping me away from booze, he's helping me out, doing me a favour, looking out for my best interests.

But how can *he* know what those are for me? Not even I know.

I'm the locomotive waiting for a new destination but never getting it. I'm the caged animal pacing back and forth, having analysed the iron bars so many times, they're embedded in my brain. I'm the criminal that wouldn't know what to do with freedom even if it were handed to me on a silver platter. Most of all, I'm a hypocrite, because I work here in a position where I pretty much whore myself out to people to make them stay around, which makes the club earn cash. Just to think, I used to insult the girls in the little dresses and the high heels, swearing I'd never turn out like "that". Yet here I am. Oh, how karma loves to turn around and sink its teeth into your heels —

All I want to do is curl up in a ball in the biggest sweatshirt I own, to hide all of the ugliness and shame I feel, and die.

God, I'm thirsty. And the longer I stare at that carbonated red drink, the thirstier I become. If only that thing was loaded with alcohol - I'd down it, and five more, and hope I'd pass out from alcohol poisoning. Nobody would miss me if I died, not even my brother. Sometimes, I wonder if Aiden remembers that I'm alive at all, that I'm still here, trying to worm my way through this awful place. Probably not. He's too busy losing himself in his girls, booze, and drugs.

Is that why I'm sitting here simmering? Because I'm angry with him? It's probably part of it, but in that case, what are the other reasons I'm not out there dancing and doing what I do best - using sexy shit to make men and women drool?

I take the base of the cold glass into my hands and down half of the fizzing liquid in three hard swallows. It burns as it trails down my hot throat and shoots into my empty stomach, which lurches with the sudden temperature change. I slam the glass back down on the counter and clutch at my abdomen with both hands, wincing against the pain. I'm seriously the most pathetic human being on this planet. I can't even drink something sweet and carbonated without wanting to vomit - what makes me think I could handle booze?

Oh. That's the problem: I'm in a state of self-loathing. *Again*. I've been doing this a lot lately. I mean, I can't help that I look in the mirror and hate what I see. I can't help that my eyes notice all the rolls of fat that hang over the waistband of my jeans and bleed through the sleeves of my shirts. It's confusing, though, because in moments like this, when my fingers bite into my skin, I feel bones sticking out like beacons in the dark. But the mirror can't be the one lying. After all, it displays all of my other imperfections with uncanny accuracy - the white lines, the red scars, and the scabs blotting my pale skin. All self-inflicted. Because it's the only way that the internal pain subsides, when I externalise it. And sometimes, all of it comes crashing down so hard, I can't hold myself up, and cutting it out, making the infected blood pour from the wounds, cleansing my tired veins of the filth, is the only way I can keep myself going. It's a purge, if you will.

And I don't get why, when most people see the scars, they say something like "You shouldn't cut yourself, Cheyenne" or "Self-harm doesn't do any good" or "Hurting yourself isn't the answer" and whatever other bullshit they can conjure. Oh, I see how it is. I'm not allowed to hurt myself, just so I can make it through another day, but all of you idiots, all of you so-called friends who promised to be there for me and you boyfriends who swore you'd never leave me no matter how bad things got — *you* are all allowed to insult me, to tear me into pieces, to slit me in two, to rip off my limbs and leave me to die?

I don't know about you — but that sure doesn't make any damn sense to me.

"*Hey*, sweetheart. You're looking pretty lonely there. Want some company? You won't be disappointed."

I turn the bar stool around, searching for the source of the voice. I see the crowd going crazy at the moves of my coworkers. I see the girls grinding against one another, the guys rooting them on, the older men hitting on every walking piece of flesh they see, and the older women clinging to their beer bottles in the way they should have clung to their failing marriages. I see the flashing neon lights pulsating with the house beat blasting through the DJ's stereo system, and the disco ball sending silver sparkles onto the walls. The pot smoke makes the atmosphere hazy, and only shadowy figures can be seen as they disappear into the back corridor. Larger silhouettes, unmistakably the bouncers, lurk near the edges of the dance floor, searching for any signs of trouble.

Maybe I imagined someone talking to me? I sigh, letting my eyelids drop to half-mast. I wouldn't put it past me; I hear voices in my head anyway. I'm just relieved that I don't have to entertain somebody.

I turn back toward the bar counter, fully prepared to enjoy the remnants of my Shirley Temple, when I hear it again. The voice is now accompanied by a whiskey and coke, served by a disgruntled Miguel - who then jerks his head towards the left.

"Wrong way, sweetheart."

I bristle and tense, shocked. Well, he just popped out of the blue. I swear he wasn't standing to my left before. He's in his mid-forties, with greying black hair slicked into what he probably thinks is an attractive style, and large coal-black eyes that look more like beads underneath those bushy hooding eyebrows. He's wearing one of those oversized trench coats that should be illegal because who knows what the hell he has in those pockets. If we're really being honest, everything about this guy should be illegal - those glimmering eyes, that cunning smile, that expression on his face as he looks me up and down and appraises me like merchandise. What a sick whore-bitch.

Oh, yeah, I guess that's yet a n o t h e r reason why I'm

sitting here and not doing my job. I'm sick of being looked at and approached as if I'm a slab of meat on the chopping block. Maybe I've asked for it by signing up for this position, but you have to remember - the reason I'm doing it is because the pay is pretty damn good, and I want to help bring money to the table. Aiden might be a partier, but he works three jobs and always makes sure that the bills and the mortgage are paid. The least I can do is *try* to help. I feel guilty when I don't contribute, as if I'm wasting space and air. I mean, I *am* a waste of air, but at least working, I can fool myself into feeling valuable instead.

But I've been working this way for a year now. An entire year of lying about my age, of being priced by old and young men alike, and even the occasional woman. Here I thought high school was bad, what with the wolf-whistling and being thrown up against the lockers and into the walls, being accosted and touched. Screw that, high school is a breeze compared to the snake pit that is this world.

"Like what you see?" I ask dryly.

I can't bring myself to sound flirtatious, but he doesn't mind. He's too busy undressing me with his eyes, peeling away the black lace corset and the black leggings and the leather skirt, imagining just what could lie underneath those layers of clothing. Oh, no, now he's analysing all of my tattoos and using that magic x-ray vision he thinks he has to make up a fantasy about what other ink might be on my body - and where. Ugh, he's probably one of those guys who enjoys rough shit during sex - you know, throwing the girl's legs up in the air, forcing her to wear her stilettos because he has a shoe fetish, rutting her against an open window? That kind of guy. He hasn't once looked at my face, but I don't really expect him to. I'm just bitching.

"Yeah — I sure do."

Of *course* you do. But finally, his eyes stop undressing and roughing me up, and his gaze rises to meet mine. I notice he shrinks back when he notices my face; most people react this way. Aiden always jokes it's because they're intimidated by the electric-blue colour of my eyes, but he probably just says that to make me feel better. After all, it's in his job description - to make me feel better about myself, to make me feel as if I'm pretty. Well - he doesn't do it that much anymore.

"What's your name?" the man tries to sound seductive.

"— Marla." I lie. Why? Because I'm not an idiot who gives out her real name to strangers at the bar — usually. Besides, making up life stories is a fun hobby, especially with disgusting, drunken creeps like this guy. I can't really tell you why, but I think it's because some are so desperate, they are willing to believe anything you tell them, so long as it ends in them nailing you to the wall.

"Marla — that's a pretty name." He grins at me, and I sneer right back. He's gaining confidence, and it makes me want to punch him in the face. Just because I gave you a name doesn't mean I want you. In fact, quite the opposite; you're not even that attractive of an older man. *Ew.* "How old are you?"

Please, tell me you're kidding. Seriously. "Twenty-five."

"Really." He doesn't sound surprised. "You look younger."

Jeez, I *wonder why*. "The beauty of foundation."

He reaches forward and slides a hand up my face. I twitch and shudder against the contact, pulling backwards, but he takes my repulsion completely in the wrong direction. "How about — you and I find a back room — away from all this noise — and get to know each other a little better, yeah?""

S e r i o u s l y. Is this *actually* happening to me right now? Does he really think that line's going to work?

I wince away from him, lips curling in disgust as his hand

jerks backward. "I think that's a terrible idea."

Plus, I am starting to get one of the most massive headaches in the history of headaches right now. Probably due to the fact that the DJ has the bass knob turned up too loud. With every beat in this new song - I feel like I'm on a turbulent flight.

"I didn't really — *ask* what you thought about it." His voice takes on a hollow, deadly tone.

"Yeah — okay, I'm leaving now. Have a nice night alone."

Because no way am I sticking around here. I shouldn't have even given him a fake name. Give them an inch and they run a mile.

I slide off the bar stool and he quickly reaches for my shoulder. His pointed fingernails puncture the bare skin.

"Not so fast, *Marla*. You aren't going anywhere."

"Actually, I am." I yank my shoulder out of his grip and point my nose to the ceiling. But though I'm putting up a good front, my heart is beating a thousand miles an hour, my pulse feels fluttery, and a sweat has broken out on top of the foundation on my forehead.

"You bitch - I bought you a drink!"

Oh, perfect. He's shouting now, drawing the attention of some nearby women, who immediately circle closer to one another and start whispering as best as they can over the loud music.

"You *owe* me!"

"I don't owe you shit!" I spew out, losing my temper and whirling on him. I can feel my pupils contracting with my anger. "You come over to me, where I'm enjoying a drink, *by myself*, and start hinting around that you want me to suck you off — and you expect a warm reception?" I raise both middle fingers, displaying my beautiful glittering red-and-black nails for his inspection.

"Suck *this,* asshole."

The next thing I know, he's rushing at me. I can see what he's about to do; considering he's drunk, he's flailing his arms, trying to grab for any body part he can manage. I balance my body weight evenly on both legs, take in a deep breath, and prepare my left shoulder for impact.

It comes sooner than I want, and I feel the wind get knocked from my lungs. Gasping from the suddenness of the contact, I'm forced to throw myself out of the way as he attempts to grapple for me. One pair of slick, sweaty fingers touches my leg, but in his fury, he loses his balance and crashes headlong into the spine of a man just wanting to enjoy his last whiskey of the night.

White knuckles against the edge of the bar, stomach heaving and threatening to dislodge all I've drunk, despite it being non-alcoholic, I can only watch through tear-filled eyes (and don't even think I'm about to start crying; I seriously just can't *breathe*) as the whiskey finds its way into the face of the perpetrator instead of the patron's mouth.

The noise level increases. I didn't think it was possible, but now, *everyone's* started to shout, to cheer, to boo the going-ons. I think that's my cue to clear out of here. Which I do, half-limping and gasping for air, using my bruised shoulder to open the door to freedom.

So much for the bouncers keeping their eyes out for trouble. So much for me having job to help out, because after this little stunt, I'm pretty much done and probably shouldn't bother showing my face inside this nightclub ever again. Which is honestly perfectly fine with me anyway. I was getting sick of staring at their vile decorations and their orange ambient lighting and hearing the overpowering bass of their music - which I can *still* hear, bleeding through the very drywall and out onto the street.

Passersby stare at me as they walk past. I don't know if it's the way that I'm dressed, or the fact that I am pressing my back against the wall, cursing under my breath at the discomfort spreading down my arm. I try breathing in the cool breeze wafting from off the Pacific, but with the smells of the different restaurants cooking up their greasy food, and the pollution exploding from the ruined exhausts of cars, its becomes more of a poisonous fume than the clean ocean wind.

Okay, I'm not breathing anymore, I'm *gasping*. And both hands are against my heart, and a sheer sweat is all over my face, beading on top of my foundation, and my stony visage is breaking, and I can feel the panic attack coming on because I forgot to take my pills before I went out tonight, and where the hell did I put that pack of Camels?

Tucked into the front of my bustier, that's where. I yank out the package and I fumble with it. My fingers tremble like leaves on the wind, but I somehow manage to get one of the white cancer sticks out and into my mouth. But I can't light it fast enough; the flashing headlights of the cars whizzing past are starting to blur, and the bass pounding through the wall slams into my eardrums, and I can feel myself falling.

But then, out of nowhere, I hear something rip, and a gigantic flame appears out of the corner of my eye, holding itself to the end of my cigarette. I freeze and am brought back to reality as quickly as I had been leaving it. I'm not falling, and there's no truly loud noises, and the flame near my face isn't big at all, but connected to a zippo lighter, which is held by one of the most callused hands I've ever seen.

Which is saying something.

"You doing all right there?" a voice, rough and dark, says from beside me. My eyes focus on the figure attached to the hand, one with a hood over his chin-length brown hair, hazel eyes glimmering at me in the lighter's light. He's tall, but not lanky; in fact, he looks more like one of those guys who went to boot camp and, if it had been a competition, won first place with flying colours. He has a deliciously snarky smirk on his bow-shaped mouth, and the flickering shadows contour his face nicely. Not to mention the all-black attire.

"Yeah, just fine, all things considering," I retort, laughing to myself. Though I'm thankful he snapped me out of my panic attack for the time being and lit up my cigarette for me, I'm still wary of this son of a bitch. (He's probably a serial killer.) "Who the hell are you?"

"I'm Asher," he says, shoving the lighter back into the pocket of his sweatshirt. "A washed-up ex-Marine who lurks around Hollywood looking for something to do. And you are?"

Looks like I was damn close with the boot-camp assumption.

"Cheyenne." Surprised that I didn't lie to him. I take a deeper drag than intended from the cigarette, but it really doesn't matter, because nicotine, holy *shit*, I love you. "Worked as a dancer at this sleazy-ass nightclub, walked out about a minute ago, not going back."

"Why'd you quit?" he asks. "I'm gonna assume, taking into account how popular this place is, it wasn't because of a low salary."

I turn my back on him and blow out another mouthful of smoke, hoping he'd get the message. But I hear him shift, and before I can walk away, he's right there in front of me, eyes shining brightly. "Oh, come on. You tell me why you quit, I'll tell you what got me kicked out of the Marines."

"See — A s h e r — I'm still trying to decide whether or not I care." I tap the butt of the cigarette, and a trail of ash flutters onto the cement sidewalk. "Oh. *Wait.* — I don't."

"*Come on,*" he says again, straightening a little. "You just burst out of that club, gasping for air, holding your heart like it was about to explode, and didn't have enough self-control to light your own cigarette. And you expect me to let you just walk off by yourself?" He shakes his head. "Nope. I was a medic in the Marines, and I know stress - and panic, and all other kinds of shit - when I see it. And you, young lady, are on the verge of losing it."

He pokes at the tip of my nose with his finger, which smells delightfully of espresso and cigar smoke. I lean my shoulder up against the nightclub's outer wall and sigh. "*Fine.* I walked out because I was tired of being looked at like meat on the market instead of a person with feelings. There. Happy?"

"That wasn't so hard, was it?" is his cheerful response as he takes a final drag on his cigar and drops the remnants on the ground, stamping it out with the heel of his combat boot. Well, he's *seemingly* pretty nice and he has a sense of humour. (This immediately makes him an asshole in disguise.) So, I'll entertain him, I guess, for the time it takes for me to smoke this cigarette. Then I'll make some excuse - invent a terrifying story that'll have him running as fast as he can in those heavy combat boots - and disappear.

It's obviously a flawless plan. (Note the sarcasm.)

"Okay, so," I say, making my voice as bored as possible. "A deal's a deal. Tell me why you got kicked out of the Marines. I'm sure it's about as interesting as shit."

"Well, I mean, I don't know, the last time I checked, my shit was pretty hot." He says this with such a blank expression on his face, it makes my lips twitch. "Anyway, yeah, I made it through boot camp and was about to get shipped off to Afghanistan when, lo and behold, some asshole ran me off the road." He gestures to his left hand, which is covered by the sleeve of his sweatshirt. "The car rolled five times down a cliff. I crawled out and started cussing everybody out. Busted all the tendons in that hand and sustained a head injury. Basically, couldn't fight or really function like they needed me to. So, I was medically discharged."

I purse my lips, and lick them when I feel the dried, crusted blood from when I had been chewing them earlier. "Yeah, that story was about as interesting as shit. I was right."

He chuckles now, and as much as I hate to admit it, I enjoy the sound. "You're funny. I like it. Girls with dry senses of humour are far and few in-between in a place like this."

In a place like this. "My sense of humour has developed over time," I tell him. "It deepened with each crack I received in my rose-coloured glasses, and when the lenses finally shattered — that's when it became a permanent fixture in my *dynamic* personality."

"You even talk *smart* while you're being funny," he says, albeit quietly, and I wonder if he means for me to overhear him. "I like it."

"Okay, *enough* of that," I snap, defences rising. I mean, compliments are nice and all, but there's a fine line between *compliments* and h i n t s, especially where guys are concerned. And since I've known him for all of five minutes, he's now progressed to stage two: seduction. (Stage three is "let's go back to my place" and stage four is sex.) And that's all she wrote about one-night-stands with hot guys and sleaze bags. Oh, wait, hot guys usually *are* sleaze bags. Actually, all guys are; sorry, hotties, didn't mean to single you out like that.

He raises one eyebrow and puts up both hands in a gesture of surrender. "Whoa, sor—*ry*, Cheyenne. Didn't mean to offend you. I was just saying how nice it is to talk to someone who doesn't want to only talk about what they wore yesterday."

"Yeah, well, this conversation has lasted all of what? Two minutes? So — you aren't fooling anyone with your —"

I notice that my cigarette has been smoked down to that point where it burns in your oesophagus because you're *literally* inhaling its fumes - and I throw the butt down on the ground. "— with your *niceness* and — stuff."

I look up to see Asher staring intently, his face contorting into an expression of confusion and realisation. I give him a strange look as I stomp out the smouldering butt. O-k-a-y, well, not really sure what you're staring at, and now, all of a sudden, everything just got super awkward. "Nice meeting you, Asher, but I'm going home now."

Almost immediately after I vacate the spot, there's a shudder in the air - that certain tension which crackles and explodes when two bodies meet and I whirl around, and the panic that had subsided quickly begins bubbling up like acid in my stomach, eating at my insides as I brace myself against the wall, backing up several paces.

I now saw for myself what Asher had stared down: the man from the club had been rushing at me from behind. Judging by the fact that the guy is now lying spread-eagled, face down on the concrete, blood pooling near his nose, it seems that Asher has bashed him in the face. The ex-Marine is now kicking something away from the fallen man, and as it glimmers in the lights of the restaurant's sign across the street, it registers in my brain as a handgun.

Yeah, okay, I'm getting OUT of here. The wind in my hair, the gawking of the pedestrians as I rush past them, my stilettos clacking on the sidewalk, tears streaming out of my eyes and ruining my makeup, hair falling out of the twisted side fishtail braid I so painstakingly wove earlier this afternoon. I have to get away. The world is spinning, the lights are dancing in my eyes, the honking horns are nothing but a malicious chorus screeching in my ears, and I can hear myself screaming, and my hands cover my eyes and my mouth, and I sob against the claws in my shoulder, fighting against them, pleading that I don't want to be beaten again, not again, please no more, I can't take it, and then he is there, the suave and lithe figure of my very first boyfriend, with his smooth voice that purrs poisonous seduction in my brain, bringing back unwanted and unbidden memories that I've long since repressed, and screw having agoraphobia, and screw having anxiety, because this street is too big and there are too many people and why the hell is everybody shouting at me, shouting about all of my faults and ripping my skin off and showing all the filth flowing through my blood?

"Cheyenne. *S t o p.*"

The voice of God rains down upon me and then someone grabs my arm from behind and yanks a little bit. I turn around, rather against my will, finding myself face-to-face with those penetrating hazel eyes. "No, no," I say, and I know I'm going to start babbling, because the single, still-slightly sane part of my mind tells me that's what's going to happen, and sits back and crosses its arms and watches as I do so, "Please don't, I need to go home, I need my meds, please just let me go home, don't touch me, please, I'm sorry."

"S T O P." He says, more forcefully this time, drawing the attention of a group of costumed girls, who whisper and giggle, and I just know they're laughing at me. He takes my face in both of his hands. "*Look at me.* Cheyenne. Where's your house? *Cheyenne.* Tell me where your house is."

I wildly look around for an easily recognisable landmark, but it's hard to focus on any one thing when your vision is swimming and your ears are blurring and your skin feels like it's on fire. Then, I see it: Somehow, I've managed to run all the way to the corner of North Hudson Avenue, and the flash of blue that glares in the streetlight is the siding of the house, *my house.*

I point, hoping he gets the gist of it. "Blue— that house, the blue one, with the lights on."

"I'm taking you there," he says, quickly shrugging off his sweatshirt and draping it around my bare shoulders as I start quivering uncontrollably. "And we're going to sit you down, and you're going to drink something, and you're going to take your meds—"

I don't hear anything else. I have my eyes tightly shut, he literally is leading me down the sidewalk toward the house, which is like a beacon in the darkness, but all I can see is the shadowed figure of my first boyfriend, his eyes bright and bushy-tailed, his words slurring as he continues drinking too much, the control he had, the way he would purr when I pleased him, the way he would hit when I didn't.

Asher continues mumbling nonsense in my ear, and I'm grateful for it, even though it isn't really doing jack shit for my panic attack. My heart beats a hundred miles a minute, and my pulse is fluttery, and I can feel my kneecaps turning into jelly. Is he dragging me up the stairs to the front porch, or is he taking me deep into the darkest recesses of an alleyway, where nobody will be able to find me?

"Okay, um, where's the key? Wait — never mind, found it. You really should put that somewhere else."

"I'll get right on that," I say, and my voice is high-pitched and I hate it. I make a grab in the air, wondering where the key is, wanting to put it in a different place, but all I'm hitting is air, and then the warm, bare arm of a human being.

"Okay, sit down." I feel him guiding me and gently pushing me, and I sink into the familiar cushions of a certain blue couch in our living room. I hear the low hum of the television, which I turned on before I left, and the odour of last night's homemade stir fry I cooked, complete with vegetables and seared chicken. My mouth waters just thinking about it. It's the thought of the food that gives me the courage to open my eyes, because maybe it'll be last night, and I won't have even gone out yet, and I'll be in my comfortable clothes and I'll be alone, waiting for Aiden to come home from — wherever.

"Take this." Asher presses a cold glass into my palms, and my eyes fly open. He's crouching down in front of me, and I'm holding a tall glass of water, complete with ice cubes floating on the top, and I notice that my hands and my legs and every part of my body is trembling, and my detached brain tells me that I need to either smoke weed or take the pills.

"Do you need anything?" he asks quietly, speaking as if I am a skittish kitten in a tree and unable to get down on my own. "Do you need me to talk you down from it? Get you something to eat?"

"Meds," I manage to whisper. My lips are shaking as well. "I'd get up and get them myself, but —"

"It's fine. You don't have to explain yourself. Where are they?"

I'll have him get the pills, because my weed is upstairs in my bedroom, and I really don't want him going up there and seeing all of that, because that's really personal and he's a complete stranger who's in my house. What's the matter with this picture? Absolutely *everything*.

"In the kitchen, on the counter to the right of the stovetop," I choke out. He rises from his crouch and strides into the kitchen, looking this way and that, finally spotting the small orange pill container and snatching it up. He looks at it as he walks back in, and the longer he studies the label, the slower his steps become. My heart skips a beat, and I clutch at my glass, the ice clinking against the sides as I stand up, ready to intercept him if need be.

"Is this the right one?" he wonders aloud, still studying the typed letters on the label. "Says here it's prescribed for Laura Kin-"

"Yeah, that's it, give it here," I quickly interrupt him, not wanting to hear my mother's married name, not wanting to be reminded that our sorry excuse for a family doesn't exist anymore, not wanting to remember that I have an addiction and that these aren't part of the actual prescription. (I buy them on the street and store them in the bottle.) I pop open the white lid and it drops onto the floor; I tap out one of the tablets and shove it into my mouth, letting it dissolve, wincing against the acrid taste and washing it down with the ice water.

Asher is watching me with a stricken expression on his face. I glare up at him. "What? What are you looking at?"

"You just ate Xanax like candy. It's asking a lot for me not to look disturbed. Considering I'm the kind of guy who can't even swallow cough syrup without wanting to vomit it back up." He's shaking his head, and I feel judged, I feel *compelled* to explain myself.

"Look, I inherited these stupid anxiety attacks from my mom, who has *long* since vacated the premises, and they've been getting worse, and since we don't exactly have extra cash for insurance, I've been self-medicating. Usually I smoke weed, but I didn't want you going up in my bedroom to get it because — *wow*, that's super weird. Not even people I've slept with have been in there." I throw my hands up in the air. "*Why* do I have to explain *everything* to you?"

"You don't," he says, clearly amused. "I didn't even ask this time. You just started talking — and I let you. Is that a problem?"

"Yeah, a c t u a l l y, it *is*," I retort, leaning forward and slamming the glass down on the coffee table in front of me. "For *some* unknown reason, I feel compelled to explain shit to you. Maybe it's 'cause you give me that look — yes, *that* one, the one that like laser-burns into my soul. *Maybe* it's because I feel as if you're judging me. Maybe —"

"Maybe you need to take deeper breaths and stop being paranoid." Asher shrugs his shoulders and crosses his arms (and continues to regard me with that *stupid look*). "And don't think about telling me to *get out*, because I won't. I just bashed some random dude in the face for you; I saved you from having a panic attack in the middle of the street; I *kindly* walked you back to your house, got you a glass of water, gave you pills (that aren't even yours), I'm *trying* to make small conversation, ask *no* questions — and how do you repay me? You jump down my throat — and that's not fair."

"Oh, *I* see where this is going."

It's going where it *always* goes. He wants to be repaid for saving my life a couple of times over, and what is he going to ask for? Sex. It's what they *always* want. I wonder if I can at least get paid for screwing him; then I can feel as if I accomplished something tonight besides making a complete fool out of myself.

"Oh, *do* you now?"

He very openly challenges me - his broad shoulders squared, his hazel eyes blazing, his jaw clenched, and as his hands form themselves into fists, I notice that his little detail about all the tendons in his left hand being busted is true; while they're clearly flexing in his right hand, nothing happens in his left.

"Yeah, I do," I say, conscious of the warmth - and the heavenly smell - of his sweatshirt still draped around my shoulders. "You're trying to be different from the other guys, which is fine. Nothing wrong with being different. But it all boils down to the same thing." I point my finger at him, sneering. "You did something for me; now I get to do something for you."

His confusion is evident as I shrug off his sweatshirt and let it drop to the floor. Well, you know what, might as well get this done. I don't want it to be *romantic*, I don't want to light candles or take him up to my bedroom. Let's just have sex on the floor in the living room — and the ten o'clock news can be our mood music!

"You *boys*," I say, reaching my hands around my back and fiddling with the zipper of my bustier, "always want something. You *always* remind me that I *owe* you something. You *want* me. You *n e e d* me. You think I'm pretty. Oh, just a little make-out session. No, not *sex*, baby, I'd *never* pressure you like that." I yank down the zipper and begin working on the lace strands. I've done this so many times without a mirror, I'm pretty sure I could do it in my sleep. (I probably have.) "And then things get hotter and heavier, and you start pushing, you slowly take off the rest of my clothes, you slowly take off the rest of yours, and before I can even think to say no, or regain my head, or wish I hadn't drunk all of that alcohol before going to your house, sex has happened. Slam, bam, thank you, ma'am, walks right out the door, never to be seen again."

Now he's understanding where I'm coming from; I can see the realisation dawning in his lined, hardened face. "No foreplay for you and me," I tell him bluntly. "Let's just get it over with. You'll get hard looking at my body, I'll do whatever you want, and then you can get the hell out of my house."

I've undone all of the lace on the corset, holding the bustier to my form, feeling vulnerable and self-conscious in the light, and if he comes any closer or looks too hard, he'll notice the cuts in my arms, he'll notice the slices in my abdomen, he'll feel the fat between his fingers. (The mirror never lies; it just reflects what's already there.)

"So, *come on.*" I speak over the internal musings, half mimicking his earlier complaint on the street. "I'll just strip and you can do whatever, or I'll do whatever if you're a lazy bastard, and then, I'll have given you what I *owe*, and you can *leave*. Happy?"

This is the second time I've asked him if he's happy, and he really looks quite the opposite; disturbed, frustrated, and, worst of all, saddened. I decide to ignore him and continue onwards, but before I can let the corset fall to the floor, Asher has dived for his sweatshirt, lying on the ground, and proceeded to put it around me again.

"No, I'm *not* happy," he says roughly. "I don't know what kind of guys you've been around, but I'm *not* like any of them. *Really.* What I said earlier — Jesus, I didn't mean it like *this.* Don't — ask me what I meant," he adds, shoving my right arm into the appropriate sleeve, purposefully ignoring when I wince, "because I don't know. Guys say shit they don't mean sometimes. *Everyone* does."

He brings the two sides of the sweatshirt together and zips it up, all the way to my chin as the corset falls, and it doesn't escape my notice that his eyes not once avert from my face. When his thumb brushes against the slant of my cheekbone, I shudder backward - even though I recognise the touch isn't searching for more. (You can't forget, I haven't felt safe in the hands of a guy ever since I was last hugged by my father ten years ago.)

"I don't want that from you," he continues, moving his hand back after a few seconds' pause. "Yeah, okay, you're super attractive to me. But that doesn't mean that I'm going to jump your bones or expect you to jump mine. That isn't how I work.

All I want is to make sure you're okay. Calm you down, make sure you don't have another panic attack. And *eventually* I want to get to know you. *You.* Not your body."

"R i g h t . . ." I draw the word out so that it lasts several seconds. "Well, feel free. But five minutes and you'll run out the door." I shrug and remove myself from how near I've gotten to him, ignoring the fact that my skin protests against the cool air replacing the warmth.

"Fine, then. I'll start out with shit about me." He presses both hands to his chest. "And then, you'll get *so bored* with it, you'll want to shut me up by saying things about yourself."

"Not how I work, army bro." I cross my arms over my chest, feeling ashamed of my behaviour (both my feverish undressing and my constant mimicking of him are lumped into that shame), vulnerable with half my clothes on the floor, and overall, like shit. I'm a lunatic, there's no doubt about it. And the Xanax hasn't started working yet, so I'm still jittery and, as much as I hate to admit it, *afraid.* But I'll never say it out loud, and I won't let him see me sweat. I fixate my face into my mask and stare him down. "Start talking."

He raises an eyebrow. "Unspoken challenge accepted." He's referring to the fact that I'm now challenging him to calm me down, because let's face it, only Aiden and my ex-best-friend-who-no-longer-speaks-to-me-due-to-various-circumstances have ever been able to talk me down. We'll see how A S H E R does.

Considering he doesn't know jack shit about me.

"So from what you've seen of me, which is this," he gestures to himself, "do I look like a guy who grew up on a ranch in the middle of nowhere?"

"Ha, *no.*" I smirk. "I've been around those kinds of people, and you don't fit the bill. You aren't wearing flannel, you don't smell of barns and fields, and your muscles are the kind that come from boot camp, not from years of manual labour."

"Believe it or not, I used to have those." Asher runs a hand through his hair and begins pacing around the living room. "I used to live in the middle of Idaho when I was a kid. I planned on going to school to be a vet. I also used to show horses; my best stallion and I won blue and red ribbons in show jumping left and right." The bitter laugh that emerges surprises me. "Then there was a freak accident in the barn, and Nautilus somehow managed to break his leg, and we had to put him down." He makes an exploding noise and a spiralling motion with his hands. "There went that hobby. I lost my love for it after that."

The droll look I sent him should've been on camera. "Wait, you had a horse named *Nautilus*?" Out of all the things I could've pointed at. But the last thing I want to think about is an animal being put down. That makes me nauseous.

"Yeah, I was obsessed with the ocean and submarines and all that kind of shit."

"Then — why didn't you join the Navy?"

"I wasn't really thinking clearly when I first signed up," Asher continues his pacing. "I just wanted to get out. I had lost my prized horse. My mom and dad fell into deep debt and could barely pay their mortgage. I didn't want to burden them with college bills. So I thought joining the military, I would be able to pay for my own school. But — shit went down, and that's not how it happened."

"What kind of shit?" I ask. When his face tightens, I backtrack. "You don't have to answer."

"While I was in boot camp, my little brother —" Asher gnaws at his lower lip. Even though he didn't say it, my heart sinks into my stomach; the implication's clear enough. Especially to someone like me. "I suddenly lost all interest in getting a better education. In fulfilling my dreams. In living, really. We had such a close relationship, yet I never knew he was being bullied at school. And why was he bullied?"

His eyes darken. "Because he wasn't athletic. Because he loved to draw. Because he wanted to go to theatre school and eventually perform on Broadway." He shakes his head. "He was the best actor *and* singer in that school, and all of a sudden, because he didn't talk to me, or because I didn't ask enough questions - or because my parents didn't - he was gone. And when he died, so did I."

My limbs begin to relax, and my shoulders drop forward as the mellowness sets in. I let my body sink back down onto the couch. Either the meds effects are beginning to sink in, or his morbid attempts at talking me down are actually working. He's making me realise that I'm not the only one going through shit. My heart hurts for him. (That's a terrible sign; it means I'm starting to *care.*) And caring about someone, and their baggage that they drag along with them, can make you weak, can put chinks in your armour, can set you up to be hurt. And the fact that I am empathising, that I understand where he's coming from, what it's like to die on the inside as your life falls into pieces at your feet — that makes me uneasy. I shouldn't be doing it.

But I am — and I can't ignore it.

"I — I'm sorry to hear that." My voice is throaty. I clear the phlegm and make sure that no tears are leaking out of my eyes before I continue. "I know that sounds stupid and meaningless, but I don't really know what else to say."

Asher shrugs. "It's more of a sore spot now. I mean, I used to not even be able to talk about his death. But it's been three years."

My eyes narrow as I scrutinise him. I want to get his mind off of the painful memories, because even though they happened long ago, I know how it feels to drudge them up again. It doesn't matter if he says it's *more of a sore spot*, I don't believe him. I think he's trying to appear strong for me, so that I don't think that he's weak.

Holy shit. He's wearing the same mask that I am. We're attempting to fool one another. Both of us can see right through the masks we wear — because they're the same mask.

Then, I notice that he's looking at me, and it's one of the most intense expressions I've ever received. Like he's marked me as his own or something. It makes me shiver — and not necessarily in a bad way.

"— What?"

"I said I'd try to calm you down and here I am, talking about things like suicide." Asher shakes his head in disgust at himself.

There's a split second of awkward silence, where both of us are scrambling for something to fill the void, and all of a sudden, I blurt out, "I get it."

"Get — what, exactly?"

I curl into myself, chest touching my knees, hands grasping my calves, massaging them. "I don't have parents here. As you can obviously tell. They up and left. I have an older brother - he's twenty-three, but he works three jobs and has his own set of problems. Right now, who even knows where he is. If he's even alive. And when my life changed, back when I was a little kid — I died inside. I died when they left. And yeah, Aiden's been around, I guess, and he's been there for me — until —" (until he found out that I'm adopted) "but — then again, he really hasn't, you know?"

"Yeah," Asher says quietly. "That's how it was with Russell. Like, I was there for him — but I feel like I could've done better. And the guilt, it eats me up, still to this day."

This admission makes me wonder how Aiden feels. Even though he chooses to drink and smoke himself into oblivion, does he also blame his deterioration on me? While it's true that I haven't committed suicide - though it's been a prevalent thought lately - I'm also not the best representation of an ever-grateful pseudo-sister. Even if things were different, I wonder if it's possible for me to be that.

What I do know is this: I shouldn't be how I am at seventeen. Yet here I am anyway, a vulnerable and weak young girl in a caustic adult woman's shell. Things make you grow up too fast.

Oh, *shit*. This isn't good. The Xanax is failing me; I can feel the panic starting to bubble back up again, and I quickly duck my head, pressing my nose into my thighs, attempting to suffocate myself. I don't want to let him see me panic *again*. (I also don't want him to see me empathising with him.) This causes so many unneeded problems.

Cheyenne, you fool. My body immediately begins rocking back and forth, attempting to defend itself against the succulent poison it hears. ***You're so* trusting, *even after everything you've been through. You know what he really wants. He's just warming you up. Not that you really need it. You never were one to keep sex from anybody who asks.***

W h o r e.

"Okay, whoa, we're not talking about this stuff anymore." Asher is there again, peeling my face away, pulling it up so that we maintain eye contact. His face blurs, and I wonder if I'm crying, but I'm not, just hyperventilating, and my hands weakly clasp at his wrists, wanting to push him away, but instead, my body decides that it needs the opposite, and I'm tugging at him, and before my logic can register what's happening, he has me in an embrace.

Neither of us say a word. There's none to say. Unfortunately, there was a strong connection, and through this small conversation, it's become undeniable. We understand each other. We get it. We've both been through a ton of bullshit. I want to explain so many things to him - I want to tell him what happened to my mom, why I think my dad left, how much Aiden and I should get along, but don't. How much I miss my lost best friend, my phobias, my fears — everything about me, I want to lay it out on the table. Is this some sort of like Stockholm syndrome-type thing, where I'm thinking that I like him more than I actually do, just because he saved my life?

Or is this finally something that's teetering on real?"

"Asher —" I want to start the conversation in that direction. Because I hate wasting time, and I want to know.

"Cheyenne, I think —"

But then, he stops, his brows furrowing. When I look around, I notice that the vases are shaking on their shelves —

CRASH! —

—BOOM!

CRASH! —

A cabinet door has fallen open, plates are jittering right out and onto the floor. Those shattering plates registered as fireworks in my kooky mind. Sirens are indeed wailing. Everywhere. Down the street, in the middle of the boulevard. Probably in the middle of Los Angeles. The television displays a ferocious stream of news, which is interrupted by grey static.

"EARTHQUAKE!"

Asher shouts this above a high pitched whine as the television screen turns blue. The lights flicker, the plates continue crashing, and I can hear furniture upstairs shifting about. He holds me in his arms and drags me underneath the nearest door frame.

No amount of Xanax in the world could calm me down now. I bury my face into his shirt and inhale his scent and try not to think about the fact that everything is *literally* falling to pieces around us. I knew good luck was a malady. Whenever I have a stroke of it, it always is followed by something terrible. Always. Never fails.

"What in the hell is happening?" I scream.

"*EARTHQUAKE!*" Asher yells again.

I twist away from him, feeling ashamed that I was clinging to him like a frightened child. Ignoring the flush threatening to break through my foundation, I rush to the front door and crane my neck. But it doesn't really offer the best vantage point.

"What do you see?"

"Nothing," I huff, then stop. I smell smoke. I distinctly remember leaving my bedroom window open before leaving to go to the nightclub. "I can't see anything from *here.*"

The shaking has slowed down considerably, but as I take a step toward the staircase, I trip over my own feet. Asher lunges forward and catches me before I can face-plant. I blink rapidly and notice that things are a tad bit fuzzy around the edges. Damn Xanax. I shouldn't have taken it. I should've just suffered through the panic attack. But no, I'm weak and I'm pathetic and I'm addicted to painkillers. My heart flutters in my chest with the admission - or is it because of the pills?

"Where do you think you're going?" Asher demands.

"Up to my bedroom," I say, my goal still clear despite my fuzziness. I look down in confusion and see that the source of my clumsiness probably isn't the pill at all; it's because I'm still wearing those stupid stilettos. I begin to bend down, just to take them off, when Asher stops me.

"Let me do it." He then crouches and proceeds to fiddle

with the buckles. I want to thank him, but my inner pride demon won't let me. I instead stand there in silence and try my best not to fall over.

I feel him slipping the shoe from my right foot, and I sigh in pained relief as my toes stretch back out. I wiggle them, resting the foot flat on the floor, and holding out the other toward him. With a smirk that he desperately tries to hide, he takes that one off as well, then tosses both of the offending heels into the nearest corner. When he stands back up, I shoulder past him and start up the stairs, clinging to the bannister. I can feel him watching me, but I press on, and finally, he begins to follow.

I go down the hallway and into the nearest doorway on the right. My floor is littered with random clothes, fallen books and hair products. I shove past these, tripping over my wastebasket in my haste to reach the open window, sheer curtains billowing in the toxic breeze.

I stare out at the cloying darkness which has consumed the twinkling neon lights of the Boulevard. Tongues of flame lick out from broken windows. Screams of frightened and wounded people reach my ears, even from this distance. And it isn't difficult to notice that the inferno is slowly spreading this way.

BEEP. BEEP. BEEP. BEEP.

Car horns echo through the stillness. The blacken sky fills with billows of thick smoke. I cough against it and slam the window shut.

When I turn, I see Asher has already found my duffel bag in the gaping wound of a closet and is throwing random shit into it. I blink at him. "*What* are you doing?"

"Packing." Asher looks up at me, shoving a shirt into the bag. "I saw over your shoulder. I *saw* that *fire*. That's coming this way. We have to leave."

"But this is my house!" I protest weakly, feeling helpless

and miserable (and what a thing to protest with: *this is my house.*) "And Aiden isn't here, and I'm not leaving without him!"

"We don't have a choice!" Asher says, raising his voice. "We'll find your brother, but we gotta be alive to do it."

I heave a great sigh, then notice what he's packing in the duffel bag and I proceed to yank it away from him. "Give me that! If we're leaving, I'm packing what I want, and there's not a damn thing you can say about it!"

I go to the closet and grab what remains in there, hangers and all, and cram it in the bag. I go to the armoire drawers and fetch out all of the undergarments, and a nice pretty pair of fuzzy socks, and I shove those in there as well. I then glance over the items on the top of the dresser, snatch up my makeup bag - which contains every bit of makeup I own - and I put that in the duffel bag with a little bit more reverence. (Packing what I *want* - not necessarily what I *need.*)

"Thought about packing shoes?"

I glare up at Asher, who fails in his attempt to disguise his amusement. How can he be laughing at a time like this? (I'd be laughing, too, if I watched someone act this dumb.) I flush, though; I almost *did* forget about shoes. (D U M B.) I go back to the closet and dig out a pair of Converse from underneath a pair of jeans. I toss those along with the jeans in the general direction of the duffel bag. I hear a zip and rustling; Asher pushes them inside and zips the thing shut.

He picks up the duffel bag, and I stand up.

"Okay, let's — "

— C R A S H !

S L A M ! —

— S M A S H !

— B O O M !

(**r u m b l e r u m b l e r u m b l e**)

All of a sudden, the entire house begins shaking and groaning. I gasp, losing my footing and crashing into Asher, who in turn loses his balance, and we both tumble haphazardly onto the bed. He quickly thrusts me underneath him and shields me with his body as the sounds of twisting metal, shattering plates, the computer smashing onto the floor, and horrified shouts and screams from outside fill our ears.

Aiden, where the hell are you?

The Twisted Metal Getaway I

October 10th
Los Angeles, California

Aiden Kinsey

I slam my elbow into the horn, applying pressure to the clutch and the gas, revving the engine of the souped-up Ford Galaxie I'm driving. Gearteeth pulls himself so that he's sitting on the ledge of the passenger-side window, and he starts yelling at the group of panicking teenage guys in front of us, who are trying their best to get their old, beat-up Buick out of the middle of the road, where it's apparently died.

"Come *on*, you jack-asses!" Gearteeth shouts, waving his arms so hard, he nearly falls out of the window and onto the pavement. Fortunately, Jam reaches over and yanks him back into the car by the waistband of his jeans. Once safely back on the bench seat, Gearteeth pushes Jam away and sticks only his head out the window this time, continuing his hoarse tirade. "We have places to be! Come on!"

They return the insults and continue their pushing, but the car isn't moving; it's blocked by one of the largest piles of debris I've ever seen. The car is *obviously* not going anywhere. (They can see it. We can see it.)

So — why in the hell am I out here, in the middle of a burning Hollywood, watching this and much more shit happen, instead of back at home? Why has a measly fifteen minute drive taken hours? Because shit's going down. Because people have gone insane. Because the world's pretty much ending as we know it. No big deal.

And honestly, unless you're a Californian, it probably *isn't* a big deal. Sure, seeing the tragedy appear on the television screen probably will be horrific to a lot of people across the states, especially if they have family living here. And sure, the news updates on the radio are probably making people in the bars talk frantically and gesture drunkenly about the craziness of it all. But none of those douches can or will do anything about it. They'll all just watch and listen as half the state of California sinks into the ocean, and the nation will grieve for the "loss of many innocent lives."

Yeah, you heard me right. Half the state is sliding into the ocean. Damn San Andreas fault. The earthquake earlier tonight, and its subsequent ones, made the plates start shifting at such a rate that the half of California on the western side of the fault line is breaking off from the rest of the state. It'll float for a bit, they predict, but eventually, it will sink. How they can possibly know that, I don't know; they probably have something like satellite pictures that tell them shit we normal people wouldn't recognise even if it were labelled and diagrammed in front of our very eyes.

None of that matters, though. I have two main goals in my mind: the first is get Cheyenne out of the house, and the second is to get out of California. I know exactly how the first goal is going to go; the second, I have no clue, and I'm not really giving it too much thought. Hell, we might not even make it that far.

But I have three friends in this car, and will soon have a little sister in here as well. I already lost one person to this destruction, and he would sock me in the mouth if he knew that I hadn't fought for our lives until the very end. I'm doing this for him, for the guys in this car, and for my sister. I'll get them out, even if it costs me my own life. I will. Just you wait.

(Aiden Kinsey's suddenly trying *super hard*.) So what? Don't look at me like that. You'd be trying, too, if you had a bunch of lives depending on you, and the threat of a friend coming back from the grave to whoop your ass. Stop shaking your head with pity and putting your hand over your mouth in horror; we'll be fine. Stop worrying.

The question is, who the hell am I really talking to?

B EEEEE P ! ! !

I lay on the horn once again, and finally, the teenage guys flip us off as they abandon the car and start sprinting away, which is a difficult thing to do, considering how much congestion there is. Most traffic is at a standstill; but I am able to weave in and out using any means I can, including using the sidewalks. I just want to reach my house. People are running, finding each other, embracing, talking frantically, walking calmly, yelling, screaming, and having panic attacks, gesturing wildly, or trying to steal cars. Someone throws their body against the passenger's side of the Galaxie, and Gearteeth shouts at them, pushing them away, pulling himself to hang out the window again, like he's some sort of monkey. Jam quickly starts chattering about how much of an idiot Gearteeth is, pulling at the waistband of his jeans, trying to get him to sit back down again.

"Man, this is shitty," Clunker says very calmly from the front passenger seat.

I glance at him. His once vibrant cerulean sweatshirt is singed, as are the ends of his hair, and his face is smudged with soot, and a long, angry burn stretches across his cheek, and his hat has long since been thrown away. But his hands are clasped behind his head, and he's leaning back, grinning sloppily. As I'm sure you know, all people have a way of individually dealing with panic: Gearteeth yells a lot, Jam talks super-fast and pulls at his hair, and Clunker gets really happy, starts making jokes.

Usually, I just get angry. You remember how I was earlier, coming down off my drugged, broken state. (I broke a mirror.) I have to tell myself to calm down and to think things through clearly, and then I sink into that stone-faced visage for which I'm so famous. But when the earthquakes started happening, and things started rapidly going downhill, I skipped all of the steps and went immediately to the stony-faced visage. And I don't know why I'm handling this differently. I mean, it probably helps that I'm not tripping balls anymore. But still.

It's almost like my mind is too busy thinking about what needs to be done, and it doesn't have any room for a strong emotion like anger, or frustration, or even fear. Fine by me; the less I feel right now, the more I can concentrate, and the better off that everyone is for it. They're all relying on me. I can't let myself lose it — again.

Must keep going. Must stay strong. Those words echo in my head, and they're in her voice. They are what's keeping me sane. I admit it. Even after ten years, it's the thought of her.

Must keep going. Must stay strong.

CA-*CLINK!*

A fire hydrant we just passed bursts open, spewing a thick stream of water high into the air. The broken, red pieces crash into cars, setting off their alarms, and into people, killing some instantly. I slam on my brakes and swerve, barely missing one of the flying shards as I turn onto a relatively abandoned side street. By some stroke of luck, it just happens to be close to the one I need.

The side-street, more along the lines of an alleyway, blocked off on both sides by crumbling and cracking buildings, lurches underneath the wheels of the car. All of us are bouncing from side-to-side, and the back bumper collides with the road on a particularly violent shake when I shove the wheel to one side, *n e e d i n g* to turn onto my street.

(Yeah, that's the problem with driving old cars. They're stacked in the back.)

Houses collapse, as though touched with a finger which disintegrates them into ash, and screams echo from opened mouths as people tumble into the darkness, attempting to scatter and flee. (Like running's gonna get you anywhere? It's not like any of them are superhuman. We certainly aren't.) Smoke seeps through the air and clusters about us, threatening to choke off our airways. I pump my brakes when we near the obnoxious blue house — home sweet home, man — but the car *refuses* to stop moving. I slam them down to the floor so hard that my foot gets a crick of discomfort in it, but it's no use; the damn tires shift every which way.

AFTERSHOCK?

Jam immediately reaches up and yanks on a chunk of hair, almost ripping it out with the first tug. Gearteeth smacks the frantic fingers away from the locks, eyes blinking furiously as he coughs out, "For God's sake, *not another one!*"

He vocalises this thought even as it runs through my head, and the tendril is followed quickly by: *Cheyenne!*

"Keep this car from running off!" I shout at the panicking motor-heads in the bench seats. "I'll be back!"

As I get out of the Galaxie, Clunker hauls himself into the driver's seat. I pump my legs as fast as they'll go, racing against the rapidly-growing magnitude of the earthquake. I push through what's left of the chain-link gate and take all four of the front porch steps in one stride. As I stumble against the screen door, I hear the walls of the house groaning. My heartbeat thuds against my chest. I feel like I can't breathe. All I can see flashing before my eyes is the blue house collapsing into a heap of rubble, with Cheyenne pinned underneath, dead.

I will not let that happen, you understand? I grit my teeth and pull at the screen door, marvelling at how easily it comes right off the hinges. I toss it out of the way. I will *not* let

California swallow us whole. I will *not* allow our final resting places to be here, where it all began and ended. I will *not* let it happen.

Adrenaline pumping through my veins, I shove through the front door and stumble onto the hardwood floor of the foyer. Looking up, I see the cabinet doors in the kitchen swinging wildly open, their contents spilling out onto the tile floor with a

S M A S H — and a

— C R A S H and then I hear

"A I D E N ?"

"SON OF A *B - I - T - C - H !*"

"HIT THE BRAKES!"

as the guys out in the car start yelling, but those cries are quickly muffled by the front door slamming shut behind me. As I pick myself up off the floor, the explosion of a nearby warehouse causes the outside to be illuminated in wicked, orange light, which flashes through the window panes, causing some of the glass to crack and even break completely. I use the wall as leverage, my sweaty fingers slapping at its surface, as I scream out,

"C H E Y E N N E!"

My voice cracks, and I cough. A billow of grey smoke flows into the house via the broken window panes, and begins covering everything in a layer of black soot, including my face and body. I cover my mouth and nose with my grimy palms, staggering like a drunken man, struggling to stay upright as the earthquake continues turning the land upside-down. With another great lurching of the earth, the old computer desk's legs snap, and the ancient monitor on top of it falls into a pile of drywall that has come crashing from the ceiling.. My ears ring with the multitude of sounds bombarding them. This will never end, will it?

"C H E Y E N N E!" I shout again, cupping my hands around my mouth. "WHERE ARE YOU?"

A **T H U D , T H U D** comes from upstairs, and an unrecognisable voice shouts back at me, saying something in response, but the words are inaudible, because sirens have just started blaring across the city. You know, those ones that they usually reserve for severe weather warnings? Those are the ones. They wail and they scream at me.

hurry — h u r r y — h u r r y . . .

I notice a pair of her ridiculous shoes. She *has* to be home. She *must* be upstairs. That voice responding to me *has* to be hers; though I admit, it sounded a little bit deeper than I remember, and it's not like I haven't seen her recently. Suspicion overrides the panic, and I manage to reach the staircase, clinging to the bannister with both hands, using it to pull myself up. The house groans and creaks, struggling to stay upright, and I push myself to hurry, my muscles shouting at me, my heart beating too fast, my vision swimming and my throat drier than Arizona's deserts.

Must keep going. Her voice is either the bane of my existence or the balm in my wounds. It depends on the situation; right now, it's balm. *Must stay strong.*   —   *A i d e n . . .*

My name. The way she breathes it. It's enough to both make a man weak in the knees and make him determined to carry on. I clench my jaw, grinding my teeth and holding my breath until I reach the top of the staircase. The earthquake hasn't died down at all, so I continue hugging the wall, feeling the house quiver under my touch. This place is going to fall down on my head if I don't get moving.

I reach her bedroom door, which has slammed shut. (Like that's going to stop me.) I throw the weight of my body against it. It flies open and crashes into the wall behind it. When I see her, a strangled cry gets caught in my throat, and I cling to the doorjambs as my knees threaten to buckle, both with shock and with the force of the earthquake.

She's in a mangled heap on the floor. Her hair is all over her face and I can't tell from here if she's breathing or not, due to the massively oversized sweatshirt she wears. She doesn't have on any shoes, just fishnets and a skirt so short, it's covered by the sweatshirt. She looks so painfully small, dwarfed by both the duffel bag near her feet and the guy hovering near her head. One of his hands is on her temple, the other rubbing her shoulder. Up and down. Up and down. A very comforting motion. He speaks quietly to her. It's then that I hear her whimpering, and see that her body shakes.

My temper flares as the guy looks up at me with a combination of suspicious and relief in his hazel eyes. (Suspicious? Of *me*? I'm not the stranger here.) His face is hard, lined, the face of someone who's seen too much too early. A face like mine. In fact, it reflects so sharply what I have seen too many times in my own face that my suspicion turns into shock and anger. It doesn't help that he's hovering over her like a watchdog, murmuring to her, trying to keep her calm. When are people going to learn that only *I* can calm her down? Only *I* know her tics - because I have the same ones. Only *I* know how to treat them - because I've done so numerous times on myself. (For two people who aren't technically related, our similarities are unlimited.)

Maybe that's why I'm so angry: because he's doing it right.

We glare at each other for a split second, his eyes flickering from my face down to the ruined left arm that's a mixture of singed skin and thick burns and raw scabs and hurts when I think about it — and after a while, his face softens.

"You're Aiden. Thank God."

"Don't know why you're thanking God. He hasn't done anything except ruin our lives." I spit out the words like venom. "What the hell did you do to her? And how do you know who I am? I've never seen you before."

"You guys are pretty much the spitting image of each other." (Oh, the irony.) He grimaces briefly. "And I didn't *do* anything to her. She's just having a panic attack."

"*She's just having a panic attack*," I quip, sneering. "Sure, go ahead and say it like it's not a big deal." I'm about to continue on, maybe throw in an insult or two, probably a lot of curse words, but she moves, bringing her hands up to her mouth and pressing them hard against it.

My face crumples, and I know that this guy sees it. He stands up, as best as he can, and backs away from her. I release the doorjamb and fall onto my knees, crawling toward her, fighting against the foreign wetness building up in my eyes. I don't know what it is about that gesture that broke me. When I reach her, I brush her hair away and her electric blue eyes feverishly stare, greedily drinking in each detail of my face. Anger is there, a little bit of surprise, some joy, and then relief, an utter blissful relief. Her hands move from her mouth toward my face, and they touch it, tracing the jawline. I take her by the shoulders and lift her into a sitting position, and her eyes never leave me.

"You came for me," she says, rather dreamily. "When I needed you most. You *actually came* this time."

It's said in that innocent voice of a child, the one long lost underneath the thick skin of too-early maturity. She's limp, and when I release her shoulders, she falls against me, and I feel her breathe in deeply, sighing when she smells the ever-familiar scent of my sweat and deodorant, a scent that has chased away her nightmares many times before. But as I tuck her into the safety of my arms, all I feel are her collar bones and her ribs pressing into me through the cotton of our clothes. Combining that with her words, the pang of guilt I feel shooting through my heart almost kills me.

She's passed out. Having a panic attack always exhausts her to that point. As I gently manoeuvre her around, so I can pick her up, I make a promise to myself, right there in the middle of that broken room filled with broken people. I will never let what I learned two days ago ruin her in my mind. I will never let her get to this point of decay ever again. I will no longer be a failure as a brother. I will throw myself right into the mouth of the monsters, if that's what it takes to save her.

Once I have her in a secured position, I stand up. I don't even grunt with the effort; it's like she weighs nothing. I cradle her head in the crook of my arm and turn around, fully prepared to leave. I have her. That's who I came here for. Mission accomplished. Time to go.

"Hey, dude, wait a second!"

I almost whirl around to face him, but I remember the still, vulnerable form in my arms, and I have to settle for stopping dead in my tracks, shoulders tense. The quake finally has decided to cease, so it's much easier to not stagger or lose my balance like a drunk now.

"Why?"

I hear him shuffling around behind me. He grunts, slinging the duffel bag over his shoulder. "Because she'll pitch a bitch fit if she wakes up and her stuff isn't with her," he says, half-joking, voice strained under the weight of whatever's been put in that bag. "And since you're carrying her, I'll carry the bag."

I start walking again, taking long strides. "What makes you think you're coming with us?" The last thing I want is a thirty-three hour car-ride with this guy. Although I guess I could always kick him out along the way — (Whoops, the doors are super unsteady, don't lean against them too hard or they might swing open.)

"Let's put it this way. I saved her ass a couple of times, and bonus points: she likes me. She'd probably have another panic attack if she wakes up to discover I'm not there. After all, I was the one calming her down."

"You weren't doing jack shit. Wasn't that obvious?" I demand, temper flaring in spite of my attempt to control it. "Sounds more like you're threatening me."

"I'm *not* threatening you." Now he's exasperated. "Damn, you both have some major trust issues. Like, I get that the human race sucks dick, but *come on* — get real here. I've had *plenty* of time to do something to her, and I haven't; you can even ask her when she comes to. It's not like she'll lie to you."

Despite knowledge otherwise (because, let's face it, she's lied a lot to me, and I've done the same to her) — his words ring out with sincerity. I grit my teeth harder. I *hate* when someone actually means what they say; because you can't really refute it. (That is, until they change their mind.) I tuck the little tidbit he's just told me into the back of my head, just in case I need it for later. Just in case he ends up becoming dangerous. "All right. *Fine.* You can come with us."

"Awesome." The house groans as we make our way down the last of the stairs. I cross the living room in a few elongated strides, hopping over shards of plates that have spilled out from the kitchen. "So — where are we going?"

"Across the fault line and to somewhere far away." I don't want to take the chance that Cheyenne is actually awake and eavesdropping on what I'm saying. Because if she finds out that we're going to visit our cousins, she'll probably have another panic attack; either that, or she'll throw herself out of the car, or sit down on the pavement and refuse to move. None of us need that kind of drama.

"Vague," the guy comments.

"I don't even know your name," I snap right back, hackles bristling. Holy shit, this guy knows how to get under my skin, doesn't he? "Don't get all mad 'cause I'm withholding information from you."

"I'm Asher," the guy says. "I'd shake your hand, but you might rip it off."

"Good call," I say, a sort of mocking praise. Maybe he isn't an idiot, like all the other boyfriends Cheyenne has brought home. Of course, that could ultimately be worse, if you think about it. Intelligence is the backbone for power, which is the sustenance for greed, the ultimate demise of the human race. It's unfortunate that people choose to use intellect to destroy rather than rebuild.

"So this far away destination," he says, purposefully keeping the sarcasm he could've used out of the sentence, which is also a good call. "How *exactly* are we getting to it?"

"Does it look like I have time for stupid questions?" is my response, complete with a snarling lip. The last person I want to answer to is some strange guy I found in my house with my sister. And don't think she's not going to get an earful once we've reached safety. "Keep up, or get left behind."

"It's *not* a stupid question. Throw me a line here, would you?"

"I already threw you one: I didn't thrash you dead when I found you with my sister. I'm out of lines to give you."

That shuts him up. *G o o d.* Last thing I need is for him to be chit-chatting like an annoying music box in a parlour. Last thing I need to do is to lose focus because of my uncontrollable anger, which he seems to be a pro at taunting. He's doing it unintentionally, I'll give him that. But that's all I'll give him. (Consider it the second line thrown.)

I shoulder my way out the screen door and onto the front porch. Clunker shouts wildly and gestures at Gearteeth, who has gotten out of the car and proceeded to throw himself against the front bumper, trying to keep it from rolling forward.

"You *moron!*" Clunker yells. I'm almost shocked; I didn't know Clunker had it in him to yell. "Get back in the car! Does it look like you're helping?"

Jam notices me approaching and quickly gets out from where he's been sitting. His face is white as a sheet and beads of sweat drip across his forehead. "You're alive."

"Ain't it something?" I remark sarcastically. "C'mon. We need to get her in the car and get out of here."

Jam's eyes avert themselves to peek over my shoulder, and his expression becomes slightly more interested. "Who the hell is that?"

"Her latest boyfriend. He's a douche."

"Gee, *thanks* —"

I don't give him a response. "Jam, put her in the back with you. And get Gearteeth off that bumper and back in the car. I'm trusting her to you two. Don't mess it up."

He salutes me, letting a shaky, sloppy grin curve his mouth upwards before he holds out his arms, bouncing onto his toes. Trying to put energy and happiness into it. I commend him for the effort. I move closer to him and hand Cheyenne over, checking to make sure she's secure in his grasp before I move back.

He looks concerned. "Dude, she weighs like —"

"I know."

He doesn't say anything more, but a funny emotion - pity or compassion or something of the like - appears in his eyes. He turns slowly, handling her much like a collector would handle his prized antique china doll. "Come on, Gearteeth."

Gearteeth somehow manages to hear Jam's quiet words, even over the sudden explosion of a nearby warehouse, which adds more light to the everlasting darkness.

He lets go of the Galaxie, and Clunker curses wildly as the car lurches forward; apparently, Gearteeth was doing more than Clunker originally thought. He goes to Jam and looks down at the still form in his arms. "Flame, is that your sister?"

"Yeah. And if you could *please* stop staring at her and get in the car, that'd be great." I say it as calmly as I can manage, but the rumbling is starting up again, an aftershock from the most recent earthquake, and I'm inwardly panicking. We need to get out of here. Now. N O W.

Gearteeth opens the passenger door and pushes up the seat, letting Jam slip in, both of them warily watching to make sure none of Cheyenne's body parts get tangled up, or crunched, or smacked into any part of the car. Once Jam is sitting inside, he sets to work moving her upper body, situating her head on his lap, and Gearteeth lifts up her legs, trying his best to preserve her modesty - shielding her painfully thin thighs from our view with his shirtless back. Once he's inside, I move back the seat and shut the door on him, and I turn around to find a rather infuriated Asher in my face, nostrils flaring like a bull's.

"Do you have something to say to me?" I ask lowly. I can tell he's angry because of the fact that I put Cheyenne in the backseat with my two friends, and now, he has to sit in the front seat with an insane bastard - me - and a guy who's throwing around jokes and insults like there's no tomorrow. Because there might not be a tomorrow. "Do you have a problem, *Ash-er?*"

I bite the end off of his name, and I feel a surge of jealousy and hatred fill my bloodstream. They're a perfect match, the Green-Eyed Monster and the Black-Eyed Succubus, and they dance around as soul mates, united in the deepest, darkest part of The Ballroom of the Human Soul. The flower of Loathing gladly sinks its roots into the soil of my heart and feeds off the very sight of the stranger named Asher. Time is frozen as I debate whether or not to leave him here. If looks could kill, he would have been strangled a thousand times over by now.

I don't know what it is about him. I don't really even think that it's because he was there and I wasn't. That's part of it, I'll admit it, but that isn't all of it. There's something much deeper that I already despise, even though it's a part I don't think I know about because I can't put a name to it nor put a finger on it. But know this - if he sticks around, I'm not taking my eyes off of him.

Hopefully, he'll (accidentally) fall out of the car, instead. Then nobody would have to worry about what might happen.

"If I say what I'm thinking right now, you won't let me in that car, and making sure I'm there when she wakes up is more important than telling you just exactly where I think you should go."

I almost rise to the challenge, I'll admit it. I *almost* respond. I *almost* dare him to tell me what he thinks, just so I can have a legitimate excuse to pound his face into the ground. But then—

Her voice.

Must keep going. A i d e n. Must stay strong.

All of the fight goes out of me, replaced by a steady calm. The memory of her voice saying those words to me gives me the willpower to just look back at Asher and cock an eyebrow. Instead of retaliating, I say, "Then keep it to yourself. Just get in the car or get left behind."

He seems taken aback by the lack of reaction he's

received, but he quickly puts that away behind a mask of concentration. "Fine — could someone open the trunk so I can put her bag in there? It'll just take up room in the front with us."

I nod. "Clunker, open the trunk. I'll take the wheel."

"*No problemo!*" Clunker shouts back at me, though I've already walked around the front of the car and reached the driver's side door. "That's *perfectly* fine! They listen to you, Flame! *Nobody* listens to *me!*"

"Shut up and get out," I say, cheerful again. These mood swings are something else, man. "Open the damned trunk, like I said."

"I'm going, I'm going!" he grumbles, opening the door and getting out, tripping over his own feet, swirling his arms in wild circles in order to regain his balance, which he does with a strange sort of awkward grace. He bows deep, from his waist, in my general direction and meanders around to the back, where Asher is waiting for him, openly staring. Clunker openly stares back, and neither of them break eye contact, not even while Clunker fiddles with the broken trunk lock and manages to get the lid halfway open. (Best staring contest *ever.*)

I slide into the driver's seat. "How is she?" I ask, turning around and looking at the three people in the back. Cheyenne seems rather comfortable, her head cradled in Jam's lap and her legs draped across Gearteeth, who flashes me a thumbs-up sign and a cheeky grin, wiggling his eyebrows. Jam gives him a reproving look, and he shrugs. "If I was into girls —" he starts, then finishes by shrugging his shoulders again.

Jam looks at me, and we both promptly shake our heads.

"I don't approve," Jam says.

"No, Gearteeth. God. Just — don't, man." I say.

His eyes widen to the size of dinner plates. "I'm just saying!"

"Well, *don't* say it," Jam tells him, reaching over and patting him gently on the cheek. "Just don't say anything at all."

We're all getting a little crazy. We're starting to act normal, we're starting to make jokes and smile more. We're all going insane. (Can you really blame us?)

I feel the car jolt and the trunk lid slams back down. Both Asher and Clunker come around the Galaxie via the passenger's side, and Clunker opens the door, bowing at Asher and gesturing for him to get in first. I grit my teeth, but remember her voice, and am immediately calmed. She's the balm in my wounds, that girl. I haven't seen her for years, but I've never forgotten her.

I stare out the windshield, peering through one of the many cracks in the glass. The distorted view of the asphalt, of the trees blowing in the hot wind of a nearby warehouse fire, fades and is replaced by the shadowy stamp of a fresh, youthful face. Her smile is wide, and two dimples are carved into her cheeks as she laughs, holding her flannel shirt in one hand and a bouquet of wild white daisies in the other, and head thrown back so that the sunlight drifts through the curls of her hair. As she runs from me, the thin white cotton of her camisole clinging to her midriff, she starts to sing, the lyrics and the melody that is a staple of all of our childhoods.

"Um, hello-o-o?" A hand is being waved in front of my face. Instinctively, I snatch the wrist and twist it a little bit, sliding a hard, annoyed glare toward Asher. The other guys look concerned and warily watch me.

I immediately release his wrist and wipe my fingers on my jeans, like I'm trying to get rid of a grease stain. "*What?*"

"I *said*, how are you planning on getting to — wherever we're going?" I feel my hackles rise at the patronising tone he's using. "Like, what roads are you gonna use?"

"Ones that you drive on. With cars. And for right now,

we're going to Arizona; because the main goal is getting out of California."

I shift the Galaxie into "drive" and press down on the accelerator, testing the motor. It's gurgling a little bit, but I think it still has some juice left. The question is whether it has enough to last us until we at least get out of the state or not. The car may have looked good when Dollar brought it in, but it sure runs like shit. As we roll down the street, a rumbling overtakes the sound of the motor. It's coming from deep underneath the asphalt, deep in the crust of the earth. The sound resembles tires rolling over compacted snow and ice, or going down a gravel driveway. It's not loud, but it's constant, and therefore, it's ominous.

"Okay, since Aiden isn't telling me, can anybody else tell me how we're planning on getting out?" Asher asks, exasperated and clearly giving up on me. Clearly labelling me as a lost cause. Fine with me. I don't give a shit.

The guys all exchange looks with one another and give their variant of a shrug. "He hasn't really told us, either," Clunker says, and the way he says it makes me feel guilty. I should at least tell them, these guys who have been with me for so much longer than just now. I can't help that Asher is in the car as well. And I was too preoccupied with driving before to really explain it to them.

I feel like I'm trapped in that cage again. Sure, the bars are melting and turning into ash at my feet, but the hole isn't big enough for me to crawl out of yet, not without me getting burned.

"We'll be on the I-10, then the I-605 and the I-210, before getting on the I-15 and then merging onto the I-40. We're going the desert route, because I don't want to deal with any more mountains than I have to. I don't think this car won't make it on those kinds of roads anyway."

I say this in a monotone, keeping all the emotion out of it, silently hoping that Cheyenne is still unconscious. I really don't need her coming awake and recognising any of the roads that I'm saying. I really don't need her throwing a tantrum.

Plus I'm grumpy because Asher went and ruined my beautiful image of *her* face. I'm inwardly growling at him, like an animal. Like a caged animal. Damn.

"That's probably the worst idea I've ever heard," is what Asher says, appearing to be dumbfounded with the description of my route.

I slam on the brakes and pound my hand on the steering wheel, whirling in my seat to face him, barely keeping the beast inside chained up and locked in his cage. "Well, *what else* am I supposed to do? It's the same route my parents took each summer! It's the only route I know! I don't know a thousand routes to get out! This is the *only one!*"

"Calm down, Flame!" Gearteeth hisses from the back, reaching forward and tapping the side of my face with two fingers. "*Calm down!* Do you want to wake her up?"

I look at the pale features with the parted lips, and how my little sister is so small and vulnerable to everything. I look at Gearteeth's white face and at Jam's hair plastered to his forehead by sweat, and when I turn back around, I see Clunker steadily looking at me, a strange sense of compassion in his eyes, and Asher looking stricken, yet determined. The image of her smiling face appears, and the tune she always hummed races through my head.

I sink back down onto the bench seat and cover my face with my hands, pinching at my skin with my fingers, taking in a deep breath, smelling the soot, the gasoline, the fire and the sweat that covers my palms along with the burning city that leaks in through the window. So close to losing it. But I can't afford to break down again. I've already broken down once tonight; twice is overkill. I have to stay strong, I have to keep going, I have to be an immoveable wall - not just for my sake, but for *all* of our sakes, including for the sake of the douche sitting next to me. I feel as if my shoulders are collapsing in on themselves, like the earth is, due to the amount of responsibility resting on them.

I want to do more than just drive. But all I can do is drive. And I'm not even doing that, because I can't seem to keep it together.

"All right," I say through my hands, finally removing them from my face and blinking away the ash that got into my eyes. My voice is strained and hoarse, and I suddenly feel very, very tired. "Do you have a better route?"

It takes a moment for Asher to realise that I'm directing the question at him, and he quickly begins his explanation, though I do notice how he edges away from me and more towards Clunker. "I don't know if it's a *better* route, but we definitely won't be caught up in the herd of cattle that will be taking the main highways."

"The herd of cattle?" Clunker interjects, pushing Asher away.

Asher stumbles a little bit, but quickly picks up where he left off. "Y-Yeah, herd of cattle. You know, people are like cows: they follow the masses. Hundreds and thousands of people from this side of California are going to be taking those main highways, all in hopes of the same thing: finding an opening, weaving in and out, somehow making it through traffic, blah, *blah, blah*.

"Well, we can beat those odds. It's kind of a — curvy road, but we won't have to deal with tons of panicking, stupid people. Take the Angeles Crest Highway through the mountains. I don't think it's that far from here, and you don't have to be on the 210 for very long. It will drop you off at the I-15 - on the other side of the Andreas fault - and you can continue the route you know."

A pause. Then —

"Did you *not* hear what I just said?" I snap, my original fire returning. "This car is falling apart! It isn't going to be able to handle the highways - much less the *mountains!*"

"It doesn't have to for long!" Asher says hurriedly, gesturing at me with his hands, which I watch with a detached expression. "Just for about twenty miles. I was a Marine, and I know for a fact that there's a hidden base along that road - with food, weapons, better cars, and all kinds of shit."

Food. Weapons. *Better cars.* Everything that we don't have, and that we'll probably need. (Except for the weapons, but —)

"Well, I hope this place hasn't been completely trashed by a rock slide or something," I growl, clenching the steering wheel hard in my hands, knuckles turning white. "And if we end up dying because of you — know that I will whoop your ass in the fires of hell."

"I believe it." Asher spreads his hands wide. "But think about it. Would I *really* suggest something that would put Cheyenne in unnecessary danger?"

"I don't know," is my response as I stare at him. "Would you?"

He doesn't seem to know what to say, so I press on the gas, and the tires spin out, smoking as I shift quickly into second and then third gear. The Galaxie begins to drift, rear end swerving to the left, and I work the steering wheel, focusing on the driving, on something that I know I'm good at, something that I know I can do, something that is solid and factual and very much within my power. Clunker sticks his hands straight up in the air, like he's riding a roller-coaster, and whoops wildly. Gearteeth ducks down, trying to keep Cheyenne from rolling off his lap, and Jam claps a couple of times, fist-bumping the air, before he does the same.

I know how to get to the mountain route, and Asher is right; it's about fifteen miles from the house. I remember one glorious vacation that my family and I went on during the spring break of seventh grade. We travelled right on up that highway and went on one of those tour-things they host at the San Andreas fault line. You can go out and look for things, or — something. Doesn't matter; the point's been proven that Asher's insane. He's basically suggesting we head straight into the fault. What kind of bullshit is that? Makes me wonder if he really does have Cheyenne's - or anybody else's, for that matter - best interests at heart. But desperate times call for desperate measures, and I do agree with him about the people being like cattle; so, I'd much rather die trying a foolish plan than die alongside the rest of a herd. I don't know; at least if we don't make it this way, I'll feel like I at least tried my hardest, because I'll have been driving frantically and trying to reach a base with a bunch of supposed supplies, instead of sitting in traffic, honking my horn, worriedly admitting secrets and fidgeting.

And at least this way, I'll be keeping my mind busy and the people in this car morbidly entertained.

Must keep going.

Her smile is bright in the sunlight. The wind whips through her hair. Those eyes sparkle at me as she touches my cheek.

Must stay strong.

I turn left onto a congested boulevard and slam my elbow into the horn. A group of people jump out of the way, and I shift down into second gear, the engine snarling as I accelerate back up to my original speed. I'm clenching my jaw so hard, I feel the enamel wearing off of my teeth. I could really use a cigarette, but

I smoked my last one at the party. (Did that really happen, before the earthquakes took over and changed everything as we know it?)

I slam on the brakes and drift again, turning onto a side street to the right. A grey truck honks its horn at me, and I wave at the driver via the window. The traffic lights are all busted, their bulbs having exploded from the earthquakes, and some of them spew sparks everywhere, still shorting out. But the darkness of the night is lit up by the multitudes of fires in the city. The four-lane road I'm on is crammed on both sides by palm trees, miniature cliff faces, and small buildings, most of which have collapsed in on themselves. The lights along the street are out. Leaving me with only the dim headlights of the galaxy in which to see. A speed-limit sign, declaring that you shouldn't be going faster than thirty-five miles per hour, has fallen across the road.

CA-CLUNK T H U M P.

The Galaxie rolls right over it, and I laugh; I'm going much faster than that. I weave around other cars who are slamming into each other, and the ones that have manage to evade wrecks, I pass them as if they're at a standstill, not moving at all.

Clunker reaches forward, somehow managing to fiddle with the radio dials as I speed into an intersection, turning the wheel with an expert hand, drifting onto Forest Lawn Drive. Most of the stations are white noise, and the ones that are working are nothing more than people speaking frantically into microphones about the impending doom of which we Californians are already highly aware, so he turns it right back off. A semi-truck slams to a stop, its loud horn screeching at us and another car, which is following us quite closely doesn't drift nearly as nicely as the Galaxie does and therefore ploughs into the driver's side of the semi-truck. It's a nasty thing, the sound of crunching metal and shattering windows and the car alarm going off, the headlights blinking. But I put it out of my mind - nothing I can do about it now - and keep speeding on ahead.

These multi-lane roads are crowded like Venice Beach's pot shops, so I can't imagine what the main interstates are like. I haven't stopped turning the wheel ever since I left the road on which our house is located. Left, right, drift, smoking tires, blare horn, flip someone off,

s c r e e c h -

S C R E A M

c r a c k

C R A S H —

Repeat.

It's monotonous. But it's something.

I can feel the clock taunting me to look at it and count down how much time is left before escape is no longer an option. **1:03AM.** The ancient dial glows an ominous green.

I merge onto a thin black strip of asphalt, passing by a building that's whistling and on fire, and get on to the interstate, blowing by a couple of trucks, who flash their headlights at me, and speed up, shifting into fourth gear, then fifth, and finally into sixth with a jerk of the gearshift, and the Galaxie settles in around seventy-five miles an hour. While there are still stalled cars and running people that I have to watch out for, I manage to get a couple of glances in, checking on the other passengers who are in here with me, having entrusted their lives into my hands.

Asher stares straight ahead, deep in thought about something. The colour is back in his face, and he bites down hard on his lower lip. His eyes narrow a tad as well, and the wind whips about his hair, framing his hardened, weathered face.

Clunker looks completely relaxed, hands clasped behind

his head, right ankle resting on his left knee, which jiggles as he moves it up and down in impatience. He nods his head to some internal music, considering the radio failed him, and if his eyes had been closed, I would've thought he was asleep.

Gearteeth bends in half over Cheyenne's legs, but his eyes remain wide and staring at the floorboard. He looks like he's in a completely different world. Jam is also bent in half, but over Cheyenne's face, and while one hand strokes away errant strands of hair from her cheek, the other rests on Gearteeth's shoulder, rubbing it. Gearteeth glances up at him, and they share a little smile, one that's known only between the two of them.

And there's Cheyenne, with her pale face and trembling, parted lips, nowhere near consciousness. And I can't help but wonder if she would be this way if I had been there for her more. ("*You came for me. You actually came this time.*")

I close my eyes for a brief second, and when I open them next, they're wet.

I cut across the lanes of the highway and get off on the exit that leads to the Glendale Freeway. It's less than five miles until we reach that damned mountain road. As the earth begins to grumble again, I can see the crash barrier to our right crumbling into dust, and a silhouette of a tree is uprooted, wailing as its tossed onto its side, and I struggle to keep the car on the moving asphalt as all the other frantic drivers around me lose control of their vehicles. I wonder if I made the best choice for us by listening to Asher.

The motor gurgles and sputters, the exhaust coughing and I internally panic, leaning toward the steering wheel, as if getting a little bit closer to the motor will encourage it to continue, to not die on me just yet. My heart lurches as it sputters once more — and then roars back to life. And we barely lost any speed. Good.

We're starting to go uphill now, and the more lanes a road has, the more traffic that seems to be on it. The multitude of headlights illuminate the road ahead. I have to press on the brakes, practically ride them, and my feet shift hurriedly in-between all three of the pedals on the floorboard as I weave around cars and people. I barely avoid being sideswiped by a massive Ford F-350, yet I get rear-ended by a another truck with a chrome bullhorn on its grill and am sent propelling forward at a terrifying speed, having to pump the brakes in order to avoid creaming the back of a van.

I just have to make it to the mountain road in one piece. I have to make it to the Angeles Crest Highway without losing a tire or a life. I have to.

Must keep going. Must stay strong.

I let my body return to autopilot, my eyes seeing things that my mind doesn't register but that my limbs make me react to anyway. I let the road become a part of the automatic absorption, and I allow the active part of my mind to wander. Because driving *isn't* enough. Even that is too repetitive for my brain to keep focused on it for long. I can do this in my sleep. I'm too comfortable with it. So I must allow myself to drift off a little bit. Or else I won't make it.

People do strange things to cope. This is my way of coping.

My memory takes me back to the summer of my eleventh birthday, when *she* was still seven. (Now I don't want any of you people gasping about the gigantic age gap, because back then, of course I wasn't really *in love* with her, but I did love her, and was comfortable around her, and didn't get annoyed with her like I did other kids that were her age, because even then, she had a strange ancientness about her, a maturity in the head that's rare in most adults, much less children.

"Come on, *Aiden*, you know those aren't the words!" she fumed, stomping her little foot. It was a hot July day, right after a church service, and we were playing out in the front yard. Or actually, she was picking flowers and I was watching with my arms crossed, smirking at her antics. (Even back then, I was broody as hell.)

"They are, too!" I teased. She had been teaching me the words to a song she had made up, and I purposefully had gotten them wrong, only because I wanted to hear her sing them again. She had this high, clear voice, much like a flute, and it trilled whenever she hit the higher notes. There weren't that many high notes, mostly low ones, but you get the picture. I liked her voice, and I wanted to hear the song again.

"Are not!" she protested, tossing a handful of dandelions at me. The yellow flowers hit me in the cheek, and I gasped in pretend shock, diving at her, wrapping my arms around her waist and swinging her around in the air. She squealed in delight as I spun her twice, three times, then set her back on the ground.

She continued spinning around herself, much slower, crossing her eyes and sticking out her tongue. "I'm *dizzy*. Now I can't remember the words! Thanks a lot, Aiden!"

"Liar!" I said, reaching forward and tickling her waist. Though not very ticklish in general, she still giggled and pushed at my hands, which was the reaction I had been hoping for. "You know the words better than anyone!"

"Of course I do!" she declared haughtily, thrusting her nose in the air, changing her stance. "After all, I'm the one that made them up!"

"Come on, just sing them again, little doe," I croon, using her favourite nickname. "I want to make sure I have them right before I sing them back to you. I don't want to mess up again."

She cleared her throat and —

"LOOK OUT!"

I blink out of the reverie in time to notice Asher and Clunker both pointing at a massive car pile-up that rapidly approaches the front bumper of our Galaxie. My eyes dart around, and I see that the exit we need is not too far after the jam, and that there is the slightest sliver of asphalt I've ever laid eyes upon directly to the right. Without further hesitation, I work the brakes and the clutch, spinning the wheel around, heart and pulse thudding like tribal drums. Jam and Gearteeth both scream and reach over, clinging to each other as they bend even further over Cheyenne, most likely suffocating her in their attempts to save her from the possible wreck that's about to happen.

"*S H I T!*" Asher shouts. "*S H I T ! ! !*"

A small car on my left has sped up and attempts to pass us, obviously not satisfied that I'm slamming on my brakes and have begun spinning. I alternate between the pedals, feeling more like I'm trying to dance with a girl at prom than driving a car, when the rear bumper smashes into the side of one of the cars in the pile-up, bouncing us forward. We're thrown around, missing the small gap of road that I was aiming for - and we watch as the other car slams head on, and becomes the just another vehicle to join the mangled mass of metal carnage. I wince, feeling for the driver and whatever passengers he or she might have had in the car with him or her — because that could've been us.

"Were you not paying *attention?*" Asher asks, shaking with either fear or anger. I can't really decide which one it is, nor can I bring myself to care enough to inquire. "That madhouse could be seen from half a mile back! Why the hell didn't you —"

"How about you shut up and let me drive?" I push the Galaxie in reverse so I can turn it around — and as the motor whines, I creep through the opening. "I don't see anybody else offering to take over the wheel and telling me that I can sit in the passenger's seat and just give the directions. So don't start throwing around questions that I can't answer and don't start lecturing me like you're my father. My father is *dead* to me. Understand? And I don't need some punk like you stepping in to do the job."

(Gearteeth had offered to drive much earlier, but I wouldn't let him.) Too proud, too far gone, too delusional to realise I can't do it all myself. But I just need to finish that daydream, and I'll be fine. I'll be fine. I promise.

Asher sucks in a deep breath and holds it there for a while. I think that, judging by most of his reactions, he doesn't exactly have the most controlled temper, either. A bunch of hotheads in one vehicle, together for over three hours is the definition of insanity. This probably will end in someone committing suicide or murder. One of the two is bound to happen. Then, he begins nodding his head, over and over, answering some internal question or maybe some question from another person in the car that I didn't hear be asked. Either way, he continues nodding, and I wonder about all of our mental health. Only for a moment, though.

I don't stay on the shoulder of the road for very long, less than half a mile, and when I see exit number twenty, which reads "CA-2/Angeles Crest Hwy." No other cars are taking this exit; all of them have become part of the huge mass of mangled carnage. Sounds of people slamming on their brakes can be heard in the darkness, their lights illuminating and painting a macabre picture of blood-splattered bumpers.

S C R E E C H ! —

BOOM. . .

We continue on unhindered, and I drift slowly to a stop

after turning the car so that the front faces the left.

And there it is. I let the Galaxie idle in the middle of the four-lane road, shifting it into "neutral," and we all drink in the sight of the shadowy mountain range towering before us, a silent guardian of a dangerous beast. The road is surrounded on both sides by trees, which fade - if memory serves me - into brush, cliff faces, and rocky walls later on. The road is almost completely deserted, and the people who are driving on it are heading away from it.

The earth rumbles underneath us, and I feel it shifting from side to side. I can feel it moving, even through the vibrating chassis of the Galaxie. My vision swims a little bit, and I swear that I can see the dark mountains in front of us moving also, shifting slightly in place, meandering inch-by-inch to the side, or even splitting in half —

I shake the foreshadowing visions out of my eyesight and blink rapidly. There's no way that's actually happening, not as I'm sitting here, pretty far away, watching it. It has to be some trick of the approaching dawn. But I still see the mountain, wavering at the edges, moving.

Moving.

I clamp my teeth together and do my best to not panic. Because even if the mountains aren't actually moving, more time has passed than I wanted and driving fast and crazy did absolutely no good.

"Well —" Asher says shakily. "This is it."

Nobody else has the words nor the balls nor the nerve to comment out loud. I resist the urge to punch Asher in the mouth (considering all of us guys end up staring at him for about five seconds, with similar looks of disbelief and "*seriously*" painted on our faces, and that's good enough for me) and instead shift back into first gear, yanking on the gearshift so hard, it shakes, and I fear for a minute that I broke it. (But I didn't. So whatever.) I press the accelerator down. I hold in my breath. Since there isn't any sort of traffic pile-up, nor semi-trailer honking at us, nor any other car speeding up to attempt to pass us, I let my mind drift back into the pleasantry of the daydream.

Because this really *is* it. And if we don't make it - which seems to be more likely to happen than I wanted to admit earlier - I want all of my last thoughts to be focused on her, the best friend I lost, the love I didn't realise I had until it was too late and I was too deep in my misery to do something about it.

"Come on, just sing them again, Little Doe," I crooned, using her favourite nickname. "I want to make sure I have them right before I sing them back to you. I don't want to mess up again."

She cleared her throat and giggled a little bit before sitting down on the ground, twirling around a dandelion by its stalk as she started to sing.

And as the little girl sings in my head, I sing quietly out loud the sad little melody with the hopeful lyrics that she made up herself.

"When the sun comes out to play,"

Asher sends me a sideways glance, confused.

"It's time to have another day."

"What the hell is he singing?" Jam whispers.

"We raise our hands to touch its face,
and we are warmed by its embrace."

I swallow hard. The curves in the road are starting, and I can feel my fingers shaking in anticipation.

"And then the dark creeps over us—"

I feel a little bit childish singing this, but its well worth the amount of tranquility and comfort I'm suddenly feeling, as if I've injected myself with morphine.

"We feel real scared and not so tough."

"This is depressing," Gearteeth mutters.

"Our covers cannot help us hide;

we feel the monsters creeping by."

I take in a deep breath and I guide the Galaxie as smoothly as I can manage around the holes in the bridge, nearly jumping out of my skin as its foundation groans and creaks and cracks.

"When in our dreams we start to run, we feel the warmth that's from the sun..."

I clear my throat.

"It chases all our fears away—"

—and I'm unable to finish it.

"It gives to us another day."

It's not my own voice that utters the final line of the song, but a raspy voice from low in the backseat.

Instead of my heart thudding faster, as it's been doing all night, it very nearly stops dead in my chest cavity. I almost cave into the urge to pull the car over now and to fold my body over the steering wheel. Instead, I grip it harder and refuse to glance in the rearview mirror.

"Welcome back, love-dove," Jam says in greeting.

"Glad you could join us," Gearteeth tells her.

Asher turns around and smiles one of the softest smiles I've ever seen on a guy, especially when they're looking at my little sister. "Hey, there."

"Nice to finally meet you," Clunker calls back.

"Aiden?" is the second thing she says. *"What* is going on?"

(—I don't even know where to start.)

The Twisted Metal Getaway II

October 10th
Angeles Crest Highway, California

Cheyenne Kinsey

Do you know how hard it is to keep your mouth shut when you hear something you *really* hate? I regained consciousness around the time that Aiden was explaining to the guys the route that he planned on taking, and ever since then, I've been lying back here, inwardly fuming at a number of different things. You can only keep biting down on your tongue for so long before it bleeds. And I've pretty much been splitting mine in half for God knows how long.

You might be wondering why I didn't let them all know I was awake before, when I actually came to. Let's be honest here. I can't handle all the testosterone that has been crammed into this car. This car isn't big enough to handle the two egos in the front seat: the overprotective brother and the stranger who apparently has something to prove. And they would've just started being all manly, and vying for my attention, because they're both hard-headed idiots who don't seem to understand that I'm not fragile and easily breakable. Yeah, I have panic attacks, big deal. Doesn't mean that I can't function as a human being. Doesn't mean I need to be treated like a porcelain doll.

Which brings me to another thing that's irking me. Why is this guy stroking my hair away from my face constantly? I mean, thank you, but no thank you, please *stop*. It's taken literally all of my willpower to not reach up and slap him across the face.

Also, I wouldn't have been able to handle sitting up and looking out the windows at the destruction around me. It's taken me a while to finally accept everything that Aiden and the other guys have been saying. At first, it was like, California can't be splitting in half and breaking off into the ocean. No way. This is just some sort of fantastic story concocted by some newscaster on meth, right?

N o p e. These earthquakes, the screaming people, the taste of panic and sweat in the air, the fires — it all points to the fact that something big is happening. And though I really don't want to imagine that it's the state splitting in half, I can't really think of anything else it could be. Except just a super-bad earthquake. But if that's all it was, then wouldn't the trembling and the groaning have stopped by now?

And besides, it does kind of feel like we're travelling uphill. Even in places where I know for a fact that there's no change in altitude.

So yeah, because of all these things, I've done a pretty good job in milking this whole "I've fainted into oblivion" act. And I haven't wanted to drop it.

Not until now.

Because Aiden had to go and start singing that *stupid song*.

That's when it all sank into my head. Arizona, he told the guys. "Arizona's where we're going for now" is how he phrased it, or something along those lines. That hadn't really seemed suspicious to me, because the other thing he said is true - it really is more important that we focus on getting out of the state first. But now, I'm onto him. I know exactly where he's planning on going.

Arizona? Ha. Arizona, my ass.

No, he's going much further. He's going back *there*.

And I can't believe it. I really can't. Not after all the shit we went through. Not after all the unopened, handwritten letters I witnessed him receiving in the mail too many times. Not after how *her* father told *our* father that he thought we both were terrible influences on his children. Not after that huge fall out. Not after a decade of not seeing or hearing from any of them.

I know I'm not making any sense. It'll all make sense eventually. Maybe. But I'm just really pissed off right now. And I'm going to make it known. Enough with the damsel-in-distress act. Enough with milking the fragility for as long as I can.

ENOUGH!

He's losing it up there in the front seat. I can smell it. That frightens me. He's never been this close to breaking before. He's usually so strong, so stable. I rely on him for my sanity sometimes. And now, he's losing it. Holy *shit*.

He can't finish the song. Before I can stop myself, the final line runs through my head, making a couple of laps around my brain, before it spills out of my mouth.

"It gives to us another day."

Son of a bitch, *why* did I finish it? What possessed me to do that!? Ah, well. I wanted to wake up anyways. I have some things that are going to be said, loudly and angrily, and I don't care *how* much shit is going down outside.

"Welcome back, love-dove," says the guy who's been stroking my hair for the past thousand years. He seems like a nice dude, though, and I feel a tad bit guilty for wanting to sock him in the face. Plus, who doesn't like that kind of bouncy optimism in the middle of chaos? I mean, probably a lot of people, but I'm certainly not one of them. Yeah, I am.

"Glad you could join us," says the guy at my feet. I raise my head a little bit to look up at him, and see that he's looking right back, half-smiling. Damn, he's cute, covered in black, tribal tattoos, with bright turquoise hair and icy, lighter-blue eyes that are crinkling even though he's just smirking, and a half-burnt bandanna all haphazard around his head. Plus he's shirtless. And it's a great view, let me tell you.

Asher turns from where he's sitting in the front seat, and his smile sends my heart into a frenzy. (I wonder if the guy named Jam can feel my heart rate, how it thuds through my chest.) "Hey, there."

I blink sleepily at him - I may have been awake for a while, but my eyes still hurt, my head still is cloudy, and I feel pretty much like shit. I swallow hard, and my throat is drier than the desert. I smack my lips together a couple of times, then feel my cheeks reddening as he continues watching me.

The guy sitting to his right stretches and turns his head a little bit. Son of a bitch, why didn't Aiden tell me he had such hot friends? I would've dated them and not wasted my time on all the losers I hooked up with during my mess of a life. Because if I know Aiden, he wouldn't hang around anyone extensively - or have strange, mechanically-based nicknames for a group of guys - that weren't good guys at heart. I think this one's name is Clunker. His ash-blond hair sticks up at random angles from his head, and he has chocolate-coloured eyes, and his sweatshirt looks like its seen better days and that burn on his face is angry and red and is in serious need of an ice pack or some salve or something. "Nice to finally meet you."

But as much as I'm enjoying this eye candy, and their various responses to me opening my eyes and saying something after a long while, only one person in this car is important right now. And he isn't saying a damn thing. I glare at the back of his black-haired head, and wonder if I can shoot daggers out of my eyes.

"Aiden." I want to snap his name, like a rubber band against my wrist. But due to the lack of saliva, it comes out all throaty and hoarse, and I inwardly curse, swallowing hard. Does it help? Nope, not at all. Thanks for failing me, saliva. "*What* is going on?"

When he doesn't answer me right away, I crane my neck, looking through the gap in-between the front bench seat and the door. I can't really see anything from this angle, except a couple of his white knuckles gripping the steering wheel, and a taut tendon sticking out of the side of his neck, which means he's grinding his teeth again.

Silence isn't going to cut it this time. It's not an acceptable answer. It never has been; not in our conflicts and there is no way it's going to be one now. Though my head swims and my limbs feel as if they weigh a thousand pounds each, still I clench my abdomen muscles and force myself to sit up. I feel Jam put one hand on my back to help me, and I inwardly fume. If I had needed help, then I would've asked!

We all know that's a lie; I'm too proud to ask anybody for help.

I reluctantly swing my legs from Gearteeth's lap. He rubs his thighs, probably trying to get a little bit of feeling back into them. I rotate both of my shoulders, trying to pop them, but I'm too tense for it to do much good. I settle into the area on the seat between Jam and Gearteeth, but I don't stay situated there for long. I have too many things to say.

I lean forward, gripping the back of the seat in front of me, balancing myself on the edge of the vinyl that I sit on. Asher's head is in my way; I can't see anything, much less be as close to Aiden's ear as I want to be. I fix a hard glare on him; I don't have time for this, get the hell out of the way. I flutter my fingers at him, hoping he gets that I'm waving him away.

He does. Fortunately he's not a *complete* moron. He sidles toward Clunker, whose lip curls in a snarl before he turns away and puts his head out the car window. Their facial expressions are made even more grotesque by a reddened light spilling in through any gap it can reach with its extensive grip.

Hmm, I guess my brother isn't the *only* one who harbours a strong hate for Asher. I really don't understand why everybody's so prejudiced against him. Maybe I'm just biased because he was there for me when nobody else was. Who knows anymore? Everyone's opinions are tainted. Probably even mine.

When Asher finally gets settled, closer to Clunker than the poor guy probably wants to be, I open my mouth. I'm fully prepared to deliver my speech. I have it all planned out, I know every single thing that I want to say, and I don't care how much peril we're in, I'm going to say it. But when the scenery outside the windshield of the car finally registers with me, all of the words I'd planned on saying die a terrible death in my throat.

The moon crawls over the horizon, a great crimson sphere, enveloping all below it in an eerie, bloody glow. The dark shadows of the mountains seem to shift back and forth. A proverbial groan from beneath our tires makes my ears ring; it's similar to the sound tires would make when crunching down layers of snow and ice. Sometimes, a crack resounds louder than the others, and something moans, as if in pain, as a section of the asphalt splits or cracks. The dim headlights of our obviously-stolen car do nothing to help with any of this; all they do is illuminate the cracks in the road, the slices of asphalt popping up in random intervals. I taste a salty dust on my tongue. The smell of poison and decay permeates the air, seeping into my skin with the same cloying texture as pot smoke. I itch at one of the tattoos on my wrist, a nervous habit, and feel that my hands are damp. I'm sweating out through my palms; I must be more scared than I think. I quickly wipe it off on the sweatshirt I wear.

See, *this* is why I wanted to remain laying down for as long as I could: because I knew that as soon as I sat up and saw all of the things that the guys had been talking about, I would begin to panic again. I didn't want to start that up, and I didn't want the guys in the car to have to deal with me in that sorry state. It's one thing to listen to them talk about it. In that case, I would only have to deal with the images my mind conjured with the words they used. But now, it's too late for that; I've seen the real deal, and that's something that no amount of words can capture nor dispel.

— Didn't I have things that I wanted to say? They've all run screaming out of my ears. I can't remember a single phrase. All I can do is repeat what I've already asked. "Aiden. *What is going on?*" There's a little more emphasis, a little more bite this time around, at least.

"Oh, boy," Asher interjects, running an unsteady hand through his hair and chuckling. "Where to even begin—"

"How about with the fact that you're sitting on top of me?" Clunker grunts at him, squirming as far away as he can manage, which is a couple of centimetres at the most. "Seriously, dude. Get out of my space."

"I can't help it! She sat up and waved me out of the way, and it's cramped in here. They say bench seats have more room, but that's obviously *not* true."

"You know what else is really obvious?" I say slowly, because everything I want to say is roaring back into the forefront of my mind. The words tumble down toward my lips now, not out of my ears and into nothingness. They're imprinted in my brain. I have to get them out. Unstoppable word vomit, commence! "The fact that you're all a bunch of shit-headed liars!"

"Cheyenne, *don't.*" Aiden's voice rasps through the quiet.

"D O N ' T?" I quip. "That's the first word you say to me, after what you've put me through tonight? *D O N 'T?* Don't make me laugh, Aiden. I haven't even started."

"Well, *don't* get started. We don't need it right now. Especially not me."

"You know what — I don't give a shit about what you 'need.'" I put quotations around the word 'need' with the pointer and middle fingers of both hands. "Know why? Because *you* stopped giving a shit about *me* a long time ago. So *why* should I give you the common courtesy of caring when *you* never did?"

"That's such bullsh—"

"No, it's not *bullshit*!" I shout, slamming both hands down on the back of the seat. Asher winces and presses himself into Clunker, but this time, he doesn't complain about the invasion of space; instead, he welcomes it, for his eyes are nearly bugging out of his head. These bitches don't know me; they don't know how rancid my temper can be. Boy, are they in for the ride of their lives. (Hint: Worse than Aiden's.)

"Don't make me bring up all the times that *I needed you* and *you weren't there!* Do you have *any* idea how many nights I woke up from nightmares, sobbing and calling out for you, and *you weren't there?* Do you know *how many times* I *screamed* your name in a stupour, and **you weren't there?** Do you *know*—"

"Yes, dammit, I KNOW!" Aiden yells, even louder than I expected him to. It shocks me into silence. "I don't need you reminding me of all the mistakes I've made! I don't need you slapping your judgment all over me. That's the *last* thing I need right now!

"Then just *answer* the *stupid question*, for the love of god: why didn't you come!?" I yell back, clenching my hands into fists, wishing I had a blade to slide through the arteries in my wrist so that I would bleed out and physically be able to display how much pain, how much loathing - of him, of myself - that I feel.

"Why didn't you *C O M E* ?!"

"BECAUSE I C O U L D N ' T!" he roars, swerving with such violence that the rear of the car fishtails and goes off the shoulder of the road for a split second. There's a collective holding of breath inside the car until all four balding, smoking tires are back on the cracking asphalt, and then, they continue holding their breath as he continues roaring, the angry and caged monster rattling its shackles. "I *couldn't* come back sometimes, no matter how much I wanted to! I was trying to pay the bills so that we wouldn't end up out on the streets!"

"Oh, yeah? And what *precious* jobs took you away so much? What kind of job was *so important* that you couldn't come home at night or something!?"

"Repo shop," Gearteeth offers quietly from behind me.

I don't bother turning around to look at him; I'm too busy watching Aiden's cheeks deepen in colour until the one I can see from this angle is a bright red.

"We ran a repo shop."

An elongated pause.

"— Our boss was a sleaze," Clunker continues, as though that little tidbit is guaranteed to make things better.

And cue another uneasy silence, because I'm hopping mad. I'm so mad about this that I'm speechless.

"He got his, though." Gearteeth finishes the short story quietly. "So, I mean, that's a good thing. *Great* thing, actually."

I sit back in-between the two guys with a loud thump. The car motor burbles as Aiden puts on the brakes and goes around a curve in the road too quickly. I grip at the hem of Asher's worn-down sweatshirt, eyes dry and mind numb. My brother had been involved in some repo shop on the Boulevard? (And from the sounds of it, it seemed pretty well-known.) So if that's the case, how had I not heard about this before now? It could be because of these strange nicknames they've been throwing around – I'm sure if they came up with code names for themselves, there more than likely was a new language developed so that they could speak of this place without the general public being aware. Then again – I just might not have been listening. Still surprised that he managed to keep this a secret. "For how long?"

"Long time," he admits vaguely, face void of emotion.

I'm secretly both impressed and perturbed - impressed that we're both skilled at hiding things like this, and perturbed for the same reason. It shouldn't be like this. Not even between pseudo-siblings.

"Well, I guess since we're admitting things," I remark, taking a different direction entirely and letting the word vomit overtake the logical portion of my brain that somehow still exists after all of these years. "Did you know I was working as a dancer down at the Cobra?"

Aiden glances at me in the rearview mirror, eyes hard.

"*Yeah*, that's right! But I mean, you can't judge me," I quip. "After all, I was just trying to *pay the bills* so that we wouldn't end up out on the *stre*—"

C R A C K — B O O M — C R A ———

The last word cuts off as Aiden wrings the wheel to the left, barely avoiding a mass of sliding debris. Vehicles speed toward us on the other side of the road, weaving around each other, trying to escape the wrath of the mountain range behind them, and here we are, heading straight towards it. The mountains loom larger and larger in front of us, and the closer we get, the more movement I can see. They're literally sliding to the sides. Splitting. Caving in on themselves. It's wondrously frightening.

"You just have to do that, don't you?" Aiden snaps suddenly, pressing down hard on the accelerator. The speedometer needle jolts up toward seventy miles an hour, and I grip the back of the seat harder, fingers whitening from second knuckle to tip. My heart beats too quickly. I lean forward a little bit, trying to relieve the pressure I imagine is on my chest.

"Every time something gets even a little calmed down, you just have to rouse it back up."

I want to apologise, but my pride throws its nose up in the air and refuses to let me say the necessary words. I instead grit my teeth and glare hard at the creases in the vinyl seat, and say:

"I get it from you."

He laughs harshly. "Oh, no. You get that from *Mom*."

My anger flares up. Kerosene has been splashed on the flame. "You son of a bitch!" I scream, hitting the back of the seat. Asher winces away from me. "Take it back! I'm nothing like her! Nothing like her!"

The road curves gradually to the right. "Oh, yes, you are," Aiden taunts. "You're a clone of her! How do you think she started out, Cheyenne? As a dancer in a club. Oh, she's just doing it for the money, she says. Oh, don't worry, it won't go any further." He snorts. "I'm glad this shit's happening. Gives me a reason to get you the hell out of here."

"And where exactly are we going to *get* the hell out of here?" I scream, fuming. All the implications — they hurt. It hurts more than you could ever imagine. "Back *there*? Out of all the states in the world, you're choosing to go back to *this* one? And you have the balls to say you're *glad* about it?"

"It's the best decision for the both of us," he says.

I'm disturbed by how calm he's suddenly become. The expression on his face tells me that he's not on this road, he's not in California, he's not driving. No, he's lost in the memories that he has, and he's in *that place*. I barely resist the urge to strangle him.

"What do you think's going to happen when we get there, Aiden?" I question, digging my fingernails into the seat. The other guys in the car look bewildered. I forgot that they have no idea we're not actually stopping in Arizona. I continue on. "Do you think that our grandparents are going to welcome us with open arms? Do you think that she'll want to see you? That she'll remember you and have missed you *so much*?" My tone becomes increasingly bitterer. "We're not wanted anymore. They made that really clear *ten years* ago, when the trouble first happened. And do you think, even if they did want us, that they'll want us when they see what we've become?"

"They'll —"

"No, just shut up and listen," I snarl. "You're not thinking properly. You're in a daydream. *Wake up*! They aren't going to want us anymore! We're tattooed. We're pierced. We smell like cigarette smoke and weed, like drugs and late-night sex, like the wrong path, like white trash. Her father thought that we were a bad influence back then. That's what he told us. What, do you think he's gone liberal or something? It's just stupid to waste time wishing for that, Aiden."

"You can't tell me that you don't want to see him." Aiden snorts derisively and I immediately know he's not talking about my grandparents. "You can't tell me that there isn't a distinct pang of excitement at the thought of seeing him again. I know how you felt about him. How you *feel* about him."

"There's nothing there." I tell him bluntly, though that pang he just mentioned immediately shoots through my body, which jolts and convulses forward with it. Surprising me. I disguise it by releasing the seat and bending forward, hugging my waist with my arms. "It was a *crush*. A stupid childhood crush. Crushes die. I'm being smart and realistic."

"*Smart* and *realistic* aren't usually words in your vocabulary —*CHEYENNE!*"

"Okay, guys, *what* the hell is going on here?" Asher

interjects, looking back and forth between the two of us. I stare at the side of Aiden's face, and he glares at me intermittently through the rearview mirror; we're locked in a vicious contest of the wills. "Does someone live in Arizona that you guys know?"

"We aren't going to Arizona, A s h e r," I say snidely, lips curling. "We're going *elsewhere*. We're refugees now, returning to our long lost, beloved grandparents."

"Is that who you're talking about?" Asher questions hesitantly.

"No, our grandparents aren't nameless." I roll my eyes at him.

He opens his mouth, obviously still curious, but I murder him with my gaze, and he decides to not ask any more questions. Which is wise of him. Otherwise, I would've cut out his tongue.

"Dude, why'd you tell us we were just going to Arizona?" Gearteeth spits out. Jam looks equally as shocked. Clunker continues nodding his head, expression unchanging.

"Because I didn't want Cheyenne to find this out," he answers in resigned frustration. "Because I *knew* this is how she would react, and I don't want to deal with it."

"You don't want to deal with it because you *know* I'm *right*." I poke him in the ear, and he cringes away, instinctively swatting at me. The devil in me is satisfied; he *hates* it when someone messes with his ears. "You know I'm right, Aiden."

"Go back to sleep."

I snort. "Not a chance."

"If this is what we're going to have to deal with—" Jam groans.

"Feel free to get out any time," Aiden tells him, shrugging. "But I'm not stopping, so it'll be a hard landing."

"—Nope, I'll take my chances with the constant bickering."

My throat hurts from a combination of the shouting and from the clouds of smoke billowing from the multitude of fires that have broken out. None of the houses and other buildings we pass are intact. Nearly none of the road signs are upright. The road has narrowed into a two-lane highway.

A sheer cliff face, groaning and trembling, stretches high above us to the left, and to the right, nothing. A drop-off. In the distance, I can make out the silhouette of the mountain range, outlined in crimson by the harvest moon casting its eerie light towards the ground. I crane my neck to lean towards the drop-off - and realise it is not stagnant, but M O V I N G. The ground - it literally is sucking itself down into impenetrable shadow. My stomach lurches, and I sit back down, covering my mouth with both hands. I want to throw up.

"Oh, Lord —" I hear Clunker mumble to himself. The moon over the mountains would be magnificent if seen during any other type of situation, but now, it's terrifying.

"Cheyenne." Aiden's too-calm voice reaches my ears. The interior of the car starts to spin. I see Asher staring at me worriedly, and I want to tell him that I'm fine, but I can tell that the anxiety is setting back in, that another panic attack is just around the corner. Aiden. I need Aiden. I just yelled at him and insulted him, and we have said too many things that we can't take back, but I still need him, especially now. "Listen to me. Cheyenne. Calm down. It's going to be all right. I'm driving. I'll get us there. I know you don't want to go there, but it's for the best." Everyone else is silent.

I zero in on the silence, and the sudden lack of sound makes my temples throb.

— Wait a second.

I whip my head up and hurriedly glance around. The car is still crawling down the mountain road, and the high-pitched whine coming from the motor doesn't sound too promising. However, the rest of the sounds - the proverbial groaning from under the asphalt, the cracking of the mountains as they shift and their foundations break, the general roar as sinkholes appear and begin eating everything above them - have all ceased.

I fling myself over Gearteeth's body, who allows me to rest my knees on his lap without much protest. I blink, my eyes adjusting to the light of the blood moon, and I pull myself out the window, clinging to the ledge with a tight grip, head sticking completely out, vulnerable to the elements. The wind whips through my tangled hair, and I hear Aiden say, "Cheyenne, what are you doing?"

"Shut up a minute," I shout back at him, and my voice reverberates down into the valley, echoing back at us. Goosebumps appear on my flesh, both from the eeriness of the atmosphere and the chilly wind accosting me. "Listen, you guys."

Clunker also puts his head out the window, listening along with me. My breath is taken by the flawless red light that the moon puts off as it continues its course in the night sky, how the redness bleeds through the entirety of the cloudless sky, and how the strange, clean scent of pine and fresh earth mixes easily with that of soot and burning wood.

"It's stopped," Asher calls out. "It's finally stopped!"

"Wait, what does that mean?" Clunker asks, pulling his head back inside the car. I, however, remain with my head and shoulders out, unable to pull myself away from the glorious, terrifying sight. I'm pretty much setting myself up for an anxiety attack, considering my fear of wide, open spaces, but for some reason, I'm not afraid. I'm mesmerised. Of course, the only reason I'm not afraid is probably because I've already accepted the fact that we're all going to die, no matter how fast Aiden drives.

"Maybe there *is* a God," I hear Aiden grumble from inside the car, "and maybe He's decided to cut us some damned slack for once in our lives."

"Well, let's not talk about it. We might jinx it." Asher says this jokingly, but the sad fact of the matter is that he's probably right.

I can't bring myself to hope. Hope is one of those highly-addictive drugs, one on which you easily overdose and don't give a damn that you do, one that you continue taking in heavy amounts, and when it wears off, when your hope goes nowhere or is stifled by circumstance or is killed by mankind, the withdrawal process can be lethal, and can result in self-induced death.

Or, at the very least, attempts in self-induced death.

"Cheyenne, sit *down*, would you? You're making me nervous."

I take in one last deep breath of untainted air and reluctantly sit myself back down in-between Jam and Gearteeth. As I make myself comfortable, pulling the hood of the sweatshirt over my hair - and it droops so low that it shields most of my face - Asher says, "We're actually almost to the base. It's just around this bend and kinda buried in the side of the mountain below the road."

"It better not be buried," Aiden says lowly, pressing on the brakes as we glide around a slight curve. The Galaxie sputters, the exhaust letting out a long, exploding noise, and we all collectively wince. "Because this car won't last the other half of the trip, that's for damn sure."

"I didn't mean *that* kind of buried. I meant more like — sheltered." Amidst a gathering of glares from my brother and Clunker, Asher falls silent, pursing his lips to keep from saying anything more. I think he's realising: one wrong move and he'll be rolling down the side of the mountain. Or left behind at the base. I could cut the tension in the air with a switchblade if I had one. I know if Aiden could find a good reason to leave Asher behind, he'd do it in a heartbeat.

Stupid men and their testosterone and their damn pride.

The mountain road takes one more curve, and we find ourselves in front of a tunnel that burrows through a section of the rock. I'm more than a little bit surprised to see that the concrete walls have held up rather nicely under the pressure and haven't collapsed in on themselves, like the rest of the whole world seems to be doing.

Asher is looking out the window, laying completely on Clunker in order to do so. "Wait, stop, *stop!*"

Aiden slams on the brakes. "Here?"

"Yeah, here," Asher says. "There's a hidden path just before the tunnel. We'll have to go down it on foot."

As the Galaxie squeaks to a stop, the motor sputters, gives a final, brave chug before dying. The headlights dim as Aiden tries the ignition a couple of times, pumping the pedals, but the engine doesn't even give us a hopeful rev. He yanks the keys out of the ignition and tosses them onto the passenger's side floor. As he does so, he gives Asher a meaningful look. "*Now* what?"

"Okay, everyone out, and quickly." His tone is clipped and that of a commander. A true military man. "We can't waste any time."

Clunker salutes him and opens the passenger door. Jam and Gearteeth wait for him to pull up the seat before getting out of the car, taking me with them. As soon as my bare feet touch the cool asphalt, my heart thuds a little bit faster.

"Leave the duffel bag in the trunk; we'll get it later." Asher barks at Aiden, who had started to go around the rear of the Galaxie to open up the trunk.

My brother stares at him with that hard, deadened expression he's so famous for. "I'm getting her some shoes. In case you haven't noticed, she needs them."

Asher lets Aiden go around to the trunk without further protest. I roll my eyes and put my face into my dirty, sweaty hands. You have to be kidding me. I'm in the middle of a power struggle. (I'm also the cause of the power struggle.) How about I throw myself off the side of the mountain, and then there won't be one? No, even that wouldn't solve anything, because that would end in them trying to pin the blame of my death on one another, and then they'd end up fighting and tearing at each other's hair, and I'm *really* tired. I need a smoke.

"Here." I don't know how Aiden managed to get the trunk open without a key, or how he managed to sneak up on me from the front without me noticing, but I don't really care. I zero in on the pair of fuzzy socks I barely remember packing and the pair of Converse. I blink at them and reach for them, but Aiden pulls them out of my reach, those fire-coloured eyes blazing at me.

"No, let me do it."

He says it gruffly, and I sigh, but gladly stretch out an aching foot. He slips the sock on first, and the soft fabric clings to my skin like a long-awaited hug from an old friend. He puts on the right, then the left and with the thick fabric of the socks, the slightly oversized converse are a perfect fit. I won't have to worry about them randomly falling from my feet.

"Way too cute," Jam mumbles to his boyfriend, who silently nods his head in agreement.

"Does anyone have a flashlight?" Clunker yells.

No one answers him.

"I'm gonna take that as a no."

"Ready?" Asher questions, and when I nod, he beckons to me and my brother. "Come on. It'll be fine without a flashlight," he adds, "I've trekked down this in the dark before."

"Yeah," Clunker mumbles to himself, "but *we* haven't."

With the aid of the dim headlights Asker leads us to a slightly trodden, crooked dirt path that leads down the side of the mountain. It's nestled amongst a few scattered boulders and fallen trees. It seems quite steep and darker than pitch. The remnants of Xanax have left me woozy and discombobulated, and I struggle to keep my footing. Gearteeth offers his hand which I gladly take and we continue, half-sliding and half-walking down the path.

After maybe a minute or so, my eyes adjust to darkness and with what light the moon gives off, we are able to reach a large grassy area. Asher stops and runs both hands through his hair. "Well — let's see what is left of this place."

I've been staring at my feet this whole time, willing them to go where I direct them and not where they *want* to go, but at the sudden sentence echoing through the otherwise abandoned forest, I look up, letting go of Gearteeth's hand. A mangled chain-link fence, one that sends a pang of nostalgia through me, as it reminds me of the one in front of our blue house, is before us, and behind it, I make out the silhouettes of a few beat-up buildings, plus a massive, gaping tunnel carved in the side of the mountain.

"It's an old missile base," Asher explains. He points at the tunnel. "That's where the missile is. Or — was. I think it was dismantled a few years back. Anyway, they keep the larger vehicles in there. The medium-sized one is — well. *was* — the barracks; you know, where we sleep and eat. And the smallest one is where all the gear was stored - the guns, the packaged food, the water bottles and whatnot. They were supposedly built to withstand earthquakes."

"They didn't do a very good job of it," Jam comments.

"Well, your mom didn't do a very good job of raising you," Gearteeth snorts.

"Yeah, I *know.*" An overdramatic sigh. "And it's *so* tragic. You know, I *tried* to tell her she'd screw me up, but she wouldn't listen." There's a loud squelching sound, and Jam gets a peculiar look on his face. "*Oh, sick,* I just stepped in the biggest puddle of shit ever."

"As in, a literal shit, or as in the type of puddle that's so murky and gloppy that it can't be called anything but shit?" Aiden questions dryly. (There's an undercurrent to his tone I can't place; he seems to be mocking someone.)

"That one," Jam says, lips twisting up. (He's in on the joke that I don't really get.) "Definitely the last one."

Everything that's being said grates on my last nerve. We walk closer to the buildings. Eerily quiet. No trees falling, no earth moving. I don't care for the silence. Is it an omen? The calm before the storm? Out of the three buildings, I find myself being drawn to the middle one, the barracks. As though there are invisible tendrils reaching out, calling me forward. The door hangs sideways on its hinges, creaking slowly back and forth, but it looks like a promise of silence.

That's what I want. *Silence.* Away from these boys. Ugh, it's bad enough that I'm going to be stuck with them for another thirty-three hours or however long it'll take to get to our grandparents' house. I need the respite where I can get it.

"Whoa, wait a second. — Cheyenne, where do you think you're going?" Asher calls. I blink in surprise. I'm somehow already standing at the threshold of the barracks, and I don't even remember starting to walk. "Stay with me."

"*Oh,* no. If she's staying with anybody, she's staying with *me.*" I can practically hear my brother balling his hands into tight fists down at his sides. "I let her out of my sight for too long already, and look at all the shit that's happened. I'm not letting her go anymore."

"Are you forgetting who was with her while you were *out?*" I sense the silent quotations that Asher puts around that word, and it makes me cringe. A distinct crawling, a bundle of itching twists, begins right at the small of my back, crawling up the base of my spine, through each little nodule. My arms twitch in response, fingers jittery, shoulders growing curved and taut. Toes curling over themselves. As though I am preparing to run screeching through the middle of this godforsaken forest. "We can have this out now if you want."

"I have a better idea: you back off, and I take care of what's left of my family. Cheyenne—"

"No," I say simply, not even bothering to turn around and face them. My voice reverberates off the solid rock wall behind the barracks. They can hear me. "I'm solving your problem for you; I'm going in here, by myself, to gather my thoughts and calm myself down. Because right now, I hate you. *Both* of you."

I hate Asher for warring with my brother. I hate my brother for warring with Asher. I hate that I trust Asher, and I hate that Aiden doesn't. I hate that Aiden wasn't there for me, and I hate that Asher was. But most of all, I hate that all of us are going to a place where we aren't going to be wanted. Surely they understand that I need to be alone — with my hate.

"— This is *your* fault," I hear my brother say as I step over the threshold and into the darkness of the barracks. "I don't know how, but it's your fault."

I shut my ears to them. I don't want to hear any more.

My eyes struggle to adjust to the sudden darkness, even

with the blood moon overhead and its ghostly beams poking through the crevice - it made for strangely dim lighting. My forehead knocks against something hard, and I curse, ducking away from it. My eyes feel gritty and hot as I stay hunkered down, one hand reaching up to feel around. The cool texture of concrete brushes my fingertips just an inch or so above my head. I feel like I'm in a cemented lean-to rather than a livable space.

Oh, what am I saying? Of course this space isn't livable anymore, it's collapsed on itself.

The tip of my shoe hits a crack in the concrete floor. Wait, that doesn't make sense. I crouch down and peer more closely at it. Hmm, I'm not surprised to see that some sections have been pushed higher by the quake than others. I'm going to have to watch my step.

But it's quiet. Unnervingly quiet.

Isn't that what I wanted?

Wait — what the —

I gasp and stumble backward, landing on my rear, both hands covering my mouth in horror.

There are bodies strewn e v e r y w h e r e.

All right, I'm being a little dramatic with the shock of seeing *any* number of bodies at all. I count three visible ones, and God knows how many are hidden behind the thicker layers of shadow. The ones I can see are impaled by the roof's steel beams, pinned to their bunk beds. They'd been sleeping. Some are still in their boxers.

Except for that guy over there on the floor. Or girl. I honestly can't tell, the corpse is so mangled, and the steel beam went straight through its skull, pinning its head down on the floor, making the face — virtually nonexistent.

It's a strange concept, not being able to feel. The skin grows numb and the pores seem to close up, absorbing salted sweat and tears spilled from eyes alike. No shivers rack the spine; no sinking of the stomach deep into the seat of the pelvic bones; no wondering what has happened or twitching fingers to dripping eyes. There's just nothing. Existence, breaths, lungs, heartbeat – and nothing else substantial. Nothing more than the human shell running as a machine in an old shop, a little sluggish and burning fuel but not at the end of its rope, not quite yet, not now.

This has transformed itself from the real to an off-camera film set. Yet despite this disconnection, I know this isn't a film set at all.

The surroundings are far too deserted; my hearing illuminates far more than sight ever could. Lungs expand as I breathe in, and deflate as I breathe out. Lashes tick as I blink. It's oppressive, and it's disturbing how shrouded it is in here. The sole of my Converse barely misses coming down on a metal nail that's managed to escape from somewhere, probably one of the bunk beds, and I gasp, kicking it away from me.

(plink —   plink —   plink)

"Someone —"

I freeze. My heart leaps from my chest. One of the dead men is talking. This cannot be happening.

"Under here —" it continues, and the last syllable turns into a wheezing cough.

No, a pile of rubble is talking. The world really is ending.

A dark silhouette shifts on the floor. I leap away and plaster myself against the wall, staring at it. This place is giving me the shivers. Why the hell did I want to come in here again? Oh, yeah, *silence*. But I was expecting one with light and without demons jumping about everywhere and disturbing me. I wasn't expecting a pile of rubble to start talking.

You really are stupid, aren't you? sneers the male voice in my head as he leans against the wall of my skull. The rubble isn't talking, you idiot. Someone's trapped.

The shadow on the floor shifts again, and this time, I recognise it as the shadow of a person, not a demon coming to suck out my soul. I reach for it this time and end up falling onto my knees; I suck in a breath between my teeth as I feel the unforgiving concrete bruising them.

"Please —"

I scramble toward the pile of rubble and start sifting through it. It consists mostly of chunks of concrete from the back wall, as well as some wooden shards from the demolished frame of a bunk bed. My fingernails scrape against the wood; splinters break off and embed themselves into my skin. Layer after layer I peel away, tossing the pieces aside.

My eyes have (un)fortunately adjusted themselves to the shrouded lighting. Beneath me, I see a dusty, war-torn face, its condition worsened by the bloodied white light of the moon shining upon it. He coughs hard and blinks up at me, and I can see some dilated pupils surrounded by something green, barely there, hardly existing. I continue removing the piles of rubble, brushing away the concrete and tugging hard at the wood and probably damaging my damp, sweating hands beyond repair, but I don't care. I want to get him out. Why hasn't he been digging himself out of there this whole time?

— O h.

I pull away the last remaining wooden board and throw it. It lands on top of a twisted corpse. The man is pinned to the concrete floor by one of the large steel beams. I quickly feel all around the steel beam; it's too heavy for me to even try and lift by myself. Panicking, I duck down, placing the curve of my right shoulder into steel beam, gritting my teeth as I silently count backwards from the number five.

"*No*," he groans, and his left arm reaches up, quick as a

flash, grasping the left side of my face. His thumb frantically feels over my grimy skin, the shape of my lips, the bridge of my nose, as if he's trying to reassure himself that yes, I am a person, and yes, I am here with him. "Don't." He's panting hard, his grip tightening on my face. "That damn thing — it's all that's holding me together."

I furrow my brows, puzzled. What does that mean? I back away from the beam and go to peer more closely underneath it, but the hand of the soldier stops me yet again.

"No." He groans again. "Come where I can see you."

Why me? Why couldn't I just have had some peace and quiet? Why am I the one who's in the room with a dying man? Can't I be spared some type of horror in my life? Can't I keep some kind of innocence to myself? Until now, I've never seen anybody in the process of dying a slow, painful death. Never.

With only the moonlight upon his face, I watch as it twists into a grotesque expression of pain. Tears stream out of his eyes, painting clear and clean streams through the mess of dirt and dust on his cheeks. Those green eyes sparkle at me, full of water and full of life still. His hair is buzzed short. His t-shirt is bedraggled and reduced to nothing more than shreds around the collar, sleeves, and middle. A thick cord in his neck bulges as he strains, trying to make himself more comfortable, or maybe even trying to get up, even after all this time.

I can't take it anymore.

"Stop that!" I cry out, bending down close to him, taking his face in both of my hands, swiping at the pouring tears with the pads of my thumbs. "You'll hurt yourself!"

"I'm already dead. Can't you see?" He blinks at me and pushes his face hard into the palm of my left hand. "I'm just glad I'm not alone anymore. I'm just — everyone else — they're all — their screams — I still hear them — echoing — echoing —"

He sobs once, coughs, then falls as silent as he can manage while still wheezing for air through parted lips. But the contact and warmth from my hands seems to be helping a little bit. His eyes dart feverishly about for a couple of seconds, and in the quiet, I too can hear the screams of his dying comrades, the names they probably called out, their hands reaching for their gear or their weapons, their feet reaching for the floor, and none of them ever making it. I'm glad when he takes in a sudden gulp of air; it breaks the damned reverie.

"Do you hear them?" he asks, his other hand shakily coming to grasp my right shoulder. His fingers tug at the fabric of the sweatshirt. "Do you hear them shouting, begging for help?"

"Hush. You stop that." I feel my lips quivering, tears forming in my eyes. I haven't cried in years; and this is what would break me. Pain I hadn't been searching for. "There's no one here but you and me. Focus on me. I'm Cheyenne."

"Cheyenne." He smiles, and it's such a beautifully tragic smile. "I think I like that name. I —"

He burrows his nose into my palm and inhales deeply. The tears continue dripping from beneath his closed eyelids as he is lost in the ecstasy of human contact for a few precious moments. "It's so nice to know I can still feel up here," he murmurs. "Because — I can't feel — my legs — they're crushed."

I don't want to look down and check for myself. I'll take his word for it. "Don't think about that now. That's not important. I'm here with you. I'm here."

"Why are you crying?" He tries speak normally, but it turns into another coughing fit, and a bead of blood appears at the corner of his mouth, trailing its dark gore all the way down to his chin. "Because of me —? Don't — do that —"

I'm not crying, am I? I take one hand from his face and

reach up to investigate. Both cheeks are wet, and as I swipe at my face, I can feel the supposedly waterproof eyeliner creasing through my fingerprints. I put the hand back on his cheek, black smudges and all, but he has been distracted; his left arm reaches around and takes my right wrist gingerly, turning it this way and that before sliding half-gentle fingers up the length of it. I see the shining, reddening whites of his eyes as he brushes over, feels intimately, the white blemishes and the pink lines and the fresh red ones that I put there yesterday, some of them especially irritated, especially deep, especially able to be sensed even through numbness. Bewilderment overcomes his face, and his dirty fingers curl around the tender skin of my elbow, and I don't care that the scars are now covered in filth, because that's why I cut; I cut to get out the filth that flows through my blood, the dirtiness, the taint.

"Don't —" he rasps, his hand going limp and smacking into the concrete floor. He doesn't even wince, though I hear several bones crack. "Don't do that — ever again."

I'm overcome with so much, too much. I can't pick out a single thing to identify, for it all blends together. Unable to resist the odd magnetic pull, tying something deep in my chest to his, I bend down until our noses are touching.

I don't know what possesses me, but I press my lips against his, closing that minute distance in a heartbeat, and he inhales so sharply, a small grunt of pain escapes from his closed throat. The hand on my face grips so hard, I know I'm going to have the shape of his palm bruising that cheek and his other hand seizes the back of my neck, holding me to him. He tastes of grime, of blood, and his lips are hot, hotter than the California sun on the beach; he's feverish. But beyond the surface, I taste more than that - I taste the salt of the earth, the metallic shells from discarded bullets, the smoke of a grenade that went off too close, the gasoline fumes from a leaking car, and a desperation tinged with desire, the desire to feel close to someone, a desire to know that he is loved even in these last moments.

And I'm all he has. All of his friends are dead.

I taste that on his lips as well - that unmistakably chilling texture of cool glass, leaking through his fever. It's the decay on the breath, a mixture of putrid and sweetness, something that both repulses and attracts, two polar opposites, two magnets opposing one another, barely coming together, barely drifting apart.

When I pull away, his sigh of relief is audible. He looks as though he wishes to speak, but no words can emerge. Nothing can be said in that moment, for it meant too much, and perhaps, in his life, he had never been near something which gave him meaning.

More tears fall from his eyes.

I make no response.

Sometimes, silence says the most.

He pulls my chin down so that it's resting on his chest. "Just lay here with me. Talk to me. I want your voice to be the — last thing I remember." His voice breaks, grows desperate, as though I don't understand, but by God, I do. "I don't want to hear them screaming anymore, and they only stop when you talk to me."

"I — I don't even know where to start," I admit, turning my face so that the right side rests on his torn shirt. His chest is so broad, I'm up where he can glance down and see straight into my eyes. His right hand stays tangled in my hair; his other rests on my shoulder blades. My lips are chapped, cursed with road dust and burnt remains of people I never knew. I'm barely dressed. I'm lying on a cold concrete floor in the arms of a dying man whose name I don't even know, listening to his shallow breathing, to the rattle of his lungs, to the steady, slowing beating of his heart deep in his chest.

Why me?

"How'd — you get here?"

"That's – kind of a long story." I pause, uncertain of how much to share, unknowing of how much time remained. Seconds dragged away as I thought, and I decided to begin with the basics; that way, if he wished to know more, if he wanted to keep me talking, he could ask questions and I would answer them. "We were trying to escape the earthquakes and our car broke down on the road at the top of the mountain and we had to go through the woods a bit on foot." I just let the words tumble out. Probably nonsense, but what can you do?

"But — this place?" He coughs. "No one knows about it."

"Well, I'm travelling with Aiden – my brother," I explain. "I'm also with three of his friends - Clunker, Gearteeth, and Jam. Bunch of damn car junkies. But we were led here by an ex-Marine named Asher, and—"

"A S H E R?"

The soldier suddenly gasps, and he heaves so far up in the air, I think that he's starting to have a seizure. "Asher *Collins?*"

"I don't know his last name—but maybe—" I lift my head from his chest and put my finger to his lips, trying to keep him quiet, not wanting him to tire out, but he won't be silenced this time. He grabs my pointer finger and pushes it away, becoming frantic in his movements. "What are you doing?!"

"I have to get up!" he pleads. "I have to see him! Oh, God, you've answered my prayers! I just want him to forgive me - and now he can. You are gracious and powerful, God. You know what I need and You provide me with it."

"Calm down. *Please.*" I cling to his shoulders, keeping him pressed against the concrete floor. "You *can't* go anywhere."

"I need to get up —" His movements grow feeble, the surge of strength gone. "I need — I —"

He collapses back onto the floor, a mangled heap, stomach heaving as he tries to gather as much air as he can into his lungs. His eyes dart about from side-to-side in their sockets.

"I'll go get him," I promise. It doesn't even matter if the Asher that's with me is the same Asher that this soldier wants to beg forgiveness from. It doesn't even matter. This man is dying, and if forgiveness is what he wants, then it's what he is going to get, damn it, if it's the last thing I do.

"Go get *who*?"

My heart stops for a split second. I whirl around, my spine cracking with the sudden, unexpected motion, and I bite down hard on my swollen, bloodied bottom lip - remember how I was chewing on it, biting it earlier? Just reopened all of those wounds. But I can't help it, because speak of the devil himself, there stands Asher, in all of his glory, oddly framed at the back of the head by the red moonlight. My flesh prickles and itches from seeing it, a sudden chill from the unexplained. He stands in the ruined threshold of the barracks. I make out in the dim light Aiden's head over Asher's right shoulder, and by the way Asher stumbles into the room, glaring back at Aiden and muttering, it's safe to say that my brother just pushed him inside.

"You." My voice breaks. I see the looks of confusion as Aiden and Asher bend down and take in my bedraggled appearance: the streams of tears on my face; the black mascara and eyeliner that are probably down to my chin by now because I've been crying more since I wiped the last batch of tears away; the quiver in my lips; the blood and the wood in my fingertips; the numerous scars on my right arm bared for the universe to stare at; the light-grey dust of powdered concrete covering me everywhere; and the panting, dying, gasping, green-eyed, nameless soldier lying next to me, with one of his hands still gripping my finger and the other gesturing weakly at Asher, trying to beckon him over. "I was going to go get *you*."

"I'm — here?" The inflection of his voice makes it apparent that he has no idea what's going on. "Cheyenne, are you okay?"

I suddenly become infuriated. "To hell with me and how I feel! This man is begging for you, Asher. He wants your forgiveness." Everyone needs to leave me alone and start thinking about others, damn it, the world doesn't revolve around me and whether or not I can survive or whether I'm actually a china doll, for god's sake.

My thought process makes me freeze for a minute. How I have changed so quickly because of one thing. Before now I would have killed to have such attention, but now, I'm sick of it, because there's attention and then there's *too much* attention and the latter is what I feel like I've been getting from everyone, and maybe I'm just being paranoid, and damn it, Asher, just forgive the poor man already.

"I don't — I don't even know this guy." Asher kneels forward and takes in the face of the man before him. Aiden stays by the doorway, leaning against the doorjamb, crossing his arms over his chest and watching this unfold with that emotionless, brooding glare of his that he gets when he's secretly analysing someone's body language. I glance up at him, then quickly back to Asher; no need to let the guy know he's being closely watched. "Why does he want my forgiveness?"

"Asher — Asher, it's me. It's Elijah." And after all this time, I have his name. My mind clings to it, forming a protective hold around it, grasping it much like I would grasp the side of a lifeboat if I were drowning in the middle of the sea and help had come to me. "*Elijah.* I'm so sorry — Asher, I should've stopped it. But please, please forgive me. I was scared. We all were! It had happened to most of us, too! And you know — you know the threats. You know what was said to us if we didn't keep quiet."

His voice rises in volume, but his body weakens. His eyelids flutter this way and that, and those beautiful green irises are losing their brightness. I turn back toward him, putting Asher completely out of my vision, and I grasp Elijah's face again. He calms a little bit at the human contact, breathing in the scent of my palm once more, as if taking his final breath.

"I'm *begging* you."

I'm no longer there to him. All he can see is the guy named Asher, who may or may not be the one that Elijah has been praying for all this time. "Forgive me."

Asher says nothing. Elijah's breathing is becoming more laboured, and something warm, wet, soaks into the skin of my calf and my knee. A pool of blood is slowly spreading outward from underneath the steel beam that has pinned him down, that has acted as a tourniquet and kept his two severed halves from being completely separated, that has kept him alive for as long as he has been. I can tell by the dimming of his eyes that there isn't much time left, at all, and that his suffering is intensifying.

"Forgive him!" I find myself crying out. "Asher, he's *dying.* Even if you're not the same guy, just — give him what he wants!"

Asher says nothing, only stares down at the soldier named Elijah with one of the coldest, hardest gazes I have ever seen on the face of a man - and believe me, I have seen many. They are locked in this battle of wills, except the problem here is that Elijah has no more will to give.

"*Forgive him.*" I cry, voice breaking. The tears fall faster than I can wipe them away, and after a while, I don't bother.

Why isn't Asher saying anything!?

I turn back to Elijah, who rests the back of his head against the concrete floor, eyes nearly shut all the way, breathing shallow and barely audible even in the deadened, heavy silence of the room.

"It's — okay." he tells me. "—I didn't really expect it." Pain racks through his body, causing his spine to seize of its own accord.

I shake my head. Back and forth. Back and forth. Several fuchsia and turquoise strands fall forward, directly into my eyes.

"But *you* were here." His voice grows softer.

His hand flutters toward his chest, trying to find something, and the tips of his fingers barely miss what I think he's looking for: a metal chain. I pull at it, revealing a pair of silver dog tags with black lettering Stamped into their surfaces. He takes the hand with the pointer finger he's been holding and puts it underneath his dog tags; I open my palm and let them drop there, rest there.

"Wear them," is his last order.

"And –

    don't –

        forget –

            me."

His eyelids don't close the remainder of the way. Because of this, I can see one last solitary tear leak from his left eye. As it rolls down the side of his face, the bright colour of his irises fades to a duller brownish-green. His breath escapes. The warmth from the pool of blood continues to spread.

I — can't —

I'm *mystified*. His face doesn't have that peaceful expression that I've seen in the movies on people, where all their muscles relax as they slip away, because everything that they wanted in life has been given to them, and they have accomplished all of the goals they set for themselves. But life isn't a movie. It just pains me to see that Elijah's face is still creased with worry, tormented with pain even though it has been relieved, and stuck in a winter of discontent.

And it's all *his* fault. It's all *Asher's* fault.

I realise that my mind and my body are separating in a mechanism of self-defence. I'm trying to protect myself, throwing my physical body into a sort of "functioning" mode while my mental one locks itself in a windowless room and paces around and around, screaming, tearing at its hair, pulling at its skin, slicing through its veins and speaking in a language that only I can understand. The dark-eyed man who usually just smirks at me prowls around outside the room, pounding on the door, demanding to be let in, whispering lies and penetrating the safe zone as best as he can with his silver-tongued bullshit. I'm withdrawing in all senses of the word - from the situation, from the medication, from the fact that I am a person and I exist and Elijah does not, will not, ever exist again.

Shock. I think that's what they call it. Remarkably simplified.

"Why?"

It's the one question my mind can form, and the one that passes through my lips, otherwise sealed until further notice.

"W h y ? ? ?"

To Contain a Mental Abscess
October 10th
Hidden Military Base

Aiden Kinsey

Well, would you look at that. Both of the Kinsey kids are attempting to stop themselves from having meltdowns. Collapsing into ourselves. Switching into survival mode. We do what we gotta do.

Asher glances towards me. He's trying to decide if he should say anything, if he should even try to apologise for what just happened. He blows out a long stream of air and shakes his head, storming out of the barracks, choosing the silent anger route. That's fine. If he *had* said anything, I would have broken his face, and none of us need that either, since he's our ticket out of here and all. Plus he's a medic.

Strange, he must only be qualified to deal with physical injuries. He sure doesn't want to handle the mental ones that have been inflicted on my sister, whom he supposedly cares so much about, and would never intentionally hurt. But how can he care? If that little episode with the soldier wasn't intentional, then I don't think anything is.

Eh, what the hell do I know? I'm not inside his head; if I were, I would have torn it into pieces and left nothing alive.

At least he's left for now, and I don't have to worry about him hovering over my shoulder. Cheyenne is pretty out of it, but she hasn't broken completely - neither have I, not really; the breakdowns earlier are nothing compared to what *can* happen - and so I'm going to fix it. (I'm going to fix her. You'll see.)

Taking in a deep breath, I cross the barracks, making my way toward the heap of a person kneeling in the still-warm puddle of blood, trying to prepare myself, wondering how I'm going to deal with a person breaking before me when I myself am not whole. When I make it halfway across something odd happens, and I slow down, eventually stopping dead in my tracks, watching curiously as a surreal transformation takes place.

The walls crumble away, disintegrating into morsels of dust, replaced by a familiar spacious meadow, with a plush carpet of green grass unrolling beneath my feet. In front of me, an area of the ground sinks, filling with a dark, briny water, laced with algae and pond slime on its surface. The wooden bunks begin constructing a dock over a section of the sizeable pond, its wood stained and worn from years of being weathered down by heavy rain, scorched by heat, and fractured by ice. By the bank, nearest to the dock, a floundering figure emerges from the water. A nymph arising from her home, wiping strands of stringy algae from her eyes, her ash-blonde braid falling out. I can see those bright, electric blue eyes, even recognisable from this distance.

More figures spring up out of nowhere - a scrawny figure who could have passed as my identical twin at the right angles, the yapping mongrel of a dog that he and I had found together, some weeks before, nipping at his heels as he sprints off the dock, shouting back at my little sister. "I got you, Cheyenne!"

"You *jerk!*" she shouts back, stomping her foot in a fit of rage. Her drenched sneaker makes a loud squelching sound that causes him and the mongrel dog to stop in their tracks. There only is a moment of silence before he roars with laughter, nearly folding himself in half, Moe spinning around in circles at his feet and barking raucously. "I'll get you back for this — just you wait, Scarecrow!"

I didn't think it was possible for him to laugh even louder than he already was, but at the sound of his nickname emerging from my sister's mouth, in that seven-year-old voice that squeaks at the end of her sentences, he manages to do just that. It bounces off the surrounding, rolling hills and reaches my ears.

"*Aiden!*" Cheyenne screeches, grabbing my attention. "Did you *see* what Scarecrow just did to me? He *knows* I'm afraid slimy stuff! There're *monsters* in there!"

"There aren't any monsters in the slimy stuff, you silly goose," I hear myself say, and I'm inwardly shocked at the voice that emerges. It's that preteen voice I remember despising, with the way it would randomly crack, especially when I would talk to the cute girls at school. I start crossing the field, making my way toward her, pushing aside a couple of the tall cattails so that I can reach her. Now that I'm a little bit closer, I can see her legs are caked in dark mud up to her knees, her hair is half out of the braid and fluttering in the breeze, and she has a dead expression on her face as she stares at me. There's a buzzing noise from somewhere, and the sight before me shifts back into the seventeen-year-old Cheyenne, now standing in that cursed, inescapable glow of the moon - in the puddle of blood that's not her own, staring at me in the same way.

But the flickering of the two situations soon stops, and my mind forces me to stay in this much more pleasant one. (Regression: replacing the unknown with something that's easier to look at.)

"There are, too!" the young Cheyenne sniffs, pulling at a strand of wet hair. "Scarecrow said so! He said that there were water monsters and that if I ever fell in the pond, they would drag me back in when I tried to get out!"

My arms reach forward, and I marvel at them for a moment; neither of them are marred with tattoos, and the skin on my left arm is still there, not having been burned off by collapsing buildings. The skin is tanned, weathered in the sense that it's been working hard and sweating a lot. I pick a couple of algae leaves from her hair and toss them into the pond behind her. "There aren't any water monsters in there, promise. If there had been, he wouldn't have actually pushed you in. He wouldn't put you in danger like that."

Her bottom lip quivers, and she crosses her arms, pouting, trying not to show that she wants to cry from relief. Cheyenne always had this little thing where if she cried, she felt weaker than the rest of us, and that just wouldn't do; a long time ago, she used to be a tomboy, climbing trees, playing in the mud puddles, getting into food fights. She didn't have OCD, didn't have a panic attack at every sudden change. She was impulsive, she was wild, and she was free. "Are you sure?"

"I'm positive."

A loud clanging resounds out behind us, sending the dogs whose name I can't remember into a chorus of excited barking.

"It's time for supper!" Grandma's voice call out.

"Oh, no!" Cheyenne cries out, eyes bulging. "I can't go in the house like this! And I won't have time to clean up, either; Grandma waits for no one!"

"It's going to be okay!" I say to her. "Here."

Quickly, I strip off my shirt, holding it up as a sort of shielding screen. "Strip out of those nasty clothes, and you can wear my shirt into dinner. She won't mind if I'm shirtless; Scarecrow does it all the time."

"So does Grey," she mutters to herself. I turn my head away as far as I can manage, wanting to give her as much modesty as possible, though my long black shirt seems to be providing her plenty of coverage. I smirk to myself as I thought about how Grey acquired that nickname, but that's a story for another time.

"That doesn't mean *you* can!" I tease her.

"Ew, Aiden, I would never," she retorts primly, grunting

a little bit as she struggles with her wet jeans. I can almost imagine the expression she's making as she wiggles out of the mud-caked fabric, the way the entire right side of her face scrunches up, one eye completely shut, the other rolling around, her tongue sticking out of her mouth in deep concentration. "I'm almost — done!"

The shirt's snatched out of my hands. Soon after, there's a cry of disbelief. "I'm *stuck*!"

I turn around and I burst out laughing. The neck hole has somehow ended up around her left arm, and some strands of ash blonde hair stick out through the arm hole. I quickly take a couple of steps, standing in front of her, gingerly fixing the shirt until she could pull it down over her head without any further complications.

When her face reappears, it is the same dead one that I've become too familiarised with.

But instead of taking a step backward in shock, I continue fiddling with the shirt, making sure it hangs straight on her shoulders, which switch rapidly from youthful and full to gaunt and unhealthy. I bite my lip, and when I speak, it's my normal, twenty-three-year-old voice, but I'm still in the thirteen-year-old body. (Very disconcerting. Like one of those horror movies, where the film strip switches back and forth rapidly between two very different scenes - one innocent, one sick and dark and twisted.)

"I'm so sorry, Cheyenne. I should have been there more."

It's a combination of both her voices when she talks, a strange distortion of sorts. "It's okay, Aiden. I know you *wanted* to be."

"You were right, you know — with all those things you said," I continue on, gently turning her by the right shoulder so that her back is facing me. I gently undo the messy braid on the one side of her hair and comb through the tangles as delicately as I can manage. "In the car, I mean. Earlier today."

"Doesn't mean I should've said them."

The surrounding environment flickers as well, a lantern deciding whether or not it has enough oil left in it to keep going. (Must keep going.) "But you did. And I responded. We can't change that."

"There are a lot of things we can't change."

The beautiful ash-blonde hair turns black, turquoise, fuchsia, platinum-blonde in my palms, then back to ash-blonde. I split the hair into three sections, recalling how Cheyenne had taught me to braid one late night when we, our family, and our friends didn't want to sleep because it was the last day of summer. Even Scarecrow and Grey had let us braid their hair; it had been long enough to sustain a bunch of tiny ones. I furrow my brows for a moment, then begin the process: left over middle, right over middle, repeat.

"I know." I finally answer her question, wondering what she thinks of the gentle, familiar tugging on the back of her head. She mustn't think too poorly of it, because she isn't telling me to leave her alone or let her braid her own damn hair, so I continue, a little less tentatively. "I wish I could."

"*Wishing* doesn't do any good."

It's odd hearing such cold, detached words coming from the mouth of a seven-year-old who shifts to a seventeen-year-old. This whole thing is odd, this projecting of the memory in the first place.

"I know," I say again, wondering if there really is anything else I could say. "But I'm still sorry. I'm sorry I wasn't there all those times you needed me. I'm sorry I let you go before you were ready."

The seven-year-old beams at me, while the seventeen-year-old just looks blankly on, silently evaluating. "Come on, Aiden, we don't have time for sorry's!" squeals the little girl, taking my hand. (The older one stays silent.) "She's still ringing the dinner bell!"

This seemed to happen in slow motion. As she pulled me around, as I spun on my heel, the beautiful meadow, with its smells of wheat, summertime, sweat, and brine spilling from off the pond and from my sister's skin; the sound of cicadas strumming their wings in the leaves, the swooping shadows of the birds above, the ancient wooden dock, the sun sinking down as the evening approached, all began to melt. The entrails of the memory dissipate in wisps of grey, revealing the sight of the broken-down walls of the barracks, the threshold with its crooked door, my sister as her seventeen-year-old self — leading me out of the building, clinging to my hand as if it's the only thing keeping her alive. The clanging of the dinner bell transforms into the sound of rumbling, the groaning noise of something dying and struggling for life. The laughing coming from near the garage or around the front of the house, and the chorus of the barking dogs is no longer those things, but the frightened shouts of a bunch of boys, yelling at each other, gesturing wildly, screaming insults, gathering up tools and supplies as quickly as they can manage, stuffing them into a large, all-terrain Hummer-type vehicle, which has a cloud of black smoke pouring out of its exhaust, as Asher is in the driver's seat, revving the engine, checking to make sure it hasn't died on him.

I'm befuddled and still detached. I glance around at the ensuing chaos, and Cheyenne turns, still holding my hand, looking at me. I notice, with a bit of shock, that her torn sweatshirt has been replaced with my shirt. Her dyed hair has been freshly braided, and though it's obvious by the thickness of the braid that it has been done on knotted hair, it looks much better than the other one.

"We don't have time for sorry's," she says to me gravely. I cock my head at her. I'm half expecting her to say we don't have time because Grandma is still ringing the dinner bell. But instead, she states, "It's started again."

Oh, no.

"Come on, we have to get going!" Asher screams, gesturing at me and Cheyenne. "We're running out of time! —"

C R A C K - C A - *B O O M* !

The adrenaline rush doesn't come. I feel locked into place instead. Lost. My good memories always get jolted away from me. I find myself looking desperately at my sister, and there is a distinct pressure in my chest, one that seems to want to implode.

"I *can't*. I can't do this anymore."

"I *can*." She grips my hand harder. "Just don't let go."

When did she become the adult, the one who had things under control, and I the teenager who acts as if he knows everything, yet is sick of pretending and now admits to knowing nothing? Does this mean that my mind has broken itself in half without me being aware of it? No, the fissure in my head merely has widened, not split. Either way, I'm relieved to let her take the reins of having strength, of having the determined expression and the stony demeanour.

Cheyenne and I jog toward the tan armoured vehicle, connected by our hands. Asher gets out of the driver's side, sending a meaningful glance toward Cheyenne, his eyes locking on the tag that's hanging from her neck. His eyes visibly darken again, and his jaw clenches so hard, a vein pops out of his neck.

"Is there a problem?" she asks quietly, voice hoarse.

His eyes dart toward me. "— *No*."

He looks over at Clunker, who's on the roof, balancing on the metal in-between two openings, shutting down the lid of the trunk, which has a spare tire strapped to it.

"Here's what's going to happen." Asher has completely switched into sergeant-general mode or something, barking at us like we're his platoon of men. "This thing goes fast, and it can cover a lot of terrain, but we're all going to have to work as a team."

Jam and Gearteeth, holding onto each other, skitter over to us, and Clunker leaps down from the top of the Humvee, rolling like a parkour expert, picking himself up and grinning like a moron as he brushes off the dust. Asher rolls his eyes skyward, and I'm going to admit, during this pause, that I'm really glad he's taken charge. I never thought I'd say that. But it's a relief to not be incessantly planning and wondering if they would even work.

"I'm driving; since I know how the vehicle. Clunker, I want you in the passenger's seat. Jam and Gearteeth, you each get a rear window. What I want you doing is constantly looking for ground that's cracking. Trees. Rockslides. Anything that'll get in our way, and when you see it, you shout it as loud as you can so I can react." He focuses that sharp gaze on me again. "Aiden, I want you in the ring mount."

"You mean, the hole in the top of the roof?" I ask.

"Yeah, that's what I mean." He glances around at the rest of us. "Any objections?"

"Where the hell am I gonna be?"

Asher purposefully avoids looking Cheyenne in the eyes. "Sitting in the cab, out of—"

Before he can even finish, she pipes up again: "Nope. Not a chance, army bro." She doesn't release my hand, yet she puts all her weight on one foot, shifting one hip to the side, cocking her head at Asher, glaring hard. "If Aiden's up in that thing then I'm standing up there with him."

Asher opens his mouth, concern filling his eyes, but she

steps forward and says loudly, firmly, "*No*. It'll be easier to watch all this ground with as many people as possible, A s h e r, and I'm not changing my mind for *you*."

The expression in her eyes hardens, and her voice lowers into a near growl as she states, "Especially not after what you did."

Asher takes in a deep breath, holding it in his lungs, cheeks burning crimson. The other three guys exchange bewildered glances, and I can tell by the way that Jam puts a finger up, inhaling, that he's going to ask what exactly we're talking about. Fortunately, Asher throws his hands into the air, frustrated yet surrendering to my sister's affirmation. "*Fine*. Now let's *go!*"

A tremendous groan reverberates down the valley, and while the other guys scramble to get inside of the Humvee, I turn around, wondering what in the hell could be making such a racket. A rockslide has begun at the crest of the mountain under which the barracks and the missile site have been built. Boulders of all sizes and smaller pebbles rain down the side, trampling down the wooded areas in their paths before —

S M A S H *CRASH* BOOM-CRA-*B A M*

"Come on, slowpokes!" I hear Gearteeth shout. The roles have switched again. I reach forward, grabbing Cheyenne's hand, pulling her away from the sight, pushing her into the cab via the door that Gearteeth left open for us. She scrambles across his lap, apologising profusely when she accidentally knees him in the stomach, to which he waves her on impatiently. I climb in after her, and Gearteeth slams the door shut behind me.

"This isn't very comfortable," Jam says uneasily, bouncing up and down on his seat, pinching his nose, positively horrified at the musty smell in the cabin, which was quickly being replaced by the odours of sweat and terror.

"It also isn't very roomy," Gearteeth adds, looking around at the crammed interior. "But nice view!"

He points toward Cheyenne's bum and torn fishnets, which is the only thing visible now, as she stands up and peers out through the ring mount, hands clinging to the sides. Asher puts the vehicle into drive, and I halfheartedly swipe at Gearteeth, garnering no reaction except buoyant laughter, I push myself through the opening forcing Cheyenne to move to the side as far as she can go.

"Everyone ready?" Asher doesn't wait for an answer. "*Good!*"

Someone has flipped on the radio just as the governor says, "The worst has passed us. We are in the clear."

"What the *hell* are you talking about?" Clunker yells at him. "It's just getting started!"

Cheyenne and I cling to the sides of the ring mount that are sticking up as Asher slams his foot into the accelerator. The back tires kick up a bunch of soil and rock, the motor whirring as he fishtails toward the hill that we originally had trekked down.

"WAIT — !" I immediately shout, pointing, though no one but Cheyenne is up there to see me. From this height, I can see the Galaxie as it sinks along with the road, which shifts and moans and falls about thirty feet below where it originally had been.

"We're taking the logging road!" Asher yells, swerving so hard, Cheyenne crashes into me. I crane my head over the side of the Humvee and inwardly panic. There's no feeling that can outdo this one: the helplessness of watching as the ground cracks and begins to sink.

"Asher, the ground's *sinking beneath us!*" Cheyenne shrieks.

He doesn't respond with words, merely slams the gas pedal down to the floor. The Humvee snarls as it accelerates, its tires jiggling as the shock absorbers do their best to lessen the impact of the bubbling ground underneath. My hands already are going numb from the combination of the shaking chassis, the trembling earth, and the strength of my grip.

Working on silent cue, and in a most ironic effort, the bloodiness of the moon thankfully begins to fade into the superb dullness of the breaking dawn. The sun itself creeps over the horizon, just beginning to bless the fractured landscape with a dimness unsurpassed. I don't care if it makes my vision fuzzy; it's much better than whatever the hell that moon was.

"Cheyenne, you take the front, I'll take the back!" I shout at her. (Even though we're shouting, it's still hard to hear over the *earth collapsing in on itself.*) I thought that it was happening fast before; but the quakes before this are nothing compared to this unfolding monstrosity. She nods, and we situate ourselves as best we can, backs pressed together, leaning our bodies together as a support system. I watch as pine trees uproot themselves, toppling over, as the crest of a hill becomes a valley, as a valley becomes a mountain, as rocks slip and slide and fight for the chance to kill something below them.

My head darts to the right. "Boulder!"

The Humvee swerves, and the grey, muddy stone passes a hair's breadth before my eyes, filling my nostrils with a murky, dense odour before it continues rolling past.

"Tree!" I hear Cheyenne cry. I feel her sliding down against my back, so I follow her lead, and not three seconds afterward, the Humvee passes underneath the splitting trunk of a massive oak tree, its branches flailing every which way, and if either of us had been standing full height, it would have swiped us right out of the vehicle.

"Asher, the right side's caving in!" Clunker tells him.

"The road is splitting!" Jam says.

"CLIFF FACE!" Gearteeth yelps, practically flinging himself against the wall to point. "CLIFF FACE! *CLIFF FACE!*"

Asher slams on the brakes, yanking the wheel to the right, and I turn, seeing that the side of the Humvee is heading toward a three-foot-tall face of rock that has decided to appear in front of us, blocking our current path. A sinkhole appears underneath the right rear tire, attempting to gobble it up, but fortunately failing.

"I really hope this isn't what's happening across the whole damn state," I hear Asher fume, "or else we're in deep shit."

"*Aiden!*" Cheyenne yells in my ear, pulling at my back. I knock my ruined arm against the protruding side of the ring mount and curse loudly. The burns are angry, red, loud as the groaning of the earth, and still blackened, charred, like ashes of a fire. (Probably infected—)

" A I D E N ! ! ! "

My mouth drops open as I watch a hill collide with another and immediately begin falling into itself, bits of soil and trees and animals yelping as they're swallowed up by the newly formed, gaping cavern.

I whirl around. "W H A T?"

"Your *arm!*" She points at it, but before she can ask after it, the axels bounce, and she's thrown forward, screaming wordlessly.

The ground ahead of us sinks, and the ground behind rises, causing the Humvee to drive rapidly downhill. Asher yells at the antics of the ground, cursing at them; Clunker screams for the first time in this entire escapade; Jam and Gearteeth start babbling about death; I hold on to the handles of ring mount, because that's the only hold I have, and Cheyenne clings to my waist, fingers biting into my skin.

"WE'RE GOING DOWN!" Asher twists at the wheel. "SON OF A BITCH, THIS MOTHERF—"

Just as he begins to curse our bad luck, the ground levels out, though the earth behind us continues rising, a dirt-encrusted tsunami pushing us forth.

"Go faster!" I hear Clunker shrieking hoarsely. "Go faster, you idiot!"

"I have it down to the floor!" Asher yells right back.

A random truck goes flying past the rear of the Humvee, the passengers inside of it hanging out their open windows, screaming as they crash into a rock wall and are immediately swallowed up by it. Birds everywhere spring into the air, cawing and chirping their alarms as they escape. A nest of foxes topples through the air, yelping as they barrel down to an inescapable doom. Other animals screech their protests, but unless they have wings (and even if they do) they aren't going to be so lucky.

Something *else* crashes, but it isn't from the earth surrounding us. My gaze goes upward, and I see clouds forming, taking away even the dull dawn, grumbling as they collide into one another, white flashes of lightning becoming the sole illumination.

The rain starts blessing us immediately after the thunderclouds form, looking more like billows of smoke from a wildfire than actual clouds. Some of them are even tinged a dark purple.

"I can't see anything!" The horn blasts for a short bit as Asher slams his hand against the wheel. "*FANTASTIC!*"

Which means he doesn't know where he's going.

"FLYING TREES!" Cheyenne hauls herself slightly over the ring-mount, hooking her hands more firmly to the edge of it.

"LOOK OUT!"

Three large trees choose to move themselves, their roots

twisting out of the ground, grunting in pain. One of the branches is especially long, reaching out and swiping me across the face, providing me with a nice bloody scratch. The water weeping from the sky quickly cleanses it for me, though.

"To the right!" Jam yells. "The ground's gonna sink!"

The Humvee swerves, and I watch as Jam's warning comes true, as the grass, the woods all fall away, peeling themselves from their original positions, sinking into a dark, angry abyss, one that swirls and emits white foam from its surface as it swallows up the little treat.

My jaw drops.

"*Cheyenne?*" I shout. "***Cheyenne, do you see this?***"

"What the hell, Aiden?" She points at the tumultuous waves.

"WHAT IS THAT?"

The road ahead of us slowly crawls upward. The engine groans, and we begin speeding up a hill that steadily increases in altitude. The roaring, foamy substance in back, creeps after us, sinking its teeth into the rear tires, hungrily washing toward us.

"*What's* going on out there?" Clunker calls.

"It —"

I can't believe what I'm about to say. I don't get a chance to say it yet, however, because Asher sees an opening and takes it, swerving quickly to the right, bowling over a couple of logs that cause the Humvee to jolt with such force that the breath is knocked out of me, as my side collides with the hard, metal edge of the mount opening. I suck in a deep breath, holding it there as pain fills my entire body, causing my knees to buckle.

Cheyenne screams wordlessly at me as I slide into the Humvee and fall onto the seat, bending in half, gasping for air, feeling the bruise as it forms on my waist.

"What's going on?" Jam asks me frantically, grabbing my

left shoulder, shaking it. "What's that terrible noise?"

Asher glances in the rearview mirror at me as the rain pounds against Cheyenne and tires to force its way through the opening.

Fortunately, I don't have to answer Jam, because Cheyenne suddenly comes to the same realisation that I had, and she screams down into the Humvee, "It's the ocean. The *ocean* is behind us! It's eating *everything*! It's coming up out of the cracks!

"*California really is sinking!*" Jam shrieks, covering his eyes.

"What, did you think we were *dreaming*?" Gearteeth pulls at Jam's hands. "*Come on!*"

"This *sucks!*" Clunker rages, slamming his fist against the dashboard. "How're we gonna get out of *this*?"

"Everyone, *calm down!*" Asher's panting with the effort it takes to drive, arms shaking uncontrollably. "The earth is shifting so much, we're probably closer to being over the fault than we think."

"The *ocean!*" Jam shouts again, pulling himself up so that his mouth is directly next to Asher's ear, his eyes wide and tears streaming down his cheeks as he finally gives into the anxiety attack he's been wanting to have since this whole thing started. "The *OCEAN, Asher!*"

"I get it!" Asher screams back. "Trust me!"

The throbbing pain in my side from the hitting the steel has faded away, and I'm able to pull myself back up next to Cheyenne, whose eyes are wide as rain streaks down her face. She's awestruck at the scene folding out before her, staring at the sight of the darkened waters of the Pacific Ocean seeping through the crevices and cracks, devouring everything in its wake. We're travelling up such a steep incline that she is nearly all the way out of the ring mount, the only thing keeping her from falling into the gathering waves is the fact that her pelvic bones are pressing heavily into the side of the opening.

"It's so beautiful," she says, and her voice is quiet, strangely calm, and I can't possibly understand what she's thinking.

"*Hold on, assholes!*" Asher sounds ecstatic, and I think for a moment that he's finally snapped. But then, a loud whirring noise, and a chorus of screaming boys rising up from below us.

As this occurs, it seems to slow down, and unlike everything before, I am able to see every single detail as it crosses my path. Cheyenne pushes off the ledge and grasps onto my waist, her mouth open in the start of a yelp. The earth beneath us falls away, the recognisable dirt, rocks, tree stumps all crumbling as we are propelled into the air. We have gone off the edge of the hill we had been travelling up, and the next bit of *stabilised* terrain is some sixty feet below us, rising up rapidly to meet our tires.

For all of ten seconds, we are airborne.

I see multiple lights winking in the distance, I see a helicopter whirring by in the air above us, attempting to navigate this terrible storm, its spotlight swooping down, encasing us in a white glow for a split second before it darts away in search of new targets. A large wave of water from behind us yawns up to meet the helicopter, which makes all sorts of terrible, screeching sounds as it is enveloped by the relentless, foaming wall of ocean water. I know the impact that is coming, and I put one hand on Cheyenne's head, shoving her down into the safer interior of the Humvee before gripping either side of the edges of the ring mount, bracing myself. Lightning flashes. The thunder, combined with the ocean, creates a proverbial, monstrous roar that will never be able to be replicated accurately. Ever. I get this strange urge, at the last second, to throw my arms out to the sides, embrace the rainfall, shout to the world that I am finally free, shut my eyes tightly, pretend that I am soaring through the air, that none of the chaos below me is occurring, that it's only me, having a beautiful dream that I am gliding to a wanted destination, gliding back to her.

B O O M CA-THUNK *SMACK*

The impact comes before I expect it to. I hear Cheyenne scream out my name as the tires collided into the hard, rock-laden earth, the nose of the Humvee dipping down, groaning, the treads of the front tires spewing out a shower of sparks before the vehicle steadies itself out. The platform I stand on departs from my feet, and while the Humvee has found somewhat solid ground — I haven't. As I turn, writhing through the air, I see the wall of black water behind us, thunderclouds fighting for dominance above, and then the front of the Humvee, the tan exterior, coming up to meet me. One hand reaches out, closing around a cold, wet metal handle, and my arm feels as if it's about to be wrenched out of its socket. As I careen back around, my legs smash hard into the windshield. I hear the guys shouting at one another. My other hand reaches up, grasping at the slick handle, and I hold on as tightly as I can manage, my lower body swinging violently back and forth.

"Flame!" I hear Clunker shout. His blonde head appears above the ring mount.

"DO SOMETHING !"

"IF HE DIES, I'M GOING TO KILL YOU!"

"Flame, hold on, I'm coming!"

I hear a raucous groaning noise that drowns out the rush of water and rain. My head whips to the right, and my heart sinks. A parking lot, one of the places where you can go to put your car and see the San Andreas fault, disintegrates into thin air, parked cars careening down into the swirling black monster below it, horns blaring and headlights flashing. My warning shout to Asher is whipped away by a gust of wind that nearly tears me from the gun; not to mention there's a distinct biting pain every time a raindrop hits my burned, ruined skin, and my left arm currently is going completely numb. I then hear Gearteeth bellow out, *"The parking lot's going down!"*

"Flame, grab my hand! Grab it — now!" Clunker is there, hanging over the edge of the vehicle reaching for me. I see Jam clinging to his legs, and most likely Cheyenne or Gearteeth underneath him, holding him in place. Just as I lift one hand from a handle, reaching for Clunker, making contact with him, to which he responds with the tightest grip I've ever felt from his callused fingers, Asher decides that it's time to start weaving away from the array of asphalt and cars melting down toward us. My other hand gets ripped away from the vehicle and I swing, Clunker's grip being the only tether keeping me here. No longer am I at the front of the Humvee, but at the back, and my legs are dangling above the splitting ground, the water springing up from the crevices, angrily foaming, stretching out long black fingers to snatch at my shoes.

"I'm going to kill you — I swear to God, PULL HIM BACK IN!!" Cheyenne screams.

"I still got you, Flame," Clunker says breathlessly. His other hand reaches further down my arm, grasping at the ruined skin. I cry out in pain, tears immediately filling my eyes and streaming down my cheeks, mixing with the rainwater as Clunker, Jam, and whoever's holding on to Jam begin to pull me back into the Humvee. "I got you, damn it."

The water stops attempting to suck me underneath, fading away from the back tires, focusing on completely enveloping the ground it's already covered instead. Clunker and company haul me into the Humvee, forcing me down inside.

"Neither of you are standing up there *again."* Clunker

fumes, pointing at the hole with a trembling finger and shaking me by the shoulder with his other hand. "Not with that crazy bastard driving."

"Oh, gee, *I'm sorry,*" Asher bursts out through clenched teeth, hanging onto the steering wheel with both hands, biceps contracting and bulging as he keeps the thing from controlling itself. "But in case you haven't noticed, we aren't driving on *smooth pavement!*"

"I haven't noticed!" Gearteeth yells, panting heavily, wiping sweat from his brow, which tells me that he had been the one holding onto Jam. We're all crammed into the back seat, Asher stares at us hard via the rearview mirror. "*Thanks* for letting me know!

"No problem!" he barks back. "I need someone up front! We can't take breathers or we'll end up flat on our asses."

Clunker huffs a hard breath through his lips and clamours into the front after slapping me on the shoulder. My entire left arm throbs; not even the rainfall soothes the aches and pains now. In fact, as I stare at it, studying it, I see it sizzling, and when I touch the skin, it's burning hot. Little wisps of smoke rise up every place a drop of rain hits the angry wound. (Is this a typical sign of infection, doctor?)

Gearteeth isn't happy — and he makes it known. "Dude, give us time to breathe; Flame almost *died* out there!"

"Breathe while you're doing something useful," Asher sneers. "Besides, he *didn't* die, did he? So there's no problem."

"— You *son of a bitch,*" Gearteeth roars, leaping toward the front. Jam yanks him back by the scruff of the neck, and Gearteeth winces against his boyfriend's tight grasp on bare skin. "You did it on *purpose,* didn't you?"

"*I didn't do it on purpose!*"

None of us are convinced.

"I think I see headlights!" Clunker crows suddenly, dispelling the growing tension. The Humvee gives a jolt, swerving to the right, barely missing a sinkhole that appeared. "But —"

"Why in the hell would there be headlights over there?"

"Maybe they're watching the earth fall away," I say jokingly. "Taking footage with their camera phones and all that bullshit."

The Humvee bounds over a large branch, causing the chassis to jolt. Asher's rear comes up out of the seat, his head knocking against the ceiling. Wincing and cussing, he grunts, "I guess we'll find out."

"If we ever get there," Gearteeth grumbles bitterly.

"Get *off* of it!" Asher shouts at him, slamming his hand onto the wheel, blaring the horn.

"No, *you* get off of it!" Gearteeth yells right back.

"Oh my *god*, you're both acting like *assholes*," Cheyenne groans, leaning forward from where she's been hunkering down. "Asher, drive and shut up. Gearteeth — just shut up." She shakes her head, exasperated. "Way too much testosterone in here."

"*Mountain slide!*" Clunker screeches suddenly.

"You mean, *rock* slide?" Asher comments drolly.

"*No*, I mean MOUNTAIN SLIDE!"

I throw myself back onto the platform as Clunker continues ranting at Asher. "If I had meant *rockslide*, I would've said *rockslide!*" I pull myself halfway out of the ring mount, peering every which way, being pelted by a rainfall that blinds me for a split second. I wipe away the water from my eyes and stare. "I meant *mountain* slide!"

"But *what* does that even mean?" Asher roars at him.

"It means — T H A T!" I yell at him, hoping he heard me over the sudden roar of a wave steadily, slowly gaining on us, rising to meet the monster of a mountain that's crumbling in on itself via multiple fissures, rocks and trees raining everywhere, the silhouettes of animals and vehicles dropping toward their inescapable demise.

"I can't go anywhere but straight!" Asher sounds bewildered.

"We're driving straight into the mountain?" Cheyenne shrieks at him. "Are you kidding me? *We're all going to die!*"

"I don't have a choice!" he screams back at her.

He isn't exaggerating. I cling to the sides of the ring mount, craning my neck. On the right side and left sides, the terrain is falling away into dark caverns; behind us, we have the merciless ocean pushing us onward; in front, we have the mountain raining down its innards and its parts on our heads.

"Everybody, hold on!" Asher yells out.

A chorus answers him:

"I hate you, you bastard!"

"YOU'RE **INSANE**!"

"YOU'VE GOT A SCREW LOOSE!"

"Please don't kill us!"

When everyone, including Asher, glances at me, waiting for my reaction to the insanity of the situation, I merely shrug, resuming a crouched position, eyes focusing on the blurring sight outside of the front windshield. I don't have a reaction, honestly. I almost died maybe two minutes ago. I don't give a shit right now.

Because I should be dead. But I'm not.

Nobody will believe me. But it wasn't just the guys pulling me into the Humvee that saved my life. No, the ocean was there, pushing me upwards, helping me before it backed off, right after Cheyenne cried out my name.

I don't even — it sounds *so* crazy to even say.

But - what *isn't* crazy about this whole thing, anyway?

The Binding of a Sulcus

October 10th
San Bernardino Mountains

Cheyenne Kinsey

There is nothing more disheartening than sinking in your own abyss alone. Not even this land mass practically disintegrating into the ocean is as painful or as heartrending or as frightening as slowly fading away into nothingness inside your own shell of a body.

I watch with as the mountain folds in on itself. It was a long shot to think that we'd make it out of here alive, I decide. I couldn't believe I had allowed myself to have even the smallest bit of hope in our survival. There's no way we're going to make it through this penultimate scenario, no way in this living hell we'll make it. The mountain in front, the beautifully dangerous ocean in back, the earth falling away from beneath our tires, the waves attempting to capture us in their powerful grips, the sky openly cursing us; there's no way.

No way.

No way,   no way,   no way.

Everybody else is screaming as we begin to pass underneath the ruins of the mighty mountain that once was and never shall be again. But I've done *enough* yelling. I've done *enough* protesting and shrieking and every other high-volume voice that you can think of to last me a dozen centuries. I'm t i r e d.

I almost let myself fall right out of that hole, you know, and into the churning waters of the ocean attempting to swallow us into its pulverising stomach. I *almost* let myself fall. And in that split second, I didn't care that I would be leaving Aiden behind. I didn't care that he would blame Asher, or that Asher would care, or that I had made a promise to ensure the memory of Elijah lived onward. I did not care about any of it.

So why didn't I do it?

Why didn't I let myself go?

Maybe I'll figure it out someday. Maybe I'll be able to admit aloud, when somebody asks me why I didn't let myself go, that there was a smidgen of hope in me, who believed that *he* was waiting for me, just as Aiden believed *she* was waiting for *him*, and that this smidgen of hope was what kept me from doing it.

I watch, entranced. What else are you supposed to do, helpless in one of the four passenger seats? What are you supposed to do, besides watch it unfold before your eyes in a trance?

Nothing. Nothing except watch.

I'm not sure at which point in time the otherwise solid wall of debris decided to part before us, allowing a hole to be made in its side, a gaping wound in the ribcage of its body. But we are suddenly encased in a multitude of shifting shadows, and the guys all duck forward, covering their heads with their hands and arms, trying to protect themselves from the shower of rainfall and different-sized stones coming in through the opening of the Humvee. I keep my gaze straight forward, looking past Asher's clenched jaw and twitching temple, right through the front windshield. I see a kaleidoscope of earth, twirling this way and that, ghosting our vehicle but never quite touching any of the tan paint. There is a strange silence, one that you might experience when sucked into a vacuum, one that makes my ears ring because it's such a dramatic shift, from the proverbial roaring to absolutely nothing within a millisecond. I can hear the blood pulsing in my ears; I zero in on it, blocking the rest of it out. Because it's a reminder to my body that I am still alive, still breathing, that the rock tsunami has not crashed down upon our heads and drowned us with its pressure.

This experience must have lasted no longer than five, maybe ten seconds, but it felt as if it lasted half of my lifetime, this oppressively relieving silence, this sensation of drowning sans being under the clawing grasp of the ocean. And when we finally reemerge into the loudness of the real world, I wince into Aiden's shirt, joining in with the rest of the screaming voices.

"We're all going to *D I E*," Jam sobs, holding onto Gearteeth, shaking him back and forth. "We're *all* going to *die!!*"

"Stop it, Jam," Clunker spits at him. "*Stop it!*"

"If we can make it out of *that* funhouse of bullshit —" Asher looks in the rearview mirror at the rest of us, tongue brushing his lower lip. "We can make it out of anything."

The vehicle continues bounding over the bumpy, shifting terrain, treads smoking as it does its best to traverse all the obstacles being thrown in front of it. Asher's going about sixty miles an hour. I have no idea where we are. My brother's just almost died. I'm tired of all the screaming and peril. Someone let me sleep.

"Your optimism *isn't helping*," Jam trills out shakily. "It's just making it worse — we all know what's coming."

"No, we don't," Aiden tells him. "We can still make it."

All of a sudden, Clunker starts gesturing wildly, insulting whatever's approaching us from the front, shouting that Jam is right for once, shouting that there's no way we're ultimately going to survive this, shouting about the stupidity of humanity, all the while intermixing a good amount of curse words and their various forms. When everyone else cranes their necks forward, wanting to see what he's making such a ruckus about, I follow suit, morbidly curious about the ends that await us, the ends that we have been running from, yet ultimately will not be able to escape, because when Death writes your name into his book, there's no escaping the embrace of his cloak, of his ever-changing face.

What I notice in the distance is the headlights of many cars shining sickly in the dim light, a lighthouse that mocks us as it gets ready to watch our ship sink down, down into the crevice of the fault. Not to mention the silhouettes of people scurrying in front of the lights like little mice, the wind whipping past the shadows of newscasters with their raincoats flying, those bright fluorescent camera lights shining on them in order for all those at home, watching the action with their nails halfway chewed off and their voices high-pitched, to clearly see how even the newscasters panic, yet how also they are brave for daring to be so close to something uncontrollable, yet how also they are stupid for the same exact reason.

"You've *gotta* be kidding me!" Aiden explodes, bursting out into bitter laughter, pointing out the front windshield. "I was right! They're *actually* filming this!"

"Oh, s h i t." Asher jams the wheel all the way to the left, and the vehicle starts spinning around in hard, tight circles. "Hold on!"

"What are you — ?" Clunker's words turn into a strangled roar as he flies headlong into Asher's lap. Jam and Gearteeth screech together, clinging to one another, rolling off the seat, one of them smacking the back of their heads on the door before they tumble into the floorboards. I plaster myself against the window, pushing myself up against it, watching out the other window in horror. Aiden joins his two friends on the floorboard, all of them cussing up a storm that could rival the one raging above us, and I stare as I see the dark patch of earth underneath our vehicle begin to slip away.

"It's not strong enough to hold us up. Not this close to the fault line." The words rush out of Asher's mouth, and he takes his hands from the steering wheel, burying his face into his palms. "Oh my god, this is —"

"*Why* did you take your hands off the wheel?" Clunker yells at him, reaching up to grip it in his own. "*Why did you do that?*"

"I —"

C - C - C - C - C R A C K!

Asher's answer is cut off by a loud cracking coming from directly beneath the treads of our tires. The vehicle shudders, engine whirring, as it begins pitching down and sideways, launching us down into the rapidly deepening cavern formed by the San Andreas fault. When my vision is met by nothing but impermeable darkness, I scream, shoving myself against the door, trying to escape from it, but as I said before, there is no escaping it, and I see his face, the shifting face of Death, sitting there in the window across from me, expressionless yet somehow still expectant, one colourless, translucent hand reaching out for me.

I cringe back from him, and as the vehicle turns through the air, turns somersaults, I catch Aiden's eye, and for the smallest of seconds, we communicate things between the two of us that can never be captured through words. His gaze, and that of Death, are both ripped away from me as the vehicle bows down, shifting all of our bodies toward the front windshield, Asher nearly crashing through it, and the bumper collides into a large boulder, which turns it into a crumpled sheet of metal, the motor choking out a few last breaths, which mix with the shouts of the boys surrounding me and the smashing of the windshield's glass and the bottomless roar of the ocean, the wind rushing past the shattered windows.

The vehicle stands upright on its busted front bumper for three seconds before it yawns backward, moaning, and I turn around, staring through the back, pointing, screaming at the churning darkness below us, mottled with white foam, and the stability from the boulder is lost as we careen through the air again, falling at a slight angle, the interior of the vehicle erupting into pandemonium as we smash into one another, as feet go into faces, as the back of my head smacks into the broken glass of the window nearest to me and I black out for a split second, still clinging to the window as if it has suddenly become my buoy, my life jacket, my fountain of immortality.

The blackness compresses against me, taking away my very breath, and I float through an invisible fog, one that shoves itself down my throat, into my lungs, constricts around my heart. I hear a beautiful, low-toned voice, one that doesn't belong to the lurking demon in my head, one that doesn't even belong to *him*, whispering my name, whispering for me, beckoning.

"C h e y e n n e. I'm here. Don't let go."

That translucent hand is there, before my eyes, and I find myself reaching for it, hanging off the edge of a cliff, and there's a shout of surprise from somewhere in the darkness. "Pull her out!"

A pair of strong hands grips the neck of my shirt, and my eyes fly open, as does my mouth, as my arms wrap around my heaving abdomen. The hands shove me down onto something hard, made of wood; I peer at it through the torrential rain and notice, as my vision clears, that I am seated on a thick branch of an overturned tree, whose roots are still securely fastened into a sheer wall of rock. The rear tires of the vehicle have landed on the tree as well, though it's about three feet to the left of me, and I see Clunker's blond hair flashing in the dim light as he reaches down, helping Jam (who has a coil of rope hooked around one shoulder) out of the rapidly-sinking machine and onto the trunk. Aiden crouches beside me - he had been the one who hauled me out of the water - and Asher stands there as well, hazel eyes staring me down, studying me.

"Are you all right?" At my nod, he continues, "You were underwater for so long. We thought you were —."

I stare at him, confused. They thought I was — what, *dead?*

I'm not even breathing hard.

"Where's Gearteeth?" Jam shouts suddenly, frantically, pointing toward our method of transport, which sends up a slight wave as it shifts, sinking a bit lower, the right tire disentangling itself from a thin branch, snapping it along the way. *"Where is he?"*

"He's not in the truck," Clunker yells at him, taking Jam by the shoulders and shaking him. "I checked! He isn't in there!"

"THEN WHERE IS HE?" Jam screeches back.

The tree groans, its roots shifting in the rock, and our bodies are thrown forward. We all manage to grab onto sturdier branches, but the corpse of our transport vehicle isn't so lucky — it succumbs to the water churning beneath us. I whip my head around, trying to take in as much as I can. We're surrounded on all sides by sheer faces of rock, which break off, crumble, and drop into the water. Trees and remnants of mountains alike crash into the waves at all angles as well, causing a ravenous current to whirl around us. The downpour still accosts us; all of us are well beyond the line of being *drenched.* Lightning flashes, but along with that light, several spotlights are seen waving around, and far away I hear people screaming.

"What happened?" I scream at Aiden, Asher, whoever's paying attention to me, gripping the branch in one hand.

"The ground went *KABOOM!"* Aiden shouts back, making a wild, circular gesture with his hand. "The ocean's eating California!"

"What are we gonna do?" I scream over the roar of the ocean and push my wet hair out of my face so I can see Aiden

better.

*"**Not drown**!"* Aiden ducks as pebbles shower from the cliff face where the roots are connected still, just barely. "If we stay on this tree, maybe it will float as the water rises; then we should be able to climb out, or swim across when it's calmed down!"

"You *seriously* think this is gonna calm down!?" Asher yells.

"There he is!" Jam's screech attracts our attention. The poor guy is falling off the tree in his fretfulness, and Clunker holds tightly onto him, gritting his teeth as he holds him back. "Someone help him!"

"It's the current!" Asher roars back, holding onto alternating tree branches as he cautiously walks down the trunk of the tree, shaking like a power line in the wind of a hurricane. "It's too strong; it'll pull under whoever tries to go to him!"

I stare at the area where Jam points, and I see a flash of white skin above the waves, a hand frantically moving back and forth, and his turquoise hair barely hovering over the surface of the water. I avert my gaze, staring down into the black depths of the water below me.

No! No, don't take Aiden's friend from him. Not Aiden's friend, too. You have enough. You don't need anymore!

(Who am I even talking to? There's no one listening to me.

No one.)

But suddenly, a strain of thought comes to me, a crazy one, one that would have all of the guys shouting at me to not do, one that would put Aiden into some sort of tirade, one that would have Asher after me, one that would put my life possibly into danger again.

What is it Asher had said? *You were underwater for so long.*

Yet I hadn't even been breathing quickly, or coughing, or expelling water from my lungs. It — hadn't affected me.

I'm not one for making snap decisions. They usually involve some sort of anxiety attack before, during, and after they've been executed. But not this time. All I feel is a rush of adrenaline, my jaw setting in determination, because I finally feel as if this will help me make up for all the things I've done to cause problems, to make my brother's life harder. "— I'll be back."

"Cheyenne, *what are you doing?*" he roars.

"Stop it, Aiden!" I tear myself away from his grasp, slipping from the trunk of the tree, holding onto the branch with one hand, my heart nearly stopping as I feel the fingers of the ocean creeping around me, moving me this way and that as if I were made of cloth, not cell matter. "Let me do this!"

"NO!" He goes to say something more, but I don't let him get any more words out, because otherwise, he might be able to successfully persuade me that I should save my crazy impulses for a time when we're not all in mortal danger.

"Y E S !" I yell right back at him, releasing the branch, allowing myself to be taken underneath by the waves, barely managing to inhale before they tugged me into their unbelievably cold embrace, enveloping me in their blackened, tightening limbs. I keep my lips pressed tightly together and my eyes wide open, though I can't see anything except shadows when the lightning flashes, shadows that dart back and forth, ripping and gnawing at each other. I am shoved up above the waves again, and I quickly begin moving my arms, my legs, swimming frantically, wondering if I'm even going in the right direction. I hear the guys on the log shouting my name, but I push them out of my mind, trying to focus on not being swept into the whirlpool forming toward the right of me, which is sucking in logs and rocks and debris of all shapes and sizes. Something grazes my left leg, and I yelp, floundering away from it. (I better not get killed by some giant squid or something.)

Through the crashing waves, I see the white hand sticking out above the black water. A smaller ripple comes toward me, and I dive into its crest, submerging myself back down. It's warmer down here; my limbs move faster, and though my eyes are open, they aren't stinging. I see more than just shadows now, can make out distinct shapes, though everything has a colourlessness to it, a greyness that belongs in the cemetery, not in something as alive as the ocean. I think that liveliness has bled into me somehow; a rush of energy overtakes me, propels me forward through the murkiness, my breath steady in my lungs, slowly leaking out in the form of small bubbles from my nose.

It's muted in here as well. Even when the Humvee finally starts sinking to the bottom, the groan that its compressing metal emits is softer than I know it should be. It's a depressing, cloudy cage, yet here is where I am freer than ever before. No older brother trying to compensate for lost time. No mother disappointing me. No father leaving me forever. No friends disappearing from my life. No relatives forgetting that I'm part of their family, too. No boys I've slept with; no girls, either. It's me, only me, and the water that seductively runs its fingertips along my skin.

It's death without departing from the world. It's flying without wings. It's the silence of the grave combined with the animation of dancing. It's peace without a proceeding war. It's sleep without unconsciousness. It's dreaming in reality.

It's true freedom.

The water shoots me forward and up, and I instinctively gasp for air as I start to tread, legs and arms furiously working to keep myself in place. The liquid immediately surrounding me is still, but twelve inches past that, the waves are angrier than before. The roar deafens me, and my left ear throbs as my hearing goes out. I cringe against it, craning my neck up, searching over the chaos for any sign of Gearteeth's hand. But it's too late to be looking for that; he's already started to drown, about to join the other ghostly shells drifting away. My hands cut through as I swim toward the general area where he had been flailing before, and after a few hard, barely executed strokes, I give up, taking in another deep breath before going back under.

There he is. His skin glows white. His wrists feebly turn this way and that, and his eyes are opened wide, nearly bulging out from his face, his legs sporadically kicking. The eyelids are sliding shut, though, and his movements are stopping. I don't have much time.

I also don't have much *choice* in regards to reaching him besides staying under the waves and just going for it. How can I manage that, though? I don't know if I can last without breathing for that long, but any break to get more air could cost him his life. I'll have to deal with the air that's in my lungs, expelling as little as possible, and just do it. Stop thinking about it, Cheyenne. Just *do* it.

I churn my arms as fast as they will go and for as far as they can stretch out, feeling my muscles shouting in protest. My legs kick just as furiously. A muted thud resounds through the water, and I see something drop to my left, a large chunk of earth, a slab of a mountain. Before I can react, the aftermath has reached me, the current snatching me and sending me twirling, spinning, and rotating just underneath the foam of the waves, out and away from the path I had been taking. I feel my mind getting fuzzy as things spin past me at great speeds, unrecognisable things, bodies of animals, those gyrating shadows again, parcels of cars and rocks and who knows what the hell else, and I gasp when I'm thrown above the surface before I'm quickly plummeted back down.

I see him sinking lower just beneath me. I have hardly any air, though I just took in what I thought had been a deep breath. Hitting the water as hard as I did had knocked it pretty much right out of me. But he is still this time around, no feeble movements or anything. I had to go down; there's no time to get more breath. *I just need to do it.*

I manoeuvre my body around and shoot myself straight down toward Gearteeth, an arrow streaking toward its target though it's hindered by a fog. Soon, though, I find myself confused, because no matter how much I thrash, he never seems to get any closer. *No!* I scream into the water, as if it cares, and I waste all of my air as I struggle even harder, my hands flailing, hoping by some smidgen of luck, they'll grab onto some part of him, even if it's a fistful of his turquoise hair.

I feel something beneath my fingers, and though I don't know what it is, I snatch at it desperately, knowing my body will begin spasming at any minute due to the lack of air. It's his arm. I don't know what happened, how I am able to grab him, and I'm not going to be asking any questions soon, that's for sure. I pull him up, gritting my teeth, glad that the current helped me a little bit, wrapping my left arm around his waist, leaving my right free to push us back to the surface. He's so limp — so lifeless.

My heart thunders harder, louder, faster. *I have to hurry.*

Don't panic right now, Cheyenne. Don't lose your head. Not now. You'll both die. You'll both *die* if you don't keep your cool.

But there's no air left. There's no air.

S t o p i t.

His voice. Not the evil person lurking in the background of my head's voice as he leers at my increasing level of anxiety.

Focus. Swim. Go.

Oh my god. Aiden and I have both lost it. He's hearing her voice. Now I'm hearing his voice. This can't be happening right now.

Swim, damn it.

I paddle my feet as rapidly as I can manage, wondering when my body will begin those painful-looking convulsions that always happen when someone begins to drown, and I force my aching bicep to continue on, scooping the water away from me, propelling Gearteeth and myself upward. I understand fully why Aiden was forcing himself to keep his cool while all these lives were depending on him. You have to. Or you'll all die. You have to.

I see Death again, face the epitome of metamorphosis, that bony, eerily intangible hand reaching toward me, the hem of his cloak drifting calmly in the ocean as he floats upward beside me with ease. God, I wish he'd just *go away*. I make a face at the apparition, looking upward toward the flickering lights, the way the raindrops patter on the ocean's surface, the way the foam moves violently this way and that. Now it's the *surface* that doesn't seem to be coming closer. I can't.

Swim.

I can't.

Swim.

I won't.

Do it.

No.

Why won't the ocean take me as its own already?

My body continues working as a machine would, though my mind detaches and hides itself away even deeper in its safe room, shying away from the two maniacs - one maliciously smirking at me through the frosted glass, the other pounding on it, shouting hoarse words of encouragement at me. I feel as if a film has been laid upon my eyes, one that has made everything murky and grey, and the dim lights from above seem to be light-years from us. Why am I not drifting? (Why am I not *drowning*?)

Then — our heads break free, liberated from the cage of the water. I don't suck in air, deeply inhale as if my life depends upon that single breath I take. I'm back to feeling energised as well, breathing harder than normal, but not so much that there's any noticeable difference. I'm not choking. The guys are probably back to thinking I was unconscious again. I had been before, though. Nah, they have probably graduated to thinking that Gearteeth and I drowned together in the might of the frothing waves. Sounds like it could be the ending to a Shakespearean drama, doesn't it?

Gearteeth, next to me, not nearly as calm as I am, gasps and sputters water out of his nose and mouth, coughing so violently, fingers scrabbling for a grip against my wet skin as his legs kick, albeit feebly, in attempts to keep himself above water. I had managed to reach him in time by something short of a damned miracle.

"Help!" I scream out, taking in a mouthful of water as punishment for my bravery. I tighten my grip around Gearteeth when I feel his body begin to slip from my grasp, and he returns my efforts with some more of his own. "H e l p!"

I spit out the water, not wanting to dehydrate my exhausted corpse more than it already probably is.

"S o m e b o d y!"

His hoarse echoes don't do much in the way of attracting attention, but still, he tries. "A n y b o d y!"

I hear the distinct whirring of helicopters, and I look up, staring straight into the weeping sky, rainwater blurring my vision. Even through the curtain, I can see spotlights, the ones attached to the front of the machines, moving back and forth on the surface of the water. But I inherently know that they won't take notice of our two bodies floating here, for they will think of us as nothing more than two pieces of debris that have conjoined together. They have more important things to be concerned about than the possibility of two people dying.

S C R E E C H !

My head whips around, eyes widening, instinctively gulping in a large breath of air and pulling Gearteeth closer to me as I watch a mountain, towering not-so-far above us now, shave itself in half, and the large iceberg of rock slide down the newly-formed break, an avalanche in and of itself, various sizes of boulders breaking off and raining down into the ocean before the rest of it finally makes impact. I watch as the water beneath it bows down under the glory of the mountain, accepting it eagerly, washing over it with its foaming waves, which continue to grow in height, in width, until their snarling undersides are hundreds of feet over our heads. I wince, feeling my eyes narrow as I stare at it, pleadingly, as if that's going to stop the monster from devouring us.

We can't get a break, can we?

It doesn't stop the monster, by the way. The wave envelops us; I feel our bodies rising. I stop worrying about staying afloat and cling to him, wrapping both arms around him, wanting to make sure that he wasn't flung away from me as he had been flung through the windshield before. I wrap my legs around him as well when I feel him slipping, when I feel the waves engaging in a game of catch, throwing us this way and that, jarring us, smacking us against their upturned palms. This lasts for so long, I lose all sense of self, not knowing whether I'm hanging onto Gearteeth or have long since let him go; my eyes staying glued shut so that I wouldn't be sick at being thrown about like a rag doll. I'm just another object, without a choice or a hope, at the mercy of the water that has had every opportunity to claim me and has yet to do so. Maybe this will be it. Maybe I'll finally be free.

The left side of my body slams into something hard, its texture bumpy, as if a chisel has made a thousand tiny ridges in it. The breath is knocked out of me, and my eyes fly open as I gasp in pain, instinctively trying to curl up on myself but unable to do so due to the sudden paralysis that strikes me, rendering me helpless on this face of rock. The waves have washed me - and Gearteeth, it looks like, for his body is a foot away from mine, sprawled in the most uncomfortable position I've ever seen, chest heaving, eyes blinking rapidly - onto the slice of mountain that had fallen and caused this whole episode of bullshit in the first place. (How ironic.) But at least there's more room to move around, and less of a chance of it suddenly sinking, like that tree that my brother and his friends and Asher are on.

My heart beats faster at the thought of what's become of them. Thunder crashes as I force my body to unwind itself; an off-key, high-pitched sound erupts from nowhere, startling me, until I realise that as it fades away, there's a distinct scratching sensation in my oesophagus. (I had been screaming in pain.) My left arm's crushed, and I hold it against my body, feeling the tears fall easily from the corners of my eyes; even the slightest movement had me gasping, breaking out into a sweat that is washed away by the rain. A place on my hip and in-between two ribs throb along with my racing pulse as I unfurl my legs, the muscles yelling at me, demanding that I stop moving, take a moment for myself.

But I've never had a moment to myself. (Not ever.) What makes me think that I should take one now, at the hour of everyone's greatest need? I pick myself up from off the ground and am forced to put all of my weight on my right leg, which trembles with the effort, for my left has become pudding, unable to withstand any sort of pressure. My shoulders curl in over the rest of my body, over the arm in its strange position, and I hear that every time I exhale, I'm making that high-pitched noise, my face creased with the pain.

Even so, there's still that strange element of detachment. I feel the pain, I *recognise* the pain, yet I'm not actually *here*, in this body that's feeling the pain. I am elsewhere; my mind is locked away, I'm more concerned about Gearteeth and the fates that have befallen the others than I am about myself. This state of being self-sacrificial is as foreign to me as the concept of wanted physical contact - I haven't been this unselfish since before I started school.

I tried to breathe in, just to gather up some air so that I could shout once more, but it was too much and ended in me curling myself in half, feeling my stomach roil as the small piece of mountain beneath me lurched a little with the impact of another wave. Fortunately, there seemed to be some mercy being given to me, for the face of rock wasn't tossing and turning as it probably should be doing, just floating along. Or maybe it shouldn't be doing that, maybe it goes down deep enough that it's stable, and stability is something you must cling to when things are going wrong everywhere.

I think I hear shouting, a barrage of indistinguishable words, and I shut my eyes, my ears against them, not wanting to start hallucinating, not now. Not now. *Please*, not now—

"*Cheyenne!* I'm coming!"

The rainfall, the sound of it, how it feels upon my skin, the trickling of it onto the ocean's surface, the waves crashing against debris and this sliver of rock, are all very calming to me, a sort of lullaby, something tangible to cling to, and cling to it I do, my eyes staying shut, my ears opening back up so that I might absorb these sounds, as well as the salty spray of the sea accosting my nose, my tongue flicking at my cracked, dried lips to taste the water upon them.

"*Cheyenne! Hold on!*"

"There's nothing to hold on to," I tell the air.

I see a tree float by, one with figures on it, ones that are moving and shouting. I blink away the rain, lifting my head, feeling my heart leap as I continue rising, breath filling my lungs and sending agony back through my body, but I don't care, *I don't care*, because there they are, on that *stupid* tree, waving at me, screaming my name, having situated themselves in the roots because the rest of it is now submerged, and they're holding on, though Jam practically hangs off of it, as it floats past the slab of rock where I lay.

"Oh, my *god*," I breathe out, wishing that I had the energy to stand back up, to wave and cuss and shout right back at them. Yet all I am able to do is sit up halfway, stare at them as the roots groan and twist, and as they all scramble around like little ants in a farm, I bury my head back into the stone beneath me, moaning, not wanting to see them all die just when I had regained hope. I don't have the strength to save them all.

"Pick her up, *get her up!*"

There's a sound of splashing that breaks the reverie, and actual voices shouting, voices that I recognise, combined with a couple of well-placed yelps and curse words. I whip my head up, blinking rapidly, in time to see the guys leaping from the log as it passes by my slab of rock. The tip of Clunker's foot hits the edge, and he goes tumbling backward, but Jam saves him, grabbing his hand, pulling him along as they all land in a mangled heap on the other side, about four feet from where I lay, directly next to

Gearteeth.

Aiden rushes toward me, stumbling over his own feet in his hurry, and upon reaching me, he grasps my shoulders in his hands, causing me to cry out in pain as he picks me up, standing me on my still-wobbly legs, shaking me as he rants. "I want to do *so* many things right now." I cower away from his well-deserved raging.

"I want to throw you right back into the ocean. I want to slap you. I want to shake you so hard that your brain falls out! I want to ask you why the hell you wanted to risk your life like that. I want to thank you for doing it." He shakes his head. "But I'm not going to do any of that shit. I'm going to hug you instead. And I don't give a damn if you want it or not!"

I can't help but gasp in surprise when he practically throws his arms around me. And it doesn't bother me as much as I thought it would, because I am far too busy enjoying the fact that I am receiving a hug from my older brother, for the first time since Mom and Dad bailed on us. I mean, I don't count all of the times that he laid next to me in the middle of my panic attacks, or when I would nurse him back to health after a particularly hard night of partying. Both of those types of displays of affection, I feel, are a tad bit on the obligatory side. But not this time. No, he *deliberately* made the choice to circle his arms around my shoulder, carefully avoiding the injured arm that I held pressed to my torso, and hug me with all the warm strength that I (didn't know) I had been craving.

"What's wrong with your arm?" is the first thing Aiden asks when he finally pulls away. "Is it broken?"

"Why should I tell you? You still haven't spilled about what's happened to yours," is my feeble argument. "— It's just dislocated."

He snorts, then glances so quickly to the side that I had

to follow his gaze, had to see what took his face away from mine for even the smallest amount of time, and as soon as I had looked up, he grabs my arm, twisting it, putting it back where it belongs with a resound pop and a scream of dismayed surprise erupting from my throat.

"Not anymore," Aiden tells me, grinning cheekily.

"Son of a *bitch!*" I hiss at him, holding the arm flat against my side. "*Seriously?!*"

Gearteeth slowly raises himself up, palms flat on the rock beneath him, arms shaking with the effort he exerts. Jam and Clunker both dive forward, wanting to assist him, but all they end up doing is knocking their skulls together, cursing at each other for getting in the way. Aiden shakes his head over and over, and I can tell by the set of his lips that he's about to say something insulting.

I duck forward in the middle of my thoughts and I wrap my arms around Gearteeth's shoulders, helping him up the rest of the way. His nose and mouth are inches from my face, and I see his grin from the corner of my eye before he plants a loud kiss on my cheekbone.

"Hey there, beautiful." He wiggles his eyebrows at me, then cocks one. "I owe you one."

"You owe her *more* than just *one*, you bastard." And there's the name-calling I have been waiting for, thanks to my wonderful brother, who has no more of a filter than I do. "You — I should just —"

"Please," I groan. "*Please* don't throw him back in the ocean. I don't have the strength to save his ass again."

There's a moment of silence where all of the other people on this makeshift island absorb what I said, and then suddenly, they all collectively decided that it was much funnier than I intended it to be. Clunker collapses in a heap, laughing so hard that tears of mirth run down his face, chasing away the ones from his previous sorrow and blending in with the rainwater. Jam falls onto his knees, hiccupping and giggling as he crawls, coming up behind Gearteeth, wrapping his arms around his middle and squeezing as tightly as he can without cutting off the much-needed air supply, burying his face in the crook of his neck. Asher swipes at his hair, the front of it now sticking straight up, all askew like a little boy's, and his mouth stretches into a wider smirk, his abdomen shaking as he contains his laughter. And then, there's Aiden, who keeps having these little surprised laughs burst out of him in-between insults that he mutters underneath his breath as he winces and turns his head to the side, popping a crick in his neck.

"I'm a comedian," I proclaim weakly as Jam and Gearteeth both collectively decide to hang on me. "Ha, ha, I make jokes in the middle of crises."

A moment of strained silence washes over us, until all of a sudden, I hear Clunker's confused voice. "Flame, what are you doing?"

When there isn't an answer, I become curious, and I lift my head, searching for my brother; it's not like he could've gone far. Then, I spot him, hunched over nearly in half, shivering and cursing quietly, dressed in nothing but his boxer shorts. I blink at the sight, feeling my eyebrows furrow. He holds his jeans in his hands, trying to rip the legs into strips and tie them together.

Clunker, who had been sitting on the ground due to his bout of laughing, picks himself up and walks over to Aiden, crossing his arms as he cocks his head at the shuddering figure. "Flame?"

"I heard you," Aiden snaps, glaring up through his bangs, which stick to his eyebrows and his eyelids. "What does it look like I'm doing? I'm ripping my jeans and tying knots in them.

We're going to tie ourselves together into a huge chain and swim for it."

"But —"

"No arguing."

"Now just —"

"I said, *no arguing!*" He flings the torn jeans at Clunker and points a finger down at the ground. "This thing is starting to crumble underneath our feet. *They're* too busy to help us, and even if they weren't, they can't reach us." He cranes his head back and shouts up at the sky. "And you can't fly in the middle of a storm! I guess no one told you that!"

"You're *crazy!*" Jam shouts, scurrying away from me and Gearteeth, staring incredulously at my brother. "*You've lost it!*"

Aiden stares him down, clenching his teeth, eyes blazing. "Do you have a better plan? A less-crazy one? What do you want to wait around for? You want something done, you have to do it yourself. I'd rather die trying than sit here and die *waiting.*"

"You're implying that either way," Clunker says slowly, uncrossing his arms and allowing them to fall imp at his sides, "we're going to die. But — hey, here's a better idea for *real.* We can just use the ropes Asher and I brought with us instead of ripping our clothes off. Jam managed to pull them out of the Humvee with him — right?"

When the addressee nods in confirmation, Aiden trains that intense glare on the blond now, saying nothing. After a few minutes of staring at one another, Clunker shrugs and begins unbuttoning his jeans, shimmying them down his nonexistent hips, soon revealing brilliant white briefs that shine like a beacon in the darkness. "But ripping our clothes off is still a good idea. Less weight to carry."

While I had been distracted by how his lower abdomen is nearly as chiseled as the rest of him, debating on what kind of steroids he took to obtain those, my mind soon registers that he's wearing white briefs, and I start giggling in spite of myself, becoming embarrassed to the point of hiding my face in my hands. Way to act like a teenager, Cheyenne. But I suppose I have to act like something. Other than the shell of broken flesh that I am.

"What're you laughing at?" I hear Clunker ask. "Listen — my mom bought them for me. You really expect me to go out and by my own underwear or something? Like I really care what I wear on my—"

"All right, *whoa,* we get it!" Gearteeth declares, two red spots burning in his cheekbones. "God, kill me now."

"Seriously?" I whisper. "Don't say that,"

"I'm pretty sure if the ocean can't kill me, nothing can," he teases as he stretches out his aching limbs and begins to rise. "Besides, if I'm dead, I can't look at you."

"Stop flirting, you idiot," Jam says cheerfully, regaining his demeanour prior to the emotional turmoil.

We're all a bunch of crazies here. Just trying to survive. Though I wonder, as I watch Jam help Gearteeth stand up on wobbly legs, if any of us will ever really be the same again.

We might act like it. We might put up a front. We might cry about everything that happened for days on end and huddle together in a tight circle, forever bonded by this experience. And then we would try to move on. But would we ever? Would we ever really be able to put this behind us, continue on with our lives? Things like this change you more deeply than you could imagine, because it's a stark realisation at just how *meaningless* you really are; how quickly your life can be torn away from you; how a second's hesitancy is the difference between a mortal wound and escaping unscathed; how minds can think too quickly or too slowly; how fragile a body is; how delicate the brain can be; how much time doesn't actually exist; how much of it is wasted on the things that don't matter.

"*Everyone* needs to strip," Aiden announces, breaking into my thoughts. "Clunker's right. The less weight, the better."

Oh, *come* on. Everything has proceeded to get *so much worse* than I ever thought it could. (I don't want them looking at me; I don't want them seeing me. They would ask questions. Sure, not now, maybe not tomorrow or even within the next week, but eventually, I would be sat down, I would be confronted about the scars and the visible ribcage and the burn marks and everything else that I have done to myself, and I would have to tell them the truth, because how can you lie about something like this, how can you lie about the pain that filled you to the point of wanting to destroy your own self before anyone else could do it further?) You can't, and I wouldn't and God, *why* are you making me go through this? *Why* are you *not* following your own rule of not putting us through more than we can handle? This is more than I can handle, I *can't* do this, I *can't* do it, I hate you, too.

"E v e r y o n e." I nearly leap out of my skin; Aiden has meandered over to me, standing above me, looking down as God will on judgment day - if either of those things actually exist.

"Yeah. It's a miracle you didn't drown with that shirt on." Asher states. "It's way too big."

"No, no." I shake my head furiously, wrapping my arms around my waist, keeping wet oversized shirt firmly tucked against my form. "No, *no*, NO."

"Cheyenne—"

"N O !" I really don't want to be shouting, but he doesn't seem to be getting it. They can't see me for what I am. I won't let them.

He struggles to keep his voice low, his hands fastening a knot in the rope at his waist. "You choose *now* of all times to be modest?"

What the words imply stings me harder than I thought it would, and I shy away from him, though he has not yet reached out for me, bunching up fabric in my hands as I fall sideways, curling into the foetal position. "Don't make me," I moan, fully aware of how pathetic I look to everyone around me. "Please, *don't.*"

"Cheyenne, really, it isn't that big of a deal." Aiden kneels beside me and hooks his hands underneath my elbows, clenching hard as he hauls me back up. I am completely limp, though, and my knees buckle; he leans forward, holding me against his bare chest as he peers down at me, studying these unexpected reactions, trying to figure out what's going through my head. He lowers his voice. "It's okay. I mean, if you're really that embarrassed, we can — I don't know, make sure we tie the material around those areas, and it'll be fine. Besides, no one's going to look at you like that. Not right now."

Something inside of me snaps at his explanation, makes me realise how much he really doesn't understand, really never understood, and probably never would. That snap makes my hands jerk up, makes them dart out toward him as if to strike, and when he backs away, alarmed by my change in attitude, I begin screaming, unaware and uncaring of my previous thoughts on the whole concept of yelling, forgetting that he and I aren't alone on this piece of rock. The break has happened. "*Why is it* that all you sons of bitches think about is *sex?*"

I gesture toward my frail body.

(Let's face it, people, it's *frail.*)

"Sex *this,* sex *that,* sex *e v e r y w h e r e,* sex on the *brain,* sex in the *eyes,* sex in the *mouth,* let's just talk about *sex* in the middle of a *freaking* disaster zone! Sure, we aren't actually talking about the deed, but *what the hell,* Aiden? *WHAT THE HELL?* Do you *really* think I'm throwing a hissy fit because I'm afraid of *that* sort of look? Goes to show me what you've always thought about me!"

Before he can tell me to calm down, to shut up, before he can throw me back into the ocean and let the frothing waves toss me about like a tennis ball, I take the hem of the shirt, and I rip it from me, yanking it over my head, throwing it onto the ground, goose bumps breaking out on my skin as the chilly wind accosts it. I tear off what's left of the fishnets and they drop, leaving me open, easily scoured.

I keep a hardened glare on my face, refusing to display any emotion to the reactions that they are about to give me. The reactions come in the form of shocked expressions, of blank recognition, of hands going over mouths and quiet gasps being heard over the downpour of the rain. And I know why. I know what they are seeing.

"*This* is why I was freaking out," I say through gritted teeth. I point to the dozens of lines that I have painted in stripes vertically on my right ribcage with the edge of a metal standalone razor; the deeper, jagged-shaped gashes that I carved into both hip bones with a serrated knife blade; the multiple burn scars induced by the smouldering ends of cigarettes and joints scattered on my right thigh. I spread my arms apart and allow them to take in the amount of ribs protruding from underneath my skin, the way that my hip bones jutted out as well, how Elijah's dog tags fell down in the centre of my hollowing-out sternum, the prominent collarbones, and the frailty of the body before them. How this waif of a person managed to save Gearteeth, they'll never fully be able to understand — and neither will I.

"*This*, Aiden. Happy now? Happy to know that I'm made of *more* than sex!?"

"What have you done to yourself?" The words emerge

from Aiden's mouth, which creases and crumples as he continues to look at me, his hands reaching out for me though they are busy with his jeans, seeming unsure of himself. "Why?"

"I'm not the one who did it. This is what the *world* did to me. These are the signs of *neglect*, of *pain*, of *heartbreak*, of *betrayal*. These are the symbols that show what the world did to me. I might've been holding the tools that created them, but the entire time, the depression, the anxiety, the boys, the girls, the people at the clubs, the lecherous old men, the voices - all of them were holding my arm, egging me on, *laughing* at me and *needling* me until I broke."

It's the worst possible time for this to have happened. But he asked — so I told. I reach for the shirt on the ground and I snatch it up, hunching over it, ferociously beginning to stretch it out into a long sliver of fabric that I could tie more easily. "The blade and the fire were there when no one else was. They never abandoned me like Mom did, like Dad did, like *you* did. *They* never left."

"Cheyenne, just —"

C   R   E   A   K—

There is a gigantic shift, and we all lose our balance a little bit, making sounds of surprise and disgust. The land beneath us groans as it struggles to support our weight in the impenetrable depths of the ocean water; this iceberg of earth isn't as stable as I previously thought it to be. I feel a little bit more of my mind shut down after all that word vomit settled into the air. I should've expected something like that to happen. Everything is being taken from me simultaneously. I'm not allowed to have such things like privacy or modesty or a functioning brain. Simply not allowed.

Everyone quickly finishes disrobing, all the way down to their shoes, in tense silence as Aiden gestures at them. We all gather about in a little circle — or rather, the guys all huddle around me, some of them glancing toward my bared wounds, others purposefully turning their faces away and concentrating elsewhere. (I don't give a crap either way.) I stand there, allowing Asher and Aiden to combine us all together, wrapping the ropes around our waists, securing them as I stare at the ground, biting down on the tip of my tongue with one of my canine teeth. I have no thoughts. I have nothing. I go from being overwhelmingly emotional to being positively nothing, and let me tell you, it's an exhausting transformation. Especially when it seems to be happening multiple times in a row.

The ocean angrily batters against the sides of the island as we shift into our places, having tied ourselves into a line. I stand on my tiptoes; looks as if they've secured me to be directly in the middle; Asher has taken over as the leader again, with Clunker behind him, then Jam, then me, then Gearteeth, then Aiden bringing up the rear. It doesn't surprise me that Aiden put himself in place behind me and Gearteeth; he has taken on the whole silent guardian thing, putting himself in charge of what he considers to be the two weakest links.

"Is everyone ready?" Asher's sharp voice interrupts my musings, and I snap back into attention. I have no time to mourn, no time to think. Just time to do, to act. "Once we jump in, there's no going back."

We all take a moment to gather ourselves, I think, letting out a collective sigh, allowing the adrenaline to begin rushing through our veins, replacing our blood, filling us with the necessary energy, causing our limbs to tremble and the chilliness of the wind to die away. At the very least, that's what is happening to me as I gaze out upon the tumultuously frothing waves, the dark of the water that wishes to devour us, the foggy sheen created by the cold rain on top of the warmer ocean waves, the blinking lights and cameras in the distance. We're much closer than I anticipated, but entirely too far away, and we're all going to die. All of us.

"On the count of three." Asher moves forward, and I feel the rope-chain tied around my waist jerk with the movement as we all begin walking.

"One."

His feet are directly near the edge of the rock.

"Two."

He crouches, and the rest of us follow suit.

"Three!"

He jumps into the air, and the rest of us have no choice but to follow his lead. When it comes for my turn, I simply allow myself to drop, do not add the theatrics of pushing my toes into the ground and gaining airtime - because what does that matter? That extra few inches of distance will honestly get me no farther. My body nearly screams in relief once it makes contact with the distinctly warmer ocean water.

And thus begins the swim for our lives. The distance is much further than any of us anticipated, and we all give a collected groan of exasperation before we begin paddling, stretching our bodies as far out as they can do, Asher basically pulling the rest of us along with his elongated strides, the rest of us frantically moving our arms, flailing our feet, feeling reassured each time the rope-chain secured around our waists jerked and reminded us that we are all connected, all a team, all working together in order to survive. My head dips underneath the surface of the water, and I swallow more salt than I ever thought I would consume in my entire life, and the waves are angry as they batter against us, trying to chase us back to the rock - or are they helping us, propelling us along, allowing our bodies to drift forward when one of us falters, when one of us doesn't have the strength to continue moving? Hard to tell, since the waters surround us from all sides and seems to constantly be changing its mind.

Water to the left. Water to the right. Water underneath. Surrounded by the very thing which is more powerful than the rest of us. It's underestimated when it's contained to little more than a shower head or a sink faucet. But this is raw. This is *unconfined.* This is death.

Aiden's head going under for longer than it needs to. Salt water spewing from his open mouth when he comes back up. The waves, with their pressure, battering against our sides. Bruising ribs. Installing abrasions on calfs. Hands slipping. Clunker being drug out of line, the rest of us being forced to follow. Asher going the wrong way, the right way, the wrong way again.

We can't make it out of this. This was a death wish from the beginning. This was a promise from the cold knucklebones pulling now at our ankles. *You're never going to leave this place.* We'd be buried under its soil and its water with the rest of them.

*You're **never** going to leave.*

Then, halfway across, shouts erupt, but not from the members of our party. These yells and screams are coming from the bystanders on the stable land in front of us, the slab of earth that we are slowly approaching, one that seems to draw closer yet still be too far away to reach.

"Throw out the lines!" someone screams. "Throw them, get them out of there!"

I nearly sob in relief when I next glance up and see thick ropes snaking out toward us, preparing to retrieve us from the unforgiving grasp of the Pacific. I feel Gearteeth grasp one of my shoulders briefly as the strands are thrown into the air and land in the water. Asher lurches forward, and the breath is knocked from me as he snatches up the cord, clinging to it, pulling himself along it and throwing the remainder of it backwards in order to enable the rest of us to grab onto it. People rush from the sidelines and gather behind the figure who originally had thrown out the line, and slowly, but surely, we are yanked to shore.

Voices all blend together into a seamless murmur of concern and questions, and camera bulbs flicker as they take candid photographs of our sorry state. I wince away from the lights as a blanket is thrown around me from behind, and I cling to the itchy wool, shuddering, inwardly panicking as it begins slipping from me. I've managed to lose Aiden in the onslaught of bodies, but Gearteeth, who had been swimming behind me, is there, loosening the knots in the rope around my waist, keeping my weather-beaten corpse pressed close to his in order to preserve what modesty and dignity the both of us have left. Which isn't much.

"It's okay," he whispers. And in the midst of body warmth, of mixing voices, I focus on him, his closeness. "It's okay."

He continues to shield me even after he's managed to fumble through the untying of the knots, allowing the rope to drop onto the ground, which quickly turns to mud beneath our waterlogged feet. I keep my arms in front of my chest, and I curl up on myself, the blanket slipping from my shoulders, and I weakly reach back for it, but Gearteeth is quicker than I am, taking the edges of it and bringing it securely about my neck, holding it there. He's mumbling something over and over and staring at me with widened, saddened eyes as he does so: "Don't let them look at me. Don't let them look at me. Don't let them look at me."

"I won't." A sliver of shock runs through me when he answers his own statement, and then I blink, realising it wasn't him who had been speaking at all, but me. Gearteeth pierces me with a stare, and I shiver underneath it. He smiles gently before motioning his chin down toward his abdomen. I follow the gesture with my eyes and suck in a deep breath, lips parting as I narrow my gaze, focusing on the areas in his side that were darker than others, the places where someone had taken a knife and stabbed, carving out his skin, making him bleed.

"I understand," he murmurs, keeping his voice low, a beautiful focal point in the mess of the situation. "I've been where you are."

"You—" I couldn't believe he had taken a weapon to his side. He didn't seem to be that sort of person. (But pain knows no labels. It has no boundaries.) "But—"

The smile upon his face makes my heart lurch and begin to sink like dead weight in my chest. "Some of those are my own; others aren't. Some boys just can't handle other boys being gay."

"—*That's* what they're from?" Crimes of hate.

He nods. "Jam came to see me once. They saw us together. Didn't like that. I took the blows for him. All of them. Used my body and shielded him from it." He shrugs, as if it's normal for something like this to happen. It shouldn't be normal, but I know it happens more than it should.

"But — you could've —" I stare at the marks in his side, and notice one deeper than the rest, just above his hipbone, right in the very slight indentation of his waist.

"I could've what? *Died?* But that's what you do, Little Bit." The nickname made my heart jolt again, but in a different way, one stemming purely from affection. "That's how it's *supposed* to be: that you would die to protect the ones you love."

I peer up at him, the similarity between the colours of our eyes causing my adrenal glands to pulse; it's eerie, merely because I felt as if I were looking into a mirror, one that reflected me my true self. It isn't the emaciated creature that they just witnessed stripping before their eyes, nor is it the cynical bitch that the rest of the world has born witness to. I'm not exactly sure — *what* I see in his gaze. But there's *something*. And I see myself in it. But neither of the selves that have appeared in public; the true one. Whatever that is. I don't even know her anymore, I've kept her buried for so long. She's gasping for air, though, sticking her hand out of the grave, trying to push through so that she might stop breathing in richly-odour soil and instead taste the fresh air, the light of day, for the first time in years. I don't know if I'll let her get all the way out, though. That could be dangerous.

My right ear twitches as I hear my name be called out. Gearteeth glances upward, breaking the connection that we had been forming, and his lips twist into a grimace of sorts. "Let's get out of this mess. Looks like the rest of our merry band of misfits is by the fire."

I furrow my eyebrows at this announcement. There's a fire somewhere? I allow Gearteeth to place his hand on my blanket-covered back and then wrap me into the crook of his arm as I think this over, then glance about, my eyes moving rapidly and my head remaining stationary, as I search for what he's talking about. But before I can take a good look around, he starts moving me forward, and soon, I'm able to see where the remainder of our party has wandered off to.

The onlookers apparently have been doing much more than standing around like idiots with their video cameras pointed at the demise of western California. Someone had set up a small rescue camp by using the upraised trunk of an SUV as a sort of shield from the rain. Aiden and the others have already gathered underneath it, still half-naked, though the rope chain is gone from their waists, wrapped up in their own entourage of blankets and towels, burrowing as close to the flames as they can manage without getting burned. Though honestly, I'm pretty sure that I personally could stand in the middle of that fire pit and not feel the heat.

I stare into the flames, and I watch them dance. The mumble of my brother's voice and his friends as they discuss an ongoing plan flows through one ear and right out the other. Gearteeth keeps me tucked against him, and I'm just fine with that.

"We need to get *out* of here," Aiden hisses to the four guys gathered around him, all of them quivering in their bare feet, clinging to their towels. Clunker tosses his from his lithe body and stretches, his muscles and ligaments popping, his face creasing in pain. "Standing here isn't getting us closer to safety."

"We legitimately *just* sat down," Gearteeth hoarsely complains. "And you're already moaning about *leaving* again?"

"Staying is putting us under scrutiny," Asher mutters, glaring hard toward the blinking video cameras and the nurses rushing about, in their scrubs, holding onto their plastic raincoats as they dig things out of the back of ambulances, preparing to come and check the six of us over for injuries. "Not to mention we'll be stuck here forever if those EMTs get over here and start analysing us. Then we'll be hauled off to some hospital, and we have no identification, and they'll ask questions, and—"

"Okay, shut up, we get it," Jam twitters nervously.

"I'm just saying how it is."

"*Enough*. No arguing right now." The both of them fall quiet when Aiden barks at them. "Okay, so, guess what this means, guys. We're gonna have to steal a car. And probably some clothes. Since, y'know, ours got torn up."

"Really." Clunker says dryly. "Is *that* where they went?"

"Clunker, Jam, you guys need to do some searching." Aiden ignores the sarcasm directed at him. "There's loads of heaps parked here. It doesn't have to be fast or flashy; just needs to have gas in it and be unlocked. Asher, you should probably get the supplies from the EMTs or wherever else we can find. You're more charismatic than I am when it comes to other people." Aiden cheekily grinned, and for a moment, I'm taken back to a time when he smiled like that every five minutes, looking more like an impish rouge than a hard-faced criminal. But things change, and so do people. "I'll stay here and—"

His voice trails off as he glances over at me and Gearteeth. The implication is clear, and the rest of the boys trot off. The two designated carjackers disappear into the darkness and Asher calmly crosses his arms over his barrel of a chest as he approaches the frantic EMTs, calling out to them and immediately putting forth the charming facade he used on me outside of the nightclub. Revulsion fills me, and I force myself to look away, to bury my face in Gearteeth and inhale the smell of his skin, the remnants of cologne long since overpowered by the odour of the salty water and sweat. I can't look at him. Because when I do, all I see is the word MURDERER imprinted on his forehead in capitalised red letters. I've known him for less than twelve hours and his body count is already up two; seems as if he's on a spree.

Aiden walks over to us, towering above me as he looks down, and the smallest, most inane detail that my eyes choose to notice is how the firelight flickers off the silver snakebites underneath his bottom lip, how interesting it looks as the colours reflect from its surface and do a little dance that belongs entirely to them. I cock my head and study it for a little bit. The motions reflecting from it comfort me. I've lost everything except him. Everything. Only he's alive, standing before me.

"Look at us," he says quietly, pursing his lips. "Just look at us now, Cheyenne. We aren't in that hellhole anymore. We're *out.* And we'll never have to go back there — ever again. This could be a good thing. It could turn into a good thing eventually. You'll see. And now that we're away from it, we can heal. We can pull ourselves out."

His optimism sounds so blinded and biased, it makes my insides curdle. The whole act of putting on a face for the good of our nonexistent mental health makes me want to tear out all of my hair and scream. But I nod anyway. Because there's nothing else I can do. Nothing I can say. Everything's been laid bare for them, exposed and revealed. I have nothing left of myself. Nothing. So it doesn't matter. Be optimistic. I *don't c a r e* anymore.

"Guys."

The three of us glance up, surprised to hear Asher's voice returning so soon. (It felt as though he hadn't departed that long ago.) He isn't coming back alone, however, and my eyes narrow as I quickly analyse the woman that he's towed alongside with him. Her silver-tinged brunette hair is pulled back into a half-ponytail with one of those toothy clips, and her dark green eyes have crow's feet that appear when she smiles, displaying that she's done it often. She has the handles of two plastic grocery sacks looped around each wrist, while Asher is carrying several smaller, folded-up bundles. I narrow my gaze when I notice that Asher also is no longer naked - he has on relatively dry clothes and a soft-looking towel draped around his neck, catching the stray drops of water falling from his hair. The crimson rock band shirt and the camouflage shorts seemed to be a near perfect fit as well.

"This is Kathleen," he says now, motioning to her as he puts the parcels down in the trunk of the car that's being used as a shield from the rain. "I ran into her on the way to talk to the EMTs — who ended up being entirely too busy for me."

"Too *busy?*" Aiden snorts. "What else could be more important than refugees?"

Asher merely points, and we all turn to watch as a helicopter, having just been struck by lightning, spirals downward, its blades being swallowed by the black smoke billowing up from the engine set afire. Aiden raises both eyebrows and turns away while I find myself enraptured by it. You know you've reached an entirely new level of insanity when you stare at accidents to force yourself to feel something — and it doesn't work. I feel *nothing*, not as I watch it collide into the ocean, not as I watch the body of the helicopter explode into smithereens, not as I mull over the lives of those pilots in there. I can't bring myself to give a damn about more people than I already do.

It might kill me.

"I saw you on the news." Kathleen's soft voice attracts our attention. "Swimming across the ocean. Getting pulled out. And I gathered up all the extra stuff I had, came here quick as I could." She nodded, more to herself than to anybody around her, as she placed the plastic grocery bags next to the items that Asher just put in the car. "I just knew in the bottom of my heart that I was meant to help you all."

Oh, boy. Gearteeth and I exchange wary glances at her words. Meant to help us. Not that I'm going to look a gift horse in the mouth or anything. Especially not now, when we've been reduced to refugee status. I guess it takes a crazy to help crazies.

"There are sandwiches from Subway in the bags," Kathleen continues, pointing to the grocery bags that she deposited in the trunk of the SUV. "And there's enough clothing to go around. Some of it might be a bit big for the girl, but at least it's clean and dry."

"Wow." Aiden already is rummaging through the

different parcels of clothing. "Ma'am, this is fantastic. Hell of a lot more than we could've asked for."

(When's the last time he called someone *ma'am* —?)

"It's no trouble at all. It wasn't being put to good use, anyways. Sitting in dresser drawers and all that, gathering up dust"

Kathleen heaves a tremendous sigh as she crosses her arms over her chest, shivering against the wind that appeared. Asher quickly ushers her underneath the roof of the trunk and out of the rainfall, and she smiles her gratitude towards him. "There's blankets in there as well. I figured they'd be loads better than the scratchy ones they'd give you out here."

"Why were these in drawers?" Gearteeth asks, leaving my side reluctantly to go and peer through the clothing. "They're nice clothes."

"They belonged to my sons, Erik and Patrick. I lost both of them due to the war in Afghanistan. Not much you can do in a bombing. Adrian was killed on impact, Ethan took several shots to the chest protecting a fellow soldier." The sudden turn of the story makes us all turn and look at Kathleen. Aiden and Gearteeth freeze, their hands immersed in the clothing, sheepishly guilty expressions on their faces; Asher clenches his teeth together and turns slightly away, as if he heard the story already yet is preparing himself to be hurt by it once more, and I don't know what my face says - it's probably as blank as the rest of me is. The way she told the story, as a basis of facts and little emotion invested in it, reminded me of myself, how I tell my own stories, pretend not to feel anything while internally I am ripping myself apart with the very thoughts.

Ah, *there's* the emotion. She blinks rapidly and looks up toward the sky, dabbing her fingers underneath her eyes, though no tears are there. I've seen a lot of people do that. I honestly never have done it myself. Thought it was pointless. Never tapped at my eyes to get rid of the tears. I either let them rush forth or never allow them to exist in the first place. No indication either way. Just doing it.

"No, it's all right," Kathleen hurriedly interjects, waving her hands toward the now-hesitant boys. "They wouldn't have wanted their things to go to waste. I know they definitely wouldn't want me to sit around and mourn about it. I'm more than happy to give these things to you. You all need it much more than they ever will."

"I'm sorry, but I don't understand exactly *why* you're helping us." I say this with much more malicious intent than I originally planned, and though it makes me cringe for a split second, I remain standing firm, half-naked, battle-scars revealed, open and vulnerable to scrutiny, and as she turns her gaze upon me, I raise my chin, tightening my jaw, dimming my eyes. She might feel free expressing her emotions, but I will not do such a thing to a stranger.

Asher's a stranger. Yeah, and look where that's gotten me.

"I thought I told you already." Kathleen seems confused by my question. "I'm meant to help you, dear. It's a simple as that."

"No one's meant to help anyone." I grasp at the towel offered to me by Asher, otherwise ignoring him, keeping my gaze pinned on this woman. "Do you live in reality? No one is meant to help anyone!" Don't know why I'm so vocal right now. "We live in a world where we all eat each other up to get to the top. Where we leave people behind to rot. Where we watch it burn and laugh about it while it happens, then turn around and complain about how we can't have nice things, how bad things happen to good people, oblivious to the fact that we're the ones causing it in the first place. No one is meant to help anyone.

We're only meant to survive. You *choose* to help people."

Kathleen slowly shakes her head. "Oh, child — what have you been through to not believe in people being *meant* to do things?"

"I'm not a child."

"Oh, no. You're all grown up." She doesn't say it meanly, unlike the snappy words I accosted her with. So much for not looking a gift horse in the mouth; I took that horse and slammed it into the ground. Why wasn't she angry? Why wasn't she grabbing away the precious belongings, the grocery bags of food, storming off toward wherever her vehicle had been left in this mess? And why was she *looking* at me like that? "You can't be older than eighteen, yet you sound older than me. It saddens me to see how the world has weighed you down."

What the hell am I supposed to say in reply to that? Hell, what am I supposed to even think? My lips part a bit as I gawk at her, my eyebrows trembling as my face debates whether it wants to scrunch up and let me scream about it, or crumple into bloodcurdling sobs. In the middle of my ghastly silence, Kathleen walks forward, looking at the dog tags that are lying on my hollow sternum, and Gearteeth glances back at me, hesitating, eyes flitting back and forth in-between us two women, trying to figure out what the best course of action is - to come to my side, or let events play out as they should. Apparently, he chooses the latter, with a little help from Aiden's hardened side glare at him, and he turns quickly back to the clothes.

Kathleen takes the two tags in her fingers and peers at them, eyes narrowing into slits as she studies the lettering on the metal surfaces. The rain patters out a quiet melody behind me, and I focus on it to the point where when Kathleen begins to talk again, it is as if her voice is echoing down toward me from an elongated tunnel. "Did you know this man? Elijah. Did you know him?"

"No." I answer her without thinking, eyes flickering back to that weathered face that challenged my very existence and the modes through which my brain function.

"How did you get his dog tags, then?"

"We found him at a base. He was trapped under debris."

"You were *meant* to save him, then."

"— *No.*" I think of Elijah's face, how my hands had been on either side, how he had asked me to make him feel, how I had lain in his blood and watched his life slip from his body. I think of him, and it makes me cringe. I think of him, and it makes me want to die. "I wasn't *meant* to save him! I *chose* to try. And I f a i l e d."

"Ah, but if you hadn't been brought to that base in the first place, then you wouldn't have had to make that choice. You were meant to find him."

What the hell is this, some religious counselling session? "What, like *God* brought me there? Bullshit. God has brought me nowhere, neither up nor down. Everywhere I've been, it's because of my own damned choices."

"So then you believe in nothing."

"Nothing but the concept of the self." I don't know why I'm bothering to explain myself to a complete stranger. But hey, it seems to be what I do best. I do, however, need to start doing something with my hands, and not something unhealthy, either. I'm still grasping that towel, so I swipe it across my skin.

"I guess it's safe to assume that you believe that you all chose to make it across the ocean and chose not to die," Kathleen ponders. "But how could you *have* chosen such a thing when the ocean can make the decision for you? You can't control everything, unfortunately. So you must've been *meant* to make it across."

I am seriously over one thousand percent done with this conversation. "S u r e . . ."

"I know you're just agreeing with me to shut me up. I had children once." Kathleen shoots me a smile. "But one of these days, you'll wake up and see it."

It's probably my best option to not say anything further, so instead of going off on a tangent, I purse my lips, fighting against it, and bring the towel around to my front, having shed the blanket since Gearteeth had walked away, trying my best to relieve that heavy feeling of moisture seeping into my pores. I doubt that all the water my skin has absorbed will ever be exorcised from me, but it's always worth a shot. I scrub at my collar bones, my stomach falling as I feel the sharpness of them poking at my fingers even through the thick fabric. Aiden walks over, having foraged enough through the piles and personally handpicked something for me to wear other than solely my undergarments, and wordlessly hands them to me. I take them, giving him the towel in exchange, and he walks back to the trunk of the SUV.

I know that look on his face. I've seen it a thousand times before. Kathleen's words are making him think about *super-deep* philosophies and all that. Making him question life and all that. Making him wonder about the purpose of this existence and all that. I don't let my expression change, but I know that he knows that I'm doing the exact same thing. I don't want her words to have *meant* anything to me. But they do.

Once again, I find myself wearing clothes that are far too big for me - and while I'm all for bagginess, for being comfortable, it's disturbing that none of these things are my own, and that this outfit I've been given belongs to dead men. Wearing dead men's clothing is more than a *little* bit weird to me. This shirt is long-sleeved and navy blue, making me feel like I'm once again swimming in the ocean; the very thought makes me swallow a panic attack. When someone hands me a belt, I haul the wide waistband of the khaki pants up to my waist and cinch it there.

"We found a —" Jam's hyperactive voice reaches my ears, and we all crane our necks upward to watch him and Clunker jog from the darkness, stopping short. His face grows sheepish and uncomfortable when he realises we have extra company. "Oh, *hello*." He directs this toward Kathleen, waving a little bit and jumping up and down a couple of times before turning his attention to Aiden. "We found — a thing."

"Real subtle," Clunker mutters underneath his breath. "Wait - I smell food."

He dives toward the grocery bags only to be smacked away by Gearteeth. "Don't be rude."

"I'm not *rude*," Clunker says slowly, crossing his arms over his bare chest. "I'm just so hungry I could eat the ass out of a rhino."

Aiden slowly closes his eyes and shakes his head at the crudeness, but Kathleen does nothing more than laugh. "That sounds like something my husband would say."

Before any of us can respond, a chorus of shouting starts up, and Kathleen's hand flutters to her mouth.

"Oh, dear," she fusses. The words that the medics are shouting about more survivors become even clearer. "It seems as if I'm meant to help more than just you beautiful children tonight."

It seems as though as soon as she ventured out of earshot, Jam and Clunker pounce on Aiden.

"Dude, we seriously found the best car."

"It's a van and it has blankets and it's totally unlocked."

"Man, it's like it's waiting for us."

(It's like they were *meant* to find it.)

Kill that thought with fire. Drown it. Get rid of it. Go away.

"Okay, I'll get the food," Aiden says, quickly gathering up the grocery bags Kathleen gave us. "Someone get the clothes and let's go."

"It — should we really just *leave* like this?" Gearteeth asks, hesitating. "I mean, I feel bad — she did get all this stuff off for us, and we're just *taking off.*"

"We can't stay around here any longer," Asher adds over his shoulder as he goes to the trunk of the car and gathers the remainder of the clothing. "It was a stroke of good luck finding her, but we need to leave. Those medics are bound to remember we're here, and like I said, being transported to some random hospital without identification will be a huge headache that none of us need. Especially not now."

Gearteeth wants to say something more, but when a bundle of clothing is tossed at him, a shirt flying up and smacking him in the face, he chooses to shut his mouth and instead don the new outfit, which hangs on him a bit, too. We're both shorter than the previous owners of these clothes, it seems. Once that's finished, he comes over to me, takes my hand, locking our fingers together.

I wish I could respond, but really, my consciousness has retreated, and there's no getting it back. Not after Kathleen's little lecture about meant-to-be shit. Odd how many breaking points a person can have; it's like, just when you think you've had it, just when you think you're going to be bouncing back from the psychotic snap, something else plunges you right back into it, right back into the insanity, the depression, the hopelessness, that feeling that it's dragging you downward with its claws, which rake deep into your skin and leave scars that never will fade, never will be gone, not until the end of time, and it buries you, it buries you alive with those marks, leaves you for dead underneath layers and layers of soil, and you don't want to dig yourself out, you just don't.

How many times can Cheyenne Kinsey contradict herself in one sitting?

When I next blink, I find myself at the open end of a van, my new clothes slowly becoming soaked from the rainfall still going strong, and I'm staring at a bundle of blankets back there.

"Get her in there." Someone says that. But I'm falling.

I'm falling somewhere.

No, I'm just being shoved into the back. Not shoved, laid down. By Gearteeth. Who reluctantly releases my hand. "I want to stay back there with her."

"No, sit up front. She needs to be left alone."

I am on the right side of my body. I am curled into a foetal position. I cannot move. Gearteeth placed me in just the right position, though. I don't need to move. Good thing. Because I can't. My eyes are open wide and staring. I feel as if my consciousness is hovering above my physical body, staring down at me with those same wide, open eyes. Staring into wide, open eyes. Wide open ones. Like a corpse. A corpse I am. Low murmurs of voices come from the front, nothing more than flies buzzing in my ears, flies buzzing about and laying eggs in my decaying ears, for I'm a corpse. A rotting corpse. I am watching myself from above my body and my body is a corpse.

When was I covered with a blanket? It's warm. Warm like Gearteeth. Smells just as good. Perhaps it's his. But it can't be. Did he bring a blanket with him across the ocean? Why is it dry? Doesn't make sense.

The bundle of blankets in front of me shifts, and my eyes narrow, wanting to focus. A small whimper that only I can hear reaches my decaying ears. One hand reaches out for the bundle and touches it, pulling back the blankets. Are we driving? The wheels are moving. There's a roaring sound in my ears. When I pull back the blankets, I see a small form. A dog. A really fuzzy dog. It whines again, then it looks at me. Looks at my wide, staring eyes. Looks right into them to my broken soul. It look to be about eleven months old. It's rather large. But not fully grown. Like me. I'm dead, and I'm not even fully grown.

It comes to me. It snuggles against me. And something inside of me softens. A hole in my heart is filled.

I feel its breath. I hear the voices. But the warmth from this life near my abdomen, as it snuggles against me, it chases it all away.

I'm free. I'm floating.

I'm free.

Part Two:

In Which We Dance on Muddy Graves

The Fissure and the Shell

October 9th
Manchester, Indiana

Ruth Reagan

Lying upon my back in a field of golden wheat that has been crushed by my weight, I stare up at the vibrant sapphire sky above me and watch as words, emboldened and colourful in their strange, square fonts, float vertically down towards me. I cock my head and make a move to sit upright, but there is a distinct tugging at both of my wrists. I glance to the side, only to see chains that extend outward from underneath a layer of fresh soil, which has an odd smell consisting of both life and death, one of charred flesh and newborn skin. I yank at them, and they scrape over the delicate skin of my undersides, chafing it, turning it a light shade of pink. Suddenly, a pale blue word bounces on the ground and rolls toward me, causing a sound similar to that of a ball colliding with concrete to erupt from its underbelly each time it made contact with the soft, malleable stalks beneath it.

My eyes follow its trail as it makes its way toward me, and I furrow my eyebrows in an attempt to clear the fuzziness from my vision, curious as to what the approaching word might be. For some reason, it continues to be out of my focusing range, appearing to meander closer while never actually gaining any distance. It leaves behind a fluorescent light blue power on the wheat, a stark contrast in hues that blinds me, and when I blink several times, I find myself back in the same position as I had been before and the process repeats itself.

The curiosity is eating me alive, gnawing through my arteries and cutting off the blood flow to the brain, constricting my lungs, swelling in a tight air sac around my heart, causing the beating to slow dramatically, I needed to know what the word had said, and but at this rate, I never would.

Suddenly, I feel as though a weight has spiralled downward in my chest. I want to press my hands above my left breastbone so as to keep that delicate mass of tissue within my body where it belonged, but alas, the shackles keep me from doing much of anything besides squirming from side-to-side. Once again, I am distracted by the words, but instead of floating down toward me, they are now being hurled at me. I still attempt to decipher what each one of them means, wanting to know who's throwing them to me like lightning as a method of torture. Whoever's doing this knows clearly that one of my biggest pet peeves is not being allowed to know something.

"Ruth."

Has the word finally chosen to vocally express itself? Has it acquired an undeniably masculine voice and revealed its identity to me? I'm unbearably confused. The word, as it had come toward me, had seemed to be much longer than four letters, so I couldn't possibly understand why my name had been spoken aloud. I crane my neck as far upward as it will go, trying my best to survey the landscape, but still horribly restrained by the shackles that emerged from the ground as hands would rip themselves out of the grave. Their cold, slender fingers dig into the tender skin, and finally, I begin to register the pain, wincing away from it and, instead, burrowing myself deeper. Because now, I am sinking, sinking lower and further away, the dazzling artificiality of the ceiling slowly pulling itself upward to reveal nothing more than a black hole, a pit of emptiness, a cavern where existence fails. I seem to even be tumbling backwards, yet that can't be possible, because still the handcuffs are there and keeping me plastered against a now-invisible ground.

"Ruth, wake up."

A warmth invades me from the left side and I attempt to turn myself toward it, whimpering in spite of myself when I find that still my access is limited. What types of hidden burdens weigh me down upon this slab of misery? When my nose grinds against something solid, I am relieved. I haven't been dumped in this wasteland to remain in solitude.

"*Ruthie!*"

Someone's hand dives down from the fading azure of the ceiling, and when my eyes fly open, I see it there, still, in my vision, a ghost that has taken on a physical form and formed itself into a tangible item that, in turn, grasps my right shoulder and begins to shake at it, moving my otherwise paralysed body back and forth. My eyelids blink, and I gasp, clinging to the person that is beside me, wanting to let the shaking being induced upon me be enough where I could snap out of this strange reverie and back into the throes of reality, but it seemed to me as though I needed something to cling to.

"Oh, my gosh." The exclamation emerges before I can stifle it, and I press my forehead against the solid, warm object, which promptly wraps itself around me and fully presses me into the security of its embrace, more comforting than any blanket, a rumble in its chest as it murmured things to me in a delicately tenor-toned voice. My wrists have been released from the throes of their capturers and my fingers flex into the shirt that they find, gripping bunches of fabric and collecting them into sweaty palms. "*Oh, my gosh.*"

"Ruthie, it's just a nightmare." As the crippling darkness of the heavy sleep fades into the background, the words being spoken are clear. "You're here. I'm here. It's going to be okay."

A hand is run through the tangles of my hair, and when callused fingers catch upon them, a tickling sensation travels to my scalp. I lean back into the unintentional ministrations and the hand continues to stroke the dark waves. "I'm here."

— Wait. *Who's* here? I went to sleep alone last night!

I suddenly sit upright, my entire body tensing against the touch that had so gently awakened me from the brutish claim of the chains, and I turn to face the unknown figure, throwing my arms up in front of my face in order to guard myself from whatever he might try next - weren't there cases of men sneaking into houses, lying down upon a bed, acting as though they are someone you know and treating you as such, then upon the victim awakening and rejecting their advances, they close a hand around their oesophagus and take the life from their lungs within a split second's time? (I saw that once in a television show.) My own hands go to my throat and I cling to it, not wanting him to gain access. I open my mouth, about to scream for my parents or for my twin brother, who would hear me despite his bedroom being in the basement, and would react more quickly than my mother and father combined, but one of those hands claps itself over my lips.

"Calm down!" His voice is a little more frantic as he hisses these words. "Ruth, calm down. It's me. It's Daniel!"

With the admission of identity, I turn my face upward toward his, eyes almost popping out from their sockets as I halfway squint through the darkness and register the lines of his face, the flabbergasted expression painted across him as he debated on how to handle my reaction without waking up the rest of the house. But now that I knew it was him, I was more apt to relax back into my original position, comforted by his warmth and that trapped by the coverlets underneath which I was covered. I have to make sure that I'm not dreaming, though. This is something that must be double checked before I continue onward.

I heave a tremendous sigh, and force myself to relax back

into the pillow, my head sinking eagerly down into it. With this, Daniel removes his hand from my mouth and slides it down the side of my face, only his palm touching the skin, as it comes to rest on my bare shoulder, his pointer and middle fingers doodling around with the strap of the violet camisole that I donned to sleep in that night. This had to be a continuation of the nightmare - but at least it had turned somewhat pleasant, with the company of one of my childhood best friends hovering beside me, prepared to deal with whatever might happen next if my mind decided to lash out again.

Leaning back like this, I am at a vantage point where I can look out upon the surrounding environment and survey the bedroom to ensure that I'm not trapped still in a dream. I see the silhouette of the desktop computer upon the pale counter of my makeshift writing desk, the assorted shadows of the items next to it, the can of writing utensils, the pile of books including my Bible tucked behind the monitor. The figure of my chair is pushed underneath the desk as it should be, the fan is turned on, the blades swivelling around and around at the fastest speed that they can manage, and there's the quiet voices emerging from the white radio on the nightstand directly next to my bed, shielded by Daniel's shadowy body. Though the words that they were singing and speaking were nothing more than garbled nonsense, even to the hearing that had been heightened by launching out of sleep so quickly, still it comforted me to know that some things were normal. No floating, unreadable, glowing letters here to torment me. Even the smells are back to as they should be — the odd mustiness that somehow managed to remain in my bedroom, no matter how many vanilla-scented air fresheners I use to fumigate the odour of old walls and ancient wood flooring, the various temperatures of fresh air with their aromas of grass and freedom that bleed through the window sill, which also is so old, it's separating from the pane and leaving a gap.

"See?" Daniel's concerned voice has faded into his normal one, which relieves me even more. He's back to being the teasing son of a gun that he's been ever since I've known him, which has been since we were toddlers. (I'm about ninety-five percent sure that we both learned to walk together.) "Everything's all right, Ruthie. Nothing big and bad out here."

I must still be addled with sleep. My mind is screaming something at me, but it's nothing more than a tainted echo as my body instinctively turns toward the warm, sidling toward it until I'm pressed against Daniel, who bends his head so that his mouth is in my hair - I can feel the corners of the lips turning upward into a smile - and threads his arms about my waist, tucking me safely against him. I push my face against his chest, and a very small, almost silent satisfactory sigh drifts through my slightly parted lips and is made known to the boy who had his arms around me.

My mind's still screeching, though, making my eyebrows tie themselves into a worried knot in the centre of my forehead. What in the world is it going on about? The words are slowly becoming clearer as I concentrate upon them, still relishing in the warmth created by the contact in-between our bodies, and finally, after perhaps thirty seconds, maybe a little bit longer, I am able to decipher what is being yelled at me, with the little voice waving a pitchfork and a burning torch, jumping up and down, high-pitched squeaks punctuating the end of each sentence as it landed back on its feet.

What are you doing?

Ruth!   *Why are you in his arms?*

You have a boyfriend!

You're dating someone!

You've been dating that same person for the past seven months!

What are you thinking?
WHAT ARE YOU DOING?

"Daniel!" My raspy voice doesn't have nearly as much vehemence as I want it to, merely sounding as a smoker of fifty years would. "What are you doing? Get out!"

"What the hell kind of a question is that?" He very nearly snorts, though at the last minute, he chooses to stifle it. "I'm lying here next to you, and I'm holding you, making sure that you're all right. What any good neighbour would do."

"This is far beyond neighbourly duties," I grumble, weakly pushing at his chest, heart throbbing a completely new rhythm at the forbidden act I'm indulging in. I shouldn't be within the confines of anyone else's arms except for my boyfriend's. Only Shane needed to hold me like this for me to be satisfied. "Get out."

"But *Ruthie*," he says, still grinning, his voice ascending into a whine. "It's *cold* outside, and I walked here in my *bare feet* just to see you! Don't be mean and kick me out of this nice, warm bed. Not even *you're* that heartless. Hell, you're not heartless at all. Have mercy on me!"

"Daniel, *seriously*, get out. My boyfriend will kill me."

"Ah, Shane, Schmane," he says easily, removing his hands from around me in order to clasp them behind his head as he lets out a long breath and relaxes further into the downy comfort of the mattress. "He isn't here. He won't know."

"Yeah, he will!" My voice cracks on the last word, and I turn toward him, lightly pummelling him in the abdomen with a fist.

He easily catches my flimsy wrist and shakes it a little bit before letting it limply drop. "What, are you going to tell him about it?"

I open my mouth to retort, then I seriously consider his

words. Have I told Shane about all of the other times that Daniel has snuck in through the unlocked door in the basement, the one Paul purposefully "forgets" to latch so that his childhood friend can enter and depart as he pleases? Have I told Shane about all of the times that I've awakened to find Daniel lurking in my chair, poking me as he stands over me, crawling on top of the covers or underneath them? Have I told him about the times that he and I have snuck out of the house to go to various places - to watch the sunrise in the meadow, to walk down the middle of the abandoned road with our arms outstretched and fingers barely intertwined, to lounge on the roof of the car and drain the battery by blasting the radio in a vacant parking lot? And have I told him about those times when I fall back asleep in his arms, in Daniel's arms, whether it be still snuggled within my bed or on the hood of that car or in the hay loft of his barn because our eyelids simply have become too heavy to remain opened? Will I ever tell him of all these things occurring?

I answer these internal musings aloud.

"No." I swallow once hard. "I won't."

"See." Daniel says this with confidence. "I knew you wouldn't. You never have. Why start now?"

Even so, still he begins to make motions to exit the bed, and while I'm wildly grateful, I'm also slightly disappointed. Which is a ridiculous thing to be. H o n e s t l y.

"Never know with me," I proclaim, still rather sleepy as I sit upright and tuck the edge of the covers around my chest. "I'm unpredictable."

"*Right*. The creature of habit going out of her way to do something impulsive. If that ever happened, I'd pay double the original ticketing price for a front row seat." He meanders over to the swivelling desk chair and sinks down in it as I reach over and I turn on the ceramic bedside lamp, illuminating what I already had observed but shedding a new, dull light on the brilliant figure turning in circles with a sheepish facial expression. "It'd be a damn day of remembrance. Right after the fourth of July."

I stare at him through blurred vision, watching as that roguish smile appears on his face in all of its glory, and I find myself relaxing, slowly shaking my head as I watch him spin around and around, catching little details of him here and there - the bronze of his skin from long hours of slaving away in the sun, the dishevelled golden-blonde hair tousled about his scalp; the lint-covered black long-sleeved shirt with the sleeves pulled to his elbows and folded under themselves; his bare and callused feet, and the sparkle of his oddly-coloured eyes, a somewhat untamed and feral hazel with ochre overtones.

"You feeling better now, Ruthie?" he asks, teasing me again, using what he calls his *baby voice*, where he shoots his tone upward more into the tenor area than the natural baritone he speaks in.

"Oh, shut up," I remark cheerfully, grasping for the nearest pillow and heaving it across the room, where it smacks him directly in the chest. "I'm much better now that you got out of my bed and went to where you belong."

"In the outcast corner. I see how it is, Ruthie." He pretends to shudder. "It's so cold. Let me get back in bed with you."

"Be quiet!" I hiss, eyes darting around wildly as if my parents or my twin brother would hear him and misinterpret his meaning. "You can't just *say* things like that!"

"Of course I can," is his quick remark. "And I do. All the damn time. Everyone loves me for it. You should try it."

"Try *what?*" I grumble, throwing back the bedcovers and stretching out the somewhat tense muscles in my calfs as I reach for the hand-woven lilac rug that takes up most of the expanse of my hardwood flooring. "Being a smart aleck?"

"No." Daniel suddenly stops spinning in the chair and bores those eyes into me. My heart immediately races, my pulse throbbing in my jugular vein, as I feel his gaze on my profile and am forced to return it, though I think that, with the widening of my eyes and the slight parting of my lips, not to mention the state of my hair most likely, I have taken on the appearance of a deer in the headlights rather than a girl worthy of engaging in a glaring contest. "Being honest. Being a smart-*ass* is a bonus."

There's a moment of silence in-between us. Something seizes in my chest, and I find that my nose has been thrust in the air as my toes touch the material of the rug that they've been seeking for a bit now. "I'm always honest."

"*Right.*"

And that single word was filled with such a vehemence that I glance up again, somewhat wildly, but in that split millisecond, his features have been smoothed over and that smirk replaced upon a mouth I could've sworn was previously twisted into a sneer, a grimace even. It leaves me wondering whether such a thing had been there at all, or if I had just been imagining things. Wouldn't be the first time.

In the silence, I turn toward the nightstand and remove the pale cloth that I use to cover the blaring blue light of the combined radio and alarm clock, staring at the black numbers until my head swims. "Daniel, what are you doing here at one-thirty in the morning?"

It's the expected question, although considering what types of things have happened before, I can almost guarantee that it involves going outside in the cold and wreaking havoc across town. Or, at least, our version of it.

"I was hoping that you'd get around to asking." He leans forward, stopping his spinning in the chair by planting his feet firmly on the hardwood flooring. "But like usual, I'm not going to tell you."

"Daniel." I feel my eyes widening, as though the upper and lower lids are drifting further apart the longer that I stare unblinkingly at his face. "This is the earliest that you've ever woken me up. There better be a good reason for it."

"My reasons are *always* the best." He stuck out his lower lip in a mock pout. "And I'm *not* telling you. It'll ruin the surprise!"

I put weight on the feet that have been hesitating upon the rug and manage to stand, though my knees wobble and a general trembling sensation spreads throughout my somewhat stiffened corpse. I inhale deeply the odours of the room, ever familiar with their mustiness, and I can just barely taste a hint of his cologne, which wafts toward me as a siren's song. I refuse to approach it, to heed its silent question, to place myself in a folded heap upon his lap, and I instead launch myself onto the tips of my toes, sighing in relief as I feel those bones and tendons stretch, my hands reaching above my head, toward the ceiling. It's an odd sort of methodical approach that the body takes, how it extends itself and slowly expands the places that had constricted during sleep, paralysis, or other such things that constitute that limbs and torso remain in the same position, or similar ones, for an extended amount of time.

"For goodness's sake, I wish you'd just tell me," I allow both hands to drop and entwine themselves in the mess of blackish-brown waves that disjointedly cascade down to the middle of my back. I bunch up the hair, winding it in my palms, enjoying in my sleepy state the feel of the oddly silken strands against my skin, and my eyelids flutter shut for a split second. When I next open them, I'm blinking at Daniel, who's smirking at me, eyeing me up and down, up and down, those eyes never resting on a particular spot - oh, there they go, positioned on my legs, then my abdomen, then my collar bones — no, not *below* them!

I narrow my eyes at him, prepared to reprimand him, but then, I look down at myself, and I feel as though my eyeballs are about to drop right out of my skull. How foolish I am, forgetting that I sleep in nothing but a violet camisole and my underwear - which, fortunately, are white and black with lace trimmings. What am I saying, *fortunately?* Shane would probably kill me if he found out that not only I'd been entertaining male company other than his in my spare time, but that I'd been half-naked while doing so.

A blush creeps from the base of my neck all the way through my cheeks, flooding them up to the bones as I squeak a little bit, darting back to the bed and diving underneath the safety of the covers, concealing my tanned, bare legs and lace undergarment from view, bringing the edge of them all the way up to my eyes this time, peeking out from just above them. I'm hiding my blush and my grin.

My *grin.* What is *wrong* with me? This is no laughing matter.

"Wondered when you were going to notice that. Nice legs." He makes the remark offhandedly as he pushes himself away from the chair, palms flat down on the arms of it, and meanders over to the middle of the floor, eyes narrowed and eyebrows hooded as he scours the pillows, arranged in a disarray. Finally, he discovers what he's looking for, and he pulls it out by the right leg - a pair of black running shorts lined in white. He tosses them at me, and somehow, they manage to land on my head, hanging there, lopsided, like an outrageously unfashionable hat. "And, y'know, other stuff." He wiggles his eyebrows. "Put those on and come on, Babe Ruth."

Babe Ruth. A childhood nickname bestowed upon me for

my love of the candy bar and my uncharacteristic adoration of baseball - the rest of my family are football fanatics. I roll my eyes at him and fixate a glower on my face. "Turn around."

"Are you serious?"

"*Yes*! Turn *around!*" I've already expended *enough* modesty for today.

"Come on, now," Daniel says, crossing his arms and giving me that look, that one that tells me he's going to say something that's unbearably true and, therefore, that I am not going to enjoy hearing. "I've seen you in less than *that* before."

At that small little mentioning, I freeze a bit, my mind taking me back to a place full of darkness and patches of absentee memories. I know what he's talking about - back around my sixteenth birthday, I had decided that it was the best idea ever to attend a party with an older senior whom I had befriended without the rather intimidating presence of my brother with me. So I went to this party, and everything started out relatively normal - I was standing in the corner, sipping at a drink. But then, something hit me - perhaps it was the different smells in the air, the burst of music from the speakers; still to this day I'm unsure what came over me - but the alcohol tasted better and better. And then I blacked out soon after that. I drank a lot; I know that much. And when I next awakened, I was being carried as a bride from the limousine by Daniel, and almost all of my clothing was missing.

I asked him what happened several times after that, and every single time, his answer was the same - he'd seen me wandering around, complaining that I was hot, and when he followed me, keeping an eye on me, I ended up in the upstairs master bedroom, passed out with an empty bottle and that current state of dress. To be honest, I was more embarrassed, and still am, about the fact that he carried me out of the bedroom in just my undergarments in front of an entire house of teenagers. But none of them seem to remember the event, either not having witnessed it or having been far too intoxicated to care about it happening. (Only Shane knows, and only because I confided it to him.)

Daniel's looking at me strangely, and I blink, bringing myself out of the odd reverie. "W—What?"

"I said, it's not like I'm watching you get *un*dressed, anyway. I'm watching you put on more clothing." He studies me a bit more intently, and I cower beneath his gaze. "You all right?"

Sometimes, I despise the way that he peers at me, as though he can see right through whatever superficial visage I choose to portray in front of him. Because he can. He can see it all. Ever since we were small children, he's delved directly into the deepest parts of me without saying a single word or asking a single question. It seems to be a talent of his, though where he managed to acquire it, I'm not sure - probably from his father, David Stamp, who was the type of man who thought about things a lot, watched quietly, and didn't say anything until he was positively sure about what he was saying. And because of that simple fact, the two of them always managed to be right nearly one-hundred-percent of the time.

"Yeah," I tell him, rather flatly. "I'm fine."

I can tell by the set of his shoulders and the way he leans toward me that he wants to ask me about what's bothering me, recount the feelings that I've been repressing toward that embittering situation, but he decides against it and merely shrugs, appearing sheepish as he looks down at the floor. "I'll look down here, but I'm not going out of the room. My luck, you'll just roll back over in the covers and go back to sleep."

"I will not," I protest, though that's exactly what I had planned on doing.

"You aren't fooling anyone."

Perhaps it is nothing more than the fog of the morning, and of my intention of sleeping for a long amount of time being reduced to nothing more than a nap. But I could almost bet money that his statement mean something else entirely. I don't want to think about it. But there's a lot of things that I don't want to think about.

"I'm not *trying* to fool anyone," I retort, pulling back the covers slowly and watching him out of the corner of my eye to make sure he isn't looking at me. Which he isn't. He keeps those eyes trained down on the rug underneath his feet. "I'm just trying to put on my shorts so that you can drag me to do whatever you have planned."

"So grumpy." The teasing tone is back in his voice. "But I think that, after whatever I have planned, you'll be smiling and back in high spirits."

"What are you planning on doing to me?"

His eyebrows wiggle up and down, and I shoot him a scathing glare, though my lips twitch, betraying the strain of annoyance that I wish I was actually feeling because it would make things a thousand times easier on the both of us. "The best sex you'll ever have in your entire life."

I'm pretty sure that my eyeballs are about to fall out of their sockets as I whirl my head upward to stare at him, one leg in the air with the shorts halfway installed upon my hips, toe pointed as though I'm about to spring upon it once more. "Oh, gosh, Daniel, you can't be serious. I haven't even —" The words stop themselves before they can fully emerge: I haven't even done that with Shane, and we've been dating for seven months. "Shane definitely wouldn't like that."

"Please. You wouldn't tell him." Daniel tries his best to keep the teasing element as a continuation throughout all of his words, but it's becoming painfully obvious that the farce is beginning to weaken. "I'm not serious. — Not this time."

The words are delivered quietly. I don't have any more glowers left in me, so I know the expression painted on my face is more of exasperation. "Daniel —"

"Yeah, yeah, I know, you love him."

"Why are you so bitter?" I persist, pulling on my shorts the rest of the way, snapping the waistband snugly around my hip bones and throwing my legs back over the side of the bed, slowly becoming more fully awake with each passing moment. "What is the problem here? Am I not allowed to love my boyfriend?"

"Listen to yourself, Ruth," he scoffs, turning his back on me and crossing his arms as he meanders his way from the room, not bothering to glance over his shoulder and ensure that I'm trailing him; he already knows that I am, and as I do so, that I'm standing on my tiptoes and trying to peek over his broad shoulder to see his face. "You sound like one of those shitty romance novels."

"Don't cuss," is my immediate, prim response, and when he turns on me, I wrinkle my nose at him, widening my eyes so that they take on an innocent air. "Words like that don't sound pretty coming from an attractive boy's mouth."

"You know what, I actually find that offensive."

He has such a wicked temper. It makes my heart throb and adrenaline race through my veins. But unlike some other guys I know who have anger issues, I'm not afraid of Daniel - because I know, despite the way that it runs as an acidic, irresistible heat through his veins, despite the way that it crawls agonisingly slow into his arteries and seeps there as a toxic balm, both soothing and grating to his senses, both filling him with a sensation of healing and tearing him apart from the inside out, that he would never hurt me. And there's some comfort to be taken in that.

"Why?"

"Because you're calling me attractive, and yet, you're somehow still choosing to date that—" He struggles for the word, making a gesture with his right hand that constitutes clenching his fingers, his mouth twisting up into a disgusted bow. "— that *dog* instead of me. I've known you for how many years now? And he's known you for, what, less than a year? There's something *majorly* wrong with this picture."

He then makes an exploding gesture by pushing his fingers toward me and then moving his hands backwards. Though he does not touch me or even brush his fingers against the fabric of my camisole that I wear, still I feel his fingerprints burning as brands directly into my skin. "See?" he continues, one corner of his mouth sliding upward into a smirk, though it isn't his normally kind, receptive one. "I didn't cuss. Just for you. And I'm willing to do a lot more."

Here, he places his pointer finger directly in-between my two collar bones, in the middle of my sternum, and his voice drops into the lowest of whispers. "A *lot* more. For you."

I know. The words die in my throat. That seems to be happening a lot this morning. I know you would, Daniel. But you shouldn't. You shouldn't be willing to do anything. Not for me. Not when I take advantage of it.

He shrugs in place of my silence and turns on his heel, ignoring his fit of temper that he nearly allowed to explode and quietly whistling as he parts the strings of multicoloured beads that hang in front of the space that leads into the small, narrow hallway which provides a direct exit into the foyer. By the way that he's dragging his feet and pressing his heels into the throw rugs that have been placed down, fuzzy cheap things that my mother bought at a hodgepodge garage sale - neither of them match - I know that he hasn't completely written me off, still wishes for me to accompany him on whatever adventure roams within his head. But I'm not exiting this bedroom until I do a couple of major things - hygienic things.

"Pit stop, there, Daniel," I tell him, lowering my voice - even though my bedroom door is tightly shut, still there is a slight draft from the air bleeding through underneath it, and I don't want to take the chance of my parents overhearing our voices at this hour. My father would be furious. "Need to do stuff."

"Girly stuff," he mutters, but he follows me, and when I flick on the bathroom light, he leans his shoulder against the doorjamb, his eyes never leaving my frame. I'm all too aware of his concentration upon me, of how those irises still don't stop in one particular place, how he constantly seems to be attempting to memorise how I look, imprint it as a stamp upon an envelope in his mind and tuck away for safekeeping.

"Even boys brush their teeth." I purse my lips at him and cross my eyes before turning to the faucet and flipping up the handle so that a gentle, cold stream of water pours out from it. I look myself over briefly in the mirror, pressing my fingers against my cheek bones, the bags under my eyes, the numerous scars in my forehead from the cystic acne I had acquired through my middle-school and early high-school years, and finally, against my swollen lips.

Swollen — ? No, not even Daniel would have been so brazen as to kiss me in my sleep. I promptly dip my head at the thought of that, bending so that he cannot view the blush that seems to perpetually be taking up residence underneath those cheekbones I had just touched. I place both palms under the stream of water, my skin immediately resisting the change in temperature as I patiently cup them together and wait for them to fill up before depositing the water across my heated features.

While this relieves the redness for the most part, I'm also doing it to wash off the oil sitting upon the surface of my skin as a result of sweating in my sleep; it's a terrible thing, being allergic to the natural oils and sweat of your own body. It's the reason behind the development of the acne in earlier years; because no soaps or antibacterial seemed to be assisting the drying out of the skin, only worsening the condition. So, I switched to a topical medication in my sophomore year, and my skin took around nine or ten months to completely clear up - and while scars still remained, visible pinkish marks even on the bronzed hue of my sun-kissed skin, it's much better than enduring the pain and infection that accompanied the pustules all over my forehead and chin.

I'm not sure why any of that explanation was necessary or relevant. I just know that I ramble to keep my mind off of the things that are either being thrust upon me or are of more importance. Such as the fact that I'm noticing, as I straighten slightly to fetch my toothpaste from the side of the counter and my crimson toothbrush from its holder, that Daniel is admiring a part of me that no one should be seeing. He catches me glaring at him in the mirror, and the impish grin returns, which fills me with a sickened sense of relief; he seems to have returned to normal after the little outburst which almost occurred, and when he sends me an apologetic shrug, I am able to return to the hygienic tasks at hand without a weight of both guilt and anxiety weighing upon my conscience.

I load the bristles with a dollop of the minty toothpaste and set to work, ridding my mouth of that terrifyingly nauseating warm feeling that makes me smack my lips and move my tongue around to remind the insides of my mouth that there's still saliva that needs to be made and a throat that needs to be hydrated. I despise that odd heat that sits directly in the back of the throat, radiating outward and coating your tongue and your teeth. Just thinking about it causes me to shiver, and I more ferociously scrub at my molars until I feel that sensation disappear entirely. Once my mouth has been satisfyingly coated in the taste and odour of mint, I spit it into the drain and watch it swirl away, a little smile alighting on my lips before I fill my mouth with cold water, further intensifying that cleanliness I so love and allowing that to swirl down the drain as well.

And yes, before you ask, I have been brushing my teeth with my facial features still depositing small droplets of icy water both in the sink and on the counter from when I had splashed them into the awakened stage. I screw the cap back on the toothpaste tube, put the toothbrush back where it belongs, and only then do I manage to use my elbow in order to shove the faucet handle downward, shutting off the stream of water. Only then do I push my face into the soft, deep-violet-coloured fabric of the towel that smells like a combination of apricot facial scrub, blackberry currant hand soap, and my mother's detergent that she always uses, and I press it against my face with the palms of my hands, inhaling all of those aromas and gently massaging the excess water from the surface of the skin and from the pores before removing it and turning to Daniel - who hasn't budged, by the way, except to let his face appear amused once more.

I can't resist from asking the simple question. "What?"

But simple questions never have simple answers.

And that much is proven to me when he shakes his head that smirk of a smile softening to something that I've seen directed at me numerous times before and have desperately been ignoring. "Just admiring the view."

He had to go and say something like that.

"Daniel!"

He puts his hands up in a gesture of surrender and turns

away from me, but I can see by the shaking of his shoulders that my reaction has reduced him to laughter. The little imp. I don't know why I bother to hope that he'll end up responding any differently. I lunge after him, wanting to plant fists against the muscles of his back, but either I'm still too lethargic or he anticipated my movements because he manages to completely evade me.

"*Daniel!*" I whisper again as he pulls open my bedroom door, and my heart hammers a furious rhythm when he turns back, eyebrows high and nearly disappearing in his hairline. I'm deathly afraid that my parents, asleep in the next room over are going to overhear my quiet screeching and come out to check on what's going on, only to discover me half-clothed and Daniel shrugging. "You can't just —"

He already knows what I'm about to say. "Yeah, I can."

Suddenly, he reaches and grabs one of my hands, tugging me out of my bathroom and barely providing me with enough of an opening to switch off the lights before I'm out of the hallway and in the foyer, alternating feet as I shiver, watching him fiddle with the brass doorknob. It's so much colder out here in the open than it was in my bedroom, even though I had the ceiling fan set to the highest possible speed. He's still holding my hand, though, so there's that little bit of warmth, which seems to traverse up my forearm, settle into my elbow, and bleed upward into my bicep.

I huff. "You're impossible."

"I try."

With that, he turns the knob ever so slightly, beginning to inch the door slowly inward, a gust of crisp autumn air flowing in through even the small opening. My shivers become more violent as he continues with this slow pace, trying his best to keep the hinges from squeaking and groaning in protest, as they tend to do

- this door is older than the rest of the house around it, or so they say, installed from the original building on the foundation and whatnot, an ancient relic, a tome attesting to the passage of time. They end up being quite vocal near the end of their journey, and I wince away from them, as if that will assist in quieting them down - which it doesn't, by the way. Doesn't help at all.

For a split second, an instinct swoops down from nowhere and warns me, sends a red alarm blaring through my body, causing all systems to cease, to halt in their tracks, my limbs to lock and my breath to seize and my mind to stop thinking. It screams that I'm making a terrible mistake, that the last thing I should do is walk out that door and into the unknown with Daniel Stamp, because I had a boyfriend that I was in love with, because this wasn't supposed to be a thing that happened once you had said boyfriend, that everything was supposed to be with the boyfriend and the fact that I was going with Daniel was wrong. But another part of me scoffs and shoves those emotions aside, treating them as flippant and childish, sticking its nose up into the air and proclaiming that we weren't doing anything except going on an adventure. It wasn't like it was a sexual adventure, despite Daniel's recent comment; that was one boundary that not even he would cross. It was just two friends, sneaking out of the house as they usually did and going to who-knows-where for some diabolical scenario that he has mapped out to occur at one in the morning when, in less than six hours, we have to get up, do the chores around our ranches, and then go to school.

But then I see his cheeky profile, and my foot decides to take a step forward, and before I can give into the odd instinct that fills me, already one of my hands has reached backward, wrapped itself around the doorknob, and started pulling the door shut behind us as we traversed outward into the chilly night air.

(Seeing his face made my decision for me.) The moment my bare feet touch the cold concrete of the front porch, an array of hardened goosebumps appear all over my flesh. Yet his giddy laughter that bounces back toward me renews my energy and my determination to follow him, to not give into the awkward instinct that I probably should listen to as a good girlfriend.

You see, whenever I'm around Daniel Stamp, I find that being the "good girlfriend" or anything of that sort, living up to the standards that I've set for myself over the years, being dedicated to the person that I'm dating and having a small circle of friends whom I socialised with during the daytime classes and sat with at the lunch table in order to gossip about certain others or assigned homework for the evening or tests gone completely awry, skitters away into the approaching nightfall and promptly commits a romantic suicide. The last thing I want to be is prim and proper around him. All I want to be is free. And he provides me with an odd sort of liberation, one that most people probably wouldn't appreciate considering they are allowed to come and go from their house as they please, allowed to attend the parties without giving excuses or making up an elaborate story. Since my parents approve of him and how he is as a person, they don't protest too loudly when they discover that I've been spending time with him - and though their attitudes and thoughts toward Shane seem scarily similar, still there is an element of difference, one that has to do with—? I'm unsure what it is, but perhaps eventually, I'll be able to put a name or, at the very least, a general label to it.

I inhale sharply as he gently tugs me along, pushing forward all of my weight onto my tiptoes and withholding quiet shrieks as we make our way onto the front sidewalk that winds all the way around the front of my house. None of the outside security lights switch on; so that meant either my mother, as scatterbrained as she has been lately - which, by the way, is not her fault, so please refrain from insulting her and I'll refrain from hurting you - or Paul, being himself and collapsing into bed after doing too much in one day, as always, forgot to flick the switch that turns them on. We're cloaked in a comfortable darkness until we reach the side of the garage where the sidewalk ends in three large steps and dissolves into the pad where we park our cars - the lights above the two large garage doors then turn themselves on, bathing Paul's ancient, seventies-style black Ford truck and my own wiry, smaller red Mazda pickup in a gentle yellow glow.

"Where are we going?" I ask again, my voice as buoyant as my steps, echoing off the side of the house as Daniel leaps from the side of the staircase instead of taking the steps as any other normal human being would do. Oh, who am I kidding? Not even my brother, or my father, use those steps sometimes; I wonder why we even bothered having them installed. "On a road trip?"

"Not tonight," is his response over his shoulder. Seeing no other way to go, I hop off the side of the landing and land lightly behind him. "We're going to my barn. I have something to show you."

We stop at the head of the driveway and he finally turns around so that he's facing me, his arms being held out toward me in a welcoming gesture. "Come on, Rapunzel. I'm not letting you walk down those rocks in your bare feet."

I glare pointedly at his own, which are shoeless, and he laughs lightly at the expression on my face, taking a couple of steps closer to me. "Don't give me that look. I might be an asshole, but even I know how to treat girls properly."

The implication in his statement is almost enough to trigger me shrieking at him and pummelling at his pectoral muscles with my fists - Shane doesn't treat me badly or with ill, malicious intentions, and how dare Daniel allude to such a thing; he doesn't know what he's talking about! - but before I can vocalise anything, I've been hoisted into the air, one of his solid, warm arms hooked into the crooks of my knees and the other wrapped around my shoulder blades, keeping me nestled against his chest.

I've become a bride being carried into the honeymoon suite, it seems.

It's amazing how quickly my sour moods come and go around this boy, how they ebb and flow as the tides of the ocean, as they wash over me and drag me under and allow me to surface to breath once more. I hitch my left arm around his neck and connect my hands together, staring somewhat dazedly out at the yard as we meander our way down the driveway, the chill of the breeze whistling past my exposed ears and causing wisps of hair to drift across my forehead and my cheekbones. I'm trying to think through the layout of his barn, curiosity once again getting the better of me, wondering what in the world he could be wanting to show me.

It isn't a new barn; it's one of those wooden ones that remain unsurpassed by time, its age only showing through the mars and the weathering of the planks. The centre area on the outside of the barn were stained a deep, ancient brown, while the other parts, directly underneath the overhangs of the black-bricked roof, had whitened and were more of a chestnut colour; neither were the original shade of the barn. The rear outside wall is half-painted crimson, but that bucket of paint has long since dried and crusted its lid shut to the rest of it. There's a small incline of grass, dirt, and pebbles that lead up to the largest of the barn doors. Underneath that incline, the stone foundation and a singular window set within it can be seen - the cellar, which houses a faded man door with a precariously broken and steep staircase, and a glass area where a greenhouse has long since overgrown, leaving nothing there to remain except the strangled remains of plants and a couple of rotten potatoes and perhaps a carrot, half-eaten by critters, scattered here and there. There are holes in the outside - makeshift windows that have the appearance of being hole-punched away - where you can see the figures of cows and horses and other assorted livestock milling around.

You can enter either through the large double doors, the man door in the basement, or through one of the windows. Daniel and I usually clamour through the foremost window, closest to the doors, because opening those doors would let loose the cows and the other animals into the rolling, fenced-in acreage that stretches out behind the house. Besides, it's much more adventurous to do something like that and allow ourselves to be deposited in one of the towering piles of loose hay. The middle of the barn is very open - there are a few walled-off sections for the assorted animals: wooden slats that separate the goats from the pigs, the two horses each have their own individual makeshift stalls and the cows are all shoved to the rightmost side, penned in by a slight groove in the floor; those morons are terrified of any dip in the ground, because to them, the smallest of open slivers looked like the Grand Canyon.

"What the hell are you thinking so hard about?"

I glance toward Daniel and I shrug. "Your barn's floor plan."

He laughs here, directly mocking me. "Are you *serious*, Ruth? What, do you think you're going to get lost in there or something? You've been in there a thousand times; what's the problem?"

"I'm trying to figure out what you're going to show me."

Then the expression upon his face became mysterious,

almost enigmatic. That little imp knows that I can't handle not knowing information; that I can't handle being in the dark; that I can't handle being aware that something is known by everyone else in the room but me. My heart swells and my arms tighten around his neck as he says, quite airily, "Oh, you haven't seen this part of the barn yet. You can't picture it in your head."

"What are you talking about? Did your dad finally build that new addition he's been talking about for the past month?"

Daniel merely shakes his head and purses his lips.

"Fine," I say primly, beginning to squirm in his arms. We're just now reaching the foot of the driveway, where the painful gravel dissolves into more traversable asphalt. The streetlight above us ticks with the effort to remain illuminated, and shadows flit across it, interrupting its stream; bats, insects, and birds who have yet to realise that it's the nighttime and not when they need to be flying about. "Then put me down and I'm going back to bed."

"Don't be such a diva," Daniel replies in amusement, though he allows his grip to loosen and slowly lowers my feet toward the asphalt, moving the arm hooked under my knees to circle around my waist and hold me against him, pressed into a close proximity, both of our pulses hammering. When I finally manage to find the solid ground with my toes, I breathe a trembling sigh of relief, though my knees seemed to have turned to jelly, and I cling to his forearms, my slender fingers digging through the fabric of his shirt and into his skin.

This causes him to stammer a little bit. "We're — we're halfway there. You can't just turn back now."

You know, you should tease him like he does to you all the time.

The little voice in my head says this, and I'm startled to hear it speak. It usually keeps quiet when it comes to things like this.

You know you like him. You know you want to.

What was this nonsensical temptation filling my head? The conflict must've shown in my face - but Daniel couldn't have any idea about the words that were starting to stream forth from the mouth of the devil himself, could he? As it were, he presses his hands to the side of my face and grips there for a moment. "It's okay. I don't—"

It's never going to be okay. Not as long as you're not with him.

But I'm in love with Shane, I tell myself. I pull my face from his hands and I begin walking in the middle of the road, making my way toward his barn, feeling my cheeks flush in embarrassment with my inability to handle conflict. I'm *in love* with Shane; why else would I be in a dating relationship with him - a monogamous dating relationship, mind you?

"Ruth, I'm sorry."

You shouldn't be apologising, Daniel. I half-turn toward him, the words appearing on my lips and ready to be released within a moment's notice. You shouldn't be apologising for my actions, for my thoughts, for my own darned confusion and muddled feeling in the brain, for my inability to make a decision and stick by it. But as it were, there is a surge of pride, one that pleasantly numbs my limbs and causes me to curl my fingers into fists at my side, causes me to plaster a smile that stretched the corners of my mouth upward, a smile that was as plastic in appearance as it felt being pasted upon my features. There was never a moment before now in my entire life when I felt as superficial as I do now.

"You are right, Daniel. It *is* okay." is what ends up emerging through gritted teeth, a statement nowhere close to the one that I actually want to say to him. And after it's been said, I find that I can't say anything else due to the squeezing of a clawed hand around my throat that wants nothing more than to throttle me where I stand for lying so easily.

I can tell that he's trying to refrain from refuting that. A scowl makes its way onto his face as he lengthens his stride and quickly catches up to me, then surpasses me, not bothering to reach out and take my hand, expecting me to now walk along instead of being led. I want to put my hands in my pockets, but these running shorts don't have pockets and neither does the shirt, so I'm stuck with them clenched into fists by my side as I dart after him, still lifting up on my tiptoes to lessen the sensation of the cold, hard asphalt underneath my feet. Something soft accosts my smallest right toe, and I squeak away from it, speeding up until I'm hovering directly behind Daniel.

"Don't be such a diva," he repeats.

But this time, the tone in his voice isn't humorous whatsoever.

I scrape my toe along the asphalt, trying to get rid of the sensation that the softness left upon the skin, and I end up taking off the top layer of flesh instead, resulting in something that feels as though it'll end up being an uneven skid mark. I withhold a whimper, not needing another gaping wound in my pride at being chastised for sounding like a *diva* or, even worse, a C O W A R D - because once he grew tired of one insult, he would grow progressively worse with the ones he assigned until you had been reduced to tears. I should know; I've seen this characteristic, this habit of his, in action. Never has it really been directed toward me, and I certainly don't want it to be a new trend that starts now.

We make our way across the street and we are moving up his driveway, past the old brick mailbox with the half-installed green sign with the reflective numbers imprinted upon them. What's most interesting about this, the house, the barn, the entirety of the Stamp household and its surrounding landscape, is that although it has a relatively unkempt, dishevelled appearance, it isn't in disarray or falling to the waste side; indeed, it's quite the opposite. I suppose the more accurate descriptive term for it would be that it appears to be lived in, and not either of the extremes - not a long-since forgotten tome of text in a foreign language that remains upon display for half-interested passersby and too-eager tourists to attempt and decipher when they see it, nor a perfectly coiffed hairstyle of the fifties with every strand tucked and smoothed neatly into its righteous place, the epitome of vanity.

His driveway consists of a faded path made by the tires of cars, small pebbles naturally churned up with the soil and the little bits of grass, which turn into towering mounds around the edges of the tracks. I move to walk by his side, and he glances down at me, his face still completely stoic, before reaching over and taking my hand again. His palm no longer holds the warmth which I had previously detected, but now had a nervousness, an anxiety within its pores, a sort of inescapable clamminess, and I was the one who held more heat there instead of the other way around. It was a mutual switching of the roles, one that our hands had apparently agreed to do after the small little exchange of commentary that caused the surrounding environment to snap as a rubber band against the side of the neck, leaving a raised reddened welt that was being soothed by the cool of a feather-light fingertip. Except now, he was the one with the welt, and I was soothing him; but perhaps, in reality, it always had been this way, and always would be.

But still, we cling to one another in the dark.

Instead of taking us through the large barn doors or through the window, Daniel leads me from the beaten, trodden path and through the taller grasses toward the man door. There's a forced cheerfulness in him now. He is regretting ever thinking that this was a good idea in the first place. "So it's down in the cellar. It's not *exactly* a new add-on, but if you've been wondering where I've been disappearing to for the past few weeks, that's it. I've been locked in this godforsaken place and basically building myself a second home."

Within a few paces, we've reached the yawning hole; the man door is hanging haphazardly upon its hinges, and there's still that sinking indentation in the second wooden stair, the area where the wood hasn't decided whether or not it's warped enough to become translucent, but bends so far inward that it's more upturned splinters and bended nails than it is a functioning step. We hesitate there for a moment, then he moves forward and leaps down all three of the stairs, bending his knees and rolling into the shadows, into the gaping darkness, which consumes him.

Immediately, I am seized by panic. I *knew* this was a bad idea. I knew I should have listened to that weird instinct that had very nearly screeched out my eardrums and clawed out my eyeballs to express itself, to tell me that leaving my bedroom and venturing out into this unknown upon this particular night wouldn't be good. The seconds stretch out more the longer that I stand there, and I quiver, wrapping my arms around myself, missing his warmth, missing his warmth, and shifting from foot to foot, constantly dissatisfied by the stance that I take, finally positioning my arms underneath my chest and pushing upward. I realise then that I had forgotten to don something unbelievably important before waltzing out of my room: my bra. A furious blush floods my cheeks and my forehead, and although no one's around to see it (and even if someone *was*, he wouldn't be *able* to see it; the light bulb above the man door flickers so many times, it's like the set of a horror movie) I duck my head, turning my face to the side so that it's concealed by my hair.

As though blinders had been fastened on either side of

my head, preventing my peripheral vision from properly functioning, I find myself concentrating on a particular plant that has sprouted close to the dip in the incline, near the stone foundation, near one of the windows. I can't tell what it is from here - it's a couple of feet away from where I currently stand - but it appears to be the makings of a weed, perhaps an unbelievably tall dandelion. Yet the longer I stare at it, the more it seems to take on a personality, to swoop and slide and make noises, to flap its leaves as wings and spread the petals upon its face as though welcoming me - or snarling at me with vicious teeth that are churning and grinding against themselves in its centre.

"Ruth. *Ruth.*"

Someone is shaking me. I'm still standing outside Daniel's barn, but he's returned, covered in dust and dirt but completely whole, having taken my shoulders in his hands and furiously taken to moving me back and forth, a glare upon his face as he stares down at me, eyes burning. "Snap out of it, Ruth."

"I'm okay," I say breathlessly. "But that's a really weird plant you have there."

"What?" Daniel turns to the area where I'm staring and he rolls his eyes. "Uh, there's no plant."

More than a little bit bewildered, I peer over his left bicep at the shadowed, darkened area where I had been staring while awaiting to see if he would return for me at all, searching for the thing that had paralysed me, rooted me to the spot, forced me to remain immobile when all I wanted to do was sprint back to the house, lock myself in my bedroom, and burrow myself under the several comfortable layers of bedcovers, maybe even accompanied by a cat or two, or the family house dog, or all of the above — but definitely with pillows, and definitely without company that could be classified as *human.*

"But there *was* a plant." I say this with insistence. I blink several times; still nothing is there. Nothing's there. Not even a strand of a leaf or the remains of a stalk. The most that's there in those shadows is grass, and Daniel says as much.

"Nothing's grown around this barn in ages," he says, sounding bitter again. "And definitely not dandelions with sharp teeth."

When I look at him, he shrugs.

"You were practically screaming about it. That's why I was shaking you; trying to wake you up before you roused the entire damn road. Including my parents and *yours*." He jerks his head toward the yawning cavern of a threshold. "Come on. Everything's ready."

READY? How long had he been planning this out, creating this room for this purpose? But there I go, being selfish and proud. What right did I have to think that he had created something that extensive and was now showing me? I wasn't his girlfriend. He didn't have any obligation whatsoever to do something like that, and I'm in the wrong to expect it of him. I shake my head slowly back and forth as he takes my hand again, helping me down the torment of a staircase, practically lifting me from the ground in order to help me over the warped area in the second stair. Upon entering the basement - which I see has been illuminated; he must have rolled in there to find the light switch, for now strands of naked bulbs were installed along the entirety of the low ceiling, and I know that the last time I was in here, around a couple of months ago, that those lights hadn't existed - I feel my entire body be coated in a layer of dust and neglect. The soles of my feet take on a gritty texture, and I wince against it. But I'm not going to be called a diva again. I'm not.

But let the records show that just because I'm a girl who's grown up on a farm, who gets her hands dirty with picking cantaloupes, watermelons, tomatoes, who buries herself in the throes of moist soil, who shovels four different types of manure, who throws her hair up in a high bun on the top of her head and wears bandannas and otherwise doesn't complain about the rivulets of oily sweat that accost her forehead, temples, cheeks, chin, neck, back of head, anywhere there's skin - just because I'm all of those things and more doesn't mean I enjoy the feeling. I just don't mind it. Not usually.

I'm still half-asleep. The last thing I'm wanting is to feel as though I've dunked my feet ankle-deep in liquid cement and am waiting for it to dry. I want a hot bath with a lot of bubbles that smell like vanilla and cherries, and I want to sneak some of my mother's Bailey's Irish Cream, which she no longer is allowed to drink due to her medication and conditions, and I want to read fashion magazines with the trends that I have no inclination to follow, and I want to soak up the warmth and have a nice sweat that's a result of laziness and not hard work for once, and I don't want to worry about anything.

But I don't think that's in the cards for me in the near future.

Or even in the distant future.

The dirt floor of the barn crumbles underneath the sluggish dragging of my feet. It's mostly a wide open space, with slatted off areas for the assorted animals kept inside: two hundred head of cattle, six horses, a chicken coop alongside some wild turkeys in the furthermost right corner from the entryway of large double doors, and an area for the three hogs and their babies, when the time comes. Deep in the heights of the roof are rafters allotted for the hay to feed and the straw used as bedding. The pellets and the wooden shavings are also stored up there, to be mixed with the straw and therefore providing a nice, warm bed for these creatures during the harshness of the winter months. Inhaling, there's the distinct odours of reminiscence and manure, of worn leather and moulding hay. Despite the shuffling around of the sleeping animals, some pressing against others, little whispers and bites being exchanged, it's eerily silent. A strange sort of comfort is what this place brings - one that teases it could be lethal if one wrong step was taken, yet I have frequented this massive structure too many times for bad things to happen. Besides, there would be no tragedy to ruin whatever surprise Daniel has planned for the two of us; just my own untrainable, buzzing nerves.

Once we've made it to the opposite end of the barn, there's a small protruding area in the shape of a square, offset by a wooden door. The leather tie on the hook is the only thing keeping the door shut. He turns, blocking my vantage point of anything beyond him and his hulking, slightly intimidating frame. "Close your eyes." All the tenseness in his voice, the snapping of the rubber band previously experienced, has dissipated. He's back to being gentle, to being Daniel James Stamp and not some monstrous, jealous asshole - though that's a part of him, too, but I digress. I much prefer him this way. How many times do I have to think those words in order to him to hear them? "I want this to be a surprise. The whole thing. Even walking in."

My suspicions are aroused, but after everything we've been through together and alongside my twin brother, even before tonight, I know that if there's one thing in the world that he deserves, it's my undying, unhindered trust.

I nod once, then allow my eyes to drift shut.

With my eyes closed, the sensation of touch is heightened, as is that of hearing. Each crick and bend in the atmosphere becomes increasingly obvious to me, and I find that my earlobes are twitching, much as a cat's would, in order to detect and analyse each and every sound. I hear the wooden door creak as he takes my hands, and I nearly jump from the contact;

my fingers have become more sensitive than they usually are, and his light touch tickles me, causing me to bite down on my lower lip in order to withhold a bout of somewhat crazed, sleep-deprived laughter. He tugs at me and instinctively, automatically, I move forward along with him. He hasn't turned around; he's walking backwards. I hear the swish of his jean legs as they grind against one another, the way that the hem of his shirt shifts ever so slightly to rest underneath a belt loop instead of on top of it, how the smallest drift of air brushes back a golden lock of hair from the nape of his neck. Everything has become increasingly prominent, obvious to me, and when he finally pulls me to a stop, I inhale.

Shavings. That's the first word that comes to mind when I breathe in - it's the most obvious, pungent odour in the place. Not just any shavings, but wood shavings. There's a distinct change in the grittiness underneath the soles of my feet as well - before it had been that of a mixture of dirt, hay and straw, and now it was that of sawdust and wood shavings. Small splinters awaiting their chance to be embedded into skin that isn't callused from wear and use. And there's a relatively moistened feeling as well that falls into my skin, perhaps remnants from the dew coating the stone foundation or perhaps because of the humidity in the cellar. But still, it's cool. Comfortable.

"Okay," Daniel whispers near my ear, and the warmth against the lobe causes me to quiver involuntarily. "Now open your eyes. And try not to shriek too loud - the walls in here are too close to handle your diva-like screeching."

The teasing had arrived back in his voice, and it's only this fact that allows me to feel comfortable enough to actually open my eyes, feeling the heavy weight of his palms upon my shoulders, the thumbs massaging, in ginger circles, the area just above the shoulder blades, the most sensitive part. And I allow my eyelids to slide open, unsure of what I would be looking at - but not displeased in the least when I realise what it is, what he has turned this room into, my hands drifting upward to cover my mouth so that my gasp of shock doesn't echo off the walls or something like that.

It's a relatively small room, a perfect square, and the singular window, which provides half a view of the main house in the distance, has been made out of part of the siding being punched out, in order to allow in ventilation. Stacked in the furthermost corner were long slabs of different types of wood, halfway disguised in shadows due to a tall lamp with a moveable neck situated to illuminate his work stands and another arranged to shed light on the portable table saw and other assorted tools. Overall, he's managed to convert this space into a place where he could invest his time and energy into a trade that would keep his hands busy and his mind occupied. His dad must be immensely pleased with this; I know I am, and the way that the expression upon his face causes him to appear as though he were the early bird who managed to eat the worm, I can tell that Daniel is too.

"Wow," is all I can really say, feeling the awe take over me.

"Yep," is his proud response as he moves away from me and puts his hands on his hips, standing as a superhero would over his saved country. "This is what I've been doing. To think you tossed and turned and fretted about me over nothing."

"I didn't fret," is my automatic response, though it's rather absentminded as I drift from my current spot, feeling what I realise now to be sawdust pressing itself against my feet as I meander about the little space, the comfort away from home. "I knew you had to be doing *something* important."

"And now you know what!" He watches me closely as I wander over to the counters and workbenches with the tools laid upon them, everything so meticulously cared for that I wonder why in the world his bedroom isn't cleaner - but I suppose that there's a difference, in his head, between his temporary living space and tools that could support a specific trade for possibly years depending on their condition. "But, believe it or not, the room isn't the best part of the surprise yet."

I wonder whether or not it would be a facetious thing to say that I figured that. Because while of course I'm interested in what he does with his spare time and I am dually impressed that he's decided to take his woodworking more serious. I also know that he wouldn't have woken me up at one in the morning to only show me around, not when he knows fully well that he could kidnap me after school in order to do the exact same thing - or, at the very least, wait until daylight. My heartbeat speeds up a little bit as I halt my perusal of the different saw blades and wood carving tools in order to turn back around to him and tilt my head to the side, hair drifting with the movement.

"There's something else?"

"Well, duh." He quickly moves to me and takes me by the shoulders, moving me forward and away from the tools. "I mean, I didn't make this room and then not *do* anything with it. So just stand there and don't turn around until I tell you."

As I inhale, my head lolls backward, and once I exhale, I start intensively studying the ceiling, ignoring the sounds of rummaging that are taking place directly behind me and close to my ears, knowing that if I listened too closely to them, I would become overwrought with curiosity and turn around, and probably end up spoiling the surprise. It amazes me how something that has supported so much weight from on top of it for so many years, the manure-laden hooves of cattle and the screeching bodies of pigs and the restless legs of horses, can be in this good of condition. Of course, by *good condition*, I mean that at the corners, the paint is peeling away, stretching down the walls in stripes that reveal a mottled grey under the white coat; there are several small holes and one particularly yawning one directly over the wood door, and threaded across its gaping surface is an unbelievably intricate spider web with several tiers of sticky, delicate thread holding all of its pieces together, a jagged puzzle left there to be seen by all. The only thing missing from the image there is the creator of the scene, the spider whose webbing was expelled and twirled and strung together in order for this to be existing in the first place.

"Alright, turn around."

The excitement in his voice causes my steps to be quick, and my eyes alight on his face, trembling and shining as though it were Christmas morning, looking down fondly at something that he held cradled in his palms and stretching outward toward me. I trail my gaze, feeling my face crease in confusion, down the front of his chest and to the little object that he held so delicately, as though the slightest movement would cause it to topple over and shatter into a thousand splinters - and upon seeing it, I gasp, covering my mouth with one hand, completely understanding now why he would be treating such an object with reverence.

It's a baby deer, standing on spindly legs, both ears thrust forward and slightly oversized for its adorable, incredibly realistic face. If it had been painted, the sanded and shaped cedar wood covered by different necessary colours, I would have thought that I was looking at a miniature clone of an actual deer - the eyes peer at me with such a depth and intelligence, I will even go so far as to comment that I feel as though I am gazing into the eyes of something with a human soul. It's painfully obvious that a lot of time and sweat went into this, and I move forward to get a closer look, my hand still over my mouth. There's an odd wetness accosting the side of my hand; I'm crying. This little gift has managed to reduce me to tears.

"Oh, *Daniel,*" I say through my hand, voice wavering, my emotions climaxing to a brand-new high of the likes that none of them have ever experienced. My fingers are trembling as I reach out with the free hand and lay my pointer finger so gingerly upon the head of the deer, feeling the softness of the wood being stamped with my print. "It's beautiful!"

He's watching me very, very closely, and the illumination in his eyes flickers as if they were the flames of candles being thrust out into the chilliness of the breeze flowing through the broken panes of the basement window. It's almost as if, instead of handing over a wooden carving that only appears to have the breath of God engraved in each and every little line and niche, he's handing over a piece of his heart, throbbing and pulsating weakly in his palm, waiting to be taken into my own hand and brought back into the furious rhythm that it wished to beat.

It is with this realisation that I know I cannot accept what he has made for me. There's playing the game, and then, there's crossing the invisible line and causing it to become cruelty; taking this, providing him with hope, would be the most tyrannical, heartless of things that I could ever do in my entire life. Saving him, telling him no now, would spare him the heartache down the road when he saw me at school still with Shane a month or so from now, and his little deer collecting dust upon one of the numerous bookshelves in my bedroom. And that isn't fair - not to me, not to him, and not to Shane.

"Daniel—" The tone in my voice is different, and that candlelight within his irises, those beautifully haunting hazel irises that I have seen more times within the confines of my dreams than I wish to remember, immediately is blown out. He knows. He knows exactly what I am about to say. Before I can continue my strain of thought, he has covered the deer with his long fingers, as if to shield it from my oncoming rejection, and he turns away from me, his body stiffening, and all the warmth dissipating from his pores, a stony expression hardening itself across his features. "I can't—"

"Yeah, you know what, this was a bad idea," he says hotly, interrupting me, his back completely toward me now. "I should've just let you go back to sleep. I honestly don't know why I bother with trying to do this stuff. It just goes a hundred-percent unappreciated and I'm constantly rejected. I'm sick of it."

"Daniel!" I proclaim, not caring anymore that my voice is carrying right out the makeshift window and into the great beyond. "I've told you a thousand times that I am *dating* someone! It isn't my fault you can't accept it!"

"Damn right I can't accept it. Because of who you're dating!"

"And what's wrong with Shane?"

"*What's wrong with Shane?*" Daniel mimics. He sets the deer down and then flings his hands out to the side. "Are you *serious?* Does he really have you that blinded by whatever bullshit he feeds you that you can't see him for what he really is?"

"He doesn't have me blinded by anything! I walked into that relationship knowing exactly what I was looking for and exactly what to expect!"

"I heard him ask you out," he seethes. "He was begging. *Begging.* Like a *dog.* I never did that to you because I have the confidence to *know* you want to be with me!"

"But I *don't*, do I?" I say this primly, even though my heart lurches. "Because if I did, then I'd be dating you instead of him."

"And that's where the *bullshit* comes into play." His eyes flash dangerously as he nears me, inhaling deeply as his cheeks flush with a ruddy ire. "He doesn't let you *near* anyone long enough to make you realise that there's better things out there than a snivelling asshole who wants to be something when he's *nothing*. He's *possessive*! He walks around with you like a prop on his arm, and you go right along with it - and hell if I know why you do!"

"I am *not* a *prop*!"

"You're right. You're not." Daniel presses a forefinger against my sternum and pushes me backward a step. "So why the hell are you with a guy who treats you like one?"

"What — *is* it with you and Paul?" I snap, flipping a hand upward toward the finger that had accosted me and missing by a mile. "What *is* it with you two? All I ever hear about when it comes to Shane is how much you guys can't *stand* to be around him, but guess what! I don't hear that whenever I ask anybody else, not even my own parents. And do you really think that my father would let me date someone that he hated? You *know* my father, Daniel. You *know* how he *is*."

"Of course I do. I've grown up around your house, Ruth. Or have you forgotten?" A long, wild laugh emerges from him, and it's high-pitched, almost unnatural, crazed. "Which is why I *really* don't get it. Your dad usually doesn't let the wool get pulled down over his eyes. Doesn't let himself get blinded by manners and all the right words said in all the right places. But I guess his bullshit radar's somehow gone faulty as well. Just like yours. *Mine* isn't, though." Here, he shakes his head several times, rolling those brilliant, glimmering eyes - which now shimmer with something closer to malevolence than mirth. "Mine's working full throttle. And whenever you bring him up, it goes off."

"Then *your* little meter is the one that's faulty." Even I can hear the confidence waning in my voice, which is incomprehensible to me. Because I believe every single thing I'm saying, and I don't understand, I *really don't*, why Paul and Daniel are *so against* Shane when no one else in the entire world can see anything wrong with him. "Because we both know my dad and he doesn't let the wool get pulled over his eyes."

"There's a first time for everything," he taunts. "And what the hell does *anybody else* have to do with this whole thing? Stop being so naive. *Wake up.* Not everybody in the whole world is looking out for your best interests."

"My parents —"

"Your mother just came back from asylum and your dad is stressed out with the farm work, taking care of her, and yelling at everyone else!" Even though he uses the polite term for it, instead of *the crazy house* like a lot of people whisper behind my back, still it feels as though he has taken the handle of a serrated blade and proceeded to drive it directly into my lethargic heart. "*Think about it:* the last thing on their minds is who the hell you're dating. Which is why you have us, me and Paul. We don't tell you this shit to make you mad. We tell you because we want to save you getting hurt."

"Oh, like every single relationship doesn't have hurt in it!"

"*Ours wouldn't!*" His hands can't decide whether they want to slam themselves down upon the surface of the nearest workbench or wrap their long fingers around my shoulders. Finally, after some hesitation and flailing, they land upon my shoulders, and he pulls me to him, those fingertips digging so deeply into my flesh that I wince against it, feeling an immobilising physical pain, the very first time that I have ever felt such a thing coming from him.

"Ours wouldn't hurt — because you're the girl for me. How many times do I have to say it? When are you going to start *getting* it? That's why I have such a problem." He shakes me. "*That's* why I'm so jealous." Shakes me again. "*That's* why I can't stand seeing you two walking around at school. Because I'm *in love* with you. And I always have been!"

"Don't say things you don't mean!" I proclaim hotly, reaching up with my hands and grasping at his wrists, trying to wrench him away from me so I can flee. "Don't say them!"

"Stop it, Ruth!" The emotions in the room are heightened beyond belief as he fights against my pummelling fists, my sharp and dangerous fingernails. "*Stop it.* I'm not lying to you!"

His voice is as the roar of the ocean waves, and it washes over me, as he has washed over me, as he always has done, and my thoughts are racing at such a breakneck speed that I fear I will crash and burn. It's coming. "Everything I say, I mean, in one way or another. Why is it so hard for you to accept this?"

I can't stop shaking my head, back and forth, back and forth, my eyes wildly darting from his face, to the ceiling, to the deer upon the counter, to the floor, and back to his face, back to that wildly passionate face that is twisted into one of the most pained, heartrending, angst-filled expressions that I have ever seen be pasted across the features of a human being.

"You *can't* love me. It *isn't possible.*"

"Why not?"

"Two people can't love me like this!"

"*Shane doesn't love you!*" he spits. "Shane's just *using* you! Remember when I said that not everyone has your best intentions at heart? He's one of those people!"

"Stop it, Daniel!" I shriek the words back at him, exchanging my name for his, and I hit him even harder. "Stop it, *stop it, STOP IT!*"

I fall silent, close to hyperventilating as tears stream down my face, causing the whites of my eyes to redden and swell. I breathe in and out hurriedly through clenched teeth, staring up at him in complete and utter disbelief. My mind is racing to keep up with all that's occurring, but failing, only causing me to have muddled, confused, mixed thought processes, none of which were coherent enough to express or think on for an extended period of time. His face is livid, beyond livid; I haven't seen him indulge in such an episode of temper since he first found out that I was dating Shane. Those strangely-coloured eyes burn at me, smouldering in their sockets, and his chest heaves as he tries to calm himself down with deepened breaths, tearing his gaze away from me and staring off into space, cords and tendons protruding in his neck with the effort to keep from completely exploding on me.

"This isn't right."

The words are short, concise, snappish, and he releases my shoulders, holding his hands up in surrender.

"You're right. This was the worst idea ever." He repeats what he said earlier and what I thought as well. "You should've just stayed in bed. I should just stay the hell away from you because this is all that happens. All we do is fight, and it's because you're too dumb to see that you're being used like a rag and that you'll be thrown out."

(Too dumb to see—)

"Jealousy makes people say things like this." I nod once in finality. "It's just the jealousy talking, Daniel."

"What now, then? Are you going to tell me that I'm gonna get over it? Because I'm *not*. I'm *not* going to get over it. I haven't for seven months, and God forbid if you walk down the aisle with this son of a bitch, don't think I won't be the first one on my feet in protest."

"What is *wrong* with you?" I shoot out, shoving my hands onto my hips, feeling the distinct flush in my face, the hot sweat on my forehead and at the nape of my neck, how my scalp tingled, how my eyes burned with unshed tears and how dampened my cheeks were from the ones that had indeed been spilled. My heart throbs painfully against my chest cavity, and I resist the urge to push my hands against it, to stop it from beating, to stop the pain and the torture that it's enduring. "If you love me and all that, then why haven't you *done* something about it? Why didn't you speak up back when I was single?"

Daniel stares at me, then shakes his head. "You never listen to me, do you? I was giving you hints. Hell, I was being *obvious* about my feelings for you and you never said anything back, you never even *acknowledged* it half the time. What'd you want me to think, that you were interested? Because you weren't showing it! You were either completely oblivious or—" He gestures weakly out toward the side, his face crumpling slightly, but he plasters one hand on his face and drags downward, as if to remove the sorrow that had been about to take root there and stain his visage. "Or disinterested. And guys are insecure, too, you know. We don't exactly know what the hell's going on or how to act all the damn time. So I decided to wait until you woke up - if you ever did. I didn't think that in the meantime, you'd be dating a horny wannabe who can't do anything else except stick his nose where it doesn't belong."

"Stop insulting him," I say tiredly. "Just stop already, Daniel. You should've been—"

I'm out of words. I know he's right; that's the problem. I knew that I was purposefully ignoring all of his attempts, enjoying the attention from him but unsure of what I wanted myself, and then, when Shane came along, nearly sweeping my feet out from underneath me like the long-awaited chivalrous knight, I thought that my decision had been made for me. I'd been praying for so long about it, every night to God about Daniel and what to do about the situation, hoping that my emotions would be cleared and indicated for me, asking for an obvious sign. I'd taken Shane's presence in my life to be the sign that Daniel isn't the one for me; I still believe that.

Don't I?

"Should've been *what*? What were you *waiting* for, Ruth?"

"I was waiting for you to *do* something!" I proclaim hotly, feeling that rush of annoyance blossom outward from a point of origin directly next to my pulsating heart and consuming my lungs, causing them to constrict, the tears hovering at the edges of my lids deciding finally to spill over and join the others upon my flesh. "Just sweep me off my feet, just walk into the classroom one day, or stalk into the barn, and tell me all of this stuff and just — just be out with it! Because contrary to your belief — *contrary* to *your belief*—"

My throat burns, my voice wavering on the edge of insanity. "I'm insecure, too. Insecure and naive and *dumb!*"

"You're not *any* of those things," he states emphatically.

"Yes, I am. You just said it yourself! It's not like I don't hear those things every day from my father!"

His facial expression changes once more, removing the stoicism and replacing it with something much worse: comprehension. The illumination of his face causes my abdomen to panic, my stomach to twist itself into unmanageable knots, and I take a step backward, reaching outward for the counter - and my finger slips on the edge of the wooden counter. A small cry of pain and a staring at the accosted appendage renders me speechless; on top of all this fighting, all of this unnecessary fighting, I've now acquired a large splinter, nestled into the fingerprint of my right middle finger, a bead of blood appearing at the bottom of it, slowly dripping downward.

Immediately, he is there before me, taking the injured hand into both of his own and cradling it there as though it were the most valuable of treasures. His eyes flicker in-between the wooden sliver that has attacked my finger, the moss-green hue of my irises, and the swell of my lips; it's the latter action that causes a rush of unmeasurably pleasurable warmth to wash over me and drown me in its wake. His gaze remains there for longer than should be appropriate, but my body and my mind, as much as I try to deny it, is addicted to him, addicted to his gazes and his touch, and I want him. Shane isn't satisfying. He never has been. And now, I truly understand why. Now I want to acknowledge this, whatever this has been and is and will be.

"No, you aren't." he says softly.

I stare down at the dot of blood that is swirling in upon itself like a reversed whirlpool, hardening and clotting around the small opening created in the skin by the splinter. His thumb traipses over the wound, the short fingernail digging at the wood and consequently extracting it, as it had not pierced the skin too deeply - and then one of his hands, quick as a light, darts up to my chin and clasps it in-between his thumb and forefinger, lifting it so that I'm forced to look nowhere else except for the flames of irises that simmer right back at me, that are dilated and brilliant, that penetrate my being and reveal to his mind my innermost thoughts and desires - one of which, according to how my body reacts, how I tremble and quiver into him, how my lips shakily allow a breath to be inhaled, how my eyelids flutter and my eyelashes tick together, seems to be him.

"Do you mean it?" He whispers in my ear, lips brushing along my cheek.

"Do I mean what?" My eyes are the ones who can no longer find a resting place now. They wander as a nomad travelling from the ends of the earth, wanting to locate a home and unable to do so because all of the places she views are breathtaking.

"That you wanted me to do something about it." It's the

shortened version of my elongated, somewhat passionate explanation.

I nod.

The hand on my chin slides up the right side of my face, pressing the palm along my cheek, the fingers splaying out around my earlobe, the thumb rubbing at the dark, deep circle under my eye, wiping away what remnants of tears stick to the flesh.

"Do you *still* mean it?"

The slight twitch downward of my eyebrows indicates my bewilderment. He clarifies. "Do you still want me to do something about it?"

All of the saliva has dissolved from my mouth. My tongue presses against the roof of my mouth in a poor attempt to formulate some. I swallow with such a ferocity that I feel as though someone has forced me to pinch my nostrils closed and let a rock slide down into my stomach, where it promptly sinks and causes the organ to convulse as it ties itself into intricate knots. A relentless heat spreads through my limbs and causes my toes to curl into themselves. The hand upon my face moves backward and entwines itself into the gnarled strands that make a crooked constellation on my head. Again, he's awaiting for me to answer, and I can do one of two things: I can continue on with the thought patterns that I previously expressed myself, or I can completely contradict every single thing that I just said to him in vehemence. It all depends on what I want to do, and what I actually mean. And while of course, the first option is the ideal one, it isn't the most appealing. I try to open my mouth further, to create syllables with them, but they are frozen in the position of being half-parted in shock. I try to remove myself from his hands, but instead, my head moves backward, tentatively enjoying the contact as I feel those calloused, hardened fingers winding about and reaching through the mass of waves to the skin of the scalp, which tingles upon contact and sends a shooting, sudden spike of adrenaline and undeniable pleasure through my veins. My body is betraying me even though my mind is fighting against it, and I know it'll only be a matter of time before my brain clicks into proper synchronisation with the rest of me and I stop battling against it at all.

"Yeah." The word comes out alongside a whimper and a rather breathy sigh, one that turns the corners of my lips upward.

He's paralysed. *"Do you mean it?"*

The more times that he chooses to phrase that question to me and await the answer makes me want to be the one to stop talking and do something about it. My head rests heavily in his palm as my eyelids flutter open and shut, eyes searing as my mouth parted a little further, my hands pressing against the broadness of his chest, and I am surrounded in a drapery of seductive heat as I quietly exhale. I look up at him and I nod.

Argument forgotten, boyfriend forsaken, ideals and morals thrown out the window, more than in just the heat of the moment, but in the utter buildup that had been aiming toward this confrontation occurring at all. His fingers curl in my hair, the immobility departs from him, and with a swell of breath that causes his chest to inflate, to emit a sound that makes me fear he's about to explode as well, he tightens his grip, bringing me as close to him as can possibly be. My heart sinks directly into my gut, pounding a furious incantation against the wall of my stomach, as an arm is threaded about my waist and using its strength to pull me upward, to lift my feet from the ground, to press my backside onto its new resting spot on top of the wooden table.

The wood creases into the skin of my upper back thigh, but I'm quickly distracted, my eyes moving this way and that to catch each of the motions he smoothly executes. He shifts forward, a hand moving to slip up the skin of my left thigh, pushing against it so that my legs part. The touch leaves a burning trail of gooseflesh in its wake, automatically causing my legs to reach for him and mould themselves around his hip bones. My ankles cross at the small of his back, one knee slightly higher than the other as I bend backwards, but his arm quickly tightens, pushing my waist toward him, our abdomens colliding, my softer one layered over the hardened one beneath it. How those hands seem to be everywhere, searing across my flesh, finally one of them gripping the nape of my neck and pulling my head upward, our mouths so incredibly close together that when he speaks, I feel him tugging ever so slightly on my swollen bottom lip, I can't understand.

"Do you *still* mean it?"

Now it's his words that come out in a breathless whisper, and I don't hesitate this time —– I find that the ability to ponder over my thoughts has been ripped from me and discarded in a thousand pieces across the barren landscape that is my logic. I nod, somewhat furiously. I know what he means. I know what he's asking - if at the end of the day, when I'm face-to-face with Shane, will the words that I've spoken still hold such a significance to me then as they do now, in this current moment of time? I find that I can't halt the nodding until I feel the tips of his fingers dig into the tender skin of my neck, and I move forward, wincing into him against the slightly disconcerting sensation of those short nails, those callused fingerprints, implanting themselves on sacred ground, our mouths colliding in something akin to an explosion, my limbs awash with adrenaline and my arteries vibrating in contentment.

Something distant whispers that I shouldn't be doing this, but the problem is that it feels so incredibly correct, so fitting to the situation, to the timeline of events that have stretched in-between us, both bringing us closer to one another and shredding us apart as one would a failed exam. Shane's hands don't make me burn wildly underneath their roughened touch. Shane's lips don't render me without breath in my lungs, without a pulse, without life; they don't force me to be reliant upon the mouth and air of another in order to gain sustenance. Shane doesn't make me feel.

Those fingernails bite and scrape against the base of my scalp as their shells trap themselves around the thicket of sepia, snarling together branches of hair to mould them into riotous knots. His mouth slants across my own, his alternate palm welding itself to the indentation of my waist, that delicate dip between the ribcage and the pelvic bone which previously only one hand had been allowed access to. But Daniel had taken that accessibility one step further than the person before him, and I shiver closer to him, sealing us completely together, removing all spaces in-between our bodies when I feel his hand dancing directly on the bare flesh of my waist and my abdomen instead of skirting over the camisole I wore.

I think that I say something, perhaps his name or a term of endearment, but the syllables succumb to the ministrations of his teeth against my bottom lip as they tug outward and, consequently, upward, releasing it so that he might hover, with an impish smile, away from my face, peering intently at my features and observing my reactions. I barely have enough of a moment to properly inhale before he layers that mouth over mine once more, immediately deepening the kiss, generating friction that sparked and ignited and made my hands slide up his forearms, taking the sleeves of the shirt with me, fingertips tracing against his flesh and causing the same amount of goosebumps to appear upon the tanned surface as had been budding on mine.

I didn't cause Shane to do this. Ever. Not even in the beginning of the relationship when all of this physical nonsense officially started. I've never had this effect on anybody of the male species in my entire life, and the fact that when my fingertips dart across him, he openly reacts, he isn't afraid to inhale sharply and push his mouth more firmly against my own, or part my lips in order to explore what is offered to him - it's all quite overwhelming to me.

"Oh, *Ruth*," I hear him whisper, bringing me out of my own head, and I peek up at him through sticky eyelashes as he positions his hands back on my face, his thumbs swiping at the tears that have fallen without my notice. "Don't cry. It's going to be all right. I'm here."

I'm here. He had been there during the nightmare and when I awakened. He has been there through my sadness and contentment, confusion and understanding, contradictions and hypocrisies, best and worst, highest and lowest. And none of these things that he has experienced, sometimes so painfully that it was as though I had taken the serrated blade upon which our relationship has balanced ever since we were children and finally decided to plunge it into the weak pulsating organ that was his splitting heart, have changed that. I'm here.

The pair of hands that reaches out belongs to me now, sliding across the sides of his face and lacing over the top of his scalp, my fingers snarling the golden field of his hair, and it is he who emits the wild gasp, the uncontrollable release of air, as I close the distance between us and cause our mouths to become acquainted, for it has been many a night since I have envisioned them meeting and now, that it finally was occurring, I'm uncertain that I want it to cease. How scintillating it is to admit these things to myself. How incredibly careless and reckless and foolish it is to let myself feel these things, and not care. Not care one little bit about the repercussions.

How could I have ever let myself be with someone other than the man who stood before me with his hands overwhelming me and his mouth an intoxication to my muddled senses, with the lips like morphine and the skin like fire, with the heart that beat pure in his chest and the blood that raced hot in his veins? I couldn't possibly understand it, not when I realise how much I haven't been experiencing while with the person that I supposedly am in love with and think I want to be with for the rest of my life. He tugs me closer with the side of my camisole, and my legs tighten around him, my right knee grazing upward along his ribcage as he leans me slightly backward, making a small sound of contentment when I become malleable for him.

You're making out with a guy who isn't your boyfriend.

You little slut.

The voice causes me to experience a miniature seizure, one that has me tear myself away from the toxicity of his mouth and lurch forward, wincing against the grating texture that scraped against the sides of my skull and threatened to provide me with one of the most massive migraines ever known. Unlike Shane, however, Daniel doesn't mistake this as a fit of passion, and he immediately pulls back, away from me, his hands still plastered on my waist and my hair, but concern overriding the rest of the feelings being portrayed upon his face.

The position of his lips and the movement of his throat indicate that he's preparing to comment or ask a pointed question, but upon further perusal of my flushed cheeks, the internalised struggle playing out upon my face as shadows on the wall, he swallows, his eyes hardening as they stare relentlessly down at me. His words have solidified as tumours on his tongue, which had so painstakingly been exploring previously forbidden territory not thirty seconds ago. Already I find myself starting to long for the sensation of him upon me, smothering me with his essence and his smell, erasing that which had been implanted as a now unwanted sedative into my bloodstream. But the both of us are frozen in the iceberg, staring with widened, unblinking eyes back at one another from across the fissure forming between us.

"It's going to be all right," he repeats with more firmness, though now it sounds as if he's also trying to convince his own head. "I'll take responsibility for this."

"*No,*" is my automatic answer. "You've been enough of a martyr for me and my choices. Besides, it doesn't matter."

"It *does* matter. Even though we try to ignore it."

I become adamant, furiously shaking my head back and forth, pursing my lips until their fullness, their swollen state, disappears into a thin line, and I take his face in my hands, my fingertips gripping at the skin and pulling down slightly, giving him the appearance of frowning. "It won't matter after today."

His eyes turn dark as his brows hood over them, his head canting to the side as he thought over the single sentence that I had offered him, and I sit here, with my legs still wrapped around his waist, keeping him pulled to me, my spine pressed against the surface of the counter, the hand on my waist absentmindedly drawing little circles with his thumb on the exposed skin there, waiting with bated breath until he either asks me for further clarification or ends up figuring it out himself. Slowly, he ponders, and as the flashes of softness indicate that he is, indeed, able to decipher what I meant, I see taking residence that hope that I initially had wanted to crush beneath the weight of my feet, how his skin almost glows and his eyes illuminate as if thrown on by a switch. There's a feverish eagerness when he wraps both hands in my hair, releasing my face and my waist, an insatiable hunger as he pulls me upward by the back of the scalp, keeping me against him, and the optimism in his expression is a sickening blow to the abdomen.

But I'm not playing games this time. I'm not manipulating him into giving me these looks so that I might feel loved and cherished by someone. I mean it. I mean what I'm implying. I mean that I'm going to be breaking up with Shane, and I'm going to be with the person who's always understood me better than anybody else in the world.

I don't know why I didn't think of this before. Perhaps it was because he and I have grown up with one another through all sizes and ages, and Shane was nothing more than a new toy, a plaything with a shiny exterior, a means of curing the edge of curiosity running through my veins. Thinking upon it, realising the harsh words that come forth in both my exhaustion and my uncharacteristic brutal honesty, is an odd thing indeed to endure, for recently I had been thinking of the different dresses, affordable of course, that I would be able to wear on the special day when Shane and I were wed for all of eternity and I was so content that I would practically dance down the aisle to him. But as long as Daniel's in the picture, that's not going to happen. I would trudge down the walkway instead, face flushing hot and stammering out the words until the fear overtakes me and forces me to run out into the wilderness, being unable to go through with the ceremony. None of my family, my brother or Daniel, would have to be concerned with shooting their hands up into the air, standing on two feet, and shouting about their rejections of the union; by the time the preacher reached that point in the middle of the rituals, I would be halfway to Mexico.

"Do you—?" His hands yank my face upwards, a little rougher than the usual contact that he uses with me, in order to better peer at the play of emotions, to look into the irises that simmer with an unspoken plan and a fierce exhaustion. I can feel sleep coming back over me, removing myself from the current moment, whisking away my head, causing my thoughts to mould over one another and infuse themselves with morphine. "Are you—you're going to—?"

I lean forward, somewhat sleepily, and I press my lips against his to silence him. He realises this is what I'm doing, and while he entertains my kiss for a few precious seconds, still he gently pushes my face away from his. "Don't make promises you won't keep."

"I'm going to keep this one," is what I tell him, more calmly than I've ever felt in making a decision before. "It's been bound to happen anyway."

Someone can be strung along as a broken puppet for only so long before they make the decision to take a knife and sever the strings in order to walk on their own. Daniel's wondering whether he should remain attached and repair himself, or cut off the ties now before either of us delve deeper into this freshly opened can of worms. He chews on the skin of his lower lip as he continues looking down at me, unable to glance anywhere else, it seems, as he thinks, long and hard, as the silence stretches before us as a densely shaded wood loaded with brambles and shards of glass.

Then, he nods. Slowly, at first. Hesitant. Each movement seems to take a century, each curving of the tendons in his neck microscopic, the unshed emotion quivering with increased instability in the reddened whites of his eyes. He is making a step forward, delicately placing one of his feet into the array of slivers and thorns that await to tear into his skin. He's peeling back the layers of the forestry and allowing the calluses in his palms to take the brunt of the pressure against the spindly obstructions that scar the branches and leaves. Then, his footsteps speed up, he ignores the pain shooting through his flesh, he presses onward. He's made his decision as I have.

"You're sure," he says, reassuring the both of us. "There's no doubt in your head, right? You're—you're actually going to do it."

I nod once.

"You're going to break up with Shane."

His tone's so incredulous that it causes the nape of my neck to bristle as a wolf's would upon being discovered while hunting for prey. Annoyance is plain as the daytime on my features as I grit the enamel off the backs of my two top front teeth and jerk my head up and down, a curter nod than the one before it.

"And you're finally going to be with me."

The situations and the tales that unfold in my head, portrayed through detailed images and snippets of sounds, cause my heart to skip several beats. But there's no way that I will let my head entertain those thoughts for longer than the couple of seconds it took for them to chase themselves across the road and out of sight. I hadn't done that with Shane, and I wasn't going to be breaking up with him to turn around and give away the one irrevocable thing that couldn't be brought back to another man. Even if I were much more comfortable with the thought of Daniel being the receiver of that gift, that's precisely what it was to me, something sacred that needed to be exchanged at the correct time and not in the heat of passion nor in a move of desperation nor directly after something so scarring as a breaking up of relations. The last thing I wanted to do was to start having it as a coping mechanism, and considering how addiction seems to run in my family, I am unwilling to even take the chance unless I know that it would be a forever ordeal. The only way I'll know that, in my head, despite all the things these boys are saying and doing, is if there's a ring on my finger and vows already exchanged.

A resounding laugh, much to my embarrassment and chagrin, awakens me back from the slumped-over position I've obtained. "Someone's tired."

"We spent all night fighting," I grumble. "What do you expect?"

His grip softens on my shoulder blades and he starts rubbing them, his hands moving expertly back and forth on the half-bared skin, which elicits a long, contended hum from the rear of my throat.

"I'm sorry," he says softly. "I really am. I didn't—but it's all better now."

I lean into him. I'm so tired. Of everything.

"Come on. Time to go night-night."

I reach out blindly for him, and somehow, my right hand lands on a slightly familiar wooden structure, a carving made for someone more than a friend and not yet quite a lover. I grasp it as he begins ushering me toward the corridor that will lead upward into the main area of the barn, where we apparently are going to be collapsing in the middle of a bale of hay, and I bring it to my chest, pressing it against the throbbing, halting heart beneath the bone.

"I love you, Babe Ruth."

"I love you, too."

There is a distinct heat that accosts me from all sides, and I soon find myself drifting through that bed of wheat once more, that golden field with the comically azure sky stretching above me - but this time, I am not chained to the invisible corpses underneath the layers of overturned, decaying soil. I am lying next to someone who has taken my hands and rubs the soreness from the welts upon the wrists.

The world is warm.

A fire burns within me, and it cannot be extinguished.

Solitary Connection to Shackles

October 9th
Manchester, Indiana

Paul Reagan

I have an itch that cannot be scratched.

No, really, because I just reached up with my hand, and I ended up knocking myself in the forehead with an empty bottle of beer.

What in the hell happened last night?

-

You know when you wake up with those words that it was either the best time of your life, with lots of memories made that you'd never want to relive; or it was another night of drinking by yourself in a hay loft.

Since I'm a thousand percent sure there wasn't a party last night, and if there was, I once again managed to not attend, it's the latter. I need to quit making a habit out of this. I don't want it to become a problem. But I can't help that the only way I can seem to get a break, take a breather, relax for a minute is withdrawing at a certain time of the night to climb into this hayloft with a six-pack and start consuming the drinks until I fall asleep—

Or, you know, pass out from too much drinking and not enough eating.

I really need to not make a habit of this.

-

I don't know how many times I'm going to pass back out before my head finally decides to wake up. There's no sunlight yet, though. So I don't think I have much to worry about at the moment.

-

Lord in heaven, I swear, each time my brain removes itself from the toxic fog surrounding it, the pounding in my temples worsens.

-

I don't know who I am or where I am.

-

Did I ever know any of these things? I can't remember.
I can't remember a damn thing.

-

There's a throbbing cadence in my head, uneven as it bounds against the walls of my skull and echoes through my ears. My temples pulsate along with it. Caged prisoners throwing themselves against the iron bars of their cells, screaming and rattling and shaking their chained fists at me. I wince against their voices and block them out as quickly as I can manage, which taking into consideration the sluggish train churning through the railroads of my thoughts translates *quickly* into *without success*. I reach upward, and it ends in a similar fashion to the first time when I went for my forehead; except this time around, the heavy bottom of the bottle collides with my right eye, and my wrist decides that it wants to give out completely on me, sagging and pressing the cold glass into the tender socket. It's like I'm trying to put a cold compress on a black eye, except all I'm doing is making it worse.

A horse neighs from somewhere below me, and a couple of cows low in response, their grumbles causing the foundation of the barn to reverberate, or so it seems. I withhold a groan as I toss the glass bottle away from me; my aim must be all right even when my eyes are tightly shut and slightly swollen, as there is no loud crashing as it shatters against the wooden planks of the loft, but rather a soft, almost nonexistent thud as it collides in the middle of a large pile of hay. A little smirk takes up residency on my mouth as I finally put both now-free hands on my face and rub at the features there, massaging the nose, the sore eyelids, the banging temples, the clammy, sweat-streaked forehead. Ah, damn, that feels good: stretching out the taut ligaments and rubbing through the tender spots of the flesh.

Then, something explodes directly next to my right ear, and I shout a few choice words that I won't mention as my right hand clenches into a fists and strikes out quick as a cobra, connecting with something soft and plushy that squawks and squabbles in protest as it flies off the side of the railing that blocks the hay loft from open air and glides down to the barn floor below. That rooster. I swear, I can't tell you how many times I've just wanted to take my shotgun down from off the wall and blow off its damn head. It'd be better off as stringy meat on our plates than being alive and annoying the living daylights out of me.

But then, I have to remind myself, somewhat forcefully, that the rooster, so affectionately named 'Dublin', is fawned over and completely, one hundred percent adored by my mother, and the last thing that I need is for her to plummet back into a downward spiral, sink into that terrifying mindset that caused her to withdraw from us and have to be committed to the asylum. The last thing that this family needs is a mother who sinks back into herself when she's just managed to get better with home therapy because that place would reduce her into nothing more than an emotionless husk that stared off into space and didn't know nor want to know how to function in everyday life, merely be content to slouch in a wheelchair with a slightly parted mouth and let the remainder of her years waste away into the daylight horizon.

I feel better now. I rant sometimes. Sorry.

But people irk me. Like, really.

I'm better off alone. Not like anybody gets me anyways.

I want to open my eyes and look around, but a beam of light streams through one of the open, second-story and hits me directly on the face. I groan again, rolling away from it and flopping out of the makeshift chair that I created using bales of old, nasty straw and layering ancient, musty-smelling horse blankets on top of in order to create a comfortable relaxation space. I drop onto the floor like a sack of potatoes, jarring my muscles and my joints together in a painful discord that causes me to half cry out in anguish and half cuss in frustration at my own lethargy and tendency to sleep in positions that rendered me stiff-legged as a newborn foal.

Something snuffles near my ear and places its black, moist noise into the tangle of my hair, whining softly as a front paw comes out and smacks me on the cheek, gripping much like a person's hand would. I groan and push at the chest of the dog who's somehow managed to get up in this loft - nothing is making sense to me right now, maybe I carried him up here with me last night, anything's possible at this rate - but he persists, his small whine turning into a full-fledged yawn, accompanied by a miffed bark, directly in the ear where the rooster had attempted to crow his own version of the morning song. "Get off, Moe." I think someone's poured half the gravel from the driveway down my throat, my voice is so dry. "Get off."

But the dog won't get off, not until I place a hand in the middle of his back, clasping at the bundles of coarse fur that come with being a sheepdog. Then, he decides to lay on me, sprawling across my abdomen and pressing my spine against the slats of the floor, panting heavily even though it's not hot. He's an old man, though, just turning sixteen this year; it's no wonder he's overheating, simply because of the amount of fur that's sprouted on him like an uncontrollable grass seed. The sound of his hot breath emerging from his throat resembles a locomotive speeding through a station, and I wince away from that as well, the throbbing in my head transforming into an unwanted, full-fledged migraine. I push my forehead against the unwelcoming wood and exhale as softly, as slowly, as I can manage.

This is just not a good way to end the week. Why the hell had I been up here in the hay loft, drinking myself into oblivion? Why do I even bother with it, when it makes me feel like this afterward, lethargic and irritated at every noise?

Because there's a reason behind it. It's the only way in the world that I can relax these days. The only way that my muscles lose their tension and my fingers uncurl from fists, the only way that the temper inside of me is soothed into compliance. The only way that my thoughts calm down and don't let me ponder over the same topics over and over again until they're well past the stage of being exhausted, die, then are resuscitated and milled around until they've been battered beyond dust. You know, the words that my father says to me multiple times, as if I didn't hear them the first time that he roars them at me from across a patch of watermelons: *You better get your act together, Paul!*

Not sure how I can get it together more than I already have. I mean, somehow without being superhuman and constantly injecting myself with antidotes that make me invincible to kryptonite, I've managed to continue getting high marks in school, putting myself at the top of the graduating class; rise at five in the morning each day, though most of the time even earlier, in order to do the majority of the work and the chores that come with living on one of the biggest ranches in the state; and attend enough soccer practices to make me think that sometimes my legs are about to fall off. I'm well-rounded, I'm not being distracted by girls or going to parties and waking up in random people's houses - I'm not sure exactly what more he wants from me.

Except, you know, to actually turn into some sort of mutant with superpowers.

I need to get up. I know that I need to get up.

I need to stop laying here and thinking about things that do nothing except flood my veins with an unnecessary amount of annoyance. It's my own fault that I've managed to induce a nasty hangover and I'm the only one that should have to deal with the consequences. I'm not going to let Ruth get in trouble because I ended up being the one who couldn't rouse himself from his stupour. It's always up to me to wake her up in the mornings. Mom's basically incapacitated, and I don't want her to have more burdens than she already has to bear. (And it's not like Dad's going to walk in and make sure she's woken up. He has the infamous attitude of "If the kids don't get up on time, not my fault if they miss school.")

If only he could understand that we're not anywhere near the level of perfection that he is. (But I mean, if I got a dollar for every time that I wished for that, I'd be swimming in that green — the green of a rich man! — instead of the one induced by nauseous envy.)

Moe whines again, and I take that as my warning that I need to really get up and moving. It's not exactly a good sign that I feel sunlight on my face. Though I'm honestly probably imagining that - and when I open my eyes, the lids slowly retracting as I use one hand in a makeshift visor pressed against my forehead, I see that my instinct's correct. There's no light on my face; it's actually the figure of the full moon still hanging somewhat high up in the sky. Don't know how my brain registered that as sunlight, but I'm not going to ask a lot of questions that have no answers. Can't waste any more time. Have to focus. Focus, Paul, get your ass in gear, and all that.

I start running through the list of chores that need to be done while staring upward at the round moon that's there, hanging somewhat half-heartedly, as though it's slowly growing exhausted and wanting to drop from the sky. I'm going to need to let out the horses and the cows into their allotted pastures. Make sure that their water troughs are full. I'll have to feed the chickens and check for eggs, see who's missing, and unfortunately check over that rooster to make sure that he isn't injured. Go through the garden and make sure nothing needs to be picked last-minute; the crops decided to come relatively late this year. Go through the fields and do the same thing. Make sure there's no barbed wire sticking out anywhere, no broken fence posts. Put the slop into the pigs' buckets. Check on Mom's incredibly pampered pet peacock - yeah, she owns both the rooster and the peacock. Should probably work the horses, too; some of them have been getting arrogant. But the horses are Ruth's territory; I only personally own one out of the seven we have. I don't know what it is about animals taking to her. It's like she's freaking Mother Nature or something.

I'm just glad she isn't one of those sisters that expects me to do all the work and that she actually helps me out, you know? Because I know someone at school who, like, has a younger sister, and all she does is sit on her ass, watch as it gets larger, and read really badly written romance novels until she's drowning in her own tears and melted chocolate and has to stuff her eyes back in her head with tissues.

I really don't understand people.

I put my hands on the wooden planks, though I have to adjust my left hand because it lands in the middle of Moe's plushy body, and I push myself upward, gritting my teeth against the strong jab that shoots through my forehead and attacks my temples, causing them to go completely numb as all the blood starts rushing there to deal with the pain. I blink furiously against the blurriness that suddenly invades my vision, and I black out, feeling the side of my head collide against the floor, though I soon am awakened by a wet tongue all over my face and a loud, raucous barking. God, you'd think that I was in a metal box with this damn dog instead of in a wide open barn, with the way that it echoes in my ears and rattles my bones where they sit. I shove him away again as I furiously shake my head back and forth, not as a hung-over man but a stallion attempting to rid his face of the pesky green flies swarming him in the heat of the day, and I position myself onto my hands and knees, allowing my head of dark hair to drop forth, pressing the crown of my skull against the wood and groaning. How much did I drink last night?

The answer to my question soon comes to me. I raise my head slightly, my stomach heaving as I try to inhale the smells of the barn - the freshness of the cut hay next to my left hand, the mustiness of the planks my palms press against, that aroma that comes with the sweat and body heat of horses and cattle, and the wet dog wafting from Moe's fur which tattles that he's been jumping in the ponds again. I see it, then. I see the line of beer bottles there, positioned with all their labels facing me, mocking me. Bud Light. Corona. Miller Light. Looks like it doesn't matter. Looks like I also have no preference, damn, the least I could do is drink good beer.

But those aren't the problems that make my heart skip a beat. It's the one that I see positioned against the area where the stacks of square bales begin, pushed against the one that's been cut open and is used to throw down to the cows and horses from up here. It's whiskey. And it's all gone. Entranced, I move forward, still on my hands and knees on the ground, reduced to a snivelling boy instead of an adult male, and my hand grabs for it.

It doesn't have dust on it. I turn it around so that the famous Jack Daniels label is facing me, and I stare at it. I don't have to look too hard at the beer bottles lined up like trophies to know that at least four or five of them have been recently handled. While that's nothing in the bigger picture - considering there are around thirty or thirty-five lined up along that ledge - it's too much for one night.

I usually only let myself have one beer or a fourth of-a bottle of hard liqueur. What the hell happened to make me drink four beers and an entire bottle of whiskey?

Oh, *right*. We got into an argument about c o l l e g e.

I don't want to talk about that. But it's a good reason to get drunk, at least.

I shove myself upward with a tremendous heave as I position myself on my knees, torso still quite wobbly. Mo decides this is the best opportunity to start walking circles around me, one of his dark eyes trained on the side of my face as his mouth opens and his tongue lolls out, as his nails click against the wood and his tail threatens to go erect like a flag on the highest point of the pole. I can do this. I've been making it for almost nineteen years; I think I can continue making it until I at least get up and find my dignity wherever I managed to drop it last - which was in the bottle, but I digress. I mean, my fingers obviously aren't small enough to fit in the neck of the liqueur, too callused and long, but maybe I'll be able to turn the bottle upside-down and dump my dignity, my pride, back out. Because a nice-sized chunk has been taken out from it.

The old sheepdog pushes himself against me, whimpering his own set of complaints, and I grasp the fur on his back with hard fingers. He doesn't seem to mind the rough contact; he allows me to use him as leverage in order to get my feet underneath me, soles flat on the ground where they need to be, and start standing up like a normal person. My knees are trembling with the effort to support the remainder of my weight, and I bend in half, continuing to push against his sturdy form as I swallow, a cold sweat breaking out on my forehead.

What the hell am I doing to myself? I really shouldn't have drunk that much, even though I was stressed. I'm not an alcoholic; I don't need to be acting like one. (Though the booze doesn't treat my bloodlines right.) What would Dad say if he were to come up here and do the hay himself, seeing those bottles lined up like figures for target practice? What would Ruth say if she found out that I'd drunk myself into oblivion? What if I hadn't woken up early enough?

All of these possible scenarios want to bombard me all at once, and as my mind has this annoying tendency to do whatever it wants, of course, all the situations are there, obvious and pertinent and rearing their ugly heads as they shout at me to pay attention to them, to think about them until I drive myself completely bonkers. I push my hands against my ears, as if that'll help, and I grimace against them, causing a blinding pain to shoot across my skull, from one side to the other, like laser beams until they die away.

It seems to have eliminated them for now.

Moe's tail is wagging back and forth, and he's peering at me with eyes that beg me to let him down from off this deathtrap of a hay loft. I'm not sure exactly how I managed to get him up here in the first place; as it were, I bend over in half and I wrap my arms around him, hauling him so that he's over my shoulder like a sack of potatoes. It's not too difficult for him to remain situated there, either, considering the lean mass of his body moulds to the crook of my neck and refuses to allow him to move as I walk, though I keep one hand pressed against his back for good measure. Sure, last night was probably awful, and the day that influenced me to intoxicate myself wasn't anything to write home about, but that didn't mean that this one, this Friday, had to be terrible. It was, after all, October; and every Friday in October, Daniel, my best friend, the guy who lives across the street (who I've known since I was little and called *Scarecrow* because he was always skinnier than a half-rotted corpse and sometimes I wondered if he had hay stuffed into his skull where his brain was supposed to be) and I would be going hunting tonight with our bows and arrows.

It isn't shotgun season yet, but that doesn't stop us; we're those two boys who go through the forests with war paint smothered all over our faces in different patterns and practise our bird calls until we're blue in the face. I think one time we even pinned feathers in our hair in makeshift headdresses; courtesy of my sister, of course, considering I didn't know how to work a bobby pin or a clip to save my life. (Still don't. Barely understand hairbrushes. Who needs that when I can just run my hands through it and get the same effect?)

I make my way through the hedge maze of stacked hay bales with a dog panting in my ear, moving this way and that to avoid the numerous cobwebs and dangling spiders which have taken up residency in the corners of the rafters and in the middle of the carved walkway. Still one manages to disassemble itself from its sticky house and implant its body in the middle of my clammy forehead. I grimace as it tiredly starts crawling upward, wanting to burrow in my nest of hair, and I reach for it, swiping at it until the small body crumples underneath my palm, reduced to nothing more than a crushed exoskeleton and half-twitching, half-severed legs.

Any other day, I probably would've screamed like a little girl. I *hate* spiders. And I mean, not those little ones that hang in the corner of your bedroom - whatever, I mean, they can make pretty big webs but they aren't obnoxious in size and most of the time, you don't really notice them. But these big ones in the barn, the ones the size of half-dollars with more fur than a horse's winter coat and long legs that grab at you as you walk by - those sons of guns need to die. Every single one of them. And guess who has the job of coming in here with the Bug-B-Gon and soaking down the cobwebs, the numerous large egg sacs, and the devils themselves. Yeah, me.

Who else? Ruth? She just runs from them. God love her.

I reach the near-vertical ladder that leads down from the loft onto the floor, and I cautiously peer over the ledge. The last time I didn't look down before I started descending, the bull had managed to open the gate which separates this small area from the rest of the barn, and was standing at the base of the ladder. (Staring up at me as I climbed down, of course, like the lout he was.) I didn't realise that an animal was down there until I heard it trumpet a challenge to me, and let me tell you something, I've never climbed back up so quickly in my life. I think I was sixteen at the time that this happened, and that bull has long since keeled over and died from some sort of shock to the heart, but still, that memory has imprinted itself so heavily in my head that there's no way I'm *not* looking down at the ground before I put my feet there.

I inhale and hold the breath in my lungs as I stand upright and put the dog higher up on my shoulder, tightening my grip on him. I don't necessarily get afraid of heights, but they aren't exactly my best friend, either; my insides start to burn with the effort as I slowly bend, extending a foot outward until I feel the sole of my boot - which I'm surprised is still on - form itself around the rung underneath it. I can do this. A little bit of panic seizes me; I can't see where I'm going. Don't be such a loon, Paul; you just looked where you were going, and you don't need to look back down at it again because you already looked once. Just get down the freaking ladder.

Okay, maybe I'm a *little bit* more nervous around heights than I want to admit. It's the whole thing with spiders, though. I know that there are things that need to be done around here, and I know that I'm the one who usually gets stuck doing them.

I quickly exhale, and the dog whines in my ear.

"Yeah, I get it, Moe," I grumble, using my free hand to grasp at the edge of the loft, temples throbbing with an inconsistence to rival that of a teenaged girl making decisions. I wince against the unevenness of the tribal drums in my head and continue meandering my way down the ladder, though I have to cling tighter to the dog when he gets frightened by the sudden lowing of a cow beneath us. I have that distinct sinking feeling in my stomach, the twisting of my gut into several individual knots, the one that signifies that this morning and this day is not going to be one that I want to remember. Just not going to be a good day. I mean, what day is, when you start it out blacked-out drunk?

There's a clock somewhere down in this area, I think, on a half-broken table. We keep it there so that we can duck in and check the time when we're out and about in the fields. The current step of the ladder that I'm on trembles a bit underneath the combined weight of my body and Moe's, and I freeze, seizing the side of the ladder. "I have no idea how I managed to get you up there last night," I grumble, half-heartedly wheezing as I turn my head slightly to the side and peer down to where the ground is, still too far to fall, not close enough for me to feel secure yet. I tend to talk to myself out loud a lot - makes me think that there's company here with me, that someone's hearing what I say, since basically no one else gives a royal care. (Or a non-royal one.)

The ladder shakes again and I hiss in dissatisfaction. Is there some sort of impish ghost that I abandoned at the top, grasping the two legs of the wooden contraption and shaking it back and forth so that I constantly am losing my balance? Ghost-man, I definitely do not appreciate what you're doing up there. Moe lets loose a whine that transforms into something akin to a low howl as I quicken my pace, my feet grasping at the slats as I descend to the pace of the migraine being thrown around in my skull. I concentrate on the pattern created, one foot underneath the other, until I no longer can execute these moves as I have managed to hit solid ground.

Breathing out a sigh of relief, I bend down and allow Moe to be placed safely next to me before I turn to the old-style alarm clock, like one of those with the two bells on top that ring out and blast everyone's eardrums with its obnoxious ding-a-ling, and grasp it in my hands, bringing the broken glass of the clock's face less than an inch away from my eyes so that they might dilate and focus on the numbers and the hands. It's either four-twenty in the morning, or two-forty—or maybe it's three-fifteen. I shake the clock for a split second, and then, a distinct ticking noise, though quieter than the cacophony that arises from the horses, a riot of neighing at the rattling of the clock's internals when I moved it so quickly back and forth, appears.

Oh. The damn thing hadn't even been working. I wonder how long it's been out of order. Probably for a while. It's humorous to me to think that all this time, we've been keeping ourselves in check by haphazardly glancing toward this broken clock on this broken nightstand-type thing and relying on it to tattle to us how many hours we had left in our day or night without ensuring that what it told us was accurate.

Huffing, I place the clock back on the surface of the nightstand and stretch my arms high above my head, clasping them, then moving my shoulders this way and that, the ligaments and tendons popping back into their correct places. It feels so damn good to stretch yourself out like a lithe cat after a midmorning meal. Feels so damn good indeed. And now I think I'm a little bit more prepared for the day than I was before. Now I think that I can face whatever's going to end up clobbering me in the face and worsening the hangover which rapidly settles into my flesh and my eyes.

But first thing's first. I'm going to have to go back to the house to check the time. (You know, I'm thinking we should start investing in watches at this point.) My upcoming actions solely will depend on what the illuminated, green numbers on the microwave read. Because as of right now, I have no idea if I need to be getting my sister up, if I need to be letting out the livestock, if I need to be leaving for a well-deserved vacation in the Bahamas, or if I need to be stripping and collapsing back into the downy comfort of my mattress.

I look over the gate before I unlatch the half-rusted hinge, needing to jiggle it back and forth a couple of times until it loosens, and swing it open. Nothing like navigating a floor filled with massive bodies to wake someone up from a hangover. I push a hand against my forehead and attempt to swipe off some droplets of sweat as I wait for Moe to follow me and then close the gate. Did I do all of my homework for school today? My mind's travelling a thousand miles per hour in-between subjects. I did my chemistry assignment, wrote half of the research paper that has its rough draft due Tuesday, completed that study guide for the World Religions' test we have coming up on Monday - I think we're reviewing that today in class, but I always prefer walking in with it completed and correcting the already-written answers to rushing, penciling them in as they're said, and breaking my lead numerous times, which results in me throwing the pencil down on the desk, where it then proceeds to bounce onto the floor and underneath someone's foot, and that *someone* is, more often than not, one of the more popular ladies in the grade, and her sneer transforms into a weird, flirtatious smile thing as she makes a show out of bending down, reaching for the utensil, picking it up, and handing it back, as though it's some sort of elaborate strip tease.

Yeah, can you tell that this has happened to me before? I don't get it. I don't have time to date. Like, I barely even have time to get hammered by myself in a hay loft, and when I do manage to set aside the hours to do it, I wake up feeling nauseous and worrying that I've forgotten to do something important. The last thing I need is to add the concern of a girlfriend on top of all of these other responsibilities.

Besides, there's no one at that school I would date. Not in my grade or the lower ones. Not a single girl that I would bother putting forth the effort to get to know and attempt to take out, or whatever the process is. There never has been, and since I'm a senior now, there never will be. But I'm actually okay with that.

I endure enough terrible migraines. I don't need the scream of someone who's being neglected, or *think*s they're being neglected, in my ear and adding to it.

The warm streams of breath emerging from the nostrils of sleepy cows accost me as I slowly make my way through the darkened barn, the sliver of moonlight previously pushing itself upon my face like an unwanted admirer having disappeared and left me to my own devices. I have my hands out slightly in front of me; whenever a finger or the side of my hand brushes against something that might be construed as the side of an animal, I move to the opposite side, not wanting to frighten one of the dumber ones and cause a stampede. Though I'm more concerned about Moe being the one to accidentally collide into a cow's legs and causing them to bolt - though from the lack of panting breaths both in front of and behind me, I think it's safe to say he's already sitting outside of the barn with his tail wagging, as waiting for the stupid human to catch up.

I'll take a leaf from his book and roll out through the ditch that's being formed by the erosion of the earth and the splaying sideways of the wooden walls of this barn. It'll save me loads of trouble from being cause by opening the large doors and accidentally letting out the animals before it's their due time, or fussing with the rusted-shut man door in the dark without a flashlight. It isn't a very large ditch, nor a wide one; it's the one that the dogs use to burrow under normally, and no one's bothered to begin filling it in because it's come in handy for us humans as well. I don't even have to look for it; in my blind feeling about with my hands, I forget that my feet also need to be supervised, and the toe of my right foot plunges headlong into a depression of earth.

The rest of me follows in a rather discombobulated manner, my knee twisting and my legs bending in on themselves, my hands absorbing the majority of the impact and elbows locking immediately, teeth rattling and nose buzzing. Nice going, Paul. I mock myself as I force my limbs to continue moving, haphazardly crawling under the wall, hearing a cricket chirp and leap from its position upon a blade of grass as I pass by it, inhaling the richness of the earth as it's overturned by my clawing fingers. You're really continuing to score high on this fine morning.

As expected, Moe has already made his way out through this ditch and is sitting there, tail slowly wagging as he notices me sidling to and fro. A whine emits from his throat.

"Oh, be quiet," I grunt, shimmying my hips when the back of my jeans gets caught on a slice of wood hanging down from the wall. "No one asked you."

Moe didn't really seem to care whether I asked him or not, considering he let loose another ear-grating whine. I glare at him as I pick myself up from off the ground, brushing through the soil and the plant particles which had plastered themselves to me as though reunited with a long-lost lover. The house stands a small distance from this entrance at the end of a dirt path, a silent, shadowed sentinel awaiting my arrival, and I start to follow it, boots thudding against the packed soil, the dog's paws a hundred times quieter than my clodhoppers as he traipses along behind me.

None of the lights are on that I can see from this angle, which means that my absence has henceforth gone completely unnoticed by the other inhabitants of the home, which was a delicate, white thing, plastered upon the landscape and sticking out like a sore thumb, its siding nearly glowing in the reflected moonlight and the shock of the contrast against the otherwise darkened environment. Maybe my streak of luck will continue, and I'll be able to slip in the side door unnoticed. The light to the garage has either been switched off manually or automatically due to no disturbances; as I move from the dirt path on the hillside to where it drops me off in the middle of the gravel driveway up to the concrete pad on the side of the house - and it does the other way as well toward the main road - I drop into a bit of a lower crouch, hunching my shoulders, preparing to scamper like a mouse caught in a trap if the lights spot me. I don't need someone coming out here with a shotgun.

Moe trots ahead of me, and as soon as he hits the sensory area, the lights flick on, bathing everything in their warm glow. I duck behind the bed of my truck and exhale, wincing against the pressure that increases in my head with the quick movement. So much for breaking into the garage door. I'm going to have to head around to the front. Hopefully someone's left that unlocked; I know I certainly didn't fasten the dead bolt. I'm terrible when it comes to that stuff around the house. Ironic, considering I'm such a stickler when it involves locking gates, stalls, barn doors, and making sure that the equipment is safely put away.

I inch my way around the two trucks parked there on the concrete pad, sticking to having my spine pressed against their beds, remaining in the darkness. If only I didn't have this pounding migraine; then I wouldn't have such a problem with rushing forward and darting around the light. But unless I want my brain to explode out of my skull, I'm going to need to be taking things relatively slow. Each forward step I take is precise and deliberate, heel to toe, making sure that no noise emits from the scraping of the textured sole against the concrete, and I manage to avoid the intruding light bulbs, taking the shortcut over the edge of the stairs' landing that leads to the path which winds around the front of the house. Only then do I feel confident enough to walk upright. I've made it past the hardest part. The next will be opening the door without alerting anyone, as my parents' bedroom is the one that's upstairs next to my sister's; I'm stuck down in the rickety basement.

None of the porch lights are illuminated as I pass underneath them, and the screen door has been propped open. Those hinges still need to be oiled, even though Dad promised that he would be the one to do them. Looks like they haven't even been touched; I swear this door has been haphazardly hanging off its fastenings for the past six months. Rolling my eyes - I really should know by now that I'm better off doing everything around here myself, I slip through the gap created and grasp the doorknob to the front door, turning it as slowly as I can manage. It doesn't make too much of a sound, not until I push against it; it swings open, much to my pleasant surprise, but a whoosh of the air escaping from the created vacuum more than likely alerted my parents to my presence.

I stop for a minute. I just realised how much of a moron I am. Like, my room is in the basement, and I leave that door purposefully unlocked. Why in the hell didn't I just go around the side of the house and enter through there? But I had followed my instincts, which had ended up leading me here, and so, I have to be at this place for a reason; and upon taking that moment of pause, it comes to my attention why I might have been directed to go this way.

There's a shuffling noise in the kitchen. An intruder. If I had entered through the basement, I wouldn't have heard the movements upstairs. But now, I can hear them, loud and clear, rushing at me from the end of a tunnel, and I freeze, mind racing through all of the possible solutions and their various consequences after execution. I could duck into Ruth's bedroom and fetch the rifle she keeps propped up on the wall closest to the door, hidden where no one else would see if they were to walk in - but that would involve opening up her door, possibly waking her up and alarming her, not to mention that she kept her ammunition in the drawer of her nightstand. No, I'm going to have to handle this with an old-fashioned touch; I'm going to have to bash the person's head into the edge of the counter.

Once I enter the house, I carefully inch the door backwards until it's nearly closed. If it were to latch in place, then it more than likely would tell the person in the kitchen that someone else was entering after them, and the last thing that I want is this moron, who thinks that he can just waltz into our kitchen and do what he pleases like some god of the planet, to know that I'm onto him. My heartbeat throbs in my ears like the soundtrack to the scene of a film, and I move forward, sidling back into that crouch which I had acquired while outside, reaching out for the bannister and grasping it in my hands as I peeked around it, squinting to better concentrate and dilate my pupils more quickly. There was that zeroing-in sensation, the feeling that the concept of time has halted dead in its tracks, and all of a sudden, the edges of the figure hovering over the counter, its side bathed in the dimmed glow of the under-counter lights which illuminated the counter space near the glaringly white stove, sharpen and allow me to very easily recognise who this person is.

My mother.

Upon further exploration of my surroundings, I note that, directly to my right, the door to the master bedroom has fully swung open, and that one of our cats, a grey furred one who always sleeps with her, currently is meandering out, disturbed by the cacophony of noise created in the kitchen where she stands now. A small meow erupts from her mouth as she reaches her front paws forward and kneads the wooden floor underneath her with her claws. When she approaches my prone form, still frozen in place, and rubs against the right leg of my jeans, I feel, even through the thick, ripped fabric, that she's warm; Mom must've literally just gotten out of bed maybe two or three minutes before I opened the door.

I stand up, feeling how my tendons and muscles stretched outward, and I swallow against the sensations as I move forward, still slowly, because I don't want to startle her, either. She isn't an intruder, not in the least; if there's anyone who deserves to be safe in this house, it's this woman who raised me and my twin sister despite dealing with a ton of personal bullshit that rose up and decided that it was time to cause her unnecessary mental trouble. But she's just been released from that god-awful place on the East coast, or wherever the hell it was. And to be completely honest, I think they did her more harm than good.

"Mom?" I let the word ring out before me, wanting her to be aware that she's no longer in blissful solitude. The cat, rightfully named Smokey, follows along behind me, and the soft padding of her paws against the floor are joined by the clicking from canine toenails. Moe must have pushed open the slightly ajar front door and entered the house, with his snuffling and his sneezing that follows him whenever he comes from the stables. But she doesn't seem to notice any of these things, instead remaining inside of the confines of her own mind, which have embraced her and whispered that she's much safer in the captivity of its arms than in reality.

"Mom?" I say it again. I'm standing by the refrigerator, which is located directly across from where she's standing; I'm in plain sight of her. I'm afraid to ask more, though. I'm afraid to say anything else. I'm walking on eggshells around her. The last thing I want to do is be the one who sets her off. The one who causes her to fly off the handle. Into a rage. Sink back into the throes of depression.

She is in the realm of her own existence as she performs the little rituals she adapted the most recent time that she had been committed. Her frothing, deep auburn waves, a black-brown at the roots from where she dyed the strands and the roots were starting to come out, framed her rather gaunt, reddish-toned face.

If there's one thing she's enjoyed doing, it's involving and raising us in our heritage, almost total immersion in our true origins alongside the Cherokee peoples. She speaks and teaches us the *Tsalagi Gawonihisdi*; she still possesses items from her great-great-grandmother, a medicine woman; she performs the traditional dances and warns us against the spiritual beings that we cannot see but still exist; she has given us names accordingly, second ones which are untranslatable into English. It is during these teachings, the relation of tales regarding her life on the reservation as a girl, the instruction of the dance and the prayers, that I see her the happiest. (And I'll be damned if I allow this to be taken from us.)

It therefore pains me to see, though, that sometimes, even her joy hasn't helped her. In the dimmed light - as she has refused to turn on the overheads - the remnants of white lines that have marred the flesh on the arms, travelling in odd patterns even upon the tender undersides and the rougher bases of her knuckles. That doesn't count the three direct, deliberate ones that had healed with serration and ridges, marring wounds that refuse to fade even after some time away from the blade that made them.

I swallow once, leaning against the side of the refrigerator. She'll acknowledge me when she's ready; for now, I'm going to comfort her with the recognition that if she no longer wants to be wrapped up in the imprisonment of her own mind, that someone would be here to take her hand and bring her out from it. For now, though, she seems content upon her task, which was chopping fruit. She's brought out a cantaloupe, a package of fresh assorted berries, four brilliant red apples, a kiwi, a peach, and two mandarin oranges. She is just starting in, brandishing the clean-edged knife in one hand and arranging over and over the plastic pink cutting board with the other before she managed to straighten it to her liking. Picking up one of the apples, she turns it, this way and that, staring at it with a practised eye from all angles; even in the shadows, those brilliant peridot irises, a shade darker than Ruth's and nowhere close to the colour of my own storm-addled eyes, snap and glow. She delicately places it upon the cutting board, as though it were something more along the lines of an idol to be worshipped instead of a simple piece of fruit, and then, with an unceremonious wave of the knife, removes the core and begins ferociously slicing it.

The logical part of my mind tries to decipher why on earth she'd be up at this hour, whatever the hour is considering I still haven't looked at the microwave or stove clocks with their blaring green numbers, chopping and dicing and slicing until her wrists ached. Then, that small little voice appears and convinces me that logic isn't suitable when it comes to my mother, not after everything she's been through; even though, to be honest, I don't know half of what that might be. I only know the snippets that the psychiatrists bother to tell us and the little morsels that she herself offers.

I want to say something to her. But then again, I don't. So many contradictions and unknowns. So many uneasy feelings I receive merely standing here, watching, as though I am an executioner waiting for the axe to fall.

She looks up at me then, and her eyes register that someone else is in this kitchen besides her own self. Her intake of breath sharpens, and the knife crashes down particularly hard upon the cutting board, but her facial expression doesn't become hostile or annoyed. She merely looks as though she were surprised, as though my presence has finally tugged on her consciousness enough to have her be forced to realise that she can't escape people in this household. Or perhaps that I'm not going to say anything, and that the job falls upon her to begin a conversation if she wants to.

There's a moment that stretches between us when we make eye contact. Even in her delirium and her controversial insanity, her irises are so — **clear.** They *snap* at you. They *peruse* you. They see *everything* you're trying to hide. My sister inherited those eyes from her; and there's only one other person in the entire world who I've met in my years of living who had a pair of those eyes. But they weren't green.

And I'd prefer not to remember their colour right now, thanks.

"Paul?" Her voice isn't as feeble as the bones protruding from her sternum portray her to be. "Why are you awake?"

Now I figure is a good enough time to look over and check out the numbers that are blinking back at me. It's currently three in the morning; too early to be awake, too late to collapse onto the downy comfort of my mattress. Seven minutes after three, to be exact.

"I—" Her acute stare causes my resolve to waver. I swallow once, falling silent.

She continues watching me as she finishes slicing the apple and proceeds to turn the knife the other way, leaning slightly over the counter, mussed waves darting forward from where they were perched behind her shoulders. "You—?"

There's that quiet again.

"I see," she says, nodding as though I've explained myself.

"Mom—"

"I noticed the whiskey was missing," is her abrupt interjection as she jerkily motions toward the door behind me with her chin. "You don't have to tell me things I already know."

"You've been practising those *observance techniques*, I see."

It had been nothing more than a generic statement, perhaps a way to plunge the conversation forward, to see if I would be able to get anywhere - but it was more than likely one of the worst topics I could've chosen, and I realised that directly after I uttered the words. I purse my lips, as though that will get rid of the fact that they hang in the air like drying stalagmites, and she slams down the blade of the knife in a particularly hard chop that sends little bits of apple flesh flying across the counter. I wince, a sheepish expression coming over my face as she jabs the knife at me, using it as a tool of gesture.

"I don't need *observation techniques* to know my own son, Paul. It's called **i n t u i t i o n**."

My jaw tightens.

"A *mother's i n t u i t i o n*," she continues muttering as she dices the apple. Using the flat side of the knife, she scoops up the pieces and tosses them into the bowl. "I may be stupid. I may be insane. Hell, I may be *dead*. But I *still* have my intuition. My instinct. And no matter what anyone else tries to tell me, it's never wrong. It's *never* wrong."

"I'm—" The words freeze.

"Don't apologise for things you didn't cause, Paul."

I don't have the heart to tell her that I wasn't going to apologise. I had planned on defending myself, on insisting that I'm not the enemy here, that if there's one person in this family that can be guaranteed to want nothing more than for her to permanently be healthy again, it's me that she can turn to, that she can trust won't belittle her or scornfully deny her existence. But there are times, more often than not around this household, that I've discovered the better of the decisions is to bite down on my tongue with so much pressure that it splits in half and refrain from speaking.

"You going back to sleep?"

The next question is literally thrown at me like a discarded towel. I catch it mid-air and answer. "I don't know if I should. I mean, I have to wake up in two and a half hours. I might as well stay up—"

"Of course not." The words rush from her as she takes the two mandarin oranges, peels them, lining the sections horizontally before beginning to slice them, her movements becoming almost frantic and hurried as she cut through the spheres. "You need to go back to sleep. Sleep off the rest of that hangover. Yes, Paul, that's what you need to do."

I can't tell if she's doing this on purpose, gently ordering me about, or if she's starting to have a bout of panic. I try to trace the lines of her body language with my eyes, but my vision still is fuzzed from the remnants of the drink I consumed. "Mom, really, it's okay. Here."

I move forward, and I put one hand over the wrist that rapidly reduces the oranges into shreds. She halts then, pursing her lips as she looks down at me, and even though she tenses, freezes in place, still the fingers beneath mine, the appendage connected to them, trembles as she is overwhelmed with a bout of nervous energy. "I'll use this old knife, and you can get a clean one." I keep any and all patronising tone out. I'm not talking down to her. I'm treating her as my equal, because she is that; she's more than that. "Two people chopping can get this done quicker, right?"

"I need to do it myself," she whispers to the hand that holds hers.

"You're obviously the best at it." I swallow hard against the discomfort of the weird pricking at the corners of my eyes. "But even the best of us need some help."

She starts nodding, then continues this as she allows me to take the knife gently from her grasp, and she turns to wander over to the drawer, which is located directly to the right of the stovetop, pulling it open, staring at its contents, canting her head to the right side in order to further analyse what lies beneath her, before she reaches a delicate hand in. I tear my gaze away and return to the work that was left behind, taking great care to ensure that my slices into the orange were as precise as hers. I start to feel my own rush of relief, a sort of odd expulsion of stress from the pores as though it were some weird liquid being thrust from the body. Like I'm sweating it out. Even though I'm not sweating anymore, just covered in what's dried.

There's an odd clunking to the left of me, and I shake my head lightly. "Mom, you don't have to dig through the drawer. Just pick one. As long as it's not serrated. I know you hate those ridges in—"

"What in the living daylights is going on in here?"

I glance up at Mom, who has seemed to been rendered paralysed, staring toward her left with a smaller, yet sharper, knife in her right hand, and it trembles uncontrollably in her tightening grasp as she bites down with so much pressure upon her lower lip that the skin ruptures and a single stream of crimson appears, beginning its lethargic journey down her chin. Her throat moves up and down as she swallows, and finally I am able to obtain the courage necessary to turn and glance over my shoulder at the newcomer who has intruded upon the private space that we'd been forming, that has ruined all of the progress I thought I was making with this.

There he stands, taking up the majority of the space which I had just vacated, with the thinning hair and the receding line upon his forehead that tattled about his middle ages rapidly approaching, with the eyes that held irises darker than the colour of the deepest gunmetal, yet still with just as much of an aim when he decided to pierce you with the bullets from his glowers. The darkly plaid flannel which he wears has all of the buttons open, revealing a soil-streaked white wife-beater under it, and his jeans have a hole beginning just above the right kneecap. He still has on his ancient work boots; the right one has all of the laces untied, and the left has been double-knotted and looped around the rear of the shoe to ensure that it doesn't come unravelled. The whites of his eyes are bloodshot. He looks like an old me.

An old, old version of me.

"W—"

"Enough, Paul," he says immediately, waving his hand toward me, and he gestures toward Mom, who still hasn't managed to become mobile again. "Laura, it's three in the morning. You should be in bed."

"So should you," is her quick reply, though I take note of how there is a distinct tremble in her voice now. "You too, Paul."

"Let the boy stay, Laura." My mouth goes completely dry at the way that he isn't slurring his words. Yes, that's right; I'm concerned because he *isn't* inebriated. Because if he wasn't out drinking, like I was doing, then what the hell was he doing? "He's a man. He'll be the man of the house and the overseer of this farm when high school's over."

I bristle automatically. As if I need to be reminded of the argument we had, the one that I don't want to talk about, the one where he blatantly told me that I wasn't going to be sent off to college, that I would stay here and run the ranch while he thought about initiating his retirement and teaching me all the last minute things. What he doesn't seem to understand is that everything that I've done around here, I've actually either learned from Daniel's parents or taught myself. So, I'm not exactly sure what he wants to give me, because he only gives things to himself.

I know, I know, I shouldn't be having such bitter thoughts about the man who raised me. Because he's better than most. He never travelled off to work and left the family behind to fend for itself; he was with my mother through all of her episodes and was one of the first ones to recognise that she needed help - even though, as you all are finding out, it didn't really help her at all. He's not entirely selfish. But he's a complicated man, and even though I've grown up with him for nineteen years, I don't think that I've managed to figure out how he functions. I know enough to keep my nose to the grindstone and stay almost completely out of trouble - and to know when I want to cause trouble, to just do it and not warn anybody that it's about to happen, and then leave no evidence that it was me.

I guess it's a little bit of payback, though, that I don't know him; considering he doesn't know me at all. I'm not the one who wants this place, as much as I love it and will always, always come back to live near here. But I don't want to be in charge.

That's Ruth's dream. She's the one who wants to stay home and oversee everything. But alas, Dad won't even imagine letting her be in charge - because as a woman, she's not cut out for that.

The thought of that little offhand comment he had made about her, to her, causes the hair upon the back of my neck to become even more vertical. I feel more like a cat that's been faced with a treacherous enemy than a boy on the verge of leaving his teenaged years behind and graduating high school and being trapped in a place that he adores and, because it will become nothing more than imprisonment, will slowly come to loathe and despise. Hmm, perhaps in that case, I am a cat, and the prospect of being tossed into a cage, yowling and screaming and clawing at those who do it the entire time, is the treacherous enemy.

Makes sense, doesn't it. And it's a crying shame for someone to feel that way in their own house. Or maybe I'm just complaining.

"Hello? Is anyone in that little head of yours, Paul?" Dad has the gall to reach over and knock his fist hard against the side of my skull, and immediately, I wince away from him, face creasing in utter agony, for there is a distinct sensation spreading throughout the area that has been touched, and that is of the blade of an axe being swung down and used to severe my cranium in half. One hand goes to apply pressure to the place which feels as though it will be bruised for the next thousand years, and tears, of which I'm immediately ashamed, make their way from the ducts, where they have been hovering since I first wobbled out of the darkened barn and made my way blindly along a pathway that I knew too well, and down my cheeks, coating them in a layer of moisture that causes him to spew out a laugh, directed at me.

"You're crying? What for?" Then, he bends down close to my face and whispers in my ear. "Drink too much last night, Paul?"

"Leav—" The word sticks in my mother's throat, but it does accomplish the goal I think she set out to do, and that was remove my father's attention from me. With a raised eyebrow, and the condescending tone in his voice as he approaches her, placing a hand upon the small of her back, makes me want to punch a hole in the wall. I hate it when he does this. I hate it when he's in the moods like this where everything is beneath him. He isn't like this all the time, admittedly, but when he is, all I want to do is kill something, throttle the life from the veins of something with my bare hands, and watch as it chokes and rattles and fades into the beyond.

"Yes, Laura?"

"He's not hung-over." She changes the sentence immediately. "He just heard me in the kitchen and came to investigate. He's nothing more than... tired. He's just tired. Like me. Like all of us. Tired. So tired." The knife still trembles in her hand. "So tired, Randy. My head is just swimming and my arm just hurts and I'm so tired."

He shushes her, increasing the pressure of his palm upon the small of her back and sidling her into the comfort of his embrace - but even in the darkness which tries its hardest to conceal them, I can see that she hasn't relaxed into him, that she remains against him, all of her muscles constricted as she maintains that disconnect which has been instilled in her since she was released the first time. It pains me to see that there's such a distance which has grown between them, even after the fact that they've been through so much together. Sometimes, it makes me wonder whether love really lasts, or if it's nothing more than an elaborate game, extended through generations, woven through lies and stories, made to sound like one of the most wonderful things in the world, too good to be true, and secretly is nothing more than someone's idea, someone's rumour that has been spread like butter on toast, with a lot of players who grow bored with the fact that everything is, indeed, loveless, and throw themselves into a fantasy in order to live more easily.

"You're fine, Laura," are his words of comfort. "You're nothing but fine now."

I'm finding that this exchange is causing me to do something extremely odd, something that is inappropriate at this moment in time, but my facial features seem to not care about that fact, and they continue twisting themselves into one of the ugliest combinations of a grimace and sneer that I have ever done. Because there's something incredibly strange about all of this. About the fact that both of my parents are awake at this hour. About the fact that my father is meandering in, looking as though he's just thrown himself into the nearest puddle of mud and afterwards attempted to scrub off the excess with a roughened, overused car towel. About the fact that he knocked me over the head and smiled about it. The absurdity of it all.

"Shouldn't you be in bed, Paul?"

The words directed at me from my father, with the way that he has tucked the minute frame of my mother deeper into the crook of his arm, and now, has engulfed me with the piercing ammunition behind those gunmetal eyes, cause me to shrug. I can't tell you why the hell I decided to take this route - more than likely, I was taking out my bitterness about the fact that I would be trapped at home while everyone else in the entirety of my graduating class, including my own sister, would travel off to somewhat distant cities and be obtaining their higher educations. But I took it, and to be quite honest with you, I can't say that I regret it.

"Oh, I don't know, Dad." The grin slides onto my mouth. "Should I?"

His face stretches across the bones underneath, and as he's distracted, there's an odd flash of light down near the area of his waist. I think for a minute that Mom has decided to snap, decided to take the knife that has been within her grasp and plunge it into the abdomen before her, feeling sickened and pale in the embrace instead of warmed, welcomed, and adored without condition. But I soon discover this is not the case, and I'm unsure as to why I had that flash of a thought, considering there is, ultimately, no reason for it to occur, as she never has despised my father enough to do such a thing; she merely has set the weapon down upon the counter behind them and turned her petrified eyes to me.

"You better put that tongue back in your mouth, boy." The warning in his tone is almost tangible. I feel as though I could reach out in front of me while blinded and still feel its throbbing surface beneath my fingertips. "Unless you want it cut off."

"Yeah, you seem to be an expert at cutting things off lately, Dad." I ignore the flash of ire that fills his irises, plunging ahead. "First, it's access to my car keys. Then, it's access to the charge card I never use. Oh, and lately, it's access to college. Now, you're threatening to cut off access to my tongue?" A dry laugh escapes. "Well, damn me to hell, why don't you? If you really want me to not talk, then maybe you shouldn't give me something to talk about."

"Oh, so you're *wanting* something to talk about?"

Dad starts toward me, releasing Mom and allowing her to stand there with her fists pressed against her sternum. "You want me to give you something to *really* talk about, boy?"

Now is the time that I make the choice to hold the tongue he wants to slice off. I said my piece, and I know that it falls on relatively deafened ears, as do all of my opinions that I choose to make known, and I avert my eyes from him as he nears me, instead staring at the surface of the right refrigerator door, staring the different magnets and assorted papers and picture frames that were suspended there as forsaken wind chimes sans a breeze to stir their respective memories. A hand grasps at the collar of my shirt, and I hear Mom emit a fearful squeak. As though she wants to say something.

I can't help but notice that he smells weird. He doesn't smell like the depths of the dusted earth, like dampened soil moulded to calloused fingers, like the remnants of the corn husks as they're walked by, like the putrid pond water when you misstep and find yourself plunging underneath the clouded green surface. He doesn't smell like any of the things that his appearance tattles he might have been doing, things that don't make sense to be out doing at this time of the morning, no matter how dedicated he is or says that he is.

"You want something to talk about?"

I almost want to laugh in his face.

"Randy, don't," I hear her whisper, and a hand is at her throat.

"Don't."

Dad has never hit any of us. I can honestly say that. He doesn't ever clench his fist and knock us upside the head, no matter what threats he mutters. He's never pulled us around, unless it's to move us out of the way of an oncoming farm machine or make us hurry up in the field. He's never even so much as backhanded or slapped our mouths when we get cheeky attitudes like this, though admittedly, Ruth doesn't have nearly as much of an inclination to display her reactions rudely. Why would she, when she's allowed to make her own decisions for the most part? It's the words that you have to watch out for, the snide remarks and the little jabs here and there that don't seem like much at the time, but end up being some of the most damaging as they assimilate over a period of years.

"I'm not going to do anything to him, Laura," he seethes, though it sounds as if this takes a great deal of concentrated withdrawal in order to say this. "He's not worth the time. He's constantly proving that these days."

There it is, the sharp words that are directed, something offhand and cloaked in the essence of an insult. He's taken the knife from the counter and he's managed to stab me right in the pulsating heart, and I go entirely limp when he releases my shirt. "I don't mean to lose myself. It's just—I got worried when I saw that you were awake." Completely changing his tune, he is. He glances at me with darkened eyes, and I know mine are the same - for if there's one thing that he and I have in common that I'm willing to admit we share, it's the eye shape and colour - and the implications are rather loud and clear. *Get out.* "You can't blame me for being a little bit on edge."

"I can blame you for a lot of things, Randy."

My mind whirls as it tries to keep up with all the changes in syntax and vocal tone, but still it's coated in drunkenness and lethargy, and all that ends up occurring is the intensification of my current developing migraine. The thing's moved all the way down into my cheekbones. Not even the pressure I put on the spots with my knuckles is making it cease and desist. Seems as though I'm shit out of luck when it comes to this, no thanks to him knocking me in the noggin.

Dad looks as though he wants to inquire, but then, he turns on me again. "Paul, I said, *get out*!"

You (verbally) said nothing of the sort. The only things that had been there were implications that you wanted me to leave, but there never, never was an explicit sentence. And I'm tempted to say this out loud, to once again state my piece, to remain with my arms crossed and stance more hulking than my dad's - I am an inch taller than him, so it could be pulled off. Yet there's this exhaustion that's been seeping into my bones, and it's decided at this moment in time to become as water weight, almost as though I have been thrown into the ocean and forced to swim for my life or sink beneath the waves. It feels as though my clothes are sodden and my cranium drowning itself in the saltwater. It's because of this tiredness that I choose instead merely to shrug, to ignore the pointed expression that's still aimed my way and the way that my mom pulls on his arm, attempts to direct his attention back onto her, and I saunter away.

"Get rid of the attitude while you're at it."

I almost turn right back around. I almost plant my feet into the ground and stare him down. I almost succumb to the little passive-aggressive attack that he offers. Yet I continue walking away, though admittedly my steps are heavier and my shoulders more rigid, but surely these things can be overlooked, considering I'm forcing myself to be the bigger person in this situation and am following orders even though every single damned nerve fiber in my body doesn't want me to. Even though he definitely deserves this attitude in my mind, I'm surrendering to his authority as *head of the house* and taking the hardened words and the snide facial expressions and going down the stairs, into the basement, toward my bedroom. Because honestly, what the hell can I do with myself at this time of the morning? I'm better off getting some sort of sustenance from the refrigerator down there, as well as a tall bottle of ice-cold water, and drinking myself into sleep, because in this state of mind, I'm not going to be anything except *annoyed.*

The darkness of the basement is most welcome to my tired eyes. I nearly fall down the last stair, one hand plastered to my forehead as I shuffle my boots toward the right, past the small, open living room in front of me and toward the kitchenette with its sink, microwave, and refrigerator. The free hand is wobbling toward the fridge's handle, and when I finally grasp it, I triumphantly throw it open, peering at its contents after scowling at the light that illuminated the inside. There are several bottles of water lying on their sides in one of the drawers; the smell of bagged cantaloupes and half-chopped sweet onions causes my nose to wrinkle. Those two scents definitely wouldn't make a best-selling perfume. But it could be worse; it could be that nasty crap that my school principal wears - or, rather, bathes in. Don't know what's wrong with her nose, but like, something rancid follows her through the hallways and walks before her, too, announcing her arrival. Makes me sneeze.

Do you know how embarrassing it is to start sneezing uncontrollably in the middle of a test? And have to get up and get tissues, all because of someone's perfume? People laugh at me, but I'm not laughing; my eyes are watering everywhere and the girls twitter in the background and the teachers tell them to be quiet and let me blow my nose, because yeah, my school is one of those lame ones that doesn't let you get up once the test starts. It's mortifying. But I make the most of it. The best of it. Like I try to do with everything.

There's no loaves of bread down here, none that have

been thawed out of the freezer, anyways, so I peruse the shelves again, and again, searching for something that might be a good substitute for the sponge-like consistency needed to soak up the rest of the alcohol in my blood. And lo and behold, there it is, looming before my eyes in a familiar white box - pizza. My old friend. My stomach growls in impatience as I first pull out a bottle of water and set it on the counter next to the opened door, then go back in for the box, yanking it out and opening the lid to see what was ordered, because for the life of me, I can't remember. Was I even home when this arrived? Did I even eat any of it?

I couldn't have. Or else there wouldn't have been leftovers.

Seems to me as though there's the all-meat pizza, due to the amount of sausage, bacon, ham, and pepperoni that are crammed onto the tops of some of the slices, and something a little bit lighter in colour, something that has a paler sauce leaking out from underneath the top layer of cheese; I inhale the pungent aroma of spices that tattles the meat is buffalo chicken. Well, there's nothing stopping me from having a few slices of both, right? I shove it onto the counter next to the bottle of water and go in search of paper plates.

Okay, there's still a chance that this evening and morning and day can turn itself around, right? I'm not that much of a pessimist. I recognise when something can turn good, if it can. I attempt to do my best and see the potential in all things. And with this pizza, which is promising to be delicious, and the bottle of water, and the fact that my migraine is settling into that stage where you can deal with it without wanting to tear out your brain matter and pull at your eye sockets, it all combined might be the push toward improvement that's necessary.

After I've found the paper plates in the cabinet

underneath the sink, I manage to slide four slices of pizza onto it. I'm glad it's one of the larger sized ones and not those pathetically small disks that barely gives you enough room to move around a fork. It's when I'm punching the buttons and hitting "start" that I hear the shouting from upstairs.

The words come nigh inaudible to my ears due to the reheating of the pizza and the throbbing of blood in my head, and so I make my way toward the staircase, moving slowly up the first one, ensuring that the sole of my boot doesn't hit that particular spot that causes the floorboards underneath to creak loudly in protest. But still, I can barely hear what's being said; some sort of eavesdropper I am. Where's Ruth when I need her? She's much better at this type of thing, having grown up with what David Stamp across the street refers to as *big ears*. Not that I really want her to—

C R A S H - - ! ! !

I'm halfway up the staircase when the screaming starts up again, and when a door slams. I fall over sideways at the sudden closeness of the noise; he's exited out the front door and has managed to shake the foundation with the force of how he shut that door, or so this is how it feels to me. Collapsed into a heap, I crawl up the rest of the way and look toward the kitchen area, panting like Moe did in the heat of the barn.

Mom's still there, though she has forsaken her fruits, her chopping, and her knife for the comfort of the floor, where she sits with her back against one of the counter doors, sobbing into the palms of her hands, which repeatedly travel up the length of her forehead and let her fingers frantically bury themselves in the now-tangled lengths of her dark hair. Her face creases in such a palpable amount of pain that it causes my own heart to seize, as though the grip of death has managed to slowly move its talons inward, puncturing the organ with the ice of the grave. This has to be one massive nightmare, I tell myself. None of this can actually be happening again.

I want to go to her, to clean up the broken shards of the plate that surround her. But she's screaming something to the ceiling, something that's beyond me, and this house, and anything in this life — and the cat is trying to climb into her lap, mewing incessantly, and she's crying out to the animal:

"I'm not *crazy*. I'm *not* **crazy**. I'm NOT!"

All moisture in my throat has permanently departed me, and I pull myself from the stairs, using the bannister as my method of rising, and go back down into the shadows, which had previously been so welcoming and were now nothing more than the personification of dread that I felt sinking into my flesh and devouring it with its sharpened, relentless teeth. Is this what depression feels like? Is this what my mom experiences every single waking and sleeping hour of her life? Is this what she's forced to deal with whenever she's in the shower, staring at the wall opposite of her, wondering if she'll have the strength to resist the pull of the razor she's dissected for the blade? Is this how she feels when she speaks of voices that no one else hears, when she comments on the oddest little things and receives patronising looks, when she's alone in her bedroom because Dad's off working his day job and has to stay late for a meeting and is seated in the centre of the mattress and gazing up, with her arms crossed, at the ceiling, a blank look upon her face as she inhales and exhales as though it's the most laborious task in the universe?

No wonder the yank of eternal sleep seems so sweet to her.

If this were my perpetual mindset, I'd want it, too.

And what pains me is that she's not the only one I know who is suffering in this sort of a mental state. The only difference: my mom's still around.

Though the microwave beeps at me incessantly, and the odour of the food approaches me as a tantalising wisp of smoke, I ignore it, my stomach convulsing at the thought of consuming anything at all, at purging the inside of my mouth and erasing the bitter aftertaste of too much booze, because I want to wallow in it as everyone else is doing; I want to be removed from the world as everyone else seems to be doing. If they're allowed to have their moments, then why in the hell can't I?

I remove my boots outside of my bedroom door, and I shuffle in my dirtied socks toward the overturned covers that encase my mattress, covers the colour of my mother's tears, a deep crimson that tattle of the wounded nature of her soul. And now, I'm sharing that with her as I encase myself in the blood of the past and ignore the seepage of the future.

The door remains ajar. Her sobs echo in the depths of my ears. A dog howls. Wind whistles past the half-opened door that leads from my room to the backyard.

And I drift.

The touch of an angel drifts along my right cheekbone through a focused and gentle pointer finger, followed by a shimmering giggle that comes as though from a great distance to me. There isn't an image painted on the backs of my eyelids, but I can conjure up the visage easily enough, for I have memorised it a countless number of times throughout the passing years. And it echoes from down the extended length of a darkened tunnel, for she is no longer here.

I shudder involuntarily as the fingerprints drape themselves across the other cheekbone now, and then, a soft voice, still in that girlish tone that I remember, saying my name before giggling once more and continuing onward, chirruping like one of the birds that perches in a branch outside the window.

"Paul, come on, you have to wake up. You're sleeping more than me, and that's a lot!"

But now, I can understand the lure more clearly than ever before. There's something really super seductive about the desire to sleep forever, to keep the eyes closed off to the bustling of reality in front of them, to remain surrendered in these shadows where your head can fantasise about whatever it wishes, where faces appear and reappear, where situations are replayed and redone a thousand times, where sentences thought are stated, and where, overall, your body doesn't feel so burdened down.

Yet the faces, eventually, fade. The body becomes heavy in its slumber. The mind succumbs to a seemingly inescapable fog, and all those things you wished you said become garbled cotton in your mouth, the words buzzing into static. Sharpness of lines fades into a blur as you are propelled around, and around — and you realise, with a jolt that causes those shields, your eyelids, to fly open, that you must wake up.

Because in awakening, there is a renewal. Your eyes can blink away the blur and features become clear again. Memories are reinstated. Thoughts are hesitant, but reemerge from their protective mists. Another warmth is found in the rays of the sun instead of the weight of the covers and sheets, and the touch upon the skin, though it becomes a phantom, promises to return when you're healthy again.

And you drift in and out as you please. Because you know you can go back in, but also come out, without falling too hard or sinking too deep. Because you know.

You k n o w.

"You *know* you need to get up. Please, Paul, just get up!"

It's not the girlish voice of my odd, half-drunken thoughts, but rather a scared one that reaches me, not from down the length of a tunnel, but from the threshold of my opened door. It's my mother, I think; because the voice isn't husky enough to be my sister's.

"Paul, wake up, quickly!"

Fan*tastic*. Has something else managed to happen after I collapsed in that really weird, philosophical stupour that I never, ever want to visit again? Because honestly, that whole thing has just successfully caused my head to start spinning again. As does the sudden movement I execute when I sit up straight in bed, both hands automatically going to the askew hairs poking out at all angles from their roots in my scalp, my eyes sleepily blinking - and holy shenanigans, Batman, are they swollen and red, I can feel the heat from here - as I look from left, to right, then stare down my mother, trying to decipher whether she's just a really detailed figment of my imagination or actually huddling outside of my bedroom door with a thumbnail in her mouth and a wide-eyed expression on her face.

"He's already out working," she continues whispering to me. "You need to go; he's doing your chores, and he's mad, he's *so mad*!"

She's warning me about Dad's impending wrath. Even though he had been the one to order me away, he still would take out his temper upon me for sleeping a little bit too late. It still isn't sunrise, though; so I doubt that I'm two or even one hour past the time that I usually awaken. But thirty seconds is enough to make him blow a gasket or three. "I'm coming."

"Hurry," she mutters again, withdrawing into herself, fiddling with the collar of her shirt - and I notice offhandedly that she's wearing a different one than when I saw her before; I did see her before, right, I didn't just imagine all of that? - She turns away from me and walks off, continuing to mutter that word. "Hurry, hurry, *hurry*."

I need to change my clothes; everything is sticky with

booze and sweat, and it smells awful. It's almost with an inhuman speed that I peel off my double-layered shirts and the pair of dirt-stained jeans that I have on, the socks sliding off alongside the bottom hems of the jean legs. It's like I'm shedding off my sins as I let them plop onto the cold tile floor that lines the entirety of the basement - except for the small living room area, which has a super ratted carpeting that makes the soles of your feet itch and tingle. The air makes goosebumps appear on my flesh as I cross the small section of flooring to the dresser draws and yank open the top, shivering as I stand just in my boxers — which— yeah, those need to be changed, too. Those first, then.

I'll exchange burgundy for black. Super hard choice right there.

Yank them off, pull them on. Good freaking God, you don't realise how cold it is someplace until you do something like that. Then, another drawer opened. Time for a shirt. That one looks good - a really old, ratted muscle shirt that I stole out of my dad's closet from spite. He never noticed, though; so much for feeling satisfied in that rebellion of stealing clothes. Next, I need to layer something over this, or else, I'm going to be freezing my arms off, even though this month's been oddly warmer than the Octobers that have passed before it. Temperature doesn't really matter when the sun hasn't risen yet, though, or is just beginning to peek over the horizon. I probably should've put on jeans before I worried about these shirts, because now, I'm going to get really annoyed having to hold the hems in my teeth so that they don't get tucked into my belt line - because there's something really stifling about that, you know? And part of our dress code at our school is that we can't wear any clothing that could be characterised as grunge or dishevelled - and apparently, ripped jeans and loose shirts qualify as that. Who installed that rule? I'm not actually sure. I just know that it's one I've never followed in my entire four years there. And yeah, the principal has literally leapt down my throat a couple of times about it - I swear that her terrifyingly pungent perfume haunted me for days after that, she had stood so close to me while yelling for the rest of the student body to hear. Of course, I received that argument with a crooked smile and a well-placed wink - and I got off without a lot of punishment.

I don't get it, honestly. Like, what's the big deal about winking and smiling? It's part of my personality, something that I've done ever since I was a toddler. At least, that's what I've gathered from the stories exchanged over dinner when Marlene and my mother used to get together, just the two of them, and cook dishes from their childhood's while adding in their own elements to the recipes, drinking lemonades and wines and laughing all the while. That hasn't happened, though, since Mom was diagnosed in the hospital a year or so back to be getting sicker with each passing day - sicker in the head, that was. Dad stopped allowing her to have company other than that of her family.

I pull out jeans from the middle drawer and slip those on; then, reopen the underwear drawer because I'm an idiot and forgot to take out my socks before closing it. My heartbeat pounds out a furious rhythm in the two-pulse pattern of the word that my Mom uttered as she left.

Hurry.   —   *Hur-ry.*

Calm down, heartbeat; I promise that I'm almost dressed.

Then, there is a trickle of a sensation along the left side of my jawline, one that graces me with such a tender care that my spine immediately straightens, my hands dropping both socks that had been loosely held in them, and all the blood drains from my face as my breath catches in my throat, and in the throbbing silence that follows, a silence that has such an impact upon me that my eardrums threaten to burst, I hear that trace of a giggle again, the one which had put me to sleep in the first place. It's as though cobwebs reinstall themselves in the gaping caverns of my mind, and for a moment, when I drift away, my eyelids dropping to half-mast, I would swear on my grave that she's standing there in the doorway, so many inches shorter than me, than everyone, with her ash-blonde hair in a bird's nest tangle and her blue-eyes bright with early morning glee. "Come on, Paul, you have to hurry. I'm ready before you and that's saying something!"

"You aren't ready," I tell her, a hint of a smile appearing on my mouth. "You're still in your pyjamas."

"So what?" She loves to needle me. "At least I'm awake! It's pretty sad when a girl's ready to go before a guy."

"But you're not ready to go!"

"I *am* ready to go."

And her voice turns much, much older, and her figure is gone from my sight.

A shiver runs its fingers along my vertebrae, and it spooks me into dressing with even more passion and speed than ever before. The last thing I want to be around right now is a ghost that roams the caverns of my mind and manifests itself in front of me.

Something streaks across the sky, illuminating the darkened basement even through the draperies that have been layered over the windows, and as I bend over outside of my drawer to retrieve my work boots, I hear Mom gasp. She's taken residency up in front of the fridge down here and peruses its contents, though when the lightning appears, her head rips out of the space and stares, half-canted to the right side, eyes wild and widened, toward the nearest window. I look toward the door that leads onto the back porch; the blinds have been drawn upward, but I don't have to gaze outside to know that a storm is approaching, for a roll of thunder shakes the very foundation of the house and causes the pictures on the walls to rattle.

"Hurry," she whispers again, closing the refrigerator door before opening it again, then closing it, then opening it. "Hurry."

She doesn't have to tell me more than those two additional times. It's almost with an inhuman speed that I lace together my shoestrings and take off out the back door, not bothering to go upstairs and properly out through the front door. When I emerge outside, I wake up the two German shepherds that we keep as guard dogs on the covered porch; one of them bonded to me, the other to Ruth. The female is the one who bonded to me, and she bounds from the old ratted couch we've pushed into the corner which functions as a makeshift bed for them, tail wagging despite the sleepiness still being in her brown irises. Her mouth opens wide in a yawn as I unhook the chain that leads outside from the back porch and shove through the door, leaving it open so her brother can walk out if he wants to; though he appears to be much too comfortable on the pillow next to the love-seat; he rolls over and extends his legs high into the air, eyes refusing to open.

Shawna, though, refuses to go *back* to sleep, and she follows me as I break into a trot, going down the hillside upon which our house has been constructed, the hem of my flannel shirt flapping in the sudden gusts of wind. There's a bellowing of cows and a shrill neighing of horses that attracts my attention, and I leap over the little ravine - one that's been created by the rivulets of erosion caused by the constant rainfall that drains downward into our pond, which is directly on my right, this side of it disguised by a crowded infestation of cattails - somewhat dramatically, arms pumping as I increase my pace. It sounds more like Dad's torturing the animals than letting them out to pasture - which I knew we would still need to do even though the sky promised to barrage us with an onslaught of wrath, since they would be much safer in the fields where they could flee or take shelter instead of being crammed into a space where, if spooked, more injury and possibly death would occur than allowing, so to speak, nature to take its course.

Her ears perk up, and she starts barking raucously at whatever she sees that I can't discern through the waving masses of leaves that fall from the trembling branches of the trees above me, a swirl of gold and oranges that threaten to blind me. When I finally get to a point, out from underneath the trees, that I'm able to see the looming grey face of the ancient barn in which I had slept for most of the night, my eyes widen to the size of dinner plates and my mouth opens, as though I'm about to shout, but nothing more than a strangled noise emerges.

So, I'm right at the fence line, and in the near distance, I can see the two massive doors, which have been opened. My father sits proudly on the back of one of Ruth's cutting horses, which is originally something that either she or I have to do - and immediately, concern fills me, because this means that my twin sister hasn't shown up, either. But here's the thing. There are two pastures, and within them are separate paddocks in which we rotate the animals. But very specifically, my father insists that the horses go more out toward the road, toward the left, and the cows go right, burrowing themselves a little bit more into wooded areas where a lot of grass continues to grow rich even into the winter, until after the initial freeze.

Yet here he is, so proud on the back of that horse, with a smug grin on his face and a roguish glint in his eyes - and people wonder where I got that trait - as he directs the cows toward the left. Of course, because my gigantic amount of terrible luck seems to be continuing, he glances up just as I stop to awkwardly stare at him, with my mouth agape and the expression of a twelve-year-old painted on my face, and he waves, so nonchalantly, as though he's doing the job correctly and not giving me more work to do.

Giving me more work to do.

Oh, so *that's* how he's chosen to get back at me for earlier this morning.

Excuse me for a minute, but —

That **bastard.**

— I thought that would make me feel better, but it didn't. Never does, not when he decides to start talking, to further antagonise.

"This is what happens when you oversleep, *Paul*," he calls to me. "Other people do your job for you, and most of the time, they do it wrong. You want something done correctly, you always have to do it yourself. Thought you would've learned that by now, but that's all right - everyone, even little snips like *you*, needs a refresher course."

Another streak of thunder attacks the unsuspecting earth below it, and the animals scatter to the furthest reaches of the pasture, leaving me only to watch as they gallop and retreat to what they consider to be much safer ground, most of them even disappearing from view. He kicks the horse into a canter and pulls up alongside the fence line, glaring down at me with those gunmetal-grey eyes. Mocking me, sorry, not glaring. Just mocking. Like the bastard he is.

Whoops, forgot to warn you about that one. Sometimes these things just sort of slip out before you can detain them.

"And *now*," he continues, as if he hasn't already managed to rub copious amounts of salt in this opened, gaping, oozing wound, "you have to clean up more of a mess than you would have before."

Retaliation is the only thing that I want to do, and my

mouth opens, fully preparing for the consequences that this impending word vomit will bring down upon my head, punishments that will make me end up wishing I had kept my temper about me and closed my lips, pursing them, even gluing them, together instead. But there is a shout from somewhere both nearby and far away that attracts my attention instead, and I whirl around to see my best friend, Daniel, and my twin sister, Ruth, running down the hillside toward us. Daniel is a bit faster, leaping over the creek with as much prowess as a ninja, and he reaches us a while before Ruth finally catches up.

I take in both of their appearances. Their clothes are rumpled and dishevelled. Ruth's hair has little bits of hay and straw scattered throughout it, though she's quickly dislodging the pieces by running her fingers through her hair and allowing the gusts of wind to carry them into oblivion. Daniel's is sticking up all over his head and makes him look about eight years old. He has no shirt on. Why, you ask?

Because Ruth is wearing it.

Both of their eyes are bright, Ruth's brilliant emeralds shining at me and Daniel's hazel twinkling, but that mirth soon fades away when they see the gauntness, or whatever they see, the raw stress, in my own face. Maybe I just look fed up with life. I hope I do. Because that's how I feel, and I prefer to look how I feel instead of putting on a mask and hoping for the best.

But I can't help but start thinking. Start getting suspicious. And I know that Dad's pretty riled up about them showing up late, too, but instead of just glaring at them, like I'm doing, and looking back and forth between the two of them and the odd crinkles in their features, he starts barking to be heard over the rush of wind.

"Where in the hell have you two been off to? Messing around in the haystacks? Is that the kind of payment I get for working my ass off and making sure you have a roof over your head? And you!" He points an accusing finger at Daniel. "Living across the street all these years and taking ad--"

"Whoa, Randy! Calm your horse!" Daniel shouts right back. The horse beneath Dad isn't moving, though, which makes me start to hoarsely chuckle. The gall of him. Calling my Dad by his first name and yelling even more loudly than he is. "Ruth and I weren't doing anything, its fine! We were out checking the crops in the fields. Brought some stuff that's fallen off plants in the garden back to the house." Ruth nods vigorously in agreement, smiling thinly, and her eyes move from Daniel out to the fields, where she no doubt notices the last of her horses disappearing into the depths of the wrong paddocks. Her eyebrows furrow, and she glances back at me, and our eyes meet; and let me tell you something. Siblings have bonds, but there's something a little bit weird about ours. (No, *that's* not what I mean; get your mind out of the gutter.) I don't know if it has to do with the fact that we're twins - because I have heard and read stuff about things like "twin telepathy" and a twin connection being established. I usually don't believe in the shit I read on the Internet, especially when it comes to things like this, but I swear to you (again) on my grave that Ruth and I can read each other's minds with a simple glare, glance, wink, hand gesture, or other small nuance that goes virtually unnoticed by everyone else around us. I know by this eye contact being made that she knows that it's been a rough morning, that Dad's in a rotten mood, that now I'm going to have to clean up a mess that's been made, that I'm really tired, and that Mom's probably not having a good day. All of this, managed to be communicated in a minuscule space. It's amazing.

How do I know all of this? Well, that's why I believe in the twin bond. I just know. I can read her body language, the little signals sent through her eyes, which dim in colour as she looks even longer at me, then down at the ground. And I also know that more than just picking the spare crops out in the fields happened this morning in-between Daniel and Ruth. I wonder if either of them will bother to tell me.

Not that I would mind, you know. Not really. Sure, Daniel's an atheist, and he tends to be a little bit of a knucklehead, but at least he knows what he's doing, in reality, when it comes to the realm of farming, and he knows a little bit about what he wants to do with the rest of his life, and he knows where he's going, how he's going to get there, and he does like her. A lot. I can't get him to shut up about her sometimes. He's talked about Ruth more than he's talked about some of the girls he's dated. Not that I blame him; even I recognise that my sister is a gem, a rare specimen in the world of today.

Of course, I could be completely delusional and not know her at all. There's that niggling sensation in my gut, too. And sometimes, I do wonder about the choices that she makes, wish that she'd come to me before executing them. But she tends to believe what society tells her. And what Shane tells her.

Now that one right there, Shane? He's the *epitome* of a bastard. No wonder he and my Dad get along so well. I really try to not loathe people, even when they're acting out and deserving otherwise, basically asking to be judged for what they're doing or saying. But I'm telling you, no matter how long Ruth dates this guy, and no matter how many times he has been invited over to the house for dinner, or lunch, or for a bonfire, and no matter how many conversations he has attempted to strike up with me in the corridors at school or at the open door of my car while I was waiting one time for Ruth to finish up with an after-school academic meeting, and no matter how many waves he gives me, no matter how much he tries to know about farming, horses, cattle, gardening, no matter how many pairs of cowboy boots he owns or dusted pairs of work boots he wears, no matter how much flannel he layers over his white tank tops or what type of hat he wears, whether it be a forward baseball cap, a backward one, or a cowboy hat - there's something, in all of that conglomerated mess, that remains the same.

I can't stand him.

Dad has been looking back and forth between Ruth and Daniel, and his eyes are about as stormy as the oncoming horizon, but ultimately, I think he decides to let the situation go. Considering they did mention they'd been out in the fields. Which I believed. Because Daniel is wearing his work boots, and they're caked in fresh mud, and Ruth has a streak of soil down the side of her left calf - though she's still dressed under Daniels shirts as though she rolled out of bed five minutes. Even though I assume Daniel kept her safe, still there is that surge of annoyance and loyalty that fills me, the whole "big brother" act that fools me into thinking that I need to keep her safe and not let her make stupid decisions. Like being with Daniel before breaking things off with Shane. I really hope that didn't happen. That'll just cause more trouble than it's worth.

She doesn't need to be doing what Shane's been doing to her. And no, I don't have completely solid proof that he's cheating - but let me tell you something, a guy doesn't chat up the same girl every day after school while waiting for his girlfriend in the hallway and respond pretty eagerly to the batting of her eyelashes unless something has been going on. I can't mention anything to Ruth, though; she's got a head harder than a bed of nails, and unless I can give her logical, solid proof, then she isn't going to believe me. She's got it in her head that God put them together, and that's the end of that. (I tried mentioning the name of the girl a while back, but I don't think she heard me.)

Honestly, it's just her insecurity that she'll never find

anything better. Though she could look in the barnyard and marry one of the hogs and be better off.

I don't know if I should apologise for my tolerance level being nonexistent today. But really, the morning hasn't been promising, and everything seems to be worsening, and having a filter probably will not improve any of the situations, so I might as well let down the walls and have the words surge forth while I can. I'll be back to pondering in my head and saying almost nothing aloud in no time.

(Wait. I just realised that I *am* saying most of these things in my head. Well, never mind that little plan of mine, then. Already it's backfired. Go me.)

"Fine," Dad says gruffly, pulling tightly on the reins when the chestnut beneath him executes an ungraceful crow-hopping motion. "Ruth, you'll have to wait to work the horses after school. The chickens and the hogs still need to be fed. And you, boy."

Of course he's addressing me. Even Daniel has a name. But not Paul. No, Paul has been reduced to nothing more than a nameless floating entity. A convenience. Another pair of hands for unpaid manual labour. A means to an end of retirement. A futureless bastard. An object. "You, *boy*, clean up this mess that you caused. I'm going to head back up to the house, check on your mother, and eat myself a little bit of well-deserved breakfast."

Excuse me while I punch a couple of holes in the fence post.

When he dismounts from the chestnut, he tosses the reins over the top of the fence, and Daniel darts forward to catch them before us other two can make a move to do the same. He doesn't bother to go to the gate, but rather clamours over the fence and lands directly in front of us, in all of his towering, intimidating glory. I keep my face from contorting into a grimace as he shoulders past me, and although my upper lip twitches, I keep it pressed into the thinnest of lines. I'm not going to let him see that he's getting to me, that his efforts to push my buttons are working. I will not let him be the one to make me crack.

Daniel keeps the smile plastered on his face until my dad disappears from view, and then, he turns serious as a heart attack. "Dude. Paul. What the hell's going on?"

"Don't you even start with me, with that whole 'what the hell's going on' attitude," I say darkly. "Where were you two? Really?"

"Whoa. Not what you think."

"Not what I think, *bullshit*," I spit. "But I'm not even going to bother getting into this right now because guess what. I have this mess to clean up!"

I gesture rather blindly in the general directions of the paddocks. I can't even be sure what time it is, but I know, I just have that inner feeling, that this is going to take long enough, to the point where I'm going to be unable to go to school. I just know it. Nothing is going to go smoothly today. I might as well have a completely clear schedule, to make sure that in case someone else's mess needs to be cleaned up, I can ensure that nothing will interrupt me.

"I'm going to help you," Daniel says hurriedly. "You think I'm going to ditch you to do this shit by yourself? Hell to the no. I usually help you out anyway."

I grit my teeth. It's my pride that makes me want to decline the offer and suffer through the impending torment by myself, even though I know that isn't going to help anybody in the long run. During this time of silence, Ruth decides to speak up. "I-I'll go to the chicken coop. Make sure the chickens are fed. Gather eggs. Check on the peacock. And I'll feed the hogs, too!"

"Ruth —"

"Don't try to deter me, Paul," she scoffs. "And don't give me that *I don't want your help* stuff, either, because I'm *not* going to believe you. You and Daniel can take care of the horses and the cattle."

"As long as you promise not to fret the entire time you're feeding them," I say, rather tiredly. I've had my fill of arguing. "I can hear your silent panic attacks from miles away."

"You're so funny, Paul," she says in retort. "You should think about going to school to be a comedian."

Ouch, she accidentally rubbed the sore spot; I know that she didn't do it intentionally, though, because she hadn't been in the house when Dad had dropped the bomb on me. I'm about to open my mouth, I'm about to explain that even if I actually wanted to be a comedian, I wouldn't be able to attend school for it, but that she should definitely, if that was one of her dreams, but before I can speak nary a word, she has turned, more than likely thinking that I'm going to protest against her helping me out or that I'll be a smart aleck back to her, and bounded in the direction of the coops and the penned area where we keep the chickens and that blasted, self-righteous peacock.

"Come on, man," Daniel says, touching me lightly on the left bicep. "We need to get moving or we aren't going to get to school."

"Not much of a point," is my short reply. "I mean, there're way too many cattle anyways. *I'm* probably not going to make it to school. But like I said, there's not much of a point. Not anymore."

I forget that Daniel doesn't know, either, until he shoots me a bewildered look and clenches the reins more tightly in his fists. "What happened last night?"

"All of my hopes and dreams were dashed," I say drolly,

expression giving nothing away. "We need to get moving."

"Dude. *No*. Not until you tell me what's going on."

I have one foot positioned on the bottom slat of the fence when he spews this out, sounding almost as though he's offended with me for keeping secrets, and I whirl on him, hovering in the air, hands clinging to the topmost slat, near the muzzle of the chestnut. "School doesn't matter anymore, Daniel, because Dad informed me I'm not going to college. Done demanding answers of me now?" I shake my head in mock disgust. "You don't see me standing here, commanding you to tell me what you and my sister were doing last night."

"That's because you and I both know we didn't *do* anything."

"*Bullshit*," I grunt as I swing my leg over and drop into the pasture. "And I'm a secret agent working to expose the underground secrets of human cloning."

"Wow—did that retort actually take time to think of, or do you have long-winded shit like that just laying around?"

"Hey, I can't help that my mind isn't a shallow kiddie pool like yours is." The banter is only a little bit on the malevolent side, at least where I'm concerned, because of the impending migraine-addled hangover that's consuming me and the rapid deepening of the rottenness of my mood. "So start paddling your feet and come on. We have animals to wrangle up."

Daniel stares after me. I can feel the weight of his gaze burning on my back like an open target. Instead of returning fire, though, I sense him shrug and decide to unload his shotgun and put down the weapon. He isn't too interested in arguing, either, even though I'm needling at him. "Whatever you say, *boss*."

Whatever you say, boss. That's the smart-aleck comment that I've given my father whenever he chooses that it's time to poke and prod at me and make sure that I know how worthless I am. Now, I'm feeling even more miserable. Dear God, why in the hell did You decide to make me like my father?

Not that I'd be better off with the mentality of my mother.

I'm a terrible person for thinking these things. I'm going to hell, I just know it.

He clamours after me over the fence, but instead of plopping onto the ground, he moves the horse so that he can slide one leg over the slant of its withers and smoothly transitions from the top slat of the fence to the dip in the horse's back. The wind has died down considerably, but the sunrise still will be unable to penetrate the thick wall of dark clouds that are clustering above this house, and more than likely, above this entire region of Indiana, and so keeping track of time will be a major problem. I didn't don my watch, even though I had gone back into my bedroom, and Daniel definitely isn't wearing one.

"I'll start by getting the cows back into this main pasture," Daniel gestures toward the right. "Since Harold's a cutting horse."

Who in the hell decided to name that poor animal Harold? It couldn't possibly have been my sister. She likes to go with fancier names. (Like Aphrodite and Benedict and Wellington and Juniper.) Not that those are much better in my opinion. Give me something simple to remember, even though simple names tend to be regarded as lame. It would've made more sense for him to be named Ginger.

"And you can close the gate."

"Whatever you say, *boss*," I return quickly, causing my voice to travel several octaves higher as I mimic him. After ensuring that I notice him rolling his eyes so hard at me, I think that they're going to fall right out of their sockets and bounce into the short grass, he kicks the horse — sorry, *Harold* — lightly in the ribcage and trots off in the general direction of the line of trees. I shake my head before I break into a jog and go toward the gate that allows access into the pastures near the road. Upon reaching it, I grasp and grunt, for the hinges are rusted (yet another thing to put on my list of things to do, since no one else will do it) as I push it shut, using all the strength I have in both my upper and lower body reserves in order to manoeuvre the bottom of the gate through the slightly overgrown weeds that have taken up residency near this area. It takes me three minutes longer than it should to finally bridge the gap and loosely wrap the chain in-between the fence post and the edge of the gate itself, but at least it's finished.

I stop for a minute, though, both hands positioned on the gate. How in the hell are we going to pull this little stunt off? Because even if we manage to gather all members of both groups, there's still the situation of transferring them through the middle and into their respective pastures. If it's done simultaneously, it could turn chaotic - but we couldn't necessarily do it separately, either. And there weren't enough halters to put one on each animal and haul them through. There are sixty or seventy head of cattle, and there are fifteen horses. I'm more worried about the cows. They tend to bowl over whatever stands in their way. I consider, for a moment, shaking grain bins and feeding them less tonight just so that I can gather them near, but that would also turn into an unnecessary bustle and hustle and fighting.

Blowing out air through my mouth, I stare off into the distance, near the road, which still is vacant, even though the morning hours grow later. Everything is so incredibly quiet in this moment. Even the hoof beats from the chestnut have faded away as Daniel has immersed himself into the depths of the brush. The wind has died to nothing more than a tranquil rustling of leaves and a darting of grass blades over one another, and the rumbles of thunder are nothing more than a backdrop to the unfolding symphony, a perfect scenery, a painted canvas. I release the gate and put one foot back on the bottom slat, draping my arms across the top, resting my chin against them as I would rest my head upon my pillow, and I let myself think, just for a minute, about how my life would be different if I were in charge of it.

I honestly don't think I would know what to do with myself, if I didn't have to deal with the constant stream of nagging and the belittlement and the reminders that I'm the lowest of the low when it comes to the familial hierarchy that has been established in the household ever since my twin sister and I were born, if I didn't have pressure on me to obtain the best grades - which is a pointless goal, now that I've been informed that I won't be allowed to attend college, that I'm expected to take over the farm and run it in the place of my dad - if I didn't have to constantly fret over ensuring that Ruth is spared the majority of Dad's wrath, if I didn't have to feel this need to protect her from everything harmful in the world, if I didn't have a best friend who was a terrible influence on me and encouraged me to let loose and reminded me that I'm not a robot, as much as I would like to believe it, that I'm a human being with emotions, blood, adrenaline, veins, and a heartbeat - though the brain, at times, is questionable, as it is with all human beings - and if I didn't have to think about the welfare of my mother, making sure that she isn't shipped back off due to someone thinking that she's relapsed, because that place isn't beneficial for her and she would relapse going back —

If none of these things existed, what would my life be?

Beautifully empty.

Of course, that could also go the other way. I would more than likely be even more callous than I already am, and there would be an irreplaceable shallowness that would take root in my pores and force me to become undeniably selfish. I would probably also transform into a narcissist, making myself believe that I needed no one except myself, and that no one was good enough to be blessed by my presence, and so the solitude which I would manage to obtain would be not only empty, but hollow, and that's what I would be as well. Experiences shape people, I guess. And I'm so deeply immersed in mine that I can't imagine living without them.

I'm not entirely sure if that's a good thing or a bad thing.

A wild frantic noise emerging from behind me is what snaps me out of this trance, and I take off, each step a stabbing sensation in the depths of my brain, toward the barn. I had just assumed that my dad probably didn't leave any horses in there; that all of them were out munching on that rich grass. But maybe one of them remained in his stall, not quite finished with his grain or wanting that last little nibble of hay. When I go through the opened doors, I quickly look around the open space — and over the half-door of one of the makeshift stalls, tucked into the left corner, I see a golden, thick-crested neck remove its attached head from where it had been hovering out in the open and lumber backwards toward the few inches of hay that still remained in the wall feeder. Of course the one left in the stall would be Ruth's beloved that she rescued from becoming mangy, flea-bitten and fly-addled in the middle of a hot, humid pasture the one that's bonded so strongly to her, they spoke to one another through glances. It's like the twin connection she and I share - except obviously not, since the horse isn't her twin. Though sometimes I wonder, considering how similar their personalities are. You'd think that they'd clash, but no, they get along far too well. Cause mischief together.

We thought when she brought him home, literally

walking him three-quarters of a mile from his original home down to our ranch, that he was a palomino gelding, a simple Quarter horse, with four gaits and a thick neck. But then, I quickly realised that he was far too tall for a Quarter horse - and asking David, the resident horse expert - he told us quite a few bits of news that we weren't expecting to hear. The first? This horse isn't a gelding; he's a stallion. The second? He isn't a simple Quarter horse; he's half-Thoroughbred, half-Tennessee Walker. And the third? He wasn't fully mature yet; due to lack of nourishment and little to no caregiving, his growth had been stunted. He was two years old when we got him; now, he's seven.

So we managed to obtain a palomino stallion with bloodlines to die for. Because when she searched his full name on the Internet, holy shenanigans, the things we saw, and his sires and grandsires and dams and all that jazz that I understand but don't feel like clarifying because I'm tired were beyond impressive. And so is he. He's a massive beast, and his chest is muscular and his back is gently sloped, and he stands at sixteen hands even, and I am only slightly intimidated by him because he isn't afraid of me in the least. We thought that it was a mistake having a stallion here - but he isn't the typical one. None of our animals, admittedly, are stereotypical. At all.

They're just *weird*. We have a pet peacock, for God's sake.

I just see one little teeny-tiny problem here. Daniel's coming, and I'm going to have no time to put a saddle on this monster - whose call name, by the way, is Xerxes - and I'm going to have to ride him that way and round up a gang of cattle and horses, and of course, the horse herd has mares in it. Some of them are, more than likely, in season.

(How many times am I going to have to state that it's a terrible day before that whole reverse psychology thing takes over and makes sure that it improves?)

In the corner where the horse stalls are, there's a small area sectioned off that's filled with nails in the walls and sawhorses, a place where all the tack is stored. I think his bridle is the one with the metal studs on either side of the noseband; I know when she rides him, she likes having him look his best. She declares it's because he's a narcissist and likes pretty things, but I think it's because she's a girl and she likes pretty things. I cross the expanse of the barn in order to remove it from its respective nail, and then, I go to him; hearing my sure-footed approach, he whirls in his stall to put his neck back out into the aisle and appraise me with a half-interested glare.

"Don't even think about giving me that look," I say warningly. "You already know we have a job that needs to be finished. And I'd appreciate it if you didn't act like a pompous ass when I get on you."

I swear that he raises an eyebrow at me, even though horses don't technically have them, at least not in the way that humans do, and he quickly snorts, still munching on the mouthful of hay that's halfway to falling from his muzzle.

"You love sidestepping and you know it. You'd think you were trained for a competition or something." It brings back all the memories of a slightly younger Ruth eagerly speaking about how she wanted to enter him in tournaments and events, but Dad putting his foot down and saying that it was bad enough she insisted on having a dozen and one horse mouths to feed without spending extra cash on what he considered to be useless, meaningless things. Well, I consider him to be a useless, meaningless thing, so I guess we should stop spending cash on him, too.

Him as in my dad, not the horse.

I glance down at the bridle in my hand, then the awaiting steed in front of me, and I hold a breath in my lungs for a split second. "*Please* take the bit," is what I grumble as I step forward and press a fist directly on his poll, which forces his head down, and begin gently pushing the Pelham bit against his teeth. After a little bit of initial pushing back against it, he takes it, and as I make sure the chin-chain is where it's supposed to be - as in, not inside his mouth alongside the bit - I also push the double-set of reins out of the way, not wanting to step on them and jerk his head down.

This is a damn chore, I'm telling you.

I pull the headpiece over his ears and allow the bridle to settle before fastening the cheek piece, securing it to where I can easily slide three fingers inside of the gap, and the noseband. All this trouble to make sure this son of a bitch doesn't rear on me. It'd be smart to completely tack him up, put on a cutting saddle and a tie-down so that he knows it's business time and there's no dilly-dallying - and even smarter would be to ride an actual cutting horse - but alas, Daniel's on the only one that wasn't released to the damn wilderness, and I sure as hell am not letting him on Xerxes.

Besides, Ruth and I have both been on the backs of horses since we were old enough to scream about it. The only time I've fallen off is when I'm being stupid - and I'm not going to be stupid. No, I don't want any comments about riding while hung-over, thanks.

"Right, old man," I say, even though he's nowhere near old.

Daniel's whooping approaches with even more rampant speed. "Don't know how this will go, but —" I open his stall door, grasping both sets of reins and tossing them over his head. He starts voraciously nodding his head, up and down, up and down, the cords in his neck stretching and contracting with the movements, as I take hold of a large, thick section of his mane.

"— it'll go."

I bend my knees a bit and pull on his mane, landing on my abdomen in the dip in his back, and as he starts walking forward, I tighten the reins, slowing him to a prancing in place as I ensure that my legs are where they need to be and that I'm facing forward, looking through the space directly in-between his ears and not at his swishing tail and rotund flanks. Then, I loosen my grip, and he comes out from the barn just as the stampede of cattle begins to flood through the wide opening of the gate and into the pasture. There's a flash of chestnut as Harold and Daniel move as one, back and forth, making sure none of the older cattle or those annoying, bawling calves break away from the rest of the herd and try to sprint back into the safety of the trees. Though I'm glad, at least, that the thunderstorm seems to be receding for the moment. Of course, that doesn't mean we're safe from a downpour; it just means that there won't be a bunch of wind making a racket and scaring the living hell out of us all as we're forced to deal with this situation.

"Okay!" Daniel shouts at me. "Uh—what *now?*"

Both gates are open. The fifteen horses are hearing the commotion and the lead mare, Ruth's second personal favourite, is coming, ears perked, to check things out, the remainder of her posse trailing a distance behind her. Xerxes spots this beautiful Appaloosa and lets loose one of the most vocal whinnies I've ever heard, sounding like a young, newborn colt who has just discovered running for the first time and wants to kick his heels up in ecstasy. Her nostrils flare, but she doesn't answer back, instead staring down the herd of cattle as though they're the most monstrous things she's ever seen in her life - and honestly, I don't understand this reaction, considering she's been around these same cows since she was rescued from someone's dilapidated lean-to three years ago. But then again, I don't think I would be exactly happy to see these old friends as they continue lumbering toward the other pasture, their actual stretch of land.

I quickly glaze over everything with a practised eye before tapping Xerxes in the right rib and shortening my reins so that he's unable to get his head. I make sure that my seat is tight against his spine before I shout back, "You keep the cows near that far fence line and I'll herd the horses past them; Raina will follow Xerxes, hopefully."

Raina, the mare. Daniel nods his consent and starts his hooting and hollering again, speeding up the last of the cows so that they meander through and he's able to follow. Then he kicks Harold and spurs him into a canter, looping around the outside of the herd, then stopping, and heading back in the direction he came, making their group push together against each other, mooing and yelling their protests, but since they're cows, and they're relatively dumb and have to be told what to do - which is *follow what everyone else is doing* - slowly, but surely, they start to press themselves together. Daniel continues rounding out the descending size of the half-circle, and once there's enough area cleared, I move Xerxes forward, past Harold, who nickers and reaches out his head toward the stallion - and Xerxes responds by putting all of his weight on his front legs and right rear, and raising his left rear to aim a high-velocity kick at Harold's muzzle.

Both of us idiots are nearly unseated from our mounts. And for some reason, we start cackling about it. What bullshit we're wading through, I'm telling you. This is ridiculous. Xerxes continues forward at a running walk, a gait he acquired from his Walker bloodlines, thank God - it means I don't have to endure that awful bumping excuse of a trot. Raina starts nodding her head up and down, and he returns the sentiments, and she approaches him, which attracts the attention of the rest of the horses, and they all start doing their little whinnies, their neighs, and the youngest one has his eyes roll back in his head. He needs to be gelded, but no, Dad doesn't want to put out any more money into these beasts. So I might have to deal with a young stallion challenging this older stallion for this group of assorted geldings and mares. Fantastic. Fortunately, though, he's taking up the rear of the pack, and nowhere near the front; all the docile ones are heading towards us.

I really hope this works. *I really hope this works.* I'm legitimately *praying* that this works. Because if there's any more trouble —

Crack. A streak of lightning causes the telephone line across and down the street a little ways to explode in an array of sparks, and the horses and the cattle go insane. The horses start pushing to get through the opening in the gate - which I'm in with Xerxes - and the stallion is terrified in and of himself, and so he spins on his heels, half-rearing, and bolts toward the cattle, which are attempting to scatter.

(THANKS A LOT, GOD!)

"Are you shitting me?" I hear Daniel scream. Or, at least, I think that's what he says. I can't hear him over the whistling of the wind in my ears. The horses are quicker and lighter on their feet than the cattle, and they make it into their paddock without much trouble - except Xerxes is out of control. I pull on his reins, sit hard in my seat, try to make him turn a circle - but that's difficult when there's a mare to your left and a gelding to your right and then —

-

"You're a moron. You know that? A righteous, Grade A moron. They should package you and sell you in stores as the face for *Stupid Pills.* What were you guys thinking? No, don't tell me — you *weren't* thinking. Now, there's a surprise. You both could have been seriously injured — or k i l l e d!"

I don't know if it's a shock or not that the person giving me and Daniel this lecture isn't his parents, nor is it my parents, but rather, Ruth, the twin sister, with her hands shoved on her hips and her hair askew from it being whipped about while she was checking on the chickens. She had come back to discover that by some unfathomable miracle - also known as Daniel's inherent patience for all things farming - the animals had been put into their respective pastures. However, there had been two problems - Xerxes had managed to run off with his bridle still on, and he also had crow-hopped with such a force that I had been knocked from him by a low-hanging branch that caught me in the forehead and literally bent me over backwards.

It doesn't hurt, though. Maybe that's because my eyebrows and features seem to be permanently creased in this glower as the bag of ice on my head, with a towel draped over it, begins to melt, and little rivulets of water race down the sides of my face. I'm too numb to hurt. We're all upstairs, in her bedroom, and she's closed the door behind us. Daniel has collapsed in her desk chair and is swinging back and forth, eyes moving from the floor to my face as he smirks like a cat that ate the canary. Ruth paces in the middle of her room, feet padding on the rug in the centre. One of the cats managed to follow us in - not the one I saw earlier, but a calico one, so affectionately named Luna - and she has decided that my lap is comfortable. I'm sitting cross-legged in the middle of Ruth's bed, and her covers are bunched all around me; I'm still in my clothes that I'd changed into before going outside, but I didn't see any dirt rubbing off onto her blankets and sheets, so I don't fret too much. Luna purrs unceasingly, her front paws digging into the leg of my jeans, kneading at the fabric as her eyes slowly drift shut.

What a God-awful day. I don't even want to look at the clock.

It looks like Ruth has showered. For Pete's sake, how long was I unconscious? She yanks her fingers unceremoniously through her dark curls; it looks like she has some sort of hair — gel stuff that she's applying. *Girls.* Daniel shakes his head. The perfume of the hair stuff makes my nostrils burn and my temples begin to throb. I want to lay back, but the minute I do that, she darts forward and shoves her hand, palm and fingers flattened, against the base of my spine.

"None of that!" she half-shrieks, though she quickly tones her voice back down into a whisper. I wince away from her regardless of the change in volume. "You almost got a concussion, Paul! Don't even think about going to sleep until the bedroom stops spinning!"

Damned twin telepathy. How else would she know that the entire world is spinning? I'm grateful for the pressure on my back; if it weren't there, holding me steady, then I know I would probably fall to the side, unconscious again, tongue hanging out like a thirsty dog and eyes rolling back in my head as if I'd been smacked with a thick tree branch. Oh, *wait.*

"Yes, Doctor Ruth," I grumble, eliciting an eruption of half-stifled laughter from the monkey in the corner. My eyes have drifted shut, much like Luna's; both of us open one to glower at that blond-haired fool, who quickly clears his throat and presses a closed fist against his mouth to stop the sound.

"I need to get to school," she frets. "Ugh, why it had to be this morning of all mornings! I have that huge presentation in my literature class, and Mrs. Stevens *hates* it when we walk in late, and I have it first period, and I'm going first!"

"Whoa, there, Babe Ruth." Now that's a nickname I haven't heard in a while. It's certainly not one that she allows the members of her family to call her. But her face nearly illuminates to the brightness of the sun itself when Daniel uses it toward her.

Despite my next-to-incoherent state, my suspicions are aroused once again. There is definitely something going on here. They can deny it all they want. And they've acted on it. I might not have dated a thousand and one girls in my lifetime, or really had a romantic experience besides that really awkward almost-first kiss that happened when I was freshman - I ended up getting up from the bleachers and sprinting out of the gymnasium, screaming about how I had stayed too late, how I needed to get home and do the chores; needless to say, that cheerleader didn't want to be with a guy who put farm work over her and her miles of dark-brown hair and glittering emerald eyes and clear braces. Nor have I ever had sex. (I'm serious. Not a single time. And no, I'm not interested in getting laid before I'm twenty.) But I'm telling you, there are some things that I know, and those expressions on their faces, I've seen them before.

I've seen them in movies. I've imagined them when I manage to sit down and read a book and it happens to have one of those romance things in it. I've seen them, at one time, a very long time ago, on the faces of my parents - and I've seen them on the faces of Daniel's parents. I saw it as a glimpse on a face I once knew, and I've seen it on that same face that floats through my dreams to this day. And these are expressions that promise something is blossoming, something that can't be stopped in its tracks no matter who else is in the picture, no matter how terrible the world is.

It's sickening. Hah. I almost can't even *look* at it, it's so sweet. Especially for my blurred, exhausted eyes. So I instead look at the top of Luna's head and reach a tentative hand toward it, rubbing her ears, causing her to purr even more loudly and lean into my callused palm.

Did they talk in this little gap of time? I think so. Because those looks are gone. And Daniel looks stricken. Not surprised, just as though he swallowed something wrong. And Ruth is very, very pale, and she inhales, and she says, "It's okay, you know. Remember what we talked about."

Oh, I have a thousand questions burning at my lips. But then, she straightens her navy-blue cardigan and gathers up her leather messenger bag, pursing her lips in a smile at Daniel before coming to me and placing a hand on the side of my face. I wince, again, at her cool touch, but at least this isn't as painful as her voice had been.

"Don't even think about going to school," she says quite fussily. "You're in no condition to do it. And don't do anything *else* stupid!"

I mumble something, I think, and her face erupts in a smile as she moves away from me and Daniel, leaving us there in her bedroom. I think I hear the door latch, but my ears are ringing, and without her hand there, keeping me supported, I fall backwards, thank God, onto her array of pillows, and I groan in a combination of agony and contentment as black spots meander into my eyesight.

There's pressure at the end of the bed, then distinct warmth beside me. Daniel's joined me. He stares at the ceiling, and I reach upward, haphazardly wrapping the bag of ice in the hand towel and clapping it down over my eyes so that I'm staring at nothing but darkness.

"She's catching a ride from Shane."

Well, that almost startles me directly out of my so-called concussion. But I force myself to remain laying down. "Fantastic."

"That's what I said." His surly tone suggests he thinks otherwise. But we both hate that bastard. We both know he's nothing but trouble. "But she's breaking up with him."

I admire that note of confidence in his voice, and I purse

my lips. "Seriously?"

"Seriously."

Unconsciousness overtakes me as I manage to utter one last little thing: "What a glorious day after all."

Blaming of the Cobwebs

October 9th
Manchester, Indiana

Ruth Reagan

Only one sound fills the space between us, and it's not the usual one of banter, of conversation that is meaningless to all except for our own selves; it is the grumbling of the half-clogged motor that needs to be either overhauled until it's unrecognisable or completely replaced. Shane has prostrated his hand to rest so that the palm is facing the ceiling of the car and his fingers are unnaturally curled. I know he's waiting for my fingers to slide into the spaces so that he can give me that cheesy line that has been used a thousand different times on a thousand different girls and somehow sounds romantic because you are both in the moment. But I can't bring myself to do it. I want nothing to do with that type of physical contact. Not with him.

So with my black cloth satchel unfastened and opened at my feet, I pull out a stack of notecards bound together by a green rubber band and unravel them, spreading them out in order upon my thighs. I have absolutely no need to memorise their contents or even look at them, because I know everything backwards and forwards. Instead of mulling over the significance of the strewn-together letters, I instead observe the ink of the pen I had used. It'd been one of those that spilt dark blue forth from its tip, but upon shaking it, I discovered that it was half-empty - and by the time I was near to finishing the outline for this presentation, the ball of the pen was starting to turn translucent from lack of colour. I'd placed it upon my tongue, I'd shaken it until my wrist felt as though the bones were jammed underneath one another, and barely, just barely, a smidgeon of ink came out.

So over half of these notecards have beautiful, rich print - and the latter four or five have this haphazard scribble where I attempted to squeeze in as much information as possible - and then the last two, the very last two, are in pitch black ink because I could salvage no more from the blue pen, which I sorrowfully threw away.

I'm not the rich blue nor the rich black ink, though my mind feels as though it's been coloured to resemble a bruise in such a manner. I'm the faded ink in-between and I don't know what to do about it. In this morning alone, I bore witness to three or four near-death experiences, narrowing ones that ended in my brother and my best friend turning into zombies on my bed as I left them. They'd probably end up sleeping all day, and I wouldn't blame them. And here I had thought that my time at the henhouse had been difficult, catching a chicken that decided to squawk and wake the remainder of the sleeping hens awake as it scrabbled around the floor of the house and pecked at nonexistent feed. Here I had thought that feeding the peacock and avoiding the way it swooshed its feathers at me had been annoying. And I'd arrived back at the fence to discover Daniel screaming a mixture of obscenities and regular words, pointing enthusiastically at my stallion, Xerxes, who had broken free from his rider and was sprinting around the pen with a bridle on and nothing else, and then seeing my twin brother sprawled out, paralysed and half-conscious on the ground, a large red welt growing in the direct centre of his forehead.

My day had been nothing compared to theirs. Though I had been the cause of some of Daniel's stress, which admittedly made me feel guiltier than I wanted to express, than I *still* want to express. Though that had all been smoothed out.

Oh, why am I sitting in the passenger's seat of this old truck, fooling myself into thinking that the situation had figured its own self out? There was still a heavy, tremendous burden that had been placed upon my shoulders, one that I had yet to dispose of out the window. Still I needed to tell Shane that we were over, that we honestly had been over for a while, but that I had not wanted to simply walk away from something we had put a lot of work into, because I didn't want to seem like some sort of a *flake*. There were so many words springing to the tip of my tongue, resembling the poison of a viper as it's about to insert teeth into the flesh of its prey - and yet nothing is expelled.

The silence stretches ever on.

I flatten one of the notecards, which has started to curl up around the edges, and my fingers go over the corners three times in a row before I hear Shane emit a tremendous, frustrated sigh. He reaches forward and switches on the stereo, and my ears automatically wince backward when the newest country music hit blasts through the tin can speakers. I never really understood why he bothered listening to that type of music when I know he doesn't really like it, but I'm not going to break the silence in order to ask him something trivial like that. I really wouldn't mind if the quiet was never breached by words at all.

Of course, though, my wishful thinking is nothing more than that, and after a couple of minutes with listening to the current hit, he suddenly swoops the volume knob to the left and nearly shuts the radio off. It startles me, and one of the notecards almost falls off my lap and flutters onto the ground, but I snatch it up before it can do that. He nearly turns fully in his seat to look at me; my eyes widen when he takes his off the road. I haven't seen his face this serious ever since the day that he asked me to be his girlfriend. This is worrisome. It sets me even more on edge than I already am. Then, a streak of hope fills me; perhaps he's going to bring it up first, say that he has been mulling it over and decided that we are no longer working, and in that case, all I would have to do is bite my lip, appear tearful, and begrudgingly agree with him.

"Ruth, is something wrong? Do you need to talk about it?"

Finally. Here is the cue I've been waiting for. Here is the moment where I am able to fully and completely express myself, allow him to know what exactly is on my mind, and there is going to be absolutely nothing that will stop me.

"Oh, no. There's nothing. Just tired."

Wait a minute—that isn't what I wanted to say at all, not what I've been rehearsing to myself this whole time. I want to continue the thread of words, but it seems as though something has sealed shut my lips together, and I only manage a half-pressed smile instead. Sure, absolutely nothing will stop me. Nothing except myself. Myself and my fear of whatever.

With a very sly smile, Shane reaches across the centre console and captures my hand in his, bringing it to rest on the cheap plastic. "You need to quit staying up and worrying about your grades, babe. Seriously, you're already on your way to being valedictorian. There's not much to worry about. You're set."

My stomach is a pit of uneasiness. It's not me who's close to being that status, but rather my twin brother. I'm closer to being the salutatorian. And no, before I am asked, I don't really mind that Paul is excelling a little bit more in academics than I am. The last time that we spoke about colleges and universities, he wanted to proceed into medical school and become a heart surgeon. I don't know if that's changed, considering the last time we spoke in depth about that was about seven months ago, before I started dating Shane, but he has to have the top marks in order to get scholarships and into the school of his choosing either way.

Was the last in-depth conversation I had with my brother,

who has been there for me the better part of nineteen years, *really* seven months ago? Has dating Shane really sucked away that much of my life from me, taken away all of these possible conversations and nuances that I could have had with others, including my own blood? The thought of this having happened, and me not noticing, me being swept away into the hypnotic stigmas of his irises that managed to capture me and unravel me as though I had been bound with ropes and twine and presented to him on a platter, causes me to almost become even more nauseous than I already am. I need to use this to my advantage. I need to claim sickness and demand to be taken home.

I need to get out of this truck.

I cannot tell you where this little blaring alarm came from, but there it is, right there in the forefront of my mind, and it is overwhelming all other thoughts, including that of Daniel and of my promise to break up with Shane today. Because there is something approaching, and I cannot say what, because I honestly have no idea, but I'm deeply unsettled and nervous, and my foot is actually beginning to jiggle in place, a habit that I haven't done since my freshman year of high school passed me by. Someone has set loose an array of scorpions and insects into my gut, and they titter about with their prickling claws along the linings of my torso. Since one of my hands is taken - and albeit becoming clammier as the seconds wear on - I use the other one to press against the flatness, wanting to quell the sensations and failing, only heightening them, it seemed.

There is only one solution, and I know it, and I have already said it. *I need to get out of this truck.*

But how? By flinging myself out of the passenger's side door? Talk about being overdramatic. No, I'll be out of the truck soon enough. We are, after all, driving to school, and there's perhaps ten or so minutes left, and then, I'll exit this cab and I'll

FROM WHENCE THEY CAME

be home free. Until the afternoon, when I can confront him in a public setting. I'm unsure as to why I'm so afraid, so phobic about this, so nervous about him possibly becoming enraged at the prospect of our breakup, considering he's never become violent or anything of the sort with me before.

I mean, not *really*.

"Oh, I know." I'm beginning to feel obligated to fill the silent void. "But I mean, there's a lot on the line, so I can't help but worry. Everything comes from hard work."

"That's something your dad always tells me."

Another twinge near my heart that causes the pulse to stutter. Dad always manages to have kind words for Shane, who isn't his son; why can't he manage to be a little bit more lenient on the guy who *is* his flesh and blood? (All right, stop this right now, Ruth. Dad has given Paul compliments before. Backwards ones. But still.)

"He's a smart guy," I hedge to cover the odd silence. "Been through a lot, seen a lot. He has a lot of words of wisdom to impart."

"Impart." Shane repeats this word and runs his thumb over my knuckles. I notice that it does not induce as shiver as it has previously. "When you use words like that, it's just *adorable*. You're like a little walking dictionary. I seriously can't get over it."

His words should not be falling flat to me.

"And so, to surprise my little dictionary, I've planned something awesome. Our eight months is coming up, after all. Of course, though, you remember."

He laughs. That, too, has no roundness, no character. I swear this is because I've purposefully forced myself to turn against him, but my gut tells me otherwise, especially as it continues sinking into my hipbones. "You write down *everything* in that little calendar of yours."

377

The blue one that always is kept contained in the side pocket of my satchel. The other one is reserved for bottles of water, soda, or sweet tea. I should've written in there for today: *break up with Shane.* Then I would be more apt to get on top of doing it, making sure it happened. Strange how that seems to register with the human mind, how writing things causes them to become irremovable as stone, etched and permanent, even though they aren't anything of the sort.

"Of course I remember." I note that the pitch of my voice is incredibly high, even for me. There is nothing girlish about this, however, nothing flirtatious and nothing in the way of attempting to be cute and giggling. I am repeating what he said and I am doing so with a very odd representation of fright. I should not be afraid of the man I'm dating, and yet here I am, very nearly cowering away from him in the seat. "You planned something *awesome*? Ah—"

I swallow. The air has become thick in here. Thick like blood.

"Something awesomely *special*," he adds with a smugness and a satisfaction that is difficult to miss.

Joyful, joyful, we adore thee, how glorious the school building is looking as we slow to a stop at the intersection in front of it. How much the scenery has blurred in my time in this truck. Usually I take out moments to inhale the changing colours of the leaves and the lines in the cobblestoned streets - for our high school is located upon the outskirts of a small town that has a nameless populace that somehow knows your business no matter how silent to the grave you keep it. Not today, it seems. The red brick of the main school building and the circular driveway that leads to its front doors never has truly claimed a welcoming feel for me, not when my heart soars in the fields and runs through the crop rows and dances in the golden heat of the seasons. But today, it certainly has taken on the appearance of knight in shining armour. I might even imagine the bottom classroom windows to be the visor of his helmet.

"Is this one of those times where I have to guess?" I don't want to ask the question, but I force myself to do it anyway, to continue with the semblance of normal. I can see students milling about, stopping to speak with one another on the front walkways, and parking on the side of the widened streets, slamming their old car doors too hard and clinging to their books as though they'll save them. Save them from what? Who knows? The ghosts that supposedly haunt the corridors of the separate cafeteria, which is housed in the old nunnery across the way.

"It's one of those times where no matter how much you guess, I'm not giving you any hints. You're just going to have to wait and see."

There is a bracing smile on my face when he turns on the road in front of the school. We are nearing the parking lot, and I will be able to drop the bomb and run for it and hide in my classes and my presentation. I begin to stack my notecards back in order, and I tie them all together with the rubber band, winding them around three or four times. "Well, then I can't wait. When exactly is this happening?"

"Now."

The rubber band snapping against the face of the nearest index card suddenly becomes very loud in my ears, reverberating and echoing and causing a pulsation in my left temple. I'm staring hard at the side of his face, and in the blurriness of the background, I see that he's passed by the entrance to the school, as well as the parking lot next to it and around behind the musical auditorium, and he's continuing to drive down the incline of a hillside that I have only been down once or twice before and my heart is pounding in my chest and I can't breathe.

"Shane." I attempt to shove some ferocity in my voice, for I am sick and tired of sounding like some frightened little girl, but to no avail. I only succeed in making my words crack like new cement. "Shane. We can't do it today. Or — at least, not right now. I have my English presentation and you have a history exam over the civil war!"

He glances at me, and there is a shrewdness to his gaze that causes all of the moisture in my mouth to run dry. I don't like that expression. I daresay I've never seen it before, and I hope that I never see it again, but there it is still, directed at me in those dark eyes. He runs a hand through the growing brunette hair, and his features are etched in an odd, hollow gaze. I fear I'm beginning to hallucinate from the lack of air to my lungs; in this, I force myself to inhale quite deeply, though I also instinctively press my back against the door.

I know exactly what this surprise is now. There's making no mistake now, not even in my naivety and lack of experience with relationships. There's no mistaking that burning in those irises.

"Live a little, Ruth." There is no derivative, no nickname, and no attempts to soothe or to comfort. "It's time to be daring."

"Not interesting in either when my grades are on the line," I say primly. My father's temper enters my veins, and I slam my fist against the window. "Turn around and go back."

He signals that he's about to turn to the left, and with a rolling stop, he executes it, quite widely, almost mowing down a car that is waiting its turn. The little green Ford blares its horn, and I barely have time to flash the driver an apologetic, panicked glance before Shane roars past them, the rear tires squealing as they leave behind blackened marks and the exhaust pours out a cloud of thickened, black smoke.

THICK LIKE BLOOD —

"Not a chance, Ruth. This is happening. Today."

"Okay, no, it's not. It's *not* happening today." I need to keep myself from having one of those infamous panic attacks that I've inherited from my mother. I will not allow myself to lose my sanity and my ability to make clear, logical choices, not in this instance. I struggle enough when I am not underneath pressure. "We have obligations elsewhere, at school. And if our parents find out we're skipping—"

"We aren't going to be skipping." He's beginning to sound frustrated. Or bored with me. Bored with having to explain himself this thoroughly. "We're going to have a nice morning and roll in around lunchtime. It's really simple, Ruth. Besides, it's coming up on that time."

"That *time*?" I almost mouth the words.

He chuckles at me. "Yeah. Back when we first started dating and I asked you about this. Remember? You said that you'd be ready around eight or nine months, that you needed to get your footing, clear your head, make sure everything was set in place, that it was what God wanted. Well, now we're certain. We've been praying about it enough." Please, Lord, *please*, that *can't* be resentment in his tone. "The time's here. You *are* ready, aren't you?"

What the hell am I supposed to say to that?

"N—"

"Don't worry." He cuts off the answer. He doesn't want to hear it. That much is becoming obvious, how much he does not want to hear anymore what I have to say because he knows that it'll be in protest. My thighs begin to quiver, and I press my palms, flattening my fingers against them, willing them to grow still once more. But they tremble ever faster. "I'll be gentle."

My heartbeat tires and pounds slowly against the wall of my chest. The beat of this music is thick. Thick like blood. I've heard you bleed the first time. I don't want to bleed. I don't want to be here at all. I've heard it hurts. I don't want to hurt. I don't want to do this, I don't, and he's not listening to me!

The atmosphere is so thick. Thick. Like blood.

"Turn around," I say again, as though it'll make any difference. "Go back."

With the way that my stomach spirals downward into the cavern between my pelvic bones, I fear that I am truly sinking underneath the amount of dread I feel. Purposefully I glare out the passenger's side window; the scenery passes by with too much speed, and by the way that the elderly truck's motor is beginning to whine in protest, I know that he's pushing the vehicle far past what it should be allowed to do. The scurrying thought of legitimately tossing myself from the cab passes through, but that would be a suicide mission. Though, come to think of it, that would be a much better fate than that which might befall me if I stay in here.

"Everything's going to be fine."

I swear upon my fast-approaching grave, if he says something of that sort one more time, I am going to flip this truck over with sheer willpower.

It's with this train of thought that there is a paralysation that shoots through me, overwhelms the nervosa taking residence in my abdomen and causes my fingers to become unsteady now, hovering in the air and quivering as I turn them this way, that way, staring at them, clenching them tightly against the palm of my hand before unwinding them, repeating the motion. Never before have I been capable of these sorts of thoughts. The amount of violence, the vehemence that fills them, is foreign to me, as though I have been thrust into an entirely new universe, where emotions run wild and unchecked, where a mind is an unruly forest instead of an organised filing cabinet, where there is not just a black shade and a white blankness but several hues of grey filling the spaces in-between, and this territory truly is frightening to me, and I am uncertain how to handle this surge of power which has been bestowed to me. It is almost as though I have been underneath the draw of a lengthened slumber and the weariness of my limbs is beginning to fade. It is as though there have been shackles around my wrists and I am yanking them free of the decaying soil.

Then, it occurs to me. *My dream.* A pale blue word floating down from the depths of the sky toward me, the edges of the letters blurred and nigh unreadable. The soaring, perpetually comical landscape that surrounded me, but the very real, tangible shackles that had entangled me into a catacomb that I knew not existed. Could this possibly be the physical representation of the elements of my dream coming true? Was Shane's hold on me the significance of the shackles, and was the pale, blue word the coming forthwith of these emotions, of these feelings that had been padlocked away into a waterlogged chest for entirely too long?

"And here we are."

Shane announces our arrival at the spot with a glorious fanfare that only he is feeling. I feel nothing. All of the emotions have been wiped away, and there is only an unfathomable amount of ire. Everything becomes very clear to me. One of these such things is that Shane is either very stupid or very much an asshole. He's ignoring the glower that has overtaken the normally relaxed lines of my face, and there is still that smugness that I noted earlier, but instead of scaring me, it only serves to fuel this very odd, very uncontrollable fire that has been set in my gut.

It seems as though he has pulled off the main road and travelled some ways down a dirt-trodden path, the rear tires having left a cloud of pale sepia dust in their wake. We are now positioned in the middle of a field which has recently been ploughed and consequently forgotten, allowed to grow over. A nice blanket of dead grass lies under the tires, as well as a couple of framing assorted bushes and shrubbery. We are also directly underneath the shade of a large oak tree, whose leaves have long since forsaken its branches and fallen onto the ground below to create a much crunchier footing. Now that the sound of the noisy, strained motor has died away, I can hear distinctly, pretty far away, the babbling of a small stream, for he has cracked the driver's side window now that the wind from driving is gone.

He reaches for my hand again. How odd that I failed to notice when he released it to yank upon the steering wheel with great force. I wonder if he handles girls' shoulders with that same amount of intimidation and fierceness. I'll not be finding out.

I'm faced with a choice. I can allow him to take the hand he reaches for, or I can lash out. And with the way that there is that warmth stirring within me, I already know precisely what decision is going to be made before I even have the words of retort to speak alongside with it.

The pads of his fingers brush against the tendons which have been made prominent by the clenching into a fist. Immediately, I pull my hand away.

"I said no."

Shane seems confused. But I'm not fooled. "You didn't say —"

"Oh, I did. But you didn't let me finish. Because you knew *exactly* what I was going to say, that I was going to say *no*, I'm *not* ready, and you didn't want to hear it."

A delicate sneer appears. This is *delicious*, this odd fit of temper, this anger that swirls so passionately about within me and threatens to officially explode into a chaotic cesspool of oil and writhing flame. I almost wish that I could pry myself open and let it become a personification, let it cascade over my skin and become officially what I am instead of a passing fancy. It would make so many things so much easier. But I suppose this wrath only comes when I've had enough.

And believe you me. I've had *enough*.

Now he's understanding. Now *he's* the one getting mad. And I don't care.

"Are you *serious* right now? *Are you serious?*"

"Not sure why this is such a big deal. You should've known— you *should've known*," My voice raises in volume when he turns away and rubs his face with his hand, "that I'd react this way. Especially considering what time it is and where we've got to be. But besides that, I'm *not ready* to have sex with you." I'll be blunt. "I *told* you that I would tell you when I was and you pushing it is *not* helping matters!"

"You're never going to want to," he sneers, and he throws his fist against the door. This causes me to flinch before he turns back to me, and his irises have darkened with the rejection. "I thought that by giving a little bit of a nudge, demonstrating that I cared enough to do something special for it, it would help. I swear to God, Ruth, I had no idea that you were such a prude!"

"A *prude*! Well, I'm so sorry that I value myself and have beliefs that prevent me from just so freely giving it out." My hands tremble ever faster. "I want to go back to school."

"You promised." Here comes the attempt at a guilt trip. Little does he know that it isn't going to work. "You promised me that at this time, you'd be ready. That you'd trust me enough. That you'd know me enough by now, and you'd be able to do it!"

"You're hellbent on a promise I'm not ready to keep." Daggers in my eyes. Daggers that are stabbing him and causing him to bleed out on the cloth seat and mercilessly churning into the pulsating organ that is his heart and killing him. "Things change, you know. Realisations take place." Implications that he doesn't catch. "And if you really knew me, then this wouldn't be an issue in the first place, would it? Because you wouldn't mind waiting. You wouldn't mind me getting myself sorted."

"Getting yourself *sorted?*" He shakes his head. "Sometimes, you speak another language to me."

"Not so cute now, is it?" I roll my eyes and I unlock the doors, preparing to get out. "Not so cute now that your little walking dictionary is denying you, is it?"

"Don't you turn your back on me!" I freeze. I've heard that line before. From my father to my mother. "Don't you *dare.*"

"Oh — what a shame," I say shakily, yanking on the door handle, causing it to open and my bag to fall out onto the crunchy leaves. "I *already have.*"

He grabs at the back of my shirt and gathers up a fistful of it, twisting me off balance so that I, too, fall unceremoniously to the ground below with a painful jolt to the right shoulder. My hip sinks into a bit of mud, dirtying my favourite pair of dark washed jeans, and my foot catches on the step-up into the truck and turns so that my ankle is caught in it. Pulling the cuff of my boot free, I straighten myself and brush off the loose bits of dirt that are caught on the fabric before snatching up my backpack and slinging it over my shoulder. I'll walk back to the confounded school if I have to.

"You're being so overdramatic about this." Shane's voice slithers at me from the other side of the truck cab. His footsteps rattle after me. "This is ridiculous!"

"You're right. It is. Shouldn't even be an issue." I retain my primness even in my fit of temper, even though the anger that courses as blood through my arteries and stems the pumping of my heart. "Shouldn't have been brought up."

"You *owe* me!" This statement causes me to halt. "I picked you up off the ground after that little incident and I promised I'd be patient as you got over it. Well, everyone's patience runs out, Ruth. And it's been a long time since it even happened."

Tendons in my neck pop out as I clench my teeth together, and I shove my hand down over the top of my messenger bag to secure its place on my shoulder blade. Images are brought forth with his words, muddled ones of a bed with pale yellow sheets and a cold blast of air accosting my naked skin from the open window, with the bitter taste of alcohol still coating my tongue and a staleness that caused my gritty eyes to be blurred and unable to focus. There was a lot of shouting, and then Daniel's warm arms underneath my bare skin, carrying me away from the scene. Daniel.

"Oh, and because it's been a *long time*, you expect me to just be *over it*?" I whirl upon him now, and I see him take a step backward. He's about a yard away from me, and he seems to want to keep this distance in-between us, but this is dissatisfying to me, and I begin to close the gap with short steps. "You expect me to just *get over* an assault?"

(An attempted rape.) I spit out the words. They're poison to me. Saying it, putting a name to it, makes it far too real.

"You expect me to get over my drink getting drugged and me having no clue *who* I was, *where* I was, *what* I was *doing?* Thanks, Shane. Thanks a *whole* lot. Best boyfriend in the world."

"I'm the only boyfriend you've ever had. You wouldn't know something better if it came along. There *isn't* anything better." His words are losing potency. I wonder what he's hoping to prove, hoping to do by continuing on in this manner. Does he want to fuel the fire, want to stem a break-up, want to separate from me? Because that's how this is going to end.

"Who in God's name do you think you are, Shane? A gift to women? The best thing that's ever graced this green earth?" I'm not sure how the discussion, how the argument took this turn, but I'm glad it did, because now, I am finally saying everything that has been bottled up inside of me for eight months and growing like a fiendish mutation. The thought of someone I knew long ago crosses my mind, and the boy with the strange-coloured eyes, Daniel, also appears. "You're not. I can tell you that. You're, in fact, the *worst* thing that's ever been *born*."

Oh, the vehemence, the hatred. He has no idea what to do with it. Blinking in surprise, he stands there, almost twiddling his thumbs as I continue toward him, and my steps quicken until I am standing directly beneath him, head craned back so that I am staring him directly in the eyes, and now, the roles have been reversed. No longer am I the afraid little girl. He is. Because he is witnessing something that he has never seen before, and that is my intolerance, my loathing, my anger.

"Don't you *dare* insult me."

"Don't you dare insult *me*. I'm tired of laying down and letting you say whatever you want when I get to say nothing that I think."

"And who's better than me? Huh? Who've you met that would put up with you like I have?"

My lips curl into a twisted rosebud, the petals curdling and blackening as they are burned. "A lot of people."

"Name *one*."

"Daniel." The name emerges. "Daniel doesn't care whether I express myself or not. He doesn't push me around, doesn't demand things of me. He stops when I say no and he doesn't ask a lot of questions about why I'm saying it!" The glare hardens further. "Nor does he kidnap me and attempt to coerce me into something I'm not ready for."

The words hang in the minute space for a moment, before his face contorts and he sneers down at me. "Daniel." He laughs harshly. "Daniel *Stamp*?"

There's another slight pause, then he leans forward, pressing the side of his nose against mine, and it would be an extremely romantic gesture if it were not for the way that his eyes seared me skinless. "I knew it."

My heartbeat slows further. It has been pumping madly and wildly for these past few moments, and with his statement, it decides that it has had enough of this nonsense. The sudden change makes the edges of my vision blur and an odd swirling to appear in my brain, as though I've been injected with morphine.

"What's *that* supposed to mean?"

"You know e x a c t l y what it means." He sneers. "Even you, innocent, naive, prudish Ruth. You know *exactly what I mean.*"

I refuse to allow myself to appear visibly shaken, and I turn away from him, once again defying the spat-out command to never turn my back on him, and I pace away a few steps before I'm able to speak again. "I don't know what you're talking about."

His grip is harsh upon my shoulder as he spins me back around, taking me by the biceps and squeezing as he shakes me. "Enough games! We're being nice and open with one another right now, aren't we? *Aren't we?*"

He seems to think that he has me cornered, seems to think that he will manage to undermine my newfound authority, and I am telling you right now—I'm not going to let this happen.

"You think I'm *stupid?* I see how he looks at you. Across the classrooms, across the hallways. And I see you, hanging on his arm, on his EVERY W O R D."

"I didn't think you were stupid until you started saying

this stuff," is my response. "Daniel and I have been best friends since before we could walk! What do you expect, for us to act like complete strangers around one another even though I'm dating someone else?"

"There's a difference between being friends and being *friends*." Friends with benefits. That's precisely what he's implying.

"Contrary to what you think, Daniel and I have done *nothing* like that." Until last night.

"You smell like a haystack. You smell like someone else."

It is in this moment that I recall an offhand comment that Paul made to me one evening, around six weeks ago, when we were in the middle of cleaning the stables and talking about people at school - gossiping, honestly. He mentioned a girl with a name that begins with the letter "M", a name I can't remember exactly right now due to other, more pressing topics being on my mind, and it caused me to take a minute, to stare at him, to try and interpret that odd little smile on his face. When I further inquired about this girl, he casually explained that he had seen Shane talking to her a lot of the time after school, while waiting for me to come down from my locker with my textbooks, or in-between classes in the middle of the corridor - even going so far as to walk with her a certain distance before bidding her farewell and returning to me at the end of the opposite hallway. I found these accusations to be weird, as Shane had never seemed to be out of breath nor flustered, and never had he appeared to feel guilty, nor had I ever seen him with my own eyes conversing with this girl. But still. If there is any moment in time to make a jab, to bring it up, to see his reaction, I think that the time is now, and although my instincts scream at me to just walk away, my temper continues to blow upon the flames, to add coal to the hearth of the fire, and it's merely out of spite that I choose to speak at all.

"It's not like I'm the only one who's innocent of having a

friend on the side. Don't think I haven't seen you waltzing around with that girl. Whatever her name is. Meghan. Morgan." I roll my eyes. "Don't think I don't see the way she hangs all over *your* every word. And unlike me, you *bastard*, you haven't known her all your life. In fact, you'd never even seen her until last year when she transferred schools."

It appears as though I know more about this girl than I thought. The more I talk about her, the clearer her face becomes in my head - the harsh line of her jaw, the curve of her nose, the brown of her eyes that mirrors Shane's, a brown that is the same colour of her short, straightened hair, and the way that she lines said eyes with a very thin black eyeliner, which unfortunately makes them appear smaller and narrower than they actually are. She tends to wear a bright blue sweatshirt, or a particular light grey one with stains on the sleeves. Yes, the image of this girl is quite clear. But not her name. Not sure why. Marisa. Morg—

-

An odd fuzziness fills my head. It's not one that belongs to anger or to frustration, but a general fog that has settled in and claimed me like cobwebs. The sky is a really annoying blue, one of those brilliant ones. I'm receiving a distinct sense, because this has happened before, and I was just thinking about the dream, wasn't I? The one where I was chained to the ground, gazing up at that comical azure?

But in this instant, my wrists are able to move, and I bring my right hand to my face, and it looks almost too large for my wrist, even though I inherently know that it is not. A deep gash has taken up residency in the fleshy tautness of the palm, one that's in a very odd shape, one that almost appears to be an evergreen tree. It branches downward with its needles, creating a trunk, and deep crimson blood oozes from the opening, trailing downward and across the veins. Maybe the shape appears to be like a tree because I'm quite dizzy, or maybe it really looks like that. But the red and the blue contrast against one another and everything seems far too bright.

—

The hand remains pressed against my chest in an attempt to keep it out of the mud. I hobble out of the shadows on three precarious, shaking limbs. The sun has brightened, filling my surroundings with a blinding white light. Everything still remains grey, so it makes no sense as to why the sunshine glares at me. When I lose my balance, despite all my best efforts, the injured hand has to push itself into the ground so I might prevent myself from completely collapsing. After steadying the rest of me, I dare to look at my right hand, to stare at the gash; it still oozes, though it now is surrounded by mud splatters and streaks of grime, promising infection. Each movement is as though I'm taking a thousand pounds with me. However, I am somewhat strangely pleased to notice the shape of the cut is, indeed, that of a tree. Which means — I'm not hallucinating after all.

Which also causes me to become bewildered as to what happened. And realise, with an even harder punch in the mouth, that Shane has abandoned me.

Other than that, I'm not entirely sure how I ended up here, on the ground. A fuzziness accosts my head, and I put my bloodied hand against the bridge of my nose to stop the pulsing. I'm certain that I look quite the mess now, all of my quick work this morning to look presentable promptly thrown out the window. I need to get up. Somewhere there's a small amount of strength, and I use it to push myself into an upright position. I scream in pain and my equilibrium immediately becomes unbalanced, and I collapse back into a pathetic heap, head smacking against my messenger bag, nape of the neck hitting the hard square of the stack of notecards.

There's a part of my face that feels swollen. Very weird, as though it has become the size of a grapefruit. My uninjured fingers reach upward to peruse the sensation, to prod and poke at it as though I am a small child inspecting some creature at the zoo that I had never seen before. Immediately, I cry out and wrench my own hand away from my face so hard, I feel a strain come on in my left bicep.

Mirror. I have a pocket-sized mirror somewhere in my bag, but that would require me turning and rummaging through it. I barely have the energy to remain in an upright position; what makes me think I can summon the strength to make my arms move, my fingers shift through items for something so small?

Come on, Ruth. You've had to throw yourself off the back of a horse and directly into a fence. You've had to ride through crow-hopping and bucking, rearing, aggression worse than that exhibited by your boyfriend - who now, by the way, is going to be your ex-boyfriend, whether you like it or not. You've been balancing on the tops of stacked hay bales, some with looser twine than others, since you were a toddler; you've been muscling your way through buckets of water and wheelbarrows full of either horse manure or vegetables from the furthest reaches of the fields. You've had to ride on combines and try not to fall into the whirring blades of tractors and covered your mouth to shield your lungs from the pesticides. You've spent hours with your mother in the gardens and even more hours standing on ladders in attempts to reach the ripest fruits on the trees. I think you can exert a little oomph in order to reach into your bag and get a mirror.

The voice in my head, as always, is correct. Should I be worried that a voice overtook me and said all of these things? I'm never certain how I should feel when it happens, or if anyone else has something along these lines to deal with.

My hand reaches out in the vague direction of the bag and finds the face of it, with its two smaller pockets tucked underneath the larger flap. The hard surface of the compact, I feel in the left one. Fingers trembling, I manage to delve into the covered pocket, fishing this way and that, until the battered texture lay beneath my prints. Pulling out the compact, my thumb automatically snaps it open, revealing the double-sided mirror, the top of which has a crack running through its centre.

When I bring it to reflect my face, I'm not sure what to expect. But not this. Never this. My eyes widen to the best of their abilities - which isn't much, I realise. Now that I'm looking at something tangible, the shock begins to register, the events of the day and the stress of the morning all snap directly into place. The left corner of my mouth droops slightly, puckered and red, swollen, beginning to pale and blacken around the edges of the circular shape. A dried strand of blood rests upon this bruising concoction, though not as dry as I think; when a finger presses against it, the wetted sensation transfers itself into the lines of my fingerprint. There's dark shadowing appearing underneath both my eyelids, and a small cut on my right temple. It appears as though the red marks surrounding the facial bruising are in the elongated shapes of fingers and knuckles spread slightly apart from one another. It seemed as though the blood flow has been stymied in addition to this, as there is a distinct flush to the bronze in my face but my neck tendons and sternum are slightly paler in comparison.

And considering how I had none of this before blacking out, I think I know exactly how I managed to get all of this on my face, plus the gash on my palm. And it is this strain of thought that breaks me down into tears. I don't even need the crack to look ugly this time.

The state of griminess doesn't matter. My fingers loosen, dropping the mirror, still open, face down into the loose soil, and I curl my palms against my eyes, shifting onto my right side, shoulders racking with concealed sobs as my knees raise to tuck themselves into my abdomen, which feels queasy, off-balanced, and twisted. I've seen the injuries, and now the pain starts, slowly, a creeping acid seeping through my body, violently consuming my mouth, overwhelming me with the urge to vomit. Nothing would come up if I did — and though my stomach contracts, though the back of my throat burns with bile, my body realises this, halting its efforts, leaving me with a bit of peace.

I did not sign up for this. *Ever.* Not back when I started dating him, not when I woke up this morning, not when I spent the night with Daniel. Nothing could have prepared me for this. Nothing I've done made me deserve this. Right? It wasn't my fault. Was it?

No, wait. That's not right. It *has* to be my fault. I did something wrong. I snapped at him, I lashed out. I didn't handle the situation appropriately. I allowed my fears to get the better of me, my anger, and because of that, he felt the need to lash out. He had every right to hit me, didn't he? I'd been near hysterical in my rambling accusations. He needed some way to get my attention.

I mean, after everything I had said, I deserved nothing less than to be lying face down in the dirt.

But that can't be right, either. He was gone. He'd just left me here. Gone to wherever else. And I hadn't imagined those trifles with that one girl. That was the reason he had lashed out - because he was guilty. He had hit me in the mouth. Done a lot more than that, by the look of my face. By the pain in my ribs. Nothing justifies that, right? No one deserves to be beat for stating their opinion.

The cycle of bewilderment and agony continues henceforth.

I need to get up.

Devastation fills me at the thought of my grades. I think

it causes me to cry a bit harder. I was supposed to have that presentation today, at the top of the morning. And here I am instead, lying in the dirt after being punched and kicked. Is this some sort of punishment employed by God for something I don't remember doing? Surely He's not that terrible of a God. Not from what I can pick up in my Bible reading. He can't purposefully induce this sort of treatment to be given to another person. No, this was the choice of man, pride and wrath combined, swimming toxically through the veins. This was all Shane. Not even I had a part to play in this.

That's what you think, Ruth. If you hadn't yelled. If you hadn't accused him. Then you wouldn't be in this position. Everything would still be perfect, as it had been. But it hadn't been perfect. Not ever since I realised my emotions toward Daniel.

I hate myself.

And that's why I have to get up. I can't let myself do what I want to do, which is lay here in my tears and my sweat and wallow in my grief. My grandmother was one of the strongest women in the nation; how else would she have meandered through the muck that constantly had been poured over her? She wouldn't have, that's how. If she were here, she would be livid, for sure, but she would not jump to encourage the hours of sobbing and wailing to the sky, asking questions that would never receive answers. She would pick me up from the ground, and she would perhaps fuss over the stains in my jeans, and then she would take me back to her house, which always smelt somehow of woodsy incense and had ancient woven decorations on the walls, and clean me up, and give me chastisement in a mixture of English and our native language. And I would understand it all, as she and Mom had ensured Paul and I were able to, and I would listen, and I would not speak, because that was the way.

She would not expect me to use her absence here as an

excuse to not follow what she would do in my place. And if there is, truly, one person I would want to make proud, even more so than my father, it would be my grandmother.

There's no graceful way to rise from this grave. I'm going to have to exert the effort and just do it without thinking about it. Taking in a deep breath, I hold it - and then I shove my hand, my injured hand, into the ground, pushing myself upward, and though a scream winds out from someplace dark and cavernous, I succeed. There's a feeling that claws have been secured into my spine and ripped out my vertebrae, but this fades into a dull throbbing, an aching, as I force my legs to unwind themselves and my shoes to press against the dirt. The landscape surrounding me is eerily quiet; no chirping of birds nor rustling of loose leaves fill my ears. It's almost as though nature is holding its breath along with me.

Only when I exhale does life return.

The wound in the palm of my hand burns incessantly; my fingers automatically twitch and close protectively around it. I can almost feel the blood oozing out, mixing with the mud and pitter-pattering onto my clothes, my bag, and the ground. I've sustained deep injuries before, such as when the skin of my arm caught itself on an overturned nail at the top of a fence. This is different. I can't tell you how. Thinking about it makes me feel thin, as though I've been stretched beyond my capabilities. And maybe pondering it is something that's passing my limits, without me being aware of it. But I have to keep getting up. Sitting here isn't getting me home, either. Getting me anywhere except further down into the pit of despair, and almost paralysed with unbidden amounts of pain. Shane did more than hit me across the mouth that was evident. One single punch wouldn't pack enough force behind it to whip me sideways and cause my limbs to splay and my spine to crack, would it?

Keep moving. I have to *keep moving*. Fists into the mud, twisting of the hip bones, stretching of the shoulder blades, the knees of the jeans further being stained, the toe of the boots digging deep, rutting holes, and finally, somehow, someway, with the balance of the world swaying this way, that way, upside-down and underneath, above, below, she stands, emerges, victorious, calves trembling, threatening to buckle, elbows bent and hands pressed against her stomach. The bag remains on the ground, but in a rush of adrenaline, I manage to bend over, scooping the muddied, dirtied notebooks and textbooks back inside before throwing the flap back over it. Still I clutch the compact mirror in my hand; I throw that inside, too, and hear a distinct crack as the corner of a history book breaks the glass further.

Visage shattered. Lenses fractured. The scenery ruined. Fitting.

I need to get to the road.

Fortunately, even though Shane had driven over hills and hollers to get to this supposedly special spot, the asphalt isn't nearly as far away from me as I thought it would be. However, every step is laden with weight and exhaustion - and dizziness. All of my senses and my injuries are working against me, and my head lolls back against my shoulders as I face upward toward the sky. Suddenly, the rays of the sun intensify in heat, and it's as though I've crossed into the desert lands instead of remaining in the scenery of the Midwest. I think in my mind I've crossed the boundary over into the badlands as well, because all of these murderous, lamenting thoughts begin nagging at me, poking at me with their needle-like tails and insisting that I pay attention to them. In actuality, I don't want to be doing any of this. I want to sit back down on the ground, and I want to cry. But I've done enough of that. Haven't I?

I wonder what Daniel would say if he could see me now.

I wonder if Paul would say "I told you so" while tending to the cuts and the bruise and handing me a bag of peas. I wonder if my father's opinion would change, or if he would demand to know what happened, then proceed to persist that it was all to blame because of my actions, not because Shane is a moron and an asshole. I wonder what my mother would say if she realised that my boyfriend had hit me in the same manner that my father had once hit her.

Domestic violence. The term arises from a lesson about women's rights we once had in our history class. *Domestic violence.* Hah. That's what this is, isn't it? A boyfriend hitting a girlfriend. *Domestic violence.*

Not a girlfriend anymore. Why do I have to keep telling myself that? Is it really so hard to believe? Yeah, it is. Because I thought for so long that he was going to be the one, and only one, that I ever would have to be with. Stupid Daniel. Stupid emotions playing tricks on me. Stupid mind being in the moment and not listening to what my instincts had been telling me all along. I cannot believe that I was ridiculous enough to push aside the little warning signs - and now, looking back, I can see them as though a film has been removed from my vision, as though I am looking upon a scene sans cracked lenses, because the lenses were smashed.

Stop beating yourself up, Ruth. That isn't going to help you. And yet, I couldn't help myself. The beating continues. I just choose to push it back and not think about it anymore.

The landscaping isn't nearly as level as it had seemed with the wheels of the truck carving through it, so I push the soles of my shoes into the tire tracks and follow them back out to the road.

Easiest way. COMPARTMENTALISE.

Easiest way. FOLLOW THE TRAIL.

Easiest way. BLOCK IT ALL OUT.

That's how my mother told me that she dealt with things one day. She said that in order to be cleared, she shoved it all into the back of her head and pretended that none of it had ever happened. She said she did it for us, for me and Paul, and that she loved us more than life.

She couldn't answer when I had asked if it were the same for my father. Now I wonder what she really was trying to tell me.

The ground turns hard beneath my feet and I stare at the patterns of the asphalt as they are swallowed by my shoes. I tug at the strap of the bag on my shoulder, situating it, attempting to make it sit more comfortably there in the niche, but it doesn't want to make things comfortable for me. If this isn't bad enough, my entire face is throbbing and my stomach hurts.

Now it seems as though God wants to rub it even more that this day is going to be the ultimate failure, the familiar rush of a motor reaches my ears, and I glance up in time to see a minivan go speeding past on the opposite side of the road. A blue car, with a pale license plate, a mother late for an appointment, I think, by the way that there's about two or three kids in the back. But the car didn't stop for me, the injured girl.

I'll give them the benefit of the doubt. Her car looked pretty full. But that's no excuse for the old man in the equally-as-ancient red truck that slowly crawls past me. He, in fact, openly looks at me, as does the ragtag Border collie in the passenger's seat with its mangy bandanna tied around its neck, and though it avidly barks in my general direction, even going so far as to cross over into his owner's lap and almost attempt to leap out the slightly-opened window, the man does nothing more than push the dog back into its place and apparently push a little bit harder on the gas pedal, for the truck wheezes, accelerates, and soon disappears as well.

So much for Midwesterners being known for their hospitality. What happened to that mentality of "taking care of one of our own?" Did it die while I was unconscious in the field? I wouldn't be surprised, honestly, with the way that the rest of the world so quickly is unravelling into pieces at our very feet. Maybe that old man took one look at me and decided I was a risk.

But what about the middle-aged couple who passed by soon after in their station wagon? The younger guy with the glasses in a convertible? Or the woman with a compact out, one eye on the road, the other in the mirror? Did all of these people think the same thing of me? Were they in too much of a hurry, did they not want the dirt in the backseats of their car, did they care? I don't think they cared at all, except about themselves.

Perhaps I'm just one of the stranger ones. Shane's told me so enough, and even Daniel teases me about my overtly compassionate nature towards both humans and animals. "I'm pretty sure someone could try to kill you, and still, you'd hover over them, bleeding out from the abdomen and the mouth, trying to make sure that they were okay and out of harm's way." One of Daniel's friends had said that to me, offhandedly, after witnessing me being the mediator of a fight that took place after school hours last year in-between two girls whom I knew fairly well, and one ended up becoming angry at me instead and lashing out before walking away. Before she could get too far, however, I had followed after her, spewing apologies and rapidly backtracking, using my charisma that I had inherited from my grandmother, or so my mother said, to my benefit. She had struck out at me, physically, and still, doggedly, I had persisted until she had calmed down.

They were right. It didn't matter how hurt someone was,

or what mistakes had been made, or what words had been exchanged, or whether the situation was my fault or involved other parties, I would always strive to make the attempts to fix it. Patch it over. Make it better. Improve it. Soothe. Comfort. It's in my nature, always has been since I was a small child and used to have panic attacks whenever one of my mother's flowers wouldn't seed, or whenever a vegetable blossom would wilt, or whenever one of the cats fell too far off the roof and screeched in surprise when they hit the ground. All of this invoked a wave of unstoppable sympathy within me, and it's as though I'm the one unseeded, wilting, fallen and startled, instead of the other object. It's as though I'm the one enduring the pain and the agony, the suffering - and it goes the other way as well, with happiness and excitement.

I have, indeed, severed this connection before with the surrounding universe. I have withdrawn into myself and resided there, developed it into being a hiding place of sorts. Yet I had felt worse. As though I were nothing more than an emptied shell. A husk sent forth to wander about the earth until it passed and time disintegrated.

I despised it, that single feeling, more than any others.

Another whirring motor approaches me, and I sigh in resignation, face and body throbbing now with each step, as though I am being punched, over and over again. Perhaps my body is reliving the trauma through which it suffered while I was unconscious. Now, there is a terrible thought, indeed, not one that I am incredibly willing to entertain. Having concentrated on the road beneath me, I tear my eyes away from the interesting flakes of colour in the asphalt and squint at the car. Instead of going by on the opposite side of the road, the dim fog lights flicker in the daytime and rapidly come toward me.

Steps slowing, I cock my head inquiringly at it, a small,

injured bird. A red Honda. I've seen that car somewhere before. It barrels down the road towards me, flittering like an angry cardinal. Well, I suppose that after everything else that I have managed to endure in such a short amount of time, I shouldn't be expecting anything less. I am going to meet my demise by the grill of this foreign car. Brilliant. I could not have thought of a better way to leave God's green earth.

I spend the next thirty seconds preparing for the impact, wondering how it is going to feel with this metal crunching against my wobbling knees, picturing my corpse toppling out and over through the air, twisting and turning this way and that, neck waddling back and forth before snapping the spine and killing me as I am impaled through the stomach with a sharpened branch. You can imagine my chagrin and surprise, then, when a rapid squealing fills the surrounding air and causes me to freeze, for the red Honda is sliding to a stop in front of me, the fog lights angrily illuminating me in pale yellow light.

The driver's door opens and remains ajar as its single occupant throws herself from the seat. My vision seems to be permanently blurred around the edges, and I startle backward, uncertain whether or not I recognise the figure as she comes toward me. Her head is swathed in a colourful kerchief, tied fashionably in a knot at the back, and I notice the strong arch of her eyebrows before the colour of her eyes, which are dark, like Shane's, but they have no impishness nor malevolence, only unadulterated fury and an unfortunate amount of understanding. She's wearing a pretty blouse, with flowers on it, big ones, flamboyant ones that put slashes of brilliance into my vision of monochrome.

"Jesus," she swears underneath her breath, taking me by the bicep. It's the same place where Shane tended to grip me whenever he was angry, but her touch is much gentler, and her fingers have a certain, pleasant coolness that makes me finally relax. "Did *he* do this to you?"

I squint up at her, and the roundness of her face, her tall, strong frame, are all so familiar to me. As is that signature twitch of her lips as she attempts to contain an outright sneer. "Figures. The douche." Even though I had not answered her question. I don't need to.

"We need to get you cleaned up." Her eyes dart around, taking in the other cars on the road - though there aren't any. She's scouring for something. More than likely checking to make sure that he wasn't returning. "You look like shit, Ruth."

I attempt to smile, but the swelling near my mouth has not reversed itself, and whatever I manage to do has her clucking at me like a chastising mother. I still cannot remember her name, however, and I would later realise this was because I had partly been given a concussion, and my brain was fighting against it. However, in the moment, I feel incredibly guilty, as though I am going to be sent to hell for not knowing her name.

She settles me into the passenger's seat, inhaling and holding her breaths in her lungs, exhaling softly, as she takes my bag from me and tosses it into the back, mud and all. And I am here, in her car, mud and scrapes and scars and all, and she does not care that I am dirtied or ruined, but rather she seems quite livid about it, and though my vision continues to swim as I press the back of my skull against the headrest, I still manage to whisper at her.

"I know you." The Honda growls underneath the prodding of her foot. "I know that I know you. But I can't remember your name."

"We've gone to school since the eighth grade together, boo," she says wryly, which makes me feel even worse. "But your eyes are both swollen all to hell. You probably just can't see me.

You're going to have some major shiners tomorrow, babes."

Boo. Babes. "Now I'm *positive* I know you. I've heard those nicknames before."

"Yep. You have."

It's right there at the tip of my tongue, at the forefront of my brain, but my thoughts swirl, racing one another to be first in line, and I shake my head, once again, quite breathlessly, insisting that I don't remember.

Then, it comes to me. "— *Julia?*"

"Guess you don't have amnesia after all."

Ignorant Greeting Cards

October 9th
Manchester, Indiana

Paul Reagan

Disrespect. Don't you ever disrespect me like that again. A hearty smack across the face with the back of the knuckles, and my body flies through the air, twisting almost completely around before it falls into a mess on the ground. Don't you be saying things that you know nothing about. Don't be thinking about this stuff. Who are you to call me names? Someone leans over me and straddles me with its knees and shakes me by the shoulders. Eyes livid and reddened at the edges, as though they have seen too much smoke. Don't you ever disrespect me like that again.

My vision darkens and the back of my head unravels at the seams, and a sharp pain shoots through my palm, up my arm, a great yawning and carving out of the skin.

I'll show you. The voice taunts me and insults me, attempting to make itself feel better. Something pounds against the side of my mouth and rings in my ears. Something jabs at my ribs and stomach.

My body has gone numb to try and still the pain. But the ghostly sensations remain.

Though my eyes fly open, I still feel as though I'm in that place, as though something in my core has attached itself to another world, and when I try to sit up, I am frozen against the mattress. I feel the way my pupils dilate, darting back and forth, thinking that these movements would help me get up from the thick layers of covers. None of it helps, not with the two massive weights bearing down on top of me at the moment. Not that just moving my eyes around in my skull would do much good with or without a person and a dog halfway to using me as a bed instead of the actual mattress. A great sense of urgency fills me, wanting to propel me upward, but I'm catatonic, it seems, and unable to do much of anything.

This is exasperating. Ruth's in trouble. I have to get up.

How do I know that she's in trouble? Because that little episode wasn't just another regular nightmare. If I wasn't a strong believer in the concept of twin empathy before, I think I definitely am now. I saw a face hovering above me, belonging to the knuckles that pushed themselves against my flesh and bruised it. I felt the squishing of the soft dirt underneath my back. I heard the words being slung at me, and it wasn't the name *Paul* being used; the receiver of this wasn't masculine, wasn't me. It was my twin sister. Shane had beat her up.

I'm *livid* right now. Not only because I had experienced it with her, but because now, she was in the middle of some godforsaken field, more than likely unconscious, without any manner of getting home or someplace safe, because knowing that bastard, he would have taken her out of the public eye. She'd be lucky, after a beating like that, if she were even able to get up from the ground and walk in a straight line. I wouldn't be surprised if she ended up with a concussion. I reach up to pinch the bridge of my nose, and find that my limbs have turned mobile, thankfully; it wasn't catatonia which plagued me, but general soreness from the morning's adventures.

Someone rewind the clock and make last night start over again. *Please!* Then maybe, if I had known all of these things would happen today, I would've stayed sober, and nothing would be as much of a problem for me as it is right now. It's really hard to function - and now, I had been in someone else's head, and that's just disorienting, especially considering I think this is the first time that it's happened. Well, perhaps not the first time ever - but definitely one of the first times that I've been aware the thoughts and dream-like projection didn't belong to my own imagination, that they were actually happening elsewhere in the world.

I only ever had it with Ruth, though. (Wait, no. There was one other, but she's gone.) I'm not a psychic or anything. Not one of those mediums, or like dream-travellers, or whatever you want to call it. I'm just a person who lives on a farm and wants a normal life but doesn't have one, you know? And yeah, I know compared to other people, our situations aren't exactly the most monumental in the universe; but they're a lot for us.

Daniel's sprawled on top of me, somehow having hooked one arm under my neck, the other lost to the rumpled coverlets. His head is directly on my chest; if I dip my chin down too far, I'll get a mouthful of that mussed blonde hair. Rolling my eyes, I push at him, arching my back and propelling my chest into the air, but he doesn't even stir, the lout. He just hitches a breath in the back of his throat, then clears it while exhaling and continues that quiet snoring thing he does, where one of his nostrils is closed by the pressure against my body and where the stream of air he inhales sounds like a whistle. As if that's not bad enough, someone has decided that it would be a good idea to let Shawna in the house - so now, there's a muddied, smelly German shepherd plastered against my legs. She rolls onto her back and promptly sticks her paws up in the air, the left front one twitching as her lips curls. It seems as though I'm not the only one dreaming. Maybe Shawna is there with Ruth right now, wanting to protect her from Shane but is unable to since she's actually here, and not there.

Man, I knew that Shane was a bastard, but not even I thought that he would stoop this low. What had happened to make him do that? Not that it matters. No one should ever just haul off and punch someone like that, not especially if you supposedly love them and want to keep them out of harm's way. He was punishing her, I think, from what I could gather. Punishing her for what? Don't you ever disrespect me like that again. Dad only said stuff like that when we get smart with him, or whenever we manage to get smart in his mind - which, by the way, we aren't actually getting smart; I swear he uses it as an excuse to lose his temper sometimes.

Wait a second.

The reason that Dad and Shane get along so well is because they're cut from the same cloth. So what if Shane was punishing Ruth for getting smart with him? What had she done, called him out on his bullshit? Decided to speak her mind? Whatever the reason, I'm proud that she finally managed to grow some balls. She's always been a little bit too compassionate, a little bit too timid when it comes to expressing herself. Blame it on the age, blame it on her personality, blame it on whatever you want, but it doesn't help when you're around a bunch of people who aren't receptive to freedom of expression. That's why I always encourage her to say what's on her mind — even though I'm usually the one who knows before she says it.

I'm going to beat the living daylights out of him when I get my hands on him. Give him a taste of his own medicine. Let's see how he'll feel when he's shoved into the ground and socked several times in the mouth and kicked. Let's just see.

My anger doesn't show on my face, though. I'm too good at masking it. Instead, I focus on what needs to be done before I can get to him. I'll need to get to the school. I'll take these two sleeping louts with me. I'll need to find him; first, we'll question about where Ruth is, and then we can beat the daylights out of him. It's a general plan, but it's much better than plunging into the dark of the cavern with no light. It's a dim light, but a light all the same. It's enough for me to grasp at.

I have to try waking Daniel up again. But maybe Shawna will be an easier target. I start shuffling my legs back and forth, a little bit at first to warm her up to the movement, and then with a bit more force. Eventually, one of the jabs catches her on the bottom jaw, and she shakes herself awake, raising that massive head of hers as she jerks out of the dream, blinking those liquid-brown eyes at me as her ears move back and forth. Too smart for her own good. She stares me down, trying to figure me out. I stare right back at her, and finally, she starts stretching out her legs, preparing to move. Mission accomplished. Now I have to move on to this lazy ass on top of me.

"Daniel."

The head of blond hair doesn't move.

"Daniel, wake up." I groan as the rag falls from my forehead, the dried coolness being removed from the hot skin, and for a moment, I wonder if I have a fever. Everything is calculated to me right now - logical, clean-cut. It makes it easier for me to not lose my head if I view things this way when I'm tampering down my anger. Do I need to take my temperature? Should I bother? I suppose while Daniel wakes himself up, I could always stick the thermometer under my tongue as I wash my hands and face or something. Yeah, that's what I'll do. I just have to wake this guy up.

"Daniel!" I raise my voice. "Daniel, *wake up!*"

He groans a little bit and shifts, flopping over with such force that he lays all of his weight on my arm instead of my abdomen, and a strained sound escapes from my pursed lips as he settles in for the morning. Or, rather, for the afternoon. I have no idea what time it is, and I'm positive if I even chance a look at the clock, I'll probably end up losing my head.

"No thanks. Too tired."

He's grumbling random things sleepily, and I could swear

that I hear my sister's name somewhere in the incoherency that follows. The last thing I want to listen to are his dreams that he might be having. Man, it seems like none of our heads shut down last night. I'm not sure if this is a good thing, considering this puts me in the middle of a bunch of people who understand what I'm going through, or if it's a bad thing, because it means we're all dealing with stuff at the same time. Kind of spooky, if you ask me.

"Daniel, seriously, you need to get off me. Right now."

"But *Paul.*" The bastard's awake. I knew it. He was just pulling my leg. He raises his head and shoots me that God-awful smirk. "You're so *comfortable.*"

The roguish grin doesn't work on me. It just causes my scowl to darken. "Daniel. I'm serious. Something's going on."

The mirth that leaked into his face begins to fade. He's realising that I'm not joking around. Or lucid dreaming. "What?"

"I had a dream. But it wasn't a dream. I was in Ruth's head. And she's in big trouble." I wanted to explain more to him, but I also know that if I were to elaborate with details, he would end up tearing apart the bedroom, throwing things, punching a hole in the wall, and generally go off into a temper tantrum. Then, we would definitely never get anywhere. He'd be fuming. Smoke pouring out of his skin. "We need to get to school. Or somewhere near it."

"Whoa, hang on a second, how do you know?? You had a *dream?*" He regards me with suspicion. "You a prophet or something?"

"D— *No!*" Why did he have to be difficult? "Dude, I'm being serious. Something's happened — with Shane."

That seems to be a trigger word for him. He shoots upright, twisting so violently that he ends up falling off the bed. Shawna follows the progression of him with those eyes that see everything, and she stops licking her front paw when he hits the ground with a resounding thud. This obviously confirms her previous thoughts about humans being complete idiots. After discarding the pillows that he's landed on, throwing one toward the desk and another toward the bed, where it hits me in the neck, he stares at me, bewildered.

"Shane? What? What happened with Shane?"

He seems to have forgotten the odd way that I know something's happened at all. Fine by me. "I don't know. But the dream - it involved a lot of hitting. And cursing. And saying things like my dad has said to us. And to my mom. And I don't like it. Even if it is just a dream, which I'm hoping it is, I still don't have a good feeling."

I add on that last part to detract from the weirdness of this day in general, but Daniel doesn't seem to notice. He has latched onto key words in the sentences and has thrown himself up from off the floor, scurrying this way and that, wanting his shoes, muttering loudly to himself in his own language, I swear, saying that he can drive, saying that he'll let me drive, on and on and on. I watch him for a moment, then move my legs from underneath Shawna's filthy underbelly and swing them over the side of the bed. He might be able to move at the speed of light, but I'm going to be the tortoise in this race. I'm an old man. I'm not nineteen; I'm seventy-three.

"Come on, Paul, we need to go, let's go." Just like him. Turning his role in the plan to be the leader, even though I'm the one who suggested it. Usually, I don't mind when he pulls a stunt like this. It's nice to not be expected to be the responsible one in the family or the friend group, believe me. Nice to kick back, let someone else do all of the difficult thinking and hard decision-making. But I'm not going to accept the backseat this time, not when I'm the one who had the dream in the first place.

"Yeah, I get it, Daniel, but I'm nursing a hangover and about ten thousand different injuries. You're going to have to give me longer than five seconds to get up from the bed."

Cursed bodies and their physical restraints, their limitations, their inability to continue even when the spirit within you is churning like an incontrollable flame and urging you to speed up, hurry up, move faster. I force my feet to shuffle me towards Ruth's bathroom, smacking at the light switch on the wall, but not succeeding in flooding the room with illumination until the third attempt. Now I'm the one who's incoherently grumbling to myself.

Run the water in the sink. Cup the hands, throw it over the face. Shiver a little bit as your body heat adjusts to the icicles pricking at your flesh and rebels against it. Watch the water droplets fall and be lost as the whirlpool dances around the drain. Wash your hands because they've become oily from the excess on your face, which has dried during your sleeping, sweating, dreaming. Wrinkle your nose against the odd scent of the hand soap, which is cranberries, or lilac, or something equally considered to be feminine, and wonder for a minute who bothered to put gender labels on soap because it smells a certain way. Make sure that all the excess is wiped into the hand towel draped across the silver ring on the side of the cabinet. Probably remove said towel to make it easier on yourself. Put it on the counter. Exit scene.

This is Paul Reagan, with today's episode of *how to wash your hands and not think about what's really bothering you.*

"What exactly did you see?"

I had been dreading that question. I should have known that he wouldn't be able to leave well enough alone. This was Ruth we're talking about. Any threat to her well-being, and he would be attached to the scent like a tenacious bloodhound. He wanted specifics now; he thought he was ready for them. Little does he know.

"I didn't *see* anything." I don't know how I'm supposed to explain a twin-pathic bond to someone who doesn't have one. "It wasn't like some epic vision that unfolded before my very eyes."

"Quit beating around the bush, man."

"The son of a bitch hit her. I *told* you that. I felt like I was being thrashed in the mouth and the eyes. I tasted dirt. I got the indication that she knew where she was, but that it wasn't a familiar place to her. I think she's somewhere by the school."

"*Thrashed?* Are you telling me that he didn't only hit her, but he legit beat her up?"

"Does it matter? As far as I'm concerned, he shouldn't have laid a hand on her in the first place."

I push past him as he leans against the doorjamb and stalk out into the foyer. A thud resounds, followed by the perpetrator, none other than the mud-covered dog. She isn't going to be left out of this misadventure if it's the last thing she does. Through the draperies in the kitchen, which have been pulled open, I can see that the weather has cleared up somewhat. There's still a distinct whiff of grey clouds hovering about, giving us with that never-ending threat of bursting open at any minute, but at least it wasn't windy and storming as it had been this morning. And at least the livestock situation had been sorted out; one less headache for me to deal with.

"I wonder if this'll be the last straw."

I walk into the kitchen and dig into the knife drawer, the clattering of the metal blades against one another reminding me about how I had seen Mom in this kitchen. The mess on the cutting board had been cleaned up, the fruit either disposed of or refrigerated. Someone, however, had left a liquid trail of tomato juice on the counter, and I stare at it, briefly comparing its consistency to that of blood, before shaking my head and moving aside one of the steak knives. I'm looking for a specific pocketknife; Mom has a habit of sticking those in with the rest of them. I hope she didn't stick it in the holder with the spoons or something. The last thing I need is to go on a wild goose hunt for a pocketknife that I shouldn't have misplaced. Why am I looking for one? Just in case I want to twist it in Shane's stomach. Never hurts to be prepared for these things.

I promise I'm not normally a violent person. Man, this is giving off a really bad impression, I'm sorry. But who wouldn't react this way?

"What do you mean?" I finally am able to respond to Daniel as he leans across the counter, watching me, staring blankly.

"She was going to break up with him today, you know. For me. Because I want to date your sister, and I come to find out that all this time, she's felt the same way. I seriously feel like such an ass, Paul."

Movements slow down, and I stare at the edge of the steak knife. "So that's what happened between you two last night." Not that I hadn't been completely, one-hundred-percent aware that it had happened. But hearing him confirm it, making it into a reality instead of something that randomly floated through the air waiting to be snatched up, is more shocking to my senses than I thought it would be.

"Um—" I don't think he expected that answer.

"You think I'm an idiot? If I know that she's in trouble, do you really think that I won't know when her good emotions are going through the roof? Besides, it was written all over your faces this morning. Not to mention she had hay in her hair."

Even Shawna stops her panting. She looks at me. They're waiting for me to give them my blessing. Well, I'm not going to do it. You know why? Because as much of a bastard that Shane is, I am actually kind of miffed at this situation. Ruth had cheated on him. She'd done exactly what he had been doing to her without even knowing it. I don't condone cheating in any circumstance.

"Should've waited until the break-up happened to throw her in the hay pile."

His face turns incredulous. "You're not going to lecture me about this."

"No, I'm not. There's more important shit to do. But you both know that it could've easily waited - or happened much earlier."

Oh, the way he opens his mouth, I know he has about a million retorts planned already. But I'm not going to stick around to listen to them. Whenever I've chosen to focus on something else, all other things get shoved to the back burner of the stove. I'm not going to waste time throwing a tantrum like my father would about this when there is something, called a life, that's at stake. Instead of stopping to listen to him, I find the knife that I'm looking for and take it from the drawer, shoving it into the pocket of my jeans as I saunter past him. No time for chit-chat. Gotta go.

I walk back into the laundry room and open the nearest drawer in search for the key fob to my truck. Daniel immediately follows after me, trailing me like a second shadow, sticking to my spine as though he's made of glue, and the next thing I know, he's sputtering out more words, more explanations. What is this going to solve?

"Look, we were arguing at first, and I was calling her out on all the shit that she was going through for this guy who doesn't appreciate her, and I made her something. I carved her a deer, man. Didn't you see it sitting on her desk in her bedroom?

And then she told me she couldn't accept it and we lost it —"

The metal of the key bites into the callused palm of my hand as I clench my fist around it and pull it out of the drawer, slamming it shut, cutting off the rest of his sentence. "Not listening right now."

I didn't mean to be so terse with him. Honestly, I'm kind of curious as to what exactly happened between them last night. In that protective older brother way. And also because I still want to yell at him, and her when I find her, after we've taken care of this problem, for being tactless and doing what Shane's been doing, sinking to his level. But I can't do any of those things; in fact, I find that I can't do much at all. I'm zoning completely out, with a free hand on the door and the weight of the knife in the pocket of my jeans increasing with each passing second.

It's hard to describe, this sensation when you're being physically pulled out of your brain and into someone else's. You realise what's happening, and something instinctual snaps into place, letting your psyche know that nothing too dangerous is happening. The rest of your body goes rigid, unable to function because the mind is deeply concentrating on this task, on confirming the connection which is attempting to be cemented. It's almost that same sensation you have when one of those falling dreams decides to pay you a visit, the one where you're trapped in a seemingly eternal darkness and there is a terrible rush of vertigo, air capturing your limbs and snagging at your clothing, if you're lucky enough to be wearing anything, and it's nonstop until you supposedly hit the ground - which doesn't even end up happening, considering you usually wake up. Except the waking up isn't the flying open of the eyelids and looking around at a familiar bedroom in this case; it's blinking several times and adjusting yourself to someone else's vision.

Ruth's eyes are a little bit blurred. She seems to be

walking. The ground underneath her feet isn't the soft mud in which she had been slammed, but rather hardened pavement. It looks to me as though she's discovered the road and is walking along the asphalt. The weight of the knife has transformed instead to represent the weight of her shoulder bag as it slaps against her hip; it, too, has drying mud encrusted on its outer flaps and pockets. Something rattles, broken, inside of it. Sounds like the clinking of glass, a mirror. Or maybe her boot had just scuffled across something in the road. There's whirring of motors as they pass her by; the sons of bitches, not a single one is stopping to help her. I barely am able to recognise the environment, which exasperates me further, a feat I had deemed impossible.

"Paul? Dude, what the hell is going on? *Paul!*"

The tables have turned. It's Daniel's turn to awaken me. He's doing it a little bit more violently than I bothered to do with him; he's taken me by the shoulders, moving me back and forth, sideways as well, as though I'm an empty piggy bank and he's searching for some change even though he hears no clinking noises.

"She's walking on the road. And I think I know where."

He freezes. "Wait, you actually saw —"

I give him an expression that unfreezes him and has him reaching for the doorknob that I had been forced to let go of when he had started throwing me back and forth like a rag doll. Of course I actually saw things. I'm not going to explain myself to him again, not when he didn't understand it the first time. Sometimes, the only manner through which people believe you is if they, too, can experience what you're describing. It's not like I can just form a connection like this to anybody that walks past me in the street and let them see through my eyes. No, this has been solidifying itself since birth, and if he doesn't believe that

I'm seeing anything, at least he believes that my instincts about Ruth are right, which is all I'm asking for.

We walk through the garage, our footsteps echoing against the emptiness, and the tick of claws against the cement following behind us, and out onto the concrete pad. Daniel grabs a baseball bat from the corner and slams the man door shut as I unlock the driver's side door of my old black truck, purposefully not looking at the red Mazda beside it, before leaning over the expanse of the cabin and opening the passenger's door from the inside. I need to fix that before the door becomes rusted permanently to the frame, but with all the other chores that have been laden down on my head, I haven't exactly had time for things that would be considered as pleasurable breaks.

He piles himself into the car and folds up his long limbs so that everything fits, laying the bat on the floor and then Shawna hops up into his lap, crawling over him with her mouth spread wide in a panting smile as she waddles into her seat right behind the gearshift. Daniel and I both inhale, getting a huge whiff of doggy breath, and despite the crispness of the autumn outside, we both have started rolling down the manual windows, which requires a bit of elbow grease, so that we don't have to smell her the whole way. When I shove the key into the ignition, I notice that my fingers tremble. Fatigued from the constant shifting in-between minds.

"Can you drive?" I'm not the only one who's noticed it.

"I did farm work when I was sick with mono and pneumonia at the same time." The engine coughs for a couple of seconds, churning over and over until it catches and rumbles to life. "I think I can drive this temperamental truck. With my eyes *closed*."

I can't handle dog breath, though. Not when it smells like a mixture of rotten meat and beef bones. And possibly the internal organs of a recent squirrel.

As I shove the truck into reverse, the radio turns on, and out of the speakers that I installed in the back windows, shoved into the door panels and whatnot, comes the gravelly voice of Ozzy Osbourne. He wants us to get aboard the crazy train, apparently, and all three of us passengers are shocked into rigidity as the opening guitar notes play. Daniel goes to flip it off, and I smack his hand away, turning up the volume a couple of notches instead. I think this is the perfect pick-me-up that we all need right now, after waking up, and nursing hangovers, and experiencing visions. Little does Ozzy know that we're all already passengers on the crazy train.

I back down the driveway, keeping my tires closer to the grassy side of the yard. Just more work that needs to be done. Every time I turn around, there's something new, staring me in the face. The slant of the gravel is starting to cave in on the left side, directly down into the massive ravine that stretches in-between the house and the barns. Basically, it's an avalanche of small rocks tumbling toward water drainage at a slow, but constant, pace. The more wheels that drive over it, the more damage that's done, and of course, I'm the one who's expected to fix all of the problems around here. That's why I can't go to college after I graduate next year from high school; I'm instead going to be sticking around while everyone else does God-knows-what and making sure that all of the issues left behind are solved. That's my apparent role in life. There is absolutely no way that I'm bitter about it or anything. I've completely accepted it.

"You know," Daniel comments offhandedly as I meander the bed of the truck through the opened gate at the base of the driveway. "I didn't think we'd be spending our Friday doing shit like this." Small talk. Trying to diffuse the tension stretching in-between us. The tension that I didn't notice because I'm preoccupied. Because that's the way that my personality is wired to handle stress.

"What did you think we'd be doing? Chores and school?"

The pause lengthens, and then, he's grinning at the side of my face. I see it as my head whips back to look through the rear window as I back out onto the actual road. "Nah. We'd have skipped school anyway."

"We would've?"

"Definitely." This is how he copes with things, I think. He just keeps talking about situations that could have happened, but unfortunately didn't, and should have, but won't now. "We would've slept in more after doing the chores and, after making sure your dad disappeared into the great beyond, we would've woken up and we probably would've washed our trucks to get all the mud off them. Especially mine, considering we went driving in the mud last week."

"Brilliant plan."

"Look, Penny wanted to go and have the experience. She's twelve. I was more than willing to take her. At least she didn't want a boyfriend to go with her or anything." Here he scoffs a little bit as I pull the gearshift down, and the clanking of the engine shoots the truck forward. "I don't understand it, man. All of these preteens wanting to have relationships and get laid. Like. Do you remember when *we* were twelve?"

He would have to bring something like this up. Although this is one of the last topics that I wanted to explore right now, specifically when I'm on the verge of losing it anyway. I prefer not to remember what happened when we were twelve. That gruesome, awful year where everything changed and nothing ever was the same in these households. Daniel apparently realises he's accidentally crossed a line, but still he waits for my answer; he wants me to remember, wants me to share in the agony.

"Yeah. I remember."

"Relationships and girlfriends were some of the last things that all of us were worried about. Sure, we had our stupid nicknames and our bantering and shit, but we never thought about breaking out of the shell and flirting and becoming boyfriend and girlfriend with anybody. You know?" (Oh, I knew.) "Like. All we wanted was to play in the mud. Pretend we were soldiers. Pretend like we didn't drool over those model cars that they sold at Tractor Supply. Remember when Ruth was still into those Breyer horses?"

"Still is." Short. Terse. To the point. Best way to be. I can't handle this right now. "I may not have seen the deer on the desk or the dresser or wherever you said she put it, but it's hard not to miss those three shelves of Breyer horses, none of them the same and all of them in mint condition, above her computer desk. Hovering like faithful watchdogs."

Shawna ensures that she sends me a sideways glance to indicate that obviously she is the best watchdog there is, and that those plastic horses with their glass eyes have nothing on her capabilities, and despite it all, I snort out a laugh. So much for short, terse, to the point. Hadn't Ruth always preached at me that talking about things made them better? That making them real helped the healing process or whatever? But she was a hypocrite, in that case, because she never talks about her relationship problems or the demons she deals with, the ones she internalises to torment her brain at a constant pace. She thinks I don't know about them; but I'm the one who goes in and soothes her from her nightmares, who's alerted during the blackness of the evening, underneath an expanse of stars, about when she's having them, following my instincts to her bedroom. And she's done the same for me. We both know about one another's darkness's and pretend like we don't. Reminds me of a couple friendships we used to have but don't anymore because those people are gone. Practically good as dead to us. Which sucks. It really, really sucks.

Wistfulness. I've never actually experienced it before. It's difficult for me to yearn for things because I remain so easily disconnected. I'm accustomed to not getting what I want; it's how the Reagan parents raise their children, to realise that the world is not going to offer us something on silver platters that we are going to have to work for it. If there is one positive lesson I can take away from growing up in this frigid household, it's that. But now, I'm yearning for something, and the ache is so strong, I feel as though it is causing my innards to cave in on themselves, to shatter and to break, to fissure, to crack open and reveal the chaotic filth inside of them. It hurts, oddly enough. I didn't think it would be such a desperate twinge located behind the heart, or the dropping of the same organ into the pelvis at the same time that the stabbing, the twinge, occurs. Very confusing, human emotions. I don't understand our own selves sometimes. Entirely too complicated, the way that we feel with both a separate entity filled just with emotions, and then, that transfers over to the physical body and we feel it there, too.

Fascinating. Complicated. Saddening. P a t h e t i c.

Daniel isn't sure where he wants the conversation to go from here. I can tell by the way that he twiddles his thumbs as I press the accelerator to the floor of the truck and push it as fast as it can afford to go, switching gears as quickly as my trembling arm can manage to execute the simple motion, which now seems a thousand times more complex to me with the twisting and churning that I'm experiencing. We both know that we're not prepared, not ready, not wanting to open up about the past experiences that we've suppressed deeply into their holes, but there was nowhere else for this topic to go except further in, exposing the rotting sores and the congealed blood and the mass suicide that this section of our lives committed after losing half of it.

"—Weather's cleared up."

Way to save the day, Daniel. Switch the subject of the conversation to be about something that only simpletons spoke about: the damned weather.

My only able-bodied response is a nod. Because *really*.

"Thought it would've stormed and blown everything around us to bits by now." He stares pointedly at some of the foliage on the side of the road, which looks a little worn-down and battered from the winds to me, but maybe I'm just seeing things. "Not that this place isn't a pit sometimes anyway."

"Hating it here again?"

Another pause. "Sometimes I just want to get out of here. I know there's more out there than this. It's not that I don't love working on the farm, but -- there has to be more out there than just this life, you know? And I kind of want to explore it. Maybe if I do that, it'll cure this itch I've been getting."

Someone up in heaven is hellbent on exposing everything that I've been trying to¹ ignore for the past however long. I wouldn't mind if it had happened on any other day, but no, of course, in typical Reagan fashion, everything had to stack up until the pile had become so tall, I couldn't see what had been placed to break the camel's back.

"Some of us aren't so lucky." I stated. "You get to go off to college. Ruth gets to go off to college."

My hands tighten on the steering wheel as I pull off our side road and onto the main stretch without bothering to flip the turn signal on. "I don't."

I can almost hear his Adam's apple bobbing as he swallows back some cutting edge remark. He and I have much different conversations when it came to colleges and universities and doing something with our lives than I had with my father. Daniel and I always talked about being roommates, causing trouble. Coming back to the farm, getting our heads back on straight only to watch them unravel again. I would talk about maybe finding a decent girlfriend; Daniel would go quiet and hope that Ruth went to the same college we did. Or, at least, relatively close.

"— Yeah, you said that this morning —"

"Everything we talked about?" I don't need encouragement to continue. "Being roommates and going to med school and all of that stuff? It's not going to happen. I mean, it'll happen for you. It'll happen for Ruth. It'll happen for, more than likely, all of the other kids in our senior class. But it isn't going to happen for me."

My hands tighten further, knuckles whitening, bloodless, like my cheeks and my neck, a pallor like death, because a part of me has died. We went from my sister being physically abused to not being able to go to college. "Dad told me yesterday. Or a couple of days ago. I don't even know how long it was now." I didn't want to know. Easier that way. "I get to stay behind. Take care of the farm."

"Are you serious?"

"As a heart attack."

He turns and looks out the window again.

"—That's screwed up."

"You're telling me."

"But we're nineteen, and we're getting older every day. That's supposed to mean we can start doing what we want, what we know that's best for us, instead of being trapped underneath some smothering thumb all the time?"

"I mean, you know my dad." I chuckle dryly. "I'm about a thousand percent sure that I could pack up my belongings, move to another state, and he'd phone me every day, hounding me about this not getting done or that needing to be fixed." My face sobers, darkens, and Daniel uneasily looks at me, and his thumbs start to twiddle. "And he probably would stop doing it. All together. Not that he does much now, in case you haven't noticed. So I'd be forced to come back, because I do love this place, and I don't want it to go to waste. Not when there are so many families relying on us."

"Problem of living on the biggest ranch, possibly, in the United States." A side-glance makes him amend this statement. "Okay, in the state of Indiana, around here at least. But you're always trapped here. Corralled and walled in and suffocating."

"Way to help a brother feel better."

"I'm just — saying. It's not like I don't feel it, too."

"Well, unlike you, I actually *am* stuck. So."

He didn't say anything more about it. And for the moment, we both managed to run out of conversational topics. All of the ones explored briefly had been far too painful. So instead, we sink into our thoughts - and to be honest, I don't know what's worse. I don't consider my thoughts to be a generally dark place. But lately, things have been changing up in there. It's becoming more difficult to completely severe my connection to my anger, and also to keep it reigned in. I know if I'm silent for the entirety of this drive, I will have executed several detailed plans about how I'm going to gut Shane and bury his body so no one can find it. One scenario even involves peeling him apart and decimating him into little bits and pieces, and then, there's some black humour sprinkled in there as I imagine someone finding this box of human square pieces and attempting to put it back together again. A bloodied, raw, decaying Humpty Dumpty who didn't have to sit on a wall to break into pieces. All that was needed was a sharp knife and a little time.

And now we know why I don't delve into my thoughts. I don't have these types all of the time, though, which is a good thing. It means I'm not a fully psychotic killer as of yet. Though Shane is one of those people that you can't help but look at as a potential target. One of those people where it doesn't take three strikes to be out of the game, only one, and it doesn't matter if it's a big one, or a small one. All it has to do is happen.

"Think you can go any faster?" Daniel stares pointedly at the speedometer, which barely manages to creak past sixty miles per hour. The rear fenders tremble with the effort.

"We have places to be."

"Daniel, for *how* long have you ridden in this truck?"

"At a time, or in general?"

"Just to tickle my curiosity's fancy, both."

"Remember that attempted road trip back last summer you and I tried to pull off? Six hours in this son of a bitch. *Never again*. We're hijacking your mom's car next time. I tried to get you to take the van, but you didn't want to make my parents angry. Oh, Paul." Daniel mockingly shakes his head at me and slinks lower into the passenger's seat. With more of his jean-clad thighs exposed, Shawna takes that as an indication that it's time for her to rest her head there, and she heaves a sigh as she rolls her eyes toward him. He nonchalantly rubs behind her left ear. "In general? I've been in it ever since you got it. When you were what, fourteen or some shit?"

"Yeah. Fourteen. So five years. And you're asking me if I can go any faster. Long story short, you should know the answer to that question."

"Yeah, but I also know that you've been trying to work on it, and hell, maybe when I wasn't looking - which is rare, I know, but it happens - you managed to pump up the engine to be a hundred times more powerful than it was."

The exhaust wheezes in protest as I pump the gas pedal, demonstrating how there is little to no acceleration now that it's maxed out at sixty-five, despite the speedometer making us believe that it can chug out up to a hundred. "Does that sound like an engine that's been worked on to you?"

"You are just *full* of sass today."

I mutter to myself. "More like full of rage."

The people on the road sense that I'm nothing to be trifled with today. The minute anyone going less than my miles per hour appeared in front of me, they step on the gas and propel themselves forward, afraid of the dark-haired, deep-skinned fool behind the wheel of a massively intimidating, growling truck. I'd be afraid of me, too. I probably look like some hot mess driving home with his high friend from one of the local bars, having stayed out all night and not slept in days. I wonder what the teachers at school are going to think when I come rolling in like nobody's business. Smoking the cigarettes that I've hidden in the glove compartment and haven't told anybody about. Halfway down the highway to hell. Then again, I wonder if I care, and if I've ever cared. Because maybe this entire respect towards authority thing is just because I'm accustomed to bending to other's willpower and not instilling my own.

Nothing much happens on the road as I'm driving. Daniel surrenders into the black of the silence and refuses any more attempts to make conversation. The things he wants to talk about, I have rapidly shut down with my concise answers and my nonchalant glares that so easily are coming to me. At least, until a Pontiac swerves in front of us on the highway and —

S C R E E C H ! !

"Son of a *bitch*," Daniel swears, pushing his hand against the dashboard, trying not to go through the windshield. "What the hell is this guy's problem?"

Unfortunately, I have an answer to that. Because the driver is none other than Shane's older brother. He's supposed to be up at college these days, a junior now. School's in session for them in the middle of October; I know for a fact that their fall break isn't for another week. So if that's the case, then why is he in front of me, with those red lights blazing into my pupils, staring in the rearview mirror with that sloppy grin that makes me always think that he's smoked too much MJ?

I can't answer it. All I know is that one thing hasn't changed. I hate him and he hates me.

Yeah, Shane's older brother, wrongfully named Matthew - and I say wrongfully because the name means "gift from God" and let me tell you right now, this is not the case - was the captain of, you guessed it, the football team, back when Ruth and I were upcoming in the high school world and his target was always the younger girls. When we were freshmen, he was a senior, and he could have anyone he wanted, because, unfortunately, there was something charismatic about the bastard. I guess everyone in that family had that quality to them; otherwise, girls wouldn't be so eager to be another notch on their belts. Matthew's supposed to be away at college, and he isn't. He's here, taunting me. Just what I need.

"Paul, look out!"

I've attempted to cross over into the other lane, after a cursory glance in the side mirror to make sure that no one would be in my way, but Matthew decides to follow, and since his Pontiac is a hell of a lot more souped up than my truck could ever hope to be at this point in time, it's relatively simple for him to speed up and attempt to cut me off all in the same acceleration. It's my turn to curse as I pump the breaks and prepare to shift backwards in gears.

"What the hell is going on?"

"Don't you recognise this son of a bitch?" I bite out a laugh, cranking the gearshift down. In the rapidly fading distance behind us, I see a couple of tractor-trailers approaching. "It's Matt."

"Matt Curtis? As in *Big Guy Matt?*' As in, the guy at the —"

I cut him off. "That's the one." He doesn't need to finish that sentence.

"The hell? Man. We just can't get away from these people."

The semi-trailers are still barreling down on us, and Matthew has set us at a snail's pace. Forty-five miles per hour. Where's a police officer when you need one? He's inching us slower still. Trying to make us go into a complete standstill. Actually, I'm not sure what he's doing except being an ass. And there's too much traffic coming up on the other side for me to signal that I need to move over. Someone trapped behind me lays her elbow on the horn and gestures at me; I gesture back in as much of a shrug as I can manage without taking my hands off the wheel. Daniel just flat-out turns around and waves at her.

"Are you seriously flirting?"

"Man, if smiling and waving is flirting, we're all whores."

I push on the accelerator, and my truck lurches forward; the battered bumper on the front, which I've modified before installing a bull's horn above it, scrapes against the dark blue paint of the Pontiac with a terrifying sound.

B A M!

Though Daniel and I barely feel anything, Matthew's neck whips back against the headrest of his seat, and his mouth moves in a long barrage of insults flung at me. This just makes me grin, and now it's my turn to wave a little bit as I back off.

"Turn the tables!" Daniel encourages this behaviour. "Hell to the yes. Show him who's boss!"

"I've got something a little bit more pressing to deal with." And it isn't Ruth. It's the two semi-trailers that aren't slowing down for any of our antics. There's no way that Matthew can't see them; one of the chassis is painted that weird, fluorescent orange, and the other has been sprayed down to be crimson. Like how our blood is going to look across the asphalt if he doesn't stop messing around with us in his damn Pontiac.

"This isn't good!" Daniel yells.

"You're telling me." Someone's still in the other lane, taking up the room that I need in order to get over. I lay on the horn, and Daniel flails his hands around at the person as though attempting to communicate with some voodoo-type sign language. I shove down on the accelerator again, and the crash into the back of the Pontiac is louder this time, more prolonged, the terrified screech of a trapped beast rather than the brief whimper of a chained pet.

CA-CA-CR E E C H !

"Jesus, get him out of the way!"

We feel the backlash of my speeding up a little bit more this time around, and the panic begins to set in. Daniel whips his head backward to stare, wide-eyed, at the tractor-trailers, one of which has a driver that reaches up and pulls on its horn. It's like the cavalry is summoning back-up soldiers, with the way that all these horns are blaring. This person in this van next to me needs to get the hell going. I need to get the hell over. A lot of things need to get the hell happening. Jesus, God, help us.

That's how I pray. Simple lines. Jesus, God. Both of them addressed in one. Jesus, God, help us.

The bullhorn is still attached to the rear bumper of Matthew's car, and he's shaking a fist at us as though this entire thing is our fault to begin with, even though it was actually him being a douche. The tractor-trailers try their best to pull on their gearshifts and push on their brakes, but I identify with them, because stopping something at that size at such a great speed isn't easy. And sometimes, its plain impossible. I've had combines go out of control. I've had massive farm equipment turn wonky underneath my grip.

There's nothing I can do. We're going to die. This is how our Friday ends. With dying. And Matthew's *laughing* about it. He doesn't seem to care that he'll be taken out with us. Neither does the van next to us. Everything's turning blurry to me, too. I'm not one for panic attacks, not to the depths that Ruth and Mom have experienced them, but this might push me to the brink. It just might have already.

Then, it's as though God himself has pushed the van up and out of the way. I release the accelerator pedal only for a moment, so that the bullhorn dislodges itself from the now-twisted aluminum of the Pontiac, before shoving it to the floor again. The truck groans, protesting against this, but does it anyway, moving from forty-five, screaming up to fifty as I forsake the turn signal and move into the vacated spot. The van appears to have floored it, now several car lengths away from me, leaving plenty of space for me to continue speeding up, passing fifty-five, and in this, coming up beside Matthew's Pontiac, which is now endangered and he realises it. With another curse - and this time, he rolls down the passenger's side window in order to fling it at us, despite us not being able to hear it over the roar of more Ozzy in the radio, which hits me like a piece of debris in the face, because I blocked all of it out - he speeds off.

It isn't much further to the exit, and the red-coloured semi-trailer pulls around me, glancing down into our truck, which although it's bigger than most, is obviously dwarfed by what he drives, shaking his head before pulling past. And neither of us, neither me nor Daniel, say a word until I signal that I'm about to turn off the highway and proceed to do so. In fact, I don't think either of us breathe until the truck, which is as worn out as we are, creaks to a stop at the light at the end of the ramp, which curves upward at a gentle slope. When the breaths do emerge, they're sharp, as though we've forgotten how to go about doing it properly, and I think in a way, we have.

I slide my eyes toward him. He has managed to sink even deeper into the seat. Shawna crawled fully onto his lap, and now her thriving mutt stink fills the entire cabin, since there's no wind whipping through the opened windows chasing it away. Her mouth partially opens, and she yawns, whimpering at the same time, creating an even further pathetic image than she had been before. One of his hands is tightly wound in the thick fur at the scruff of her neck, and the other is lost in his own hair, as though he's been trying to yank it out by the roots. And maybe he has. I stopped paying attention. The song that the radio blasts out at us is in the middle of a guitar solo. I don't have the energy to turn down the volume. The person who pulls up beside us looks in at us and shakes his head. Why is everyone mocking us?

Well. We do look kinda pathetic. The wind tousled our hair; I'm pretty sure half of mine has been ripped off. My eyebrows raise high on my forehead, and Daniel's hunker low over his eyes, which have darkened several shades. Our cheeks are flushed and our foreheads are sweaty, and we have a massive dog in the front seat with us and this truck looks like it needs to go on an episode of one of those television shows where they overhaul and refit a vehicle to look like an actual vehicle instead of a death trap or a bomb about to implode.

And we both start laughing. Uncontrollably.

The light switches to green at that time, and the person

next to us pulls away as though we've become possessed and are going to drag them down into hellfire. Maybe we are. I mean, after all, we did just escape imminent death. The words to the song start up, and we can't help but sing along, even though we can barely understand them. We only sing along for a couple of verses until Daniel breaks the odd tension and says, still halfway to insanity, "Man, what a damned day this is."

"Dude. We're on our way to kill Shane, and Shane's brother tries to kill *us* instead." I think that's the most hilarious part about this entire thing. "What are the odds?"

"A thousand to one, and we were on the losing end."

"Tell me about it. Should've just stayed home."

"Don't look at me, psychic boy. You're the one who had the vision." Daniel moves his hand from the dog's neck and to her ears. Immediately, her pupils cloud up and she blinks sleepily, and I could almost swear that her mouth curves upward in a contended smile as he starts to rub the bell of one ear. "You're the one who saw something and woke me up."

"You're right. It's *all* my fault." Thinking again of Ruth, putting past the situation that had sent my heartbeat into a frenzy, something hits me even harder than the realisation that the radio had been going this entire time and yet, I hadn't heard it. "I haven't seen anything lately."

"Are you taking this as a bad sign? Because last time you saw something, you collapsed against the door frame and I had to halfway haul you out to the truck."

"I was able to walk after a few seconds, and you know it. Quit being difficult."

The radio switches from Ozzy to Joan Jett. I slam my hands on the steering wheel in time to the beat, causing Daniel to roll his eyes so hard, I swear they fell out of his head and rolled underneath his seat. He hates it when I do this. "Okay, so you haven't felt anything." He prompts me, silently, to go on.

"Yeah. Like the connection's been put on mute or something. Like the phone was hung up, but then it fell out of the receiver, and now, I'm just getting a dial tone from her. Does that make sense?"

"Now that you compared it to something I've done and have had happen to me? Uh. Yeah. Now I actually get it." He removes the hand from his blonde locks and rubs it over his face, ridding the skin of the delicate sheen that covered it. I continue pounding against the wheel. "Would you stop that? You're going to give me a headache."

"You love me."

"Yeah, yeah, about as much as I love a dog bite."

I glance at Shawna, who has been pulling back her lips in a delicate snarl and flea-biting at Daniel's jean leg as he continues to rub her ear. "That's not a dog bite, you pussy."

"Don't make me push you out of the truck."

"Your death and mine."

Only we would be able to banter, somewhat forcibly, about the same thing that had almost taken us into its chilled embrace.

"Thankfully, we're almost there." This part of town is known as the outskirts; if we had turned left, we would have been heading toward the inner city. And I'm using that terminology lightly, because Batesville isn't exactly the size of Indianapolis, yet somehow still manages to have a slums and a rich-people line. By turning right, we're avoiding all of that, and meandering past the grocery store, a couple of gas stations, and a dermatology place set back, far away, off a side road, before rounding a curve to the left and heading toward the even smaller town where the high-school is located.

"Yeah, I mean, we only had to go through fire and water

to get there."

"Are you quoting Tolkien at me?"

"Dude, it's been so long since you picked up a book, I'm surprised you even halfway recognised that."

"*Dude.*" My sour mood returns. Yes, this is what it takes to make me plunge back down into the fray. Comments. Offhanded comments unintended to mean anything except how they sound. "I don't have time these days."

"Yeah. I know." I think he received the message that he's being an insensitive dick. (Or that I'm being a sensitive one.) "So, are you going to try to beat me to Shane, or can you just let me get a couple of good hits on that face of his before you break out the knife?"

"Actually, I'm thinking that Shawna will beat him for the both of us." Once she acquired a target, it became her sole focus. In fact, Daniel and I had taken her out on more than one of our yearly hunting sprees in the woods, simply because she had turned out to be better at some things than the actual hound dogs we'd bought. Though slowly, those had either run off or managed to become part of the piles of road kill we buried. "And she'll sink his teeth into his arm, or maybe his calf."

"Shame it isn't meatier."

"She isn't a cannibal. It's probably good that it's mostly bone and no muscle. Because the injury will be worse that way. It'll snap the bone immediately, since there's no cushion in-between the incisors, and it's not like Shane has loads of calcium in his system." The guy had never drank a glass of milk in his life and sneered at the thought of cheeses and creams. "At least, I don't think he does, from what I've seen."

"I wasn't disturbed until you went into detail."

"Someone who skins cow hides for leather and butchers chickens and pigs for their meat is disturbed by the fact that I'm talking about how dog teeth scientifically work?" I scoff at him. "Think about it. It's all murder."

He had nothing to say in response to that.

We make it down the nauseating hillsides that lead into the smaller town, and the trip is even worse than usual because I refuse to let up off the gas pedal. We lost valuable amounts of time with those activities on the highway, and I blatantly remind myself to take the back roads when we're finished with what's happening here. I'm not going to find myself entrapped like some fish on a hook again. Daniel keeps his hands buried into the dog's fur as I take the curbs at too-quick speeds and mash the pedal to the floor. This truck, even though it needed a lot of work before, is definitely going to need an extreme makeover after I'm through with it today. There's absolutely no way in hell that it's ever going to run again once I switch off the ignition for an extended amount of time. I don't blame it. If someone shoved me into the ground like this, kept slowing me down, speeding me up, pushing me past the limits I didn't think I had, I probably wouldn't bother to start up for them again, either.

Oh, wait. I know exactly how the truck feels. I go through this all the time when it comes to pleasing my father. Relatively depressing to be able to sympathise with a truck that shouldn't have feelings at all. It isn't Ruth or my mother who has the insanity of the family; it's me.

I turn at the stop sign in front of the school just in time to see the students milling out of the main building and from the auditorium. It seems as though we have arrived in time for school to be letting out. Is that really how late in the afternoon hours it was? Is it really even the same day? Because it sure feels to me as though about six or seven days have passed in the last few minutes. I hate this concept of time that humans have developed. I think we have it all wrong.

Someone has cleared out a parking space on the hillside in front of the school. Since we're a little bit wanting when it comes to actual lots, we have to make do with what we're given, which usually involves parking on the street or squeezing into the gravel-covered area next to the auditorium. When I slow to a stop, I ensure that the emergency brake is pulled and that everything is in order before I shut off the ignition. The last thing I need is for the truck to roll backward and into the great beyond. The engine provides me with a tremendous, relieved shudder as it shuts off, and with the lack of vibration rattling through my bones, I suddenly feel quite empty.

I don't have to say a word. Daniel has already propelled himself out of the truck, grabbing the bat and slamming the door behind him. Shawna barks happily in my face, tail wagging voraciously as she waits for me to follow suit. The last chords of the rock song echoing in my head, despite the radio having been turned off alongside the ignition, I lean against the driver's door, which faces the school, and I feel around as nonchalantly as I can manage in my pockets. There has to be a spare cigarette around in here somewhere. Unless I can sneak back around to the passenger's side and retrieve them from the glove compartment. But Daniel appears to have the same mentality as me; he holds out the package of battered Camels and I notice that his hand is trembling, the lid rattling against the filters of the cigarettes inside. I snatch it from him and quickly open it, extracting two of the cancer sticks and putting one right in his mouth before balancing my own between my lips and rolling the package up in the sleeve of my flannel shirt I don't remember putting back on.

"They're going to kill us for smoking on school property." Daniel jerks his head toward the front doors of the school, where some of the students are beginning to take more notice of our presences here. They were more looking toward the massive black truck with the loud radio, but now that it's disappeared, and we're standing in front of aforementioned truck, they're looking at us instead. "Here comes Rossman."

Sure enough, the principal makes an appearance. Today she has on a navy skirt that hits just above her knees and a matching, long-sleeved blazer, with an ivory collared shirt on underneath and tucked into the skirt's hem. The clack of her high-heeled pumps against asphalt and cobblestone can be heard reverberating against the houses behind us as she makes her way toward us truants and the truck. You know, I just realised that Dad probably thinks that we're all at school, as does Mom. I just realised that the principal could have called them and told them we weren't, since high schools require parents to call in for absences. I'm toast. We're all damned toast.

Without butter. Which sucks.

"Mr. Reagan. Mr. Stamp." Principal Rossman's voice brings more attention to us than we thought it would. "Ah. I was wondering if you two would show up."

"Is—there a problem, ma'am?" Have to keep cool.

"Oh, yes, I think there are several problems, Mr. Reagan. The first of which involves you explaining to me why you were absent today. And you as well, Mr. Stamp."

She still is in the center courtyard in front of the school when she begins speaking to us, but she quickly closes the distance, crossing the road and coming to stand directly in front of us. "The second of which involves you explaining your sister's absence. And then the third of which involves both of you hopefully convincing me that I don't need to call your parents and report this."

She's good at issuing out threats. She does it with this compassionate sternness in her eyes that you can't ignore. Daniel and I exchange glances with one another. We both probably want to leave out the part where I was drinking last night and am now hung-over.

Then, something sinks in.

"Wait, ma'am, Ruth isn't here?" Of course, we already know this due to my vision. But if we expressed our lack of knowledge on the subject, we might be able to pull this off without our parents being called about our truancy and instead about Ruth being kidnapped and disposed by her bastard of an ex-boyfriend.

"No. She hasn't been here all day. And Shane came in without her." She raises an eyebrow, asking all of the questions without saying anything, until she continues. "Is something going on?"

"Ma'am, the initial reason why I was absent today was because of farm work. Which Daniel helped me with. And it went wrong, and I ended up being injured." I point somewhat haphazardly toward my forehead. "Daniel stayed behind to make sure that I would wake up, considering I had a concussion and fell unconscious. Neither of us skipped school on purpose."

"Ruth wasn't going to skip school, either," Daniel adds in, rather darkly. "She set off in Shane's truck with him this morning. The both of us saw them pull out of the driveway before the accident happened. We're pretty blind when it comes to knowing what happened to her or her reasons behind not being her. Uh. Ma'am."

His relationship with authority and their usage of proper terms toward them isn't as frigid as mine. He adds on the respectful title like an afterthought. Which, to him, it probably was.

She regards us for a minute, her gaze switching in-between us back and forth like a small child fascinated with a light switch. Turning on her lie detector. Trying to see through the thinly-webbed story we provided her with. The only problem is that I don't know what to tell her if she decides we aren't telling the truth, since we are. Ironic how I'd be lying to her to give her something more believable.

Fortunately, she thinks that we're telling the truth. "All right, then." The gears in her mind churn ever faster. "Do you need my help with this — drama?"

Oh. That was what she was debating. Whether or not she should get involved. It's not as though my father's reputation hasn't preceded him. This is, after all, a small town. We all know how those places function. Everyone somehow knows everyone else's business, even if you forsook telling anybody about it. I think we've been over this, and if we haven't, then we have now.

"No, ma'am. Just please don't tell our parents." Daniel pipes up again to make up for my sulk. "We want this handled quietly. Don't want to worry them or anything. Considering we're sure it's all fine. Do you, ah, know where Shane is?"

"Where he's supposed to be." She's still miffed we didn't show up today, it seems, despite our problems. And she isn't going to offer up any more details. "And I suggest you gentlemen take care of things and then go clean yourselves up."

She cares. In a really weird way. And apparently isn't very good at expressing it, either. I can relate. I watch her as she stalks back toward the school, pulling in on the filtered cigarette, before I realise that she didn't even tell us to put out these things before I polluted the entire school. Seems as though we're not the only one with issues that needed to be dealt with. Maybe something huge had happened at the school that none of us knew about due to our absence. Huge, as in one of the rich parent's kids acted out and they were forced to discipline them, which would result in the loss of some funds. Not that they couldn't afford less money here. Then they'd be a little bit pickier about what they spent it on.

"Well, that was helpful," Daniel mutters through his cigarette.

And then I realise she didn't tell us to stop smoking because neither of the sticks had been lit up yet. I shake my head at my scatterbrained thoughts before yanking the lighter out of a pocket and flicking it, the flame very small, almost invisible in the gust of wind that appeared. "More helpful in the fact that at least we might be able to escape Mom and Dad's notice with this."

"Do you know Shane's last class?"

I shake my head, watching a pair of boys, ones who played on the basketball team with Matt when they were freshmen, meander their lanky selves out from the side door of the gymnasium. "No idea."

"Fantastic. Well, it's not like the school is some huge maze. We'll figure it out. And it's not like we don't know what he looks like."

"Unfortunately."

We stand there in the autumn wind with the trails of smoke whipping about our face, inhaling on the cigarettes and people-watching. If one were to stand here long enough, one would see the entire population of the school. We aren't going to be embarking on a wild goose chase when there is a higher chance of Shane coming directly to us, without much work involved at all. Daniel and I stand close to one another, shoulders brushing, our stances relaxing as time passes, and Shawna spreads herself out in front of his, head and ears erect as she takes in everything and does some observations of her own. Our cigarettes rest in-between our pointer fingers and thumbs when they aren't in our mouths, and we don't make much conversation. In fact, we don't make any at all. It's unneeded.

Some of the junior cheerleaders whisper behind their

hands, never taking their eyes from us. A girl with red braids tucks her books against her chest, taking advantage of their distraction and hurrying past them. Someone in their brand-new yellow sports car that they received for their sweet sixteen turns on the ignition, grinding the gears a little bit and wincing in the driver's seat, though immediately recovering when a couple of her friends look at her, enough to slip on a pair of sunglasses and roll down the tinted windows. Even from here, I can hear strains of the music she's listening to; one of the more popular pop songs. Considering my areas of expertise lie in the eighties and nineties, I can't tell you the name of the song or anything. But I think I've heard Ruth singing this at the top of her lungs in the shower. Something about poker. Weird.

I think we've been standing here about ten minutes or so. The cigarettes are long disintegrated and turning into mashed particles of the asphalt. The air is no longer comfortable, but growing cold, and we've crossed our arms in an attempt to keep body warmth closer to us, and of course, this isn't doing us any good. Even Shawna is beginning to look displeased, her eyes halfway shutting against the breeze, which blows into her face, and a regal rigidity to her spine. And there's still no sign of the bastard who brought us here with his stupid fists and his stupid reasons for hitting my twin sister, whatever those might be and I don't care what they are, I just want to stab this knife into his heart and ask where she is and go back home with her in tow.

"Okay. We need to get a move on." It's like three-thirty in the afternoon. Even lazy bum should've been out and about by now. "We should try by the lockers first."

We start off at a quick pace toward the front school doors. By this time, there are few stragglers remaining, and none of which are interested in making conversation to us, so we're unhindered as we push our way through the doors and make our way toward the stairwell. The school has its entrance, then splits into two hallways, one that goes right and the other that goes left. Both eventually lead to a stairwell. We go left, past the social studies room and the two English classrooms, then rounding a corner that takes us to the left and heading past the student lounge on the right and the gymnasium on the left before entering the double door stairwell. One door on this landing leads outside; there's two flights of stairs leading down into the basement and the locker rooms, as well as the maintenance rooms and the weight room. Then, there are two flights of stairs leading upward, which are what we take, in order to get to the second floor. We pass by the biology and chemistry rooms on the left, the women's bathroom on the right. We round the corner which takes us even further to the right, and there is the elongated stretch of lockers; on the left are more classroom entryways.

We stop. We don't even have to go down there. Because there's no one up there. The ticking of the dog's claws against the cheap linoleum and the screeching of our worn work boots as we halt our walking are the sole noises. As those fade, we hear the murmur of a teacher speaking to a student in the classroom nearest to us, but upon further eavesdropping, we hear that the voice which responds back to her is feminine as well. Shane isn't up here at the lockers like he usually is. He isn't in the school at all. But Principal Rossman said that he came in this morning.

Daniel and I exchange glances with one another. Things have just decided to escalate even more quickly than we imagined. The single word appears in our minds at the same time, and we both say it aloud in a chiming ring as well: "Auditorium."

He's in the orchestra, now that I think about it. The orchestra practices are held during the last period of the day, as a seventh class, right before the final bell, and the same amount as the other courses: fifty minutes. Since of course there's no classroom large enough to house all the members, they practise in the auditorium.

We turn on our heels and go down back the way we came, but instead of going all the way around to the front of the school again, instead we go down the flights of stairs and exit out the back door on the main floor. This opens out onto a concrete sidewalk, which leads to the auditorium's side door toward the right. We hurry along the path. I haven't even felt the connection to Ruth tighten, or release, or anything. That could mean too many things. Unconsciousness. Mental blockage. Death. I really hope it's not death. Because I will kill Shane, if that's the case. I won't just mortally wound him and *leave* him to die. No, I'll make sure that he's dead.

Daniel reaches the side door before I do and pulls at it. I hope it isn't locked; the teachers in this building tend to leave early if they don't have any private lessons to give the students, which means that the auditorium goes on lockdown. God continues to be with us on this day, however, and the door eases open after some taut tugging. We go into the small landing, then open the ancient metal door, which squeaks in protest, and then burst into the main auditorium.

We don't have to look very far. Shane is right there, maybe three feet in front of us. And he's not alone. Even better. Catching him in the act. Neither of them seem to notice that Daniel and I are standing right here, gawking at them, and blinking as though we've had soap thrown in our eyes. He's with that girl. Of course he is. She's the one he's been chatting up the most these last few weeks. His hands are all over her, too. Her shirt is untucked and her pale waist is revealed - and more that I don't bother to look at because frankly, I don't find it interesting. Not when the person attached to her is supposedly madly in love with my sister. Not when the person is attached to her neck like a leech, leaving marks there that won't disappear for a long time. Not when Ruth is missing and Shane is still cheating on her, and not when everything is his damn fault.

Daniel and I look at one another, long and hard. He forms his lips into a thin line; and throws the bat over his shoulder. My eyes narrow until I can barely see. The dog begins to growl, hackles on the back of her neck rising as the stare down continues. Shane continues to not notice and not care. But he's going down. Six feet under down.

His lips twisting into a sadistic grin, Daniel removes his flip-up cellphone from his pocket and opens it, pointing the camera directly at them, and when the flash illuminates the shadowed visage of the backstage area, finally their attention is captured by something other than one another. Shane blinks at the phone, having looked up at the time that the phone had emitted the snapping noise that all camera shutters make when they're capturing a moment to be remembered forever. The girl shrieks and flings herself away from Shane, as though this'll prevent us from blaming her. Unfortunately, it takes two to tango. Oldest rule in the book.

She manages to get away, but only because we're not focused on her. It might take two to tango, but she isn't the core of the problem here. When Shane attempts to dart underneath our arms, he's interrupted by the dog; I step forward, take two fistfuls of his shirt, pick him up off the ground, and shove him back against the piano where he belongs, bending his back into the curve of the instrument, yanking out the pocketknife and withdrawing the blade, pressing it directly against his jugular vein. Right above the pulse that tells me whether he's alive or dead.

Shawna lunges at his exposed ankles, and a loud, wild burst of laughter erupts from somewhere dark. Daniel has decided to lose it. Officially.

"Where's my sister?"

Shane doesn't appear to understand what I'm saying to him. His eyes dart back and forth, and as my eyes readjust to the darkness – The girl has opened the door to the hallway, briefly flooding the area with light before the door slides shut again - it's like his iris and pupil have flooded into one. He looks demonic. More crazed than I do. Though perhaps his reaction is influenced by my appearance.

"H E Y! You son of a *bitch*!" I carve the blade even more closely against that fluttering spot and he grounds his teeth together, whimpering. The dog prowls behind me, back and forth. Daniel approaches us, swinging the bat, lazed in his pace, Cheshire grin in place. "I asked you a question!"

"I don't know." It comes out as a mumble.

"The kid says he doesn't know." It's one of the worst insults you can give to someone like him, who has an ego the size of the state of Texas and about half the maturity. "Hear that, Daniel? *He says he doesn't know.*"

"Oh, I'll bet he doesn't know," Daniel taunts.

"Of course he doesn't," is my agreeable response. "He didn't drive off with her or anything."

A thin line of crimson bursts from underneath the rusted blade. The edge hasn't punctured the vein itself, but it's breaking through the skin, and the shallow slice causes blood to trickle down into the collar of his shirt and onto my hand. "You better try again."

He squirms beneath me, trying to break out of my grip, which only tightens. One of his legs comes up, and I shove it aside with a knee, and then, I do what he planned on doing to me, with an immensely gratifying crunch emerging from his groin as both my knee and shinbone bury themselves there. His breath whips out of him in a wheeze and it's apparent that his eyes are watering. That he's crying. Shame on me. "I'll give you a third time. It's the rule in baseball, you know. Three strikes and you're out. Well, you're on your third one. So you'd better actually give me an answer now."

He looks at me, then looks at Daniel, and he says nothing. The spasm in his cheek muscle belies how hard he clenches his jaws together.

"Get rid of the knife." Shane rasps out the words.

"Fat chance." Eerie calm spreads through my limbs, starting at my core. I can feel it seeping outward in a definite trickle, ink reaching its tendrils through water and colouring it. This ink decidedly colours me with all of the anger I have suppressed, but in such a tranquil manner that I don't realise how white my knuckles are and how my knees tremble with energy until our voices fade from the echo of the auditorium. My skin flushes; the center of my chest turns ice-cold while the rest of me is boiling over. "Start giving us answers and I'll think about it."

I'm not sure why he's holding back information. We managed to catch him in the middle of the cheating act, and now because of Daniel's quick thinking with the camera function on his dinosaur of a cellphone, we also had evidence to use against any claims he might make that it hadn't happened. It's also apparent that Daniel and I are aware that some altercation happened between him and Ruth. So what does he think he has to gain by glaring at us and staying silent? There's no big secrets here. There's nothing that he can do to protect himself in this case. There's no ammunition he can use against us that's going to divert us from getting what we want. He might as well just work with us so that I stop thinking through the detailed manner in which I want to use this knife and pry out the pulse in his vein.

"Look, I don't know what you guys want me to say. I

don't know what happened to Ruth, all right? I saw her this morning and that's it."

He has to be stalling for a reason. Then, it hits me. "Your girl isn't coming back with the cavalry, Shane. You think she's going to head toward Principal Rossman's office and say, 'Oh, Principal Rossman, Shane was attacked in the auditorium while I was in there in the dark with him after school hours.' Get real, man. She's abandoned you in this one. There isn't any help coming for you. And there's no story she can make up that'll sound believable and shift the blame from you both, and you know it."

Shane glares down at the knife still at his Adam's apple, then slides his glance over toward Daniel, who is staring at the photograph on his mobile phone, then turns so that the display screen shows us the flash-encrusted picture, with a leering grin and a slanted eyebrow. This type of malevolence comes easily to him. He's been allowed to express his feelings in whatever form he wants ever since he had been old enough to scream and formulate coherent sentences. It's more difficult for me to tap into it, to let it go, to let myself feel anger. After all, expressing myself, doing what I think is right, isn't encouraged in my household. Emotions aren't masculine unless shown through violence and verbal assaults. And if this bastard doesn't start talking, that's what I'm going to end up resorting to. The spitting image of my father.

I think the worst part about it is that I don't care. I'll do whatever it takes to find Ruth and make sure that she's safe. Even if it means transforming into the monster that has haunted my footsteps and the temper which remains dormant.

Visibly shaken, Shane exhales sharply and rolls his eyes so hard I think they're about to pop out and bounce onto the wooden, scuffed stage. "Look, just take the knife off my throat so

I can talk without feeling that shit about to cut me, okay?"

"You're being vocal about the wrong things." This results in no removal of the weapon at his throat.

He gives up. Somewhat. "I don't know what happened to her."

"And I don't know why you're still being a lying sack of shit!" Words explode from me, and I remove him from the lid of the piano, tossing him away, nothing more than another hay bale to stack on top of the numerous others in the barn. He stumbles, losing his footing, twisting over the tops of his own feet. "You think we don't know you have something do with the reason she wasn't at school today?" I shove him hard in the right shoulder so that he trips backward and collides with the wall behind him. He's in the perfect position where someone could open the door and smash him flat into a pancake. "She was in your car this morning, Curtis. She *left* with you." I grab the side of his face. "So I don't know why you're standing across from me and claiming to be innocent."

When I bring my knee up, aiming it toward his groin and the satisfying crunch it'll emit when the bone makes contact with the appendage he doesn't need, he whips his hands out and slaps at it, quite weakly, trying to push the knee away. He manages to force its collision to happen on the interior of his thigh, and though he winces, he has escaped irreparable damage. "Keep away from me! Crazy bastard!"

Crazy bastard? Does he think that amateurish insult is going to distract me from my extraction? It's going to take a little bit more than throwing around the word crazy like a soiled dishrag to derail me. "Once you tell me what you did to Ruth."

"Yeah, and if Paul isn't convincing you, let me." Daniel steps out of the shadows bat in hand, where he faded and was watching us with that feral glow to his irises, and he waves the phone about in the air as though it is a trophy won, and it is with what it now has on it. He puts his bat directly in the centre of Shane's chest, as though sighting down the barrel of a shotgun and targeting the place to blow out his innards. "So, you can either help us out, and I'll pretend like this picture isn't on my phone, or you can continue to be a complete douche bag, in which case I'll do a bit of online posting about you." He shrugs. "Your reputation will be ruined. Not to mention you'll never get laid. Ever."

"Ooh, I'm so scared." It doesn't work, either. Shane leers at us, pressing his spine against the wall and panting, great gulps of air that make his chest heave. "Doesn't matter either way. It's not like I was getting laid before. She's a prude. Not to mention," and this last part he addresses to Daniel directly, "I'm not you. So there's no chance that she'll ever give it up."

Shawna growls and as he becomes distracted by her, I manage to pummel him in the abdomen with both fists and his shirt rips down the centre in the front as I pull at the hem and crack him one on the back of the neck, using the weight of my entire arm, sending him to the floor, groaning. "Don't you insult my sister like that again!"

"It's her fault," he wheezes out in-between boisterous hacking and clearing of the throat. "Damned tease is what she is. She blinks those green eyes at you and makes you believe that the world revolves around you; but you're nothing special. You're just another name on the list to be checked off once she's finished messing with you."

"You —!" I go to kick him in the mouth with the top of my boot, but Daniel grabs a fistful of my undershirt and thrusts me away with a warning look. Again I am being told to tamper down the ire, to ensure that it doesn't explode in everybody's faces, because it isn't the right time. I would make the worst police officer. I would always end up resorting to this type of coercion in interrogations.

"Don't blame your problems on Ruth, Curtis," Daniel says instead in a bored voice. "Just tell us where she is, and what you did with her, and none of this ever happened."

"I didn't do anything with her. Don't you guys get it? That's what I'm trying to say!" He slurs out the words as he swipes at the saliva in the corner of his mouth. He heaves several times before he's able to continue, placing his palms flat on the ground. "Look. We've been dating a while. Time to get things moving. I was giving her space to get over that thing that happened at the party when she was a freshman. Like any well-mannered, respecting boyfriend would. But it's been — long enough, don't you think?"

He pushes himself into a kneeling position, as he rubs a hand over his sweat-covered face and exhales one final time, glancing first up at Daniel, then at me, with that annoying brunette scalp of his and those eyes that look like cesspits. *But it's been long enough, don't you think?*

As though this is some regular chat between a trios of gang-banging best friends. Boy, has he got the wrong idea. He's chumming us up. Who does he think he is?

He takes mine and Daniel's riveted silences as a good sign, and barks out a chuckle, shifting one leg so that the sole of one boot replaces a knee. "I had a great morning planned out and she freaks out and just jumps out of the truck."

"You—" I say again, but without the accompaniment of a threat toward his mouth, and in a lowered tone of voice, as though I'm sharing secretive information with him. "You pressured her."

"I didn't." His glances in-between us two harbingers of death turn more frantic. "I didn't pressure her, I swear to God."

"Lying through your teeth." Daniel turns away from him as I spit out these words, and he clasps his hands on top of that mussed golden head. "I can see it in that scared-as-shit glare you have on your face. And she said no. Didn't she? Made you mad, didn't it?"

Even if I hadn't been plagued with the unfortunate vision earlier, I still would have been suspicious of his behaviour, the unnatural manner in which his fingers twitch against his extended leg, the way that he looks at either of us as though awaiting some extensive approval, a nod, an acknowledgement that he isn't giving us a load of falsities. But he is. Which makes him even more of a douche bag. I didn't think that even this guy could sink this low on the totem pole, but hey, we learn something new every day. And it becomes more obvious to him that we aren't accepting his excuses that he offers up like sacrificial lambs.

With this stark realisation, he withdraws from the situation, and with another rub across his features, erases that genial expression which he has adapted from the front cover of a gentleman's magazine. There is the Shane that I have seen a thousand and one times peering from the driver's side of that blue Toyota, the one that I have seen walking up the driveway as though it's a chore and a half to even think about coming down to our house and parking on the street when a late March snow had appeared and sent all of us into a frenzy about planting and made Ruth screech for several days about how she had wanted to head down to the Versailles trails for riding with the Stamps. This is the Shane with the lines at the corners of his eyes that have appeared from scowling too much. This is the Shane with the slight twitch in the upper right corner of his lip, as though he constantly smells something repulsive in the air. The one with the pupils that blend into the iris. The demon within.

"Yeah, fine, whatever. Doesn't matter now, does it? She

was asking for it." He clenches a hand. "Asking for every single bit of it. She's a tease. And since my name isn't Daniel Stamp, there's no way she'll ever give it up. I said that already, but I guess I have to say it again in order for you two blockheads to get it. And she got an attitude and I put her in her place."

"Stop bringing me into this!" Daniel exclaims angrily, bursting out and rapidly pacing back to us; he had been walking away, trying to ignore the words. "This doesn't have anything to do with me!"

"Right. And I'm the president." Shane points an accusing finger at him. "You're the whole reason this happened. If you guys hadn't gotten it on last night, then I wouldn't have had to put her in her place. She wouldn't have been a bitch. I mean, I guess I could be thankful. You *did* break her in for me."

His face drains of all colour, as the pocketknife finds its way back at the pulse in Shane's throat. This guy has the audacity to call me crazy while he spouts off things like this and expects us to take it well. He gets off on soliciting power over others, on making them squirm, on angering them, and by the glint displayed in his eyes when I shove that blade against his vein, he knows that I have figured him out. But still he rejoices in the fact that he's able to get me riled up at all, and one side of his mouth slants upward. "Is that how you solve all your problems these days, Reagan? With idle threats?"

"Keep talking and I'll make sure it isn't idle." It wouldn't be difficult, either, to pull it off. I could make it both soundless and painless, or I could draw it out, and considering who we're speaking of, I think I'd more than likely choose the latter. The pulse flutters against the edge of the knife, the heartbeat of a hummingbird, a small finger tapping its fleshy imprisonment as it attempts to look for an opening. I could help it out. I could make sure that it's extracted and doesn't helplessly beat in such a manner. I could release that suppression, and in doing so, release mine. An easy process. Prepare the flesh, if you're feeling merciful, with a shallow slice underneath the nodule itself, and then insert the tip of the knife into the created cut, pushing ever deeper until you can feel the weight of the sphere against the flat of the blade, and then, you start carving upward —

"You're a walking idiot, Reagan. First you threaten me to talk. Now you're threatening me to *not* talk. But I don't really give a shit what you want or don't want, because I'm just going to tell you how it is anyway." No more niceties, it seems. "She went off, accusing me of cheating on her, and how did she find out about *her* anyway, I wonder? Doesn't matter. Thing is, she's being a hypocrite, and we all know it. Who does she think she is, coming around and telling me that I'm a cheater, that she's seen me with this, watched me do that, when she herself had a nice little tumble in the hay with none other than Daniel Stamp last night? And God knows how long it's been going on underneath my nose."

I'm not sure what I can add to this conversation except a more firm press of the pocketknife against his throat, but not even that's going to stop him at this point. It's not like he's pulling this out of the air. Even I could see this morning that Daniel and Ruth had experienced something with one another. While I doubt it involved actually having sex, you'd have to be, frankly, blind to not see the way they looked at one another. But I don't care what she did or didn't do. She's my sister; she comes first, no matter her poor, heat-of-the-moment decision that resulted in her and Daniel falling asleep in the hay together. And this twerp doesn't have any right to judge her.

"You don't have any right to judge her." Leave it to Daniel to vocalise exactly what I'm thinking. "We just caught you getting it on with someone else. Don't shift all the blame onto her, and don't bring us into your problems."

"Oh, see, you're not even denying it. Real smooth, Stamp. I like the familiar way you use the word us. Which means there is an "us" going on. That's fine, though. Just wish you'd told me. Oh, and by the way, you're going to have to accept the fact that she's going to come crawling back to me, despite me getting a little bit rough with her."

"She's not going to go back with you." Daniel keeps staring Shane down, as though he can disintegrate him with his eyes. If only. "She broke up with you this morning. And she's definitely not going to go back with you after this."

"You're right. She did break up with me." Wincing, he stands upright and glowers at me. "But guess what. Despite all my running around, I'll go back with her. And she's going to do the same with me. You think fights like this between us haven't happened before?" He sniffs and runs a wrist underneath his nose. "Hasn't she told you the reasons behind the little bruises on her wrists? Well, shit. I would've thought she'd made some story up about how it was nothing and how I just don't know my own strength. But I do know it. And I know girls like her need to be put in their place."

"I think its guys like you who need to be put in their place," I snap before Daniel can comment further.

"Yeah, well, what can you do? Just you watch and wait, Stamp. She might've had a nice roll with you last night, but you'll always just be the second man."

"You're a liar!" Daniel screams, rushing forward. I intercept him and slam him against the wall as he struggles, clawing at me, and raking lines down the front of my chest, nails tearing through my shirt and going for the flesh, a ravenous, unfed beast. "You're a liar, you son of a bitch! I'll kill you! *I'll kill you!*"

Shane takes advantage of our distractions and wastes no time in heading for the door out of which Morgan managed to make her escape. As he pulls it open, I pin Daniel there with one arm across his sternum and turn toward Shane as best as I can. "Don't forget that we know the *real* reason behind why you're still bothering with her, Curtis."

He freezes in the open threshold, hesitating with one hand on the door jamb, and I can see that true fear flicker in his irises, chasing away the psychopathic glee that had been there moments before, and the ruddiness in his cheekbones is replaced with a distinct white, the colour of stale cream wheat. When he glances at me through his peripheral vision, I smirk at him. "I suggest you clean yourself up and pretend this didn't happen. Or else that story will be unearthed so fast, you'll be suspended before you even have time to say the word, Oops."

He'd forgotten. Not necessarily the fact that the situation occurred at all, but the fact that Daniel had witnessed it and relayed to me what had happened. And despite there being no physical evidence to back up the claims, it wouldn't be hard to coerce people into believing the truth. Not when so many rumours had been whispered about it from the get-go. I just want to bring him down, you know? He's one of those people who walks around with a burgundy target painted on his back, constantly threatening his own life with his stupidity. He's just one of those people that somehow manages to renew his reputation and charm the knickers off those he sees while secretly being a snake in a pit. He's just like my father. And bringing Shane down would be me bringing my father down. Exacting authority I was never given.

"Have a nice day, Curtis." I say it as a cool dismissal, though my veins throb hotly with vigorous energy. And he flees, leaving us two crazy bastards in the dark.

Shawna calms down from where she had been standing, rigid, waiting a command that never came I begin to think: that could've gone worse. But let's face it, it also could have gone much better.

What a fail of an interrogation.

"I'm going to kill him," Daniel seethes as he shoves at my unrelenting arm. I grit my teeth against the pain - because I still have a substantial hangover and every single movement is as though I'm riding on some abandoned railroad tracks - and refuse to move. "Just let me go after him, Paul, and rip his tongue out."

"That won't do any good," I say amiably. I thought I would have been able to lose my temper, but no, it had once again turned into one of those situations where I have to keep myself underneath as tight of a control rein as possible because two of us uncontrollable hotheads would result in something tragic. Boys aren't supposed to express their anger in violence anyway.

Be a man. Grow some balls. Stop being such a pussy. That's what my dad would say to me whenever I cried to relieve my stress. Be a man. What does that even mean, you know? What does it mean to be a man? He certainly doesn't know, does he?

"Castrate him instead."

"I thought you were going to," Daniel comments darkly, turning those eyes on me, and the hostility in them makes me break out in a cold sweat. It's one thing seeing it painted through the irises of your sworn enemy; it's another thing completely to see it reflected in the pupils of someone you consider to be closer than a blood brother. "Then you turned into a pansy on me. Why didn't you cut his throat?"

I know he doesn't mean those in any other manner except for the current situation, and that there are no ulterior motives telling me to grow up in there, but still, I wince away from him, releasing them as though his body temperature had soared to the point where he had burnt me. Because in a way, he had. That single cutting sentence had singed something in me that I had hidden. "Because I thought eventually he'd say something useful. Sorry, Captain. Won't let it happen again."

Daniel doesn't continue this line of conversation, instead straightening the sleeves of his shirt and glaring at something past the drawn curtains on the stage, past the front doors of the auditorium. "And we still don't know where Ruth is. This was pointless. We should've just stayed home. Or not bothered with that bastard."

I narrow my eyes at him. "— You don't actually believe him, do you?"

He whirls on me and shoves me in the chest, right above the heart. "Believe him about what? About the fact that Ruth doesn't know how to leave him? Yeah, I believe him on that front."

I move backward, and he follows me, and his eyes are more crazed than that of my mother's before she had a psychotic break, and I swallow once, hard, cowed. He took that string of nonsense more seriously than I thought he would. "Daniel. Come on. You know Ruth. He doesn't. I doubt he's hit her like this before. He was bluffing, man. He wants to get a rise out of you."

Daniel goes to swing at me again, and I put my hands up, palms facing outward, in the universal gesture of surrender. This seems to calm him more than my words, which also seemed to have some invisible effect as his shoulders relaxed, and he ran a hand through his tousled golden locks before he manages a tremendous sigh. "Yeah. Okay. I guess you're right. I'm just on edge, all right? And that ass running his mouth didn't help matters."

There's a moment of silence, and I push the blade of the knife back into the handle and inserting it into my pocket. "Come on. Let's go clean up and -- wait, did you call her?"

Daniel stops. He had been walking ahead of me and about to pull the door open. I can see him silhouetted by the different shades of shadow. The way that his face belongs to a ghost, something of the dead world. "Call her?"

As though this is the most incredible idea in the world. As though I'm a god for suggesting it. Then, he turns to look at me, and we stare at one another, and with a choking laugh, he pulls open the door and holds it so that I don't leave behind bloody fingerprints from punching Shane by accident. "We're both morons, man."

"Let's not even talk about it," I tell him as I shove my way into the bathroom directly across the hall, despite it being designated for girls only. "Let's just pretend that we were doing this on purpose."

"I mean, I thought that's why we were. How long have we been waiting to jump Shane's bones and make him regret the day he was born?" Daniel laughs. "You have your cellphone?"

With my elbow, I switch on the faucet. I glare at him through the reflection in the mirror. He leans against the wall opposite the stalls, shoulders resting there as he crosses his arms over his chest and balances on one leg, the other foot angled at about ninety degrees, shoe pressing into the wall. "Do I look like it?"

"Just saying. She might not want to answer if we call from my number. Considering she's still apparently dating Shane and whatnot."

I startle from this so quickly that soapsuds splatter onto the floor. "Daniel! Come off it! She's not with Shane anymore! And if you think I'd let her get back with him, even if she were stupid enough to still want to be with him, then you're an idiot! Jesus."

I swear underneath my breath as I swipe at the white bubbles on my forearm, and then, as though someone has shoved me from behind - though the culprit isn't Daniel, considering he hasn't moved since I started staring at him - my right hand catches wrong against the mouth of the spigot and I'm graced with a gash that mirrors Ruth's where depth is concerned but differs in shape.

"Are you serious right now?" I stare at it, the heavy stream of water causing more pain than I assumed it would. Quickly I switch it off and pull one of those brown paper towels from the dispenser.

Daniel moves forward to look at what I managed to do and whistles as I dab at it with the paper towel, which doesn't do much good except to stick to the gaping, bleeding wound. "Paul, you're just not having a good day."

"Neither are you," I say shortly, switching back on the water long enough to dampen the entire paper towel before moulding it into a straight shape and wrapping it about the gash. That'll have to do. "And neither is Ruth."

When we exit the bathroom, he flips open his cellphone again. Pressing the number three on the keypad - the first two numbers are reserved for David and Marlene - he shifts the phone so that it's on speaker, each ring bouncing from the walls. On the third ring, Daniel smacks the phone shut again.

"What the hell are you doing?" I ask him sharply, retrieving my truck keys and jangling them in my palm as I shove open the door to the stairwell opposite the one we entered in. "Hanging up like that. Didn't even give her a chance to answer."

"She's not going to answer."

"Don't be such a Debbie downer. Here." I snatch the

phone out of his hands and throw him the truck keys. "You're driving this time; I'm in charge of the phone."

I repress the number three, and as the phone is still on speaker, those rings accost us again as we make our way across the gravel parking lot. I notice with an inadvertent glance that Shane's truck is gone from its space. The phone continues to blare those annoying tones at us, all of them going unanswered. There's a hitch in the connection, which makes my steps slow; usually that means that the phone is being handled, I've found, moved out of a pocket or drawn out from underneath papers or swiped at to remove the mud from its screen. And then her voice emerges from the speakers in a shrill, bewildered tone.

"Hello?"

"Oh, my God." Daniel backs away from the phone as though it's become possessed. He truly hadn't expected her to answer. "Ruth."

"Ruth?" I ask, halfway to shouting, drawing the attention of the track team, who are stretching out their muscles at the front of the school. Before they can notice my dishevelled appearance, I duck my head away from them and bring his phone closer to my mouth. "Ruth, are you okay?"

"Hello? Oh, this isn't how you do the thing, is it? Ugh. Um, hi, it's Ruth. I'm not here right now, but leave me a message and I'll call you back as soon as I can."

I'm frozen in the middle of the street. The monotoned woman takes over. *"At the tone, please record your message. Or, you can hang up, or press 'one' for more options."*

I don't bother to leave one, slapping the phone shut in a similar manner to how Daniel had done so, and he shakes his head, slowly, mockingly at me, dangling my keys from in-between two fingers, and the clanging noises from all the metals smacking against one another make Shawna bark in happiness and run around in a circle. "Shame. You gave up your driving privileges for voicemail."

He's already started the truck by the time that I move my legs, which feel as though someone has submerged them in molasses, and manage to get over to the passenger's side. Shawna follows me, and I let her up in the cab first before following. The radio blares out some random eighties' disco, and he's bouncing back and forth in the seat, swaying as though someone has injected him with happiness pills, and I stare at him for a minute. "You're awfully wired."

"Might as well not be angry," he says, quite cheerfully. Oh, I know what he's doing. He's actually so incredibly angry that he's forcing himself to go manic. I think that's what it's called. That extreme state of euphoria, where you fool yourself into thinking that there is absolutely nothing wrong with the world around you, and you view all of these rampantly darkening corners as unexplored misadventures instead of venomous flytraps. "So let's dance, right? Anyway, where are we going?"

"Um. Field. Straight, then a left." Since Shane wasn't much of a help when it came to gaining an actual location, I resort to the memories that I had been provided with. Which is what we should have done in the first place. But I couldn't leave well enough alone in my hot-headed fit. Which still threatened to rise up again, considering how harshly it had been tampered. "Not too far. Maybe a couple of miles. It's got this path, I think, leading off the road, and it's just this muddied mess unless it's been nice weather. Lamest place ever to take a girl for their first time."

"Yeah." Daniel dismisses this last part, though I inserted it as nothing more than a halfhearted attempt to get him to let loose and scream like I know he wants to. Hell, he can even slam his hand against the horn if he wants to and scare the elderly neighbour out of their afternoon naps for all I care. I just don't want him to turn into me. Oppressing everything he feels for the sake of appearing strong. And the radio blasting out "She's a super freak!" isn't helping matters. He's bouncing so violently that the chassis shakes back and forth on the axis's, and the entire track team, including the coach, stares down this black truck that bounces like a pimpmobile and is blaring eighties' disco as it starts rolling up the hill as nonchalantly as an old truck can.

"Okay, we're switching to something else." And I move the dial so that there's a wave of white static, and then an explosion of guitars. Def Leppard.

"No, we're not. I'm driving. I get the radio." As soon as my hand leaves the knob, he moves it back, just in time for the finishing chorus. Which is just like the rest of the song. And he continues being an idiot.

So I stare out the window at the side of the road, looking for something that could possibly trigger more memories. He can't have taken her far from the school itself, and what I managed to see looked familiar, as though I had seen it once or twice before, perhaps a third time in a nightmare or a dream sequence. I'd be able to identify it if I saw it, but the whole problem is that first, in order to see it, we have to find it and know where we're going. If this isn't the place that I'm thinking of, then I'm going to be at a loss and have to blow up her phone until she answers.

"You said left, right?"

"No, just left."

"You're a smart-ass, Paul, you know that?"

"Better than a dumb-ass."

The mud-filled meadow appears more quickly than I could have anticipated, and before I know it, I'm punching at Daniel's shoulder, reaching across the panting dog in the middle to do so, and he's screeching at me to quit with that before he knocks my teeth out as he pulls over to the side of the road. Of course, I don't bother getting out of the truck - not when I realise that the meadow is as empty as it's supposed to be, that there is no prone, dark-haired form trudging her way toward us with a torn backpack and a fat lip. Immediately, my spirits, which had lifted when I had seen that the scene of the crime was not a thousand miles away, spiralled. The music switches to the King of Pop, as he's known. You've been hit by a smooth criminal. Not us, Michael Jackson. My twin sister. And to think of Shane Curtis as anything other than a worm that needed to be split in half made my mouth fill with acridity that couldn't be erased, not by the cigarette I shakily pulled from the carton and lit without thinking much about the consequences which would arrive when my dad poked his head into my truck and smelt it. The windows were down, anyway.

"Well."

"Dead end and a half."

Daniel and I glare at one another before glaring at the cell phone resting on the top of my left thigh. "I guess," he says, as easily as he can manage, though now his agitation is starting to overwhelm the manic mood swing, "we should try again."

I make a turning motion, and he shoots the volume of the radio down into the subzero numbers as I press the number three again and we wait through the rings. One. Two. Three. Four. A hitch in the connection. Five. Six. Another hitch. Then, her voice, piercing in the atmosphere, which swells into a sweltering briar about us. But this time, we aren't fooled into thinking that it is a live person speaking to us, but instead, a remnant, a husk that can pose as such, and when the mechanical woman takes over the speaking, I snap the phone shut again, and I peek up at Daniel.

He's staring out the front windshield while the truck idles

in neutral, tapping his fingers halfheartedly against the steering wheel, and a muscle in his right cheek twitches. They had switched to some disco song now that didn't even have vocals, just that cheap instrumental made completely from those sound systems that made all the backtracking very obviously outdated. The whirring synths. The high-pitched noises that stand in for what would be the melody.

As he gazes out that windshield, as I continue to watch him, as I see the way that the sunlight begins to slant and the shadows start to become more prominent, something ominous overwhelms me. Something that tattles about how wrong this is. It is as though I have been walking along a path for years and years, and all of a sudden, I reach what I think is the destination, only to stop with one foot hovering over the edge of a cliff, leg dangling somewhat sickeningly over the black gap of an endless cavern. As though I have barely escaped something, as though my back is pressed against the trunk of a tree as I pant quietly and pray to God that the beast won't find me as I listen to it snuffling about in the brush not five feet from me. And I'm struck with a very weighted sense of foreboding. It confuses me, sends me into a panic, and I press a hand against my heart as though to still the fluttering beat, the hummingbird effect which has transferred from Shane to me.

I know this has to do with washing someone else's blood off my hands. Or rather the fact of the matter being that it was human blood in general, and not animal blood. There is, believe it or not, a difference. At least, there is to me. Both are living things, yes. But there's an extreme amount of disconnect when it comes to skinning something after a long hunt and getting the blood of your hard work on your hands. There's also a different sort of care when it comes to tending to the wound of an animal that you love, a pet with a scrape in the top of her paw or a neck wound in a kitten. They're animals. You find them resourceful, or you love them. You treat them with respect, of course. At least, I do.

But it's different than human blood. When you bind up the chest wound of a friend who was shot in the shoulder with an arrow, and the bandages are bloodied, it isn't just another thing with crimson pouring from it. It isn't just another life slowly ebbing away as you work your hardest to keep it from going. There are memories in that blood, memories that you've shared with them, and when it runs into your fingertips, you start to remember the things you think you've forgotten, the moments that didn't seem so important but now are the things that stick out most. When you see someone wincing as they limp with a thorn in their foot, the empathy pain is stronger and more passionate than it is with an animal; you might find yourself having a pulsating, stabbing sensation in the sole of your foot, mirroring the injury seen.

Animal blood doesn't have as much instilled in it. Not to me. But human blood? It holds the secrets and the dirt that you don't share. It holds the good things and the bad. It holds the friendships, the broken hearts, the things you lost, and the things you found. When it flows onto your skin and into the small pores there, it brands you in a way that makes it not matter how much you wash with soap to remove that copper smell and that sweet tang if you get it in your mouth.

You can know a human's blood. You can make a pact, a promise, with it. And having Shane marking my hand where his bloody mouth spewed on me is disconcerting. Because the blood feels almost corrupted to me. Full of that hidden dirt. Not the kind that comes from abuse, not the kind that can't be controlled because it has been inserted by life. But the kind that has been put there on purpose, with choices and malevolence.

The dread intensifies, weighing down on the interior of
the truck, not flowing out through the windows like the breeze
but remaining stagnant. A haunted smog. It drowns out the
music and makes it sound dissonant to my ears, as though the
station playing the tracks has gone out of tune. As though an
orchestra is winding up.

I begin to panic. Slowly. Then all at once. But Daniel
breaks in.

"So, what the hell should we do now?" He slams his
hands against the steering wheel, breaking off that repetitious
beating he had been doing in time with the music, and glares out
the driver's side window as he continues angrily talking. "Our
lead's been destroyed. We've wasted God knows *how* long
interrogating a son of a bitch that told us nothing. Ruth isn't
picking up her phone. So, Paul, what the hell do we do?"

I don't have an answer for him, though I wish I did. All I
do is hit the number three again and make sure that his cellphone
is on speaker, so that we can both listen to the heart-stopping
peal of the phone ringing and going unanswered, so that we can
wince simultaneously when we hear that breathless "Hello?" that
we desperately want to believe belongs to her, but only belongs
to her ghost in the machine, and then scowl as I snap the phone
shut against the woman's mechanical voice that just doesn't
understand our plight.

Daniel has a different solution in mind.

"Let's just go home, okay?"

He isn't asking for my approval. And I say nothing as he
puts the truck out of neutral and pulls onto the road again.
"We're better off there than here," he says. "At least we can do
something to pass the time," he says. "Maybe she'll be there," he
says.

And I continue to say nothing. I just stare out the

window, arms folded over my chest, cigarette stale and cold in-between my lips, as I try very hard to ignore the weight in my chest, the weight against my heart that threatens to stop it forever.

Impersonal Wind Chimes

October 9th
Manchester, Indiana

Ruth Reagan

"Don't even think about answering that phone."

The latest Lady Gaga tracks blast from the oversized desktop computer in the corner of the living room, the neon lights of the screensaver dancing along to the infectious beats. Julia's voice floats from where she stands in the kitchen, which has one of those lowered bars where those within can glance over it and see into this room where I have been seated, with both feet propped up off the bland, beige carpet, a package of peas plastered against my face where the majority of the damage had been done, for the past however many hours. My body hurts and my spine aches at the base, near my tailbone, from remaining in such a heavily slouched position without much shifting in place, due to my astounding lack of energy. Despite this discomfort, my hand drifts toward the cell phone placed on the fake leather cushion beside me, where it has been buzzing almost nonstop for the past fifteen minutes. Perhaps even longer. When she speaks, my fingertips freeze. They had barely managed to touch it.

"I mean it." She glowers at me over that lowered ledge. She's in the kitchen making the two of us something to eat. Her meal, hopefully, will be relatively more substantial than what I will be eating, which will consist, according to her, of *chicken broth and maybe some noodles, if you're lucky.* "The less drama, the better."

She had exchanged the earlier kerchief for one that was emerald in colour, with blazing gold accents, and it brought out the hazel flecks in her eyes, that impishness that I remembered her always having when she was smaller, when I would catch her eye during the middle of a math lesson and be reassured that someone else was as confused as I was, despite the rest of the class seeming to understand the concept. Now that the mud and the crimson liquid - I refuse to think of it as blood, because that makes things entirely too personal for me - has been washed thoroughly from my face, with much groaning in agony and chirping from my caretaker about how I have such clear skin and how I should use a moisturiser from here on out so that the scarring will be less, I am able to have a nostalgic feeling towards her. It had been difficult to recognise her through the layer of grime which had covered me, but she hadn't blamed me, considering how disoriented I was.

Might even have a concussion, she had said, without any joking tone to her voice. He really hit you hard, baby girl.

He really hit you hard, baby girl. Every time I think about the one who put his fists on me and did this to me, I want to curl up into a ball and die.

Julia hadn't pursued the subject after she had managed to wrestle his name from in-between my sealed lips, with their cracked surfaces and their burgundy lines; even though she had known who had done it, she wanted to hear me admit it. It made a difference, she said. Made it real.

But I knew the discussion was coming. I can tell by the tautness to her shoulder blades and the way that she surreptitiously glances at me while over by the toaster oven, fiddling with the temperature dials and cooking something that wafts its delectable odour toward me. She has things to say. And when she has things to say, nobody can stop her. No matter what the topic of discussion is.

The music on the computer switches to another Gaga song.

I can't help myself, though. It's as though someone has

been experimenting with magnets, inserting one into the surface of my phone and its opposite into my palm, and soon, after a subtle look upward to make sure that Julia isn't hawking me from the toaster oven - and it seems as though she has departed for the stove to check on the chicken broth, which I can smell combining with whatever bakes in the oven - I pull the phone toward me, so that it looks as though my sagging weight in the cushion made it slide down next to me, as though I didn't do it on purpose, before pressing the "home" button at the bottom of the phone.

When the backlight illuminates, my heart drops.

(12) Missed Calls. Daniel Stamp.

(2) Voicemails.

"Is it Shane?"

I have been caught red-handed in the middle of the crime. Guilty as charged, I grit my teeth together, which sends a wave of pain up through my jawline and makes my eyes water, before shaking my head. "Daniel."

She grunts before going back into the kitchen. She doesn't approve of either of them. Says that I need to focus on myself (and spend more time with her) instead of worrying about these idiot boys who don't actually understand what they want past their daily hard-on. I swear those were her exact words, dropped like atomic bombs right before we exited the car. Or, before she exited the car, came around to my side, and pried me from the seat, putting my arm about her shoulders and continuously cursing at the added dead weight in that good-natured way she does.

I feel as though I have heard these words be said to me before, to some similar degree. So if this is the case, then why am I just now actually listening to them, or wanting to? Why am I just now bothering to care about myself and my state of being?

"You're going to spend time with me — even if I have to force myself down your throat."

Her smile is wry as she walks from the kitchen balancing a tray. It's one of the cheap trays, with the images of fruit painted on the sawed wood, and it has a crack on one side, but it fits the overall haphazard décor throughout the rest of the house, from what I have managed to see through these swollen eyes. Her parents were both at work, and her little brother in school, an eighth grader; I hadn't seen him in ages, either. Her older brother lives in Cincinnati now, making a name for himself. She had been excused from school because she had been going to the hospital for her treatment. She's an outpatient, she told me, and the disease she has is so terrible, so monumental to me, that I cannot name it — because if there is one thing in the world that I don't want to make real, it's the fact that she has it. It had been pure luck, though, that she had seen me at the time she had, that she had decided to take the back roads to her house instead of the main highways. Or else I probably would have been walking home.

I tried to tell her, when she had settled me into her couch with a similar maternal manner as to when she had put me into her car, that it wasn't just luck, that she had been a Godsend, a miracle, and the expression in her eyes had darkened to such an extent that I had feared saying anything after that for quite some time. "Leave God out of this," she told me, not offended, but angry at something else, something more than just my offhand comment and subsequent insistence. "He's the reason I'm here now." I didn't have to ask for details to know what she really meant.

God is a forbidden topic. As is politics. But sex and relationships, however, that's completely fine to talk about. And it's what she brings up now.

"Last thing you need is a thousand guys knocking at your door. Look at you. God. Son of a bitch. I want to castrate him." Her stream-of-consciousness manner of speaking is a welcome change from the so carefully arranged sentences that Shane always used, as though he had instilled much thought into each conversation, thought about how they could pan out and conjured up answers, solutions, for each problem. I used to fool myself into thinking that this was just his mechanical mind working; he had, after all, shown extreme promise in the engineering field, was even thinking about forsaking the country life to live in the city and work for one of the big-name companies. But I realise that all I have been doing throughout the extent of this relationship, if that's what it can even be called, is telling myself lies, making myself feel better, and instead of listening to what God really had to say on the matter, thinking my own thoughts and believing they were answers to prayers instead.

It's humbling to realise this. Also disconcerting. Because then you begin to question everything and anything that you have ever prayed. And wonder, like Julia, if there is really any sort of thing up there in the sky listening after all.

"Woman, get out of your head. Not a good place to be."

My eyes, which have drifted shut, fly open, and when I see her staring at me, I must give her a riotous look back, because all of a sudden, she bursts out into laughter, a deep, rich tone that manages to fluctuate from high to low all at once, a sound that I like more each time I hear it, especially when it's because of something I've said or done by accident. "Don't give me that look. Talk to me. Tell me what you're thinking about."

She winces as she leans back into the couch, and makes a little bit of a hand motion toward the tray on the glass table which separates us, as she has decided to sit across from me. A pang of guilt overwhelms me again, but this time, it's because she is in pain at my expense. "I'm thinking," I say, and I nearly startle at how hoarse my voice is, as though I swallowed half of the dirt that had been caked on my face, and perhaps I had, "that I'm intruding on you." A vague start.

"*Intruding* on me?" She rolls her eyes and picks up the glass of ice water, with a green extendable straw, from the tray, bringing it over to me, not bothering to wait for my body to decide whether or not it can function. "We've been best friends for how long and that's what you think this is? — Don't tell me that you're having a pity party for me. The pain's not too bad."

Now I really do give her a glower.

"Not today, at least," is the most she'll amend her statement before she pushes the straw's opening at my mouth, trying to get me to be receptive. "It's pretty shit the rest of the time, though, so I'm just being thankful for the fact that I'm not nauseous and throwing up as soon as I see something edible."

I don't want to think about the medications that she so nonchalantly listed off, using their official names as though they were old companions from childhood. There's too many of them. A cocktail sloshing about in her veins, one that is supposed to help her, but causes more agony. How screwed up is that? No pain, no gain, they say, as they inject you with the needles. And you wonder whether it's worth it at all. Of course, you can't tell this to anybody, she said, rather thoughtfully, because they'll just encourage you that life is the best option. But is it? Is it really, when it's coated in prescriptions that you can't escape? But talking that way, she said, bitterly, made the others think that she was suicidal, that she didn't want to live anymore and that she was giving up. So instead, she shrugged, she kept it bottled up inside, where it rotted and festered like a dead limb.

"I was also thinking," I tell her, after she has removed the straw from my mouth and the iciness of the water coats my insides, "that I should be getting home. They're calling me nonstop. Probably worried sick that I didn't show up at school."

"Goes to show you that Shane didn't own up to what he did. That bastard. Really, just say the word, and he'll wish he'd never been born. I promise. All it takes is a few well-placed punches." She puts down the tall glass of water and eyes the other things that are on the tray. She had been dealing with those bagels in the toaster oven, the ones coated in cheese, as well as meats, depending on the kind that was bought. There also is a small bowl of broth, with the noodles and chicken strained out, and another glass of water, without ice, but still with a straw. I'm assuming that's hers. "Make a choice. You're not leaving until you get something in your stomach. Take it from me that painkillers make you want to vomit."

"Vomiting comes up a lot," I say, sounding reproachful even though I don't mean to.

She isn't offended. "Yeah, especially in this line of work. Chemo is a drag."

I move my chin toward the broth, because there's no way in the world that I'm going to be able to chew something crunchy when I am barely able to formulate words, and as she retrieves it, I scoot myself up higher on the couch so that my abdomen loses the ripples in its flesh and so that my spine nearly screeches out in relief from the C-shape it has been stuck in. I remove the ice from my right eye, and turn my face fully toward her so that she might take inventory of the injuries, which she does with a keen eye and a cluck of the tongue. "Your right eye will probably be swollen for a few days, but your left one's going down."

I could tell that much, considering my left one is how I am doing the majority of the seeing around the house and watching her for her reactions. Though my ears still ring, the music has helped in getting rid of that, and though the pressure in my head hasn't completely dissipated, the migraine medication she gave me has helped it considerably. At least I don't have the constant urge to tear my brain out.

"And the lip?" It still feels as though someone has attached a grapefruit to my mouth. And considering the narrowing of the eyes that she does, however invisible to the faraway eye, tells me that the lip won't be so lucky, that there is no way in hell that I will be able to disguise these injuries if I were thinking about it. Which, admittedly, I had been. "Great."

"*Great* is the *wrong* word," she says dryly, extracting the spoon from the bowl and holding the spoon up in the air so that I might blow on it to cool the liquid off. I think I forgot to mention that she has been wearing a face mask this entire time. As a precaution, she tells me. The last thing her immune system needs is something that might have been on my clothing; the facial masks covers her mouth and the tip of her nose, concealing her nostrils from the floating, unseen atrocities. Another reason for me to feel bad. I'm contaminating her sterile environment. And no matter how many times she tells me it's okay, I don't feel like it is. "Open up, boo."

I slant an eyebrow at her as she pushes the spoon into my mouth. I feel a little bit like an invalid, but I admit that it's quite nice having someone be a caretaker for me, for a change. It's always me who is the one of the family that remains most responsible when it comes to healthcare matters. I'm the one who pats closed the cuts on the boys' foreheads, the one that wrapped my mother's bandages when they needed changing; Paul had tried a couple of times, but become queasy at the depth of the lines there and, unable to stand it, walked out of the room. Mom used to do these types of things when I was sick with an influenza or a pneumonia, but not anymore. None of us have had terrible diseases like that recently; not to mention she, well, hasn't exactly been feeling like herself. I don't expect her to be able to take care of us when she is having difficulties taking care of herself.

"So. Do I need to give you the lecture?" Here it comes. "Do I need to tell you just how poor of a bastard your boyfriend is? Do I need to tell you that I told you so?"

"Told me so?" I ask lamely, wracking my brain for a trigger word as to what she might be talking about. As far as I can remember, she and I never discussed romantic relationships at any length, not walking down the hallways together at random or sitting next to one another in class. I think the most we did was speak about the guys we found to be semi-attractive. Which, unfortunately, weren't many. Nor did we agree on half of them. "What are you talking about?"

"Oh, shit. Concussion. Right." I still don't believe her when she keeps saying that I have a concussion. But with the way that my thoughts are unorganised, maybe I do. "Um, so, back in junior year of high school. You — Well. I'm sure you remember the party. We talked a little bit before everything got rough and wild. And we were talking about how the guys looked cuter in the dark, and you got all prophetic on me or some shit, talking about how the shadows in their cheekbones made them look like ghosts, and then you pointed at Shane and you were like, 'He's attractive, yeah?' And I told you he was bad news then. Told you straight up."

My heart almost stops. "Yeah. You did." No wonder it hadn't come immediately to the forefront of my mind. Almost everything about that party I couldn't remember - or didn't want to remember.

But I did. The way that the pulsating synths had surrounded us, music much like what emerged from her computer speakers in the present day, with something iridescent in a plastic cup half-dangling out of my hand as I leaned to the side, leaned against her, and giggled, pointing out Shane, who had been eyeing me too, which pleased me. No boy *ever* eyed me. "Be careful," Julia had said. "He's bad news. Likes to play games and shit like that." And my drunken response had been of satisfaction that he and I could play a game of cards, perhaps poker or rummy since my dad didn't like those anymore.

That was how I had taken her comment. As that type of game. How ridiculous I had been. How stupid. Let's be blunt. I was stupid to think that. Stupid, stupid, *stupid.*

"Hey. I'm sorry. I didn't mean to bring it up." The sepia ring around her pupils seems more pronounced when she's this close to me. "It's in the past. And so is he. Just so long as you're not planning on going back with him."

My cellphone buzzes again. More difficult to ignore this time, considering it's pressed up against my thigh, embedding itself into the space in-between jeans and fake leather.

"You're not planning on going back with him. Are you?" Julia dips the spoon back into the broth and holds it to my mouth. I make the split-second decision to swallow it before I answer.

"———— No."

The answer should've been automatic, and she catches the hesitation, the catch at the end, the lift that means I am uncertain about this being my official ending answer, and with a clatter, the spoon drops back into the plastic bowl, her hand trembling as she puts it back on the tray, pinching at the bridge of her nose and grimacing for a split second. Panicking, I sit upright too quickly, coming away from the backrest of the couch in an attempt to grab her by the shoulders and get her to lean back, and all of a sudden, all of the dizziness which has remained dormant springs forth, released from its cage. The ceiling is beneath me, the floor is above me, and I am reminded of how I felt upon initially awakening from unconsciousness, and the next time that I blink too slowly, I find myself leaning over the arm of the love seat, and just as I topple over, going sideways off the couch, I catch a glimpse of my face in the mirror, the reddened and inflamed mouth, the pallor of the dead.

"Jesus, Ruth!" Julia stands up from the couch, and though birds fly around my head, tweeting out their cacophony, my wooziness doesn't prevent me from seeing that her knees tremble about as much as my fingers do as I reach upward to shove hair out of my face - and then I see the gash, the one shaped like a tree, covered in white gauze, and I am distracted in staring at it. "Did you land on it?"

She's pointing at my hand, leaning against the arm of the love seat I just vacated. "No, no," I say weakly, gravelly, wanting to curl up here in this position and never move for as long as I lived. "I just - I forgot it happened at all, really."

Her expression is grim. "Your concussion might be even worse now. What the hell were you thinking? Flailing like that?"

"I - just - I thought that I had said something to make you hurt or something, I don't know!" To my befuddled mind, it had made sense. I had responded to her question and she had been sent into a near convulsion. Therefore, it was my fault. Just as Shane hitting me had been my fault. Right? Because I had provoked him with my attitude. He shouldn't be blamed for me, and neither should she.

"You need to chill, babes." She folds her tall form so that she's lying next to me on the floor, and the two of us are curled up, face-to-face, with arms draped across our stomachs. "But hey. Better down here, anyway. Now you can't look anywhere except right in my face, and I want you to do that, and I want you to say that 'No' as though you really mean it. Do I need to ask again?"

I swallow hard, the scalding broth now a remnant on my taste buds. "No. And I mean that in more than one way. No, you don't need to ask it again. And no, I'm not going to go back with him." I can almost feel my pupils expanding. "No matter how much I blame myself for what happened."

"You are *not* in that place."

"I am." I like her rugged manner of talking. The way she proclaims things as though they are true, but then, I end up contradicting them. It's a natural interaction with her, it seems. Reminds me of a film where the girls say *"Shut up"* as an exclamation of surprise; I wouldn't be surprised if she eventually drops that line with that significance behind it. "I'm definitely in that place."

"Girlfriend, you have got to realise something. Speaking your opinion isn't any reason for a guy to haul off and punch you across the mouth. Okay? And from the looks of it, lay a couple more hands on you after that." She pointedly takes in the injuries again, which causes me to become self-conscious, and I look down at the fibers of the carpet, for they have become interesting, indeed. "No one should do that. Got it? Don't be blaming yourself for him being a complete douche bag."

There's a moment of silence that stretches in-between us before she sighs heavily, and lays one of her hands, which is sweat-covered and clammy, on my bare arm, and goosebumps erupt at the change in temperature. But despite the state of her palm, the touch comforts me. "You do know this has happened before, right?"

Fervently, I shake my head. If there was one thing that Shane and I never discussed, it was the relationships in which he had previously invested himself. "He always said they didn't matter. That it was me and him which mattered, because it was going to be forever."

"I'm sure it was," Julia says, quite good-natured in expression but acrid in tone. "Until he popped you one. But there's a reason beyond that, you know."

"No, I don't know." Which exasperated me more than it should. Because I am coming to the realisation that the person I had been dating for the past seven months has been a complete stranger to me, that the things he had woven to me all those nights could possibly not be true, that he could be an entity composed entirely of falsehoods. "Please, just tell me." I only say this because she looks quite reluctant, as though she regrets bringing up the train of conversation at all.

Resignedly, she rolls her eyes upward, as though she is trying to look at the ceiling. "Well. He had this last girlfriend before you. I'm sure you've heard about her. Phoebe? She went to the public high school. Tall, athletic, blonde, had a lot going for her."

The way that this girl, Phoebe, whose name did indeed sound incredibly familiar, is being referred to in the past tense disturbs me, causes a tight knot to wind up, bind up, rubber bands clasped into a ball, in my stomach. One that belongs to a different type of nausea. "Wait — went?"

"She would be a senior now, yeah." Julia's odd eyes, with their majority of blue and that aforementioned ring of sepia around the pupil, penetrate me. "She committed suicide. Like two weeks before you started dating Shane."

"What?" My throat constricts closed. "—She *what?*"

"Yeah. Hung herself in the closet. Her mother found her apparently. I don't know for sure, of course. I wasn't there. This is just from what I could gather through the rumour mill." And now, I understand why she seems so familiar to me. Because, and the memories are coming back to me, her photograph had been plastered on the windows of the local schools, with those Latin inscriptions underneath, the in memoriam that testified the life above it had been lost, and the thought of that blonde hair splayed about a face more pallid, more lifeless than mine, made me want to vomit. I cover my mouth with a hand as Julia continues.

"They say he drove her to it. With the constant needling. The whole *'You'll never be good enough'* thing after telling her that she was the best thing since sliced bread. I don't know. The whole situation is a little bit muddled, and you know small towns; anything considered to be semi-controversial, and underneath the nearest rug it goes as soon as possible. But she had been coming to school with bruises around her neck and finger-shaped red marks on her wrists. They'd thought that, you know, the sex life had been rough, but turns out, after autopsy - because yeah, I guess some of them lasted that long, again, I don't really know - that the coroner discovered that some of them had been self-defence wounds. That he'd been physically abusing her.

"Look," she hurries to say when she notices the sheen of sweet on my cheeks, which can be felt through my fingertips being plastered across my face as I shift my hand up to cover my eyes. "I'm not telling you this to make you feel guilty or anything. I'm just warning you. I'm telling you that this is just the beginning. She kept going back with him, okay, and it never got better. And she ended up dead. And yeah, suicide is a choice in the end, but I don't want you to make that choice. Not because of him. He isn't worth death, not worth crossing over to the other side, you know, not when there are uncontrollable things more than willing to kill us."

"I know." The words come out strangled. As though it is my throat that he has wrapped his hands around, and not Phoebe's. As though I am the one being bruised underneath his heavy weight after telling him that he's gone too far. As though I am the one being subjected to his violent outbursts. And now that she has mentioned such things happening, it brings to me so many little things that I should have noticed, signs that I should not have so flippantly addressed, red flags that I had previously claimed to not have existed, and now, there they all are, blatant beacons in the impermeable darkness, the shadows accosting me from all side, and I want to sink into the created oblivion and, perhaps, never come out. But she's correct; if there is a reason to go down into that place, it isn't going to be because of someone like Shane Curtis.

"It's just - I never knew about any of that. He never told me about any of his ex-girlfriends. Not a single one."

"Yeah, and that's just the one that we know about," Julia remarks, mincing no words, relentless in her quiet persistence that even thinking about him from now on is a terrible idea. "I know he's had a couple before that."

I narrow my eyes, then, suspicious. "How do you know so much about him?"

"We all do." Her tone turns droll. "We're just not as good at ignoring it as you are."

The blinders of love, as they are called in all the romance novels. The shields which are placed over the eyes of those involved, as though they are horses attached to a carriage, and the extent of the relationship is the length of the journey upon which the horses embark, and the entire time, only can they see the road in front of them, and not the dangerous that lurk around. They are able to ignore everything except what is presented to them. And it's up to the driver, the placer of the blinders, to make sure that they are well-informed, that they are soothed, that they realise they can trust him. And what if that trust is broken? They spook. They rear. They charge away in an attempt to escape from the newfound, unexpected danger.

"You know what else you're really good at ignoring? Me."

The rap music playing in the background doesn't fit this train of thought nor the topic of conversation at all. At any other point, it might have even proved to be comical. But when we both lie on the floor in pain, grieving over the losses and pressing our arms against our stomachs - there's nothing funny to be found.

I grit my teeth and close my eyes briefly.

"Yeah, you *already* know what I'm gonna be saying. Cause you know what else make it hard on Phoebe? The fact that she didn't have any friends to talk to about it all. Know why she didn't have any? She decided Shane was *too important.* She ditched all of her girlfriends, stopped talking to her parents. She curled up into herself and became a whack-job clone of Shane Curtis. Man, if I was like him, I'd probably get driven crazy, too. The point is — don't pull this shit on me again."

She sniffs once, closes her own eyes as I open mine.

"I can take it once. But I'm not taking it twice. Not now."

I reach for her hand and touch her knuckles, clammy and lukewarm from her heavily fluctuating body temperatures. "I won't."

(And I mean it.)

And then, the cellphone rings again. We can hear it vibrating against the couch cushion, even from here. The eyeliner underneath her eyes runs from how tightly she has been squeezing her eyes shut in pain, and she swipes at the moisture, glaring toward the phone. "Can't even have a decent conversation without that thing going off. Sometimes I hate technology, you know?"

"Yeah, I know," I say, absentmindedly, trying to follow her advice to stay out of my own head and failing. Because there's something relatively nice about being up in there with floating clouds and nonchalance.

She doesn't allow me much solace. "Look. I'm sorry you have to find out about him this way. But better late than never, right? And hopefully this is helping rest my case as to why you shouldn't think about going back with him."

"I'm not thinking about going back with him!" I'm irritated. "I get the point. I see the evidence. I was dumb. I was stupid. I was blind. I was this. I was that. I was in love. I thought he was different. I thought it'd be different with me. I stayed with him. I stuck through it with him, and it ended up not being any different. And it's happened before, and it's ended poorly. I get it! I'm not going back with him!"

The coolness in her gaze softens a little bit, and her hand goes to perhaps drape itself across my cheek, but all I can see, instead, is the back of Shane's hand coming at me, the shock and the impending red mark on my face, the way that I had stepped backward, how he had come at me again, how I had tripped and ended up on the ground, and then, he was still there, still coming for me, and I could do nothing to stop him, could only throw my hands in front of my face to have them knocked aside, weightless, and I float again. And then her hands are on my shoulders and she's shaking me, but it's him who's shaking me, telling me to snap out of it, and I scream and I bury my eyes into my wounded palm and blink into the coolness of the bandages, look at their stark, slightly stained surfaces, and breathe through my mouth.

"Ruth, snap out of it. Come on, babes. Come on."

She hadn't been slapping me at all. She hadn't been shaking me by the shoulders. Her hand remains layered on my arm, replaced there when she noticed that I wasn't particularly receptive to a hand near my face, and she just looks at me, and there was never any coolness in her expression except that which my own imagination had implanted there, and I exhale, shakily, as she says again, "Come on. Nothing's happening. He's not here. We're good."

"What is wrong with me?" I stammer out, and realise that my entire body's shaking. "Julia, *what's wrong with me?*"

"There's nothing wrong with you," is her vehement response. "You were strung along and played like an instrument and beat up by someone you thought you could trust. You're in shock. No one's blaming you here. No one's rushing you. Just breathe. Okay? I'm not going to let him come in here."

And even though I know that he is nowhere near this house, that he has high-tailed it elsewhere, for some reason my mind had thought that he would come to me, that he would find me again and do that apology thing and then I would fall for it. The last thing I needed to do was see him. If I had my way, except for accidentally in the hallways and in the classrooms, I would never see him again. That way, there would be no opportunity for me to fall for the trick that he has pulled several times over. Too rough of fingers on the arm, immediate release and an apology. Then it happens again. The aggression about sex. The falling back, then the asking again. Not understanding the word No unless it was reiterated a dozen and a half times.

Panic is still in my voice. "Don't leave me alone with him."

The phone vibrates again on the couch cushion. We both ignore it now.

"What do you mean?"

"Like at school." I have to get the words out. "We're in classes. We sit next to one another. Oh, God, help me, I don't think I can even stand to look at him."

"Hey, it's going to be okay. I said that already. I'll be there at school. And so will your brother, and that other guy—"

"Daniel—"

"Yeah, Daniel. Which, by the way, don't you be getting into a relationship with him, understand me? Nothing but trouble waiting to happen."

"Daniel?" It's strange to describe what my heart does at this current moment, but it's almost as though I have taken it and dropped it down a garbage chute. "You don't have dirt on him, do you?"

"No. But dating someone after this nasty of a break-up and relationship, especially right away, is not a good thing. No matter how much you and the other guy get along." Julia turns so that she is looking at the ceiling and I mimic her, and we both stare at that weird pattern that seems to be in everyone's houses these days, in the Midwest, where someone has aimed a paintball gun at it and thought it was a good idea to leave it like that. "Just promise me that you'll stay single for a while. Think about yourself. Have some girl time. With me. Your best friend. Remember me? Hi, I'm Julia."

My heart hurts. In fact, my entire body aches, and it isn't from being hit. It's from the realisation that there is a possibility that this friendship will be ripped from me — and I'll be forever maimed with the guilt, with the realisation that I'd been ignoring it, taking it for granted, throwing it into the churning tempest for the grace of a relationship that ended up turning sour. The phobia of loss is cloying and weighted. But we made a pact. And I promised, and I meant it.

"I can't have girl time with anyone else?" I tease, trying to keep myself from thinking too hard, thinking about (death.)

"Bitch - you don't *need* anyone else. I'm all the best things rolled up into one Julia-sized package."

Then we just lay there on the floor through three more Gaga songs and a Kanye song, both of us immersed in our own separate worlds of pain, connected by a simple touch on the arm and the weight of one another's presences. And I don't know what she's thinking about, but I know that I am seriously contemplating the things which could have happened if I had been picked up by anybody else on that road. Because I had been in a bad enough way where it wouldn't have mattered; the first person who had taken my arm and guided me to their car, I would have gone with, because I wouldn't have cared. I wouldn't have cared. That frightens me a bit. The fact that a person could have absolutely no care in the world for their well-being.

And in the middle of the Kanye song, the phone starts to ring again. Buzzing in the little dip that it fell down into.

I feel like a small child asking for permission, but I do it anyway. "Can I answer it now? I need to tell them that I'm not dead."

She grunts in disapproval, but doesn't say anything open in protest, and with this, I pull myself into a hands-and-knees position on the floor, crawling back to the couch and snatching up the phone on the last ring, sliding the "answer" button over and shoving the earpiece to my ear. "Hello?"

"Oh, Jesus, if this is your voicemail again—" The voice erupts at me in static.

"Um, Paul?" I clear my throat, aware of how it grates in the back of my throat, and I lean my shoulders against the front of the couch, sighing. "Paul, is that you?"

There's a silence on the other end, and then a roughened, detached voice. "—Ruth? Wait, really?"

"Yeah, really. Julia finally let me answer my phone."

Another pause, and then, his voice sounds far away, as though he has pulled the phone away from his face. And he has, because soon after, he shouts, **"Daniel?** *Daniel!* **What the hell are you doing? Daniel, come back!"** An exasperated sigh.

"God, Ruth, we've been looking for you everywhere. We confronted Shane —"

"What? You did *what?*" Julia has scooted herself over to sit next to me and I hold the phone out – putting it on speaker - so that she can eavesdrop on the conversation.

"—And he didn't tell us anything, but oh, thank God, Ruth, we have the twin bond. Because I saw where you'd been, but then you weren't there, in that field, and everything has just gone to shit over here."

"Paul, what are you talking about? Slow down!" Julia shoots me a concerned glance at the winding up in my throat, as though I am a music box and being twisted to play the recorded melody. "Just—one thing at a time."

He exhales sharply. I can almost imagine him running his hands through that deep chocolate hair, the sheen of sweat and leftover ash from the secret cigarettes he smokes - as if I don't know about it - dotting his olive skin, reddened from the amount of sun he receives. "Okay, we woke up, and I had this thing. I had this vision, I guess, and you were being hit, but it was like I was being hit, right, like I was in your place. Are you okay? He didn't do anything too bad, did he?"

"Um —" Julia fervently shakes her head. "Nope."

"Thank God." This is the third time he's said that. "So we went to the school to talk to him, and things just went badly - and so we went to the field, and we didn't know what to do, so we went home and—Daniel's just lost it."

"*Lost it?* What do you mean, *lost it?*"

"Look. Shane isn't a nice guy. Obviously." My brother sighs again. "And he needled at us. Said not nice things. I didn't think it'd get to Daniel, but it did. Badly. And he's mad. Like, absolutely livid. I don't think at you. Just in general that this had to happen at all. Because it didn't have to happen."

"Do I need to come home?" My voice turns panicky when he's silent. **"Paul!"**

"Yeah. You do. Soon. No matter what you look like. He needs to see you. And you need to tell him that you broke up with Shane. Because he believes it - but he doesn't believe it, you know?"

"Why *wouldn't* he believe it?" I feel as though someone has stabbed me. Julia puts a hand over mine which lies limply upon my thigh, and I barely feel it.

"Because Shane said that little things like this have happened before, and that you've always gone back with him no matter how much you guys fight, and so on, and it irked Daniel because - well, because of what happened last night."

I close my eyes. "Jesus, help us."

"Yeah, uh, this is a mess. Wait —" He pulls his mouth away from the phone again, and the words rip out from him in a roar. **"Daniel! Get back here! RIGHT. NOW!"** Then, back to me. "Ruth. I have to go. Okay? Come home. *Please.* Just come home."

And the connection goes dead.

"What exactly happened last night?"

I stare down at the phone as the backlight turns itself off. "Daniel made me a little deer and kissed me and we fell asleep in the hay." The shortest summary of the events that I could have offered. "I guess it was obvious to everyone else, even Shane, that something had happened at all."

"Ruth, girl, you manage to get yourself into some tight situations, you know that?" She pulls herself up from off the floor using the arm of the couch as a balancer, and then offers a hand down to me. "Good thing you have someone to pull you out of them."

And even though she was doing nothing more for me in

the current moment than pulling me off the ground, I feel as though she was also dislodging me from the cesspit I accidentally had fallen into, and though the liquid still coats my limbs and my skin and I won't be able to forget about the experience as easily as I would like, I know that she's going to be there to swipe at it and get it off of my clothing, and disinfect the wounds created, and I am bittersweet about her proffered friendship, but I wouldn't reject it for the world.

"I'll drive you home." She takes one of the used washcloths to the kitchen sink, scrubs at the plasma and the dried blood and the leftovers from the wounds it's been pressed against until all of the particles dislodge and flow down the drain, then re-wets it in cool water and rings it out. "You're taking this, and you're keeping it over that eye and that lip. Does anything hurt? I mean, I know everything hurts, but like, is it pain you can't stand?"

"No," is the automatic answer, one that emerges more easily than the one before it, despite my eyes feeling as though they are three-dimensional and my lids are pieces of fabric I'm attempting to pull over a bloated stomach. "Just *weird*. Never had a black eye before."

"And the lip?"

As though someone socked me in the face with a baseball and the baseball has yet to fall from the corner of my mouth, so that I'm just walking around nonchalantly as possible with a baseball on my face. "It's fat and swollen. But not painful." As long as I don't brush a hand against it as I accidentally did on the couch.

"— And the hand? How'd you even get a gash like that, anyway?"

I stare down at the white gauze and shrug. "I don't remember." Because I didn't. All I remembered was looking down at my palm as I went to brush my hair out of my face, and seeing the massive, gaping hole there. And for the life of me, the memory as to how I managed to acquire it has gone completely blank. "And I really don't," I emphasise, when she gives me that glower again, the one that tattles she knows that I'm hiding something. Except this time, I'm not.

"All right, fine. You can keep the clothes, by the way. Just wash them and bring them to school whenever."

I look down at myself, having forgotten that she had undressed and redressed me in my half-conscious stupour. I wore a lilac shirt, a plain one, with holes in the sleeves, and the hem traipses all the way down almost to my knees. She's also slipped on a pair of basketball shorts, blue ones with black splashes on the sides, and though I'm pretty sure those aren't supposed to be this long, they hit at my mid-calf. Then, there's the black ankle socks. Which are warmer than any pair I have. Odd.

"Let's get moving, homie."

Another term of endearment. I fear that I won't be able to keep up with all of these different nicknames being designated for me. Homie. Babes. Boo. Girlfriend. All except my name, which she seems to only use when I am in deep turmoil or slipping backward into the *bad place* in my head.

She readjusts her face mask, which came undone after slipping on a pullover sweatshirt, and then holds the front door open for me. I realise that I haven't even moved a single muscle, and the cool autumn afternoon tickles at me even from here. Sighing heavily, I scoop up my phone and stand up, scrunching up my face when the dizziness comes on stronger than ever, standing there until it subsides, and then continuing on.

You've been kicked by horses before. You've been almost trampled by angry cattle. You've had to run from one house to the other over the expanse of twelve hours when the Stamps' best mare was giving birth. Your body can withstand a lot.

I tell myself these things as I force my feet to move forward, as I make myself go through the front door and toward her red Honda as she locks the door behind me. You've hauled several pounds of textbooks on your shoulders throughout high school. You can handle this. Your body can withstand this. Yes, I can do this. You aren't being constantly drug under by actual medicines. These are physical wounds that can heal. Ruth Reagan, you are a fighter, and you can do this.

I manage to open the passenger's side door to the unlocked car, though I fall into the seat instead of sliding in like she does, and by the time I reach over to pull the door shut, I'm breathing hard. I look over at her, but as she starts the car and puts it in reverse, she doesn't seem to notice my internalised distress; and if she does, she's purposefully ignoring it. My satchel still lays across the backseat, not having moved since it was thrown there, and it slides all the way to the other side when she turns sharply out of her driveway. "Whoops."

"You're insane," I say, staring at the speedometer. She definitely knows how to utilise the acceleration benefits of foreign cars. "This isn't even a main road."

"I just ask myself, what's the worst it's going to do? Kill me?"

But the needle inches down toward the speed limit nonetheless.

"I'm going to try and call Paul again," is my abrupt not-response, and I open the phone, inputting the password, so that I can dial him, forgetting that iPhones have the capabilities to dial people without putting in the password, because it's called emergency calling. "I didn't like the way he sounded on the phone."

"Hey, at least he did my job for me. You know, teaching

Shane a lesson. Probably more appropriate that your brother did it, anyway." She shrugs. "I hope he comes to school looking worse than you do. Because then, everyone will know what happened. And I'm pretty sure he'll never have a girlfriend again."

She turns down the radio as I freeze in place. "Oh, Lord."

"What?"

"Everyone's going to know what happened."

"It's the best thing ever about living in a small town, isn't it? You legit have no business of your own. And I doubt anyone will believe the *horse kicked me in the face* story."

"I could've come up with something better than *that*," I say dryly as I find Paul's name in the contact list.

"Not the point."

I slap the washcloth she hands me over the swollen eye and push the earpiece of the phone against my ear as I listen to the rings. Counting them, one by one, and my heart threatening to stop a little more with each one that goes unanswered. I know he's going after Daniel, and I realise that they need me physically there, but for some reason, I couldn't help myself from dialing his number again. I expect nothing, but still there is an uneasy knot in my gut when the voicemail picks up:

"What's up? Paul Reagan. I'm not here to take your call but, uh, leave a message with your name and number and I'll get back to you." Indistinct shouting elsewhere. *"As soon as I can. Thanks."*

I don't bother to leave one. And I'm not going to call him a thousand and one times as he did to me on Daniel's phone. Which I should probably try calling as well.

It's the same results. *"Daniel Stamp here."* Laughter fills the background. *"Don't laugh at me! Assholes. Anyway, sorry I didn't pick up. Call back later, leave a message, I promise I'll get back to you."* I can hear him smiling. *"And if it's Ruth calling, know you're top priority."*

I hang up and nearly throw the phone at the glove compartment, but I stop myself short, clenching it despite the sudden sensation which makes it feel like a hot brick in my palm. *Know that you're top priority.* I am so *blind*. I am such an *idiot.* How could I have thought that he didn't have feelings for me? How could I have so openly ignored him pouring himself out in the littlest ways? Who was I, accidentally playing a game with him, acting the same as I always have? There shouldn't have been any games played. There shouldn't have been other relationships. Daniel and I should have been together from the time that we were old enough that our families would let us. Dad would have approved of him. Mom definitely does. Daniel's parents adore me as though I am one of their children, and Penny thinks of me as a sister, and I think of her as the one I haven't had. We mesh together. We've known each other for a long time and are comfortable with one another. What had I been thinking? All along the person I needed has been right there in front of me.

Are you sure about that?

And there it is, the doubt! Which will probably plague me henceforth because of my idiocy. But then, I realise, that this is not just any other amount of doubt. This is a particular thread, one which I thought I had severed from the tapestry of my life, and yet, here it is, when I least expect it to appear, with its glaring, fluorescent colours that threaten to throw the rest of the design out of proportion.

Are you sure that Daniel isn't just a stand-in, in his own right? You know exactly what I'm talking about, too. The voice turns pretentious. *Guess you didn't forget like you thought you did. Sure he isn't just a representation of what you've actually lost and -*

"Stop it." My fingernails dig into my jeans with such force I can feel the skin underneath being pinched. "Stop it."

"I'm going to assume you're talking to yourself, because I

swear I'm not speeding anymore. Just a one-time thing, promise."

I blink, and I am back in the passenger seat of Julia's Honda, and she's giving me a side-eye glance with one eyebrow arched, and my shoulders are tense, and my spine is rigid, and those nails dig into my thigh and I force them to relax. I have control over myself. I have control over my own thoughts. Everything up there is safeguarded. I don't need to snap again. I had my mental breakdown. That's what it had been when I had fallen off her couch, right? So I didn't need to have another one. Not so soon. "Yeah, I was just talking to myself."

"Don't look so sheepish. It's okay. I do that all the time. Especially in the shower. I don't know, I guess I like to hear the echo of my own voice back at me." She unleashes that buoyant laughter of hers. "Do *you* sing in the shower? Sometimes I feel like I'm the only person who does it every day, even though I know that's not true because, come on, almost everyone sings in the shower, right?"

Girl talk. Small talk. I'm uncertain how to handle it. And it's another pang that fills me with the recognition, the acceptance, of how awkward I am when it comes to intimate social situations. I can't remember the last time I was with someone, just me and them, in a car or somewhere else, just talking. Paul is more silent with me; our communication sometimes solely remains mental. Daniel chatters a bunch; you can barely keep up with him sometimes. Having an actual conversation, where someone proffers something, and where I respond, and where there is a constant back-and-forth in the interaction, is foreign to me, so foreign that ice rushes through my veins and I feel as though I have been rendered catatonic. What if I do something wrong? What if I say something that ruins everything? What if I manage to express an opinion that's considered to be off-the-wall and unpopular? The number of *what-if's* overwhelms me.

But I'm not going to back away from this challenge. I'm not going to throw away all these years. Friends since grade school. Gone because of me. And all friendships should be a give-and-take. I won't stand for her giving and giving and me doing nothing but the taking. That is a stark reminder as to how it was with Shane. I was always the one giving to him, always trying to curb his appetites, satiate his fancies. No more of that. Equality is what I want. And I think here is a good place to start. Though it's going to be strange to me, I don't care. I want it more than anything else in the world. I crave being seen as a person. I just crave it.

"I - I think everyone sings in the shower." Come on, Ruth, this is just talking about singing and showers. "I know I do. Like, I like to sing those really overplayed songs. You know? Because in the shower I don't have to worry about anybody groaning and being all like — Oh, here she goes again, I've heard this song a thousand times, I'm sick of it. I don't have to ask for anybody's approval."

I think that was a good response. Right?

I guess so. She continues the conversation. Without a pregnant pause. "*Right?* Like, okay, don't tell anybody, but I have a really soft spot for Ke$ha. Like, her newest CD? One of my guiltiest pleasures in the universe. I know all of the raps and stuff. And I can tell you that people would get tired of hearing 'Crazy Kids' all the time. And girl, don't tell me you've asked for approval to sing things."

"I like Selena Gomez." I blurt that out. My cheeks flush with the admission. "I listen to that song, 'Birthday,' about twenty times a day or something." Over-exaggeration. That's part of small talk. "I've never told anybody that, oh Lord. Paul would get after me so much right now. *What the hell are you doing, listening to that stuff?* And then make me listen to The Black Keys to purge me."

"Girl, we can listen to The Black Keys, Selena, Ke$ha, and Queen Beyoncé, and ain't nobody going to tell us differently."

"And no, I don't really ask for approval. I mean, I used to get really shy if I were caught singing. I still do. Kind of." It's hard talking through this fat lip, but for this, I'm willing to make an exception. And interruptions, going back and forth between topics, that's allowed. I think I'm doing okay.

"Own it. Who cares if you're off-key? Own those words, feel that music. Here. Let's start with right now. Hear this song? We're going to scream it at the top of our lungs." She rolls the windows halfway down, and I blink against the contrast of the heated interior to the cold outside. "Okay. It's just starting out. We're in luck. You know this song, right?"

"Of course. Who doesn't?"

"Right. So don't ask anybody for permission. Don't look at me with those sad eyes and don't plead silently with me to say that it's okay. You don't need permission. You get a couple extra points since you have a fat lip for doing this. Ready, go."

And she spends the next twenty minutes of the car ride convincing me that it's okay to scream out the chorus when we're at a stoplight, to not pay attention to the way that some of the drivers in their cars stare at us, because who really cares what they think, anyway? It's our song, she tells me. It's our song and we're making it our song, and if they can't afford to appreciate that, then oh well. It isn't as though, she says, pointing out an older gentleman in his Volkswagen that glared at us openly, we're ever going to see any of them again. Though initially it's as though someone has extracted me and set me outside of my own skin, soon I'm able to settle into the routine, and by the time a mutual favourite comes on the radio, my voice is hoarse and my lip throbs and yet I am happier than I have been in a long time, and not once have I thought about Shane and his inability to be a human being, or my brother and what drama could be unfolding, or Daniel and how I'm going to have to convince him of something he should believe in the first place. None of that seems important when I am nestled here and protected from the outside world and feel nothing but nature's caress in the wind and listen to the way that sometimes mine and Julia's voices blend together well, naturally harmonises, and other times, purposefully shoot higher or lower than the other in order to create a terrible, dissonant sound that sends us into fits of laughter, and I could almost swear that mine is as lively as hers.

As she turns onto the road that leads to my house, with me pointing in the direction that she needed to go as we slid to a stop at the three-way, she drapes her wrist across the steering wheel and smiles a little bit. "Now, see? Was that so hard? Letting loose for a little bit? And don't tuck into yourself. Come on. Live proud. Live loud."

"It was hard," I admit. "Like. You wouldn't think it would be." I clear my throat past the phlegm that has been created and swallow hard, wincing and slapping the washcloth back on my face, this time on the lip, despite nearly all of the moisture having evaporated, leaving behind a stiff fabric instead of the softened dampness that I need. But the cool seems to be helping with the pain, so I'm not going to complain. "But it was. I'm so used to being inside myself, you know? I have to be. I have to hold myself together for the rest of my family."

"Ruth, ah, you don't have to talk about this if you don't want to." Julia didn't know much about my family, but the fact that my mother had been sent to asylum for a time isn't too much of a secret.

"No, really. Not just because of Mom. But because, like, Dad. You know? He's one of those guys who's really strict, and I swear he just wants the best for us, and it's the whole concept of tough love, but then again, I feel like there's something else. So I always hold myself in, never let fully loose, because I hear how he rags on Paul and how he doesn't approve of half the things he does even when they're done to perfection." I blink slowly at the window as though I have been given new eyes, and perhaps I have, in a metaphorical, unfortunate manner, in a similar one as a child would experience when her rose-coloured lenses had been shattered by hands she thought she had known. "Do you think that's abusive?"

"—What?"

"I mean, the way that my dad always pushes Paul. Tells him to be a man and stuff. And he's really rough. Rougher than he ever has been with me. Do you think that's abuse?"

Her hands, which like to skim across the top of the steering wheel, as though she's smoothing down invisible fabric, go very still. "Not my place to say, babes."

I would have to think about this some more when my head stopped hurting so much, when the concussion subsided. I think this episode with Shane has tainted me more than I want to accept. I might start seeing examples of abuse everywhere now.

She sings quietly along to the song on the radio, and then leans against the steering wheel, quite heavily, heaving a tremendous breath from the darkest part of her stomach, and when I look over at her, her foot has come from the accelerator, and the Honda coasts slowly, losing speed. "Julia?" Guilt. There it is. Again. "Julia, are you okay? Oh, Lord, what can I do?"

"Just give me thirty seconds," she spits out through clenched teeth, and though I know she doesn't mean the words with any amount of hostility whatsoever, my attitude which I thought I had shed the layers of, the reserved and the withdrawal and the offence, the taking everything personally, the sensation of being attacked, comes roaring back to me and devours all of the hard work that I had done in singing along to the car radio. It's a pallid, cowed Ruth that leans back in the seat and watches her old friend warily, instead of a stronger Ruth that demands to know what's wrong and pushes more for a solution as to how to assist her through the pain.

But no matter weak or strong, this Ruth does have one thing in common - she reaches out for the clammy hand and she takes it, removing it from the steering wheel, and though Julia grinds her fingernails into my palm, with tears streaming out of her eyes, peeling through the calluses there and gouging old scars open, I leave it there for her to hold. Because we should always have a lifeline which responds back to us instead of inanimate objects which simply cannot understand us. "Thirty seconds."

"Thirty seconds is over," I say, as calmly as I can manage. "But you can take more than that if you need to." A very strange, maternal sense overtakes me, and the gash in my right palm tingles, uncomfortably until the flesh surrounding it goes numb, and then it is as though I have been injected with morphine, and I relax, and the grass blades at the side of the road become greener and the sky bluer and the breeze more purposeful. "If I can take a long time, so can you. Especially you."

Another ninety seconds or so passes. No cars fly through the roadways. It's simply us two and nature. And there are no overwhelming sounds and nothing to fear, just us basking in our pain and dealing with it and connected, once more, through hands, and hands are so incredibly healing in their own right. And then, she peels her hand away from mine, and she exhales, and she begins to drive again, and though her face is bloodless, her body curling toward the steering wheel, and tears marring further the eyeliner underneath her eyes, she continues on.

I want to be strong enough to withstand it all. And I think that's why she keeps so much of her internalised pain exactly that, never expounding upon it unless it is the physical kind that she cannot mask. Because she wants others to think that she is immortal, that she can get through it no matter how hard it gets and no matter how much closer the axe of death nears her neck. She doesn't want others to cry for her or feel sorry for her. She doesn't want others to feel pity or make her cookies or treat her like a china doll. She just wants to continue to be treated equally, as normally as possible, and if it means masking the pain, then she will. And she does. And I don't think nearly enough people appreciate this.

I just hope that eventually she can realise that she doesn't need to be strong all of the time. That once in a while, it's okay to question her own existence and the existence of God, and it's okay to think that she has no friends and wallow in the self-pity and the guilt and the unanswered questions. I just hope she realises that she needs to let it go, let it out, and stop with the bottling up because - and I am a hypocrite, because I do it, and still will do it and have done it - it's harmful. Look at me. Look at how I exploded. Look at how I ended up. I don't want her to be the same.

So maybe, yeah, I want to be strong enough to withstand it all. But I also want to be able to know when it's okay to crumble. Infuriating, though, because everyone admires you when you're strong for them, and always is asking, *"How do you do it?"* and you can't give them any answer but a smile, or an "It's all for you" or something alike these answers. And then when it's your turn to display your cracks, no one is there to collect the pieces and sew them back together.

She pulls up into our driveway, right next to Paul's truck.

The driver's side door is open, and the cellphone lays in the seat. No wonder he isn't picking up. He doesn't even have the phone on him. Through the half-opened windows, when Julia turns off the ignition, we remain in silence for a little bit - and the silence returns to us. There's no voices, no shouting. There's no telltale sign that anybody's even here. If it weren't for the three little furry heads of the outdoor cats that I see from here, peeking at us with their dilated pupils from underneath the front shrubberies, I would think that this place had been abandoned. Mom has to be at home somewhere; maybe she's out in one of her gardens. Dad, too; he's probably out doing work. And to think they think I've been at school. I wonder what Dad will have to say when he realises that the boyfriend he has idolised and considered to be the best thing ever for me is nothing more than an arrogant schmuck who hits girls.

"Where is everyone?"

I continue staring at Paul's cellphone. Daniel's is in there, too, it seems, and there's dog hair all over the seats. "I don't know. Maybe across the street?"

But the Stamps' property is quiet as well.

"Man, I remember the last time I came out to your house. That sleepover in, like, eighth grade. Do you remember that?"

I didn't want to. "Yeah, I do. It was pretty great."

"I've been to lots of sleepovers since then, but - none of them compare to that one."

"Come inside." I turn to her.

She stops, not expecting me to say something that abrupt. "Sorry, what?"

"You're coming inside. And you're going to rest."

"Um—"

"You've had — chemo." I open the passenger's side door and then pull the seat forward so that I can reach into the backseat to retrieve my school bag, plopping the dried washcloth down on the vacated leather. "And you almost passed out on the road. Come inside."

"I don't —"

"Julia." My eyes, as wide as they can go, hopefully pierce her in a similar manner as to how hers pierced me. "You took care of me. Now it's my turn. Friendship is give and take."

It doesn't take much more convincing. It's apparent, even despite her attempts at staying outwardly strong, that she's tired, that she can't go on without some respite. So, she follows me around to the front door of the house, which has more of a guarantee to be unlocked than the garage door, and I'm relieved when the knob gives way underneath my hand, allowing us entrance into the foyer.

"Anybody home?" I call. There's no answer. Feeling a little bit awkward and foolish, especially by the way that my voice cracked on the last word, I shut the front door behind Julia and lead the way into my bedroom. Upon entering, I am overwhelmed with a combination of relief and memories, as though I have walked into a sanctuary, a secluded place of remembrance. The covers are rumpled from where Paul and Daniel had been sprawled across them, asleep. I can smell their sweat, Daniel's cologne. I can feel the ghosts of their presences although they've left. The little wooden deer he carved me is on the desk, and Julia goes to it, picking it up, looking it over, and half-smiling.

"This is cute. He made this himself?"

I nod. "Worked all night on it, I think."

"Damn." She twists her mouth and glances around my bedroom. The lavender walls. The wrought-iron bed against the wall. The built-in computer desk and bookshelves above it. The clothes cabinets on the wall opposite the bed with their glass doors. The bookshelves with their solid doors.

"You're going to lay down. *No* protesting. Get comfortable."

I trudge into the kitchen as she stands there, looking about her, wanting to protest but, having been shut down, instead choosing not to. I don't know what meds I can give her that won't mix poorly with the chemotherapy drugs, so I skip over that and instead retrieve some water from the little dispenser on the inside of the fridge. By the time that I get back to my bedroom, with the glass of water and a red straw, and a dampened washcloth, she has already curled up on the bed amidst the coverlets that smell like my brother and my best friend, and her chest moves up and down methodically, as she already has given way to slumber. Sleeping away the pain.

I set the glass of water on the nightstand, next to my alarm clock, and then I fold the washcloth in half and rest it on her sweaty forehead. She's still dressed in her shirt and cardigan, as well as her jeans, so I don't bother covering her up with a blanket or anything. If she shows signs of shivering, I'll cover her up.

I myself am not tired. In fact, I'm oddly energised. Pulling at the hem of the shirt of hers I wear, I make my way back into the bathroom and take a good look at myself. Take in all of the damage which has been done. The left eye is all right. The right eye is swollen, the lid above it a deep red, the skin underneath bruised and purplish. There are a few shallow scrapes, as well as the massive bauble of tender skin that is the right side of my mouth, shiny and puckered at the edges as though someone has glued it there and done a poor job and the glue is coming undone. My hair is a mess; all the blackish strands fall to one side, and very little is on the other, and when I try to pick at the strands, they stick together, muddied and filthy, and I sigh as I pull at a knot in the ends of my hair, resulting in that painful cracking noise as it's unwound. I should shower - but I don't want to chance Daniel and Paul coming in while I'm still dressed in a purple robe or anything.

So, instead, I go to my desk and I sit at the chair in front of it, and I look through the contents which surround me. The massive book by Donna Tartt I have yet to read. A couple of bottles of nail polish, one a deep emerald and the other a translucent gold, more of a second coating than an original colour. An old Spanish binder from my freshman year of high school, a white one, with multicoloured tabs on the inside separating the content which I have yet to clean out. A couple of notebooks I started to write things and make lists in, and forgot about. Paul's blue iPod. My black one. My unwound earphones. A bottle of vitamins. A salt shaker. A snow globe I received as a stocking stuffer from my mom this past Christmas.

And an ancient copy of Romeo and Juliet. One with yellowed edges from the oils of my fingerprints having decorated it so much, possessed it, little splotch marks in certain paragraphs where my tears caused the ink to run. And I know instead of reading something which has never been touched, I will be picking up this gem and ruffling through it and re-reading, for the hundredth time, my favourite parts.

I unfasten my boots and am left wearing the socks Julia gave me; I stretch out my legs and prop my feet up on the desktop, reclining in the desk chair. I reach for the tome which calls to me, and I flip through it - but I don't have to flip for long. When I rest the spine of the book against my thighs, it flops open to the place which is my favourite part of it all.

I begin to read, though, several pages before this. The last thing I want to do is allow my eyes to scan the text for my favourite line, and then I would be finished with it until the next time. I needed to draw this out; needed to pass the time. I force myself to read more slowly than to which I am accustomed, taking in each word as though it is a pill to be swallowed, and the minutes tick by, ever onward, as I crawl through the text, the pink and blue highlighter marks, the annotations in the margins and in-between lines. And I think to myself about them before continuing, challenging my mind, and then, I lose myself to the train of thought, How am I going to explain this to my English teacher when I go back to school on Monday? Because this is the literature I had planned on giving my presentation about, and those notecards, curdled and damp and soiled in the bottom of my bag, with a broken mirror, had been put to absolutely no good use.

Though I think she'll understand. Make an exception. Maybe she'll even let me give her the presentation in private, instead of standing up in front of the entire class with this busted eye and lip. I hope so. I really hope so. I don't think I can take much more embarrassment. I'm just glad that Shane is in regular English - and not in the advanced placement.

Then, I reach the line. And I read it aloud in a whisper:

**"Death, that hath sucked the honey of thy breath,
Hath had no power yet upon thy beauty."**

And then, everything changes.

As if on cue, as if it had been waiting for this moment, when I look up at the blue-lit alarm clock on the nightstand, and I see that an hour or more has passed, and still no one has made an appearance, the front door opens, and my head shoots toward it, watching it from this position as it swings on its hinges to its fullest extent, only stopping when it gently smacks against the arm of the decorative chair just outside my room. One of the cats darts into my bedroom, shaking her head and twitching her ears, and hisses, diving underneath the bed.

Something is terribly, terribly wrong.

Heart turning into dead weight in my chest, I put the book down, closing it, knowing I'll be able to find my place again if I want to, and I advance slowly from the bedroom, down the corridor, unable to see who stood behind the opened door as they had not fully entered into the house yet. I swallow hard, pulse thudding, and my hands come to clasp themselves at my abdomen as I begin to lean, to peek around the door, and what I see, I could not have been prepared for.

It's Paul. Staring straight ahead with a vacant expression. Denim jeans torn into tatters at the knees and the backs of the thighs, scuffed boots an explosion, a conglomeration, of moss, grass, dirt, and general forest grime. White undershirt almost nonexistent, revealing great slabs of that beautiful red-toned skin we inherited from our mother's side of the family. His abdomen and chest slathered in brown and red. Drenched in it. Dripping it onto the rug. The red especially. My nose crinkles against the rusted smell. The tangy scent. Blood. He's covered in blood. His elbows are bent, and the palms of his hands face the ceiling as he holds his arms out in front of him, and his hands, too, have rivulets of burgundy running through them. His hair is more dishevelled, more in a state of panic, than usual. There's a brown paper towel wrapped on his right hand, but it didn't seem to do much good; and I doubt that single wound caused this much to happen to him. There's a gash on his right temple, recently acquired.

And those eyes, so like my father's, and yet nothing like them, such a steely contrast to the dark sepia of his hair with the light-brown streaks, are empty. The grey irises don't notice my face. Nor my presence. There's no recognition. There's no proclaimed cry. *"Ruth, I'm glad you're safe." "Ruth, oh, thank God, you made it home."* No words are spoken at all. There is only the eerie quiet, broken by the pitter-patter of the blood onto the floor around him.

"Paul?" I whisper his name tentatively. But he doesn't hear me.

I step a little bit closer to him. His eyes don't even flicker down toward me. I'm uncertain what I should do. I'm quite uncertain what I'm seeing right now. Is this even real? No, perhaps I fell asleep. Yes, that would explain everything. So, then I have to touch him. I have to have my hand pass through this apparition, and then, I will wake up with my nose in the spine of the book, and that distinct smell of use wafting up my nostrils, and I will shake the crawlies from my skin, dispose of the cobwebs of the nightmare that this is, and then he will come tromping in with Daniel in tow, as usual and everything will be fine. Yes, all right. I just have to touch him.

His face. It seems so much older now. Lined. Grim. It's foreign to me, seeing a face which mirrors mine in all aspects except for gender, looking so much different than I am used to seeing. Swallowing again, I reach upward, slowly, so as not to startle him, and I go to place my middle finger against the cut on his forehead, the shallow slice which he has managed to get since I last saw him this morning. That, combined with the bruising on his forehead, and the scars, the wounds, he received from last night, and he is a sight, indeed. Covered in blood.

Not his blood.

"Paul?" I ask again.

There's enough time for my fingerprint to register that the appendage did not drift through his head as I expected, that he is not a ghost as I desperately want him to be, before he reacts. Violently. One of those blood-covered hands whips up and grasps at the arm; I gasp as the stickiness, still warm, seeps into my skin, and when I glance back up at him, the frenzied expression in those irises makes me cringe.

"What happened?" My voice threatens to break. I can hear Julia stirring on the bed inside of my bedroom, apparently alerted by some sixth sense that something is the matter out here, perhaps glancing upward and wondering where I had disappeared to, but all I can see is my twin brother looking as though he has seen hell. "Where were you? And where's Daniel? **What's *h a p p e n e d*?"**

These last two words come out in a shriek as his hand tightens about my forearm. I pull myself away from him, stumbling backward and into the wooden bannister which separates the foyer from the basement staircase, leaning heavily against it, staring at the blood dripping down my arm and then back at him, bewildered by his behaviour. Julia, fully awakened now, lumbers out of the bedroom, cursing quietly underneath her breath, but stops in her tracks when she sees Paul standing there. The hand which I have ripped myself away from clenches its fingers into a fist, and all of a sudden, there is emotion in his gaze, such a riotous mixture that I cannot look at his face, and yet, I look at it, I look at it fully because I am unable to look away. I am frozen. Catatonic. Paralysed. Tears well up behind his eyes. And they spill over. My brother. My brother is crying. Paul Reagan doesn't know how to cry.

And yet he is crying.

"We have to get help," he states in a strangled whisper, as though someone has fastened a hand around his throat.

"We have to get help."

"Help for what?" I want answers. I *need* answers. "Help for what, Paul? *What's happened?*"

"9-1-1. Call 9-1-1. We need to call 9-1-1."

Julia has already started for the kitchen in order to gain access to one of the portable phones, so that someone who knows the number can dial it. I still can't, for some reason, though I think it begins to settle into my knowledge, comprehend what the matter is, what's happened to him, whose blood he's covered in. And so I peel myself away from the bannister, and I start toward him again, and I demand, and there are tears behind my eyes as well, but they are tears of exasperation, tears that come from being tired of not knowing what needs to be known, and I ask him again, in an urgent whisper:

"Paul. *What happened?*"

He shakes his head, back and forth. His face, it crumples. He looks down at his hands and he clenches them, unclenches them, and he clamps his lips and his jaw quivers, and it's so alien to me that I gape at him, through the tears running down my cheek and trailing down my own injuries. How did we all get so hurt? How did we all suffer so much in one day?

"It's—" Pause.

"This—" Another pause.

"It's Daniel. He's——"

You know that moment in life when you feel like you're falling? You know that moment in life when you're given something that you just can't carry? You know that moment in life where everything you've ever known has suddenly been shattered?

I don't remember collapsing on the rug. I don't remember the people who walked past me. I don't remember the screams I emitted, the terrifying banshees that surround death when it comes, with their wails and their nameless noises. I don't remember the names, the words, and the numbers. I don't know how long I sit here. I don't know who has their hands on my shoulder. I don't know what I'm screaming at the top of my lungs. I don't know anything.

    I just know that everything I have ever known has just

        been

            destroyed.

Broken Glass Irises

October 9th
Manchester, Indiana

Paul Reagan

"D A N I E L !"

I trip over a root that stretches across my path and am sent to the ground, sputtering and cursing. Heart beating erratically in my chest, I shove myself back upward and continue my avaricious sprint through the woods.

"D A N I E L! Damn it, this is *not necessary!*"

I stop, panting, leaning against the nearest tree, my hand with the paper towel from school catching on the weathered bark, chest heaving and head reeling.

Everything that *could've* gone wrong — *has* gone wrong.

The drive home was awkward and tense. The singing along with the radio that Daniel had been doing, it sounded forced and prerecorded. The dog kept acting strangely, shifting back and forth in her seat, unable to find a comfortable position, whining whenever her head laid on one of our laps. Conversation had been irrevocably impossible, and I'd reclined in the passenger's seat, ever so often dialling Ruth's phone number in an attempt to get her to answer

After we had pulled up in the driveway, come to a stop on the concrete pad next to Ruth's car, he had taken a moment, he had clung to the steering wheel, and then, all of a sudden, he had *exploded*. Completely exploded. Into a thousand pieces. His face had reddened and all of the ire which he had been disguising, not too well to me who knew him too thoroughly for his own good, revealed itself in the messiest way possible, and amidst the dog barking, because she too had been rioted up by his shift in demeanour, he had let it all hang out. All of it. All of the dirty laundry for me to see, and I could only stare at him as he went off. As though he had been *possessed.*

"That son of a *bitch.* Who does he think he is? But you know what. I think he might be right. Just a *little* bit. Let me finish, Paul." I hadn't interrupted or even moved. "I think he's right about her going back to him because, *let's face it,* there's been *plenty* of opportunities for her to leave him and *reasons* to do so, and come to me like she should have been *all along* and then, she *stays* with him. It really *pisses me off.*"

"Daniel," I had said, finally, after overcoming my shock. "You can't be serious. You can't think she's going to go back to him. What's the matter with you?"

"I love your sister, Paul, and if she steps on my heart one more time, I'm not going to be able to handle it! *That's* what the matter is!"

When he had started to get out of the truck, Ruth had picked up her phone, with a voice that had sounded a thousand miles away. Julia finally let me answer my phone. It had to be one of the most chaotic phone calls I've ever had in my entire life. She was asking a hundred and one questions, it seemed like, and I was trying to explain things to her, and I'm screaming at Daniel to get back in the truck as he stalks off around the front of the house, nearly running.

Do I need to come home? And I can't imagine how she felt when I told her that Daniel didn't believe she had broken up with Shane. She had sounded close to tears when she'd demanded to know why he didn't. Sounded as though she wanted to be the one screaming and throwing her hands about and gnashing her teeth. Jesus help us.

And then, I had seen something terrifying. Daniel had

come out of the front of the house again, without the dog, who had left with him - and he was carrying a shotgun. Shoving shells into his pockets. From the looks of it, it had already been loaded before he had come back outside. And instead of coming back to the truck, he stormed past it, heading down the side of the driveway, through the grass, toward the patch of woods behind our house. When I'd screamed at him: *Daniel, get back here! Right now!* he had quickened his pace, broke into a run, a fast run, with the gun tucked underneath his arm, and by the time I had hurriedly hung up on Ruth, thrown the phone into the driver's seat, stumbled from the truck, onto the concrete pad, followed in his footsteps, he had already disappeared amongst the trees.

You wouldn't think that it'd be difficult to find someone when the trees were shedding their layers of clothing, their colourful leaves painting the muddied ground, but it was a hell of a lot harder than I thought it would be. Hence why I had been shouting out his name for the past ten minutes. And he isn't answering me. There's only that foreboding silence, and that ominous weight on my heart increases, though it never left - it only had seemed as though it was gone, but it isn't, it's still there, threatening to kill me. My voice echoes back at me, and that's the sole sign of life. Not even the breeze rustling through the barren branches seemed to infuse nature with breaths and heartbeats; it only adds to the depleted appearance of the dying forest. And dying it is. Everything is dying, actually. The one drawback of the autumn season. Everything dies and is buried in winter.

"Daniel!" I holler again, shoving myself away from the trunk of the tree and running full-speed through the nearest patch of brambles, shoving them aside, barely feeling the pricks of the thorns as they rut against my skin. "Daniel, damn it!"

Then, the detonation of the shotgun rings out. And it's as though I'm the one who has been shot. My entire body is filled with an icy shock, yet despite this, I continue to run, fixing my path so that I am heading in the correct direction, and the tears which I didn't know existed threatened to blur my vision as I screamed his name again, voice breaking at the end, mouth open as I take in great gulps of air to prevent myself from sobbing. Why hadn't he just stayed in the truck until Ruth had come home? Why had he believed Shane? Why did he think it was necessary to kill himself over it? He'd snapped so viciously. I'd never seen anything like it, not even from my mother. And that sense of foreboding had grown and now it came to a climax, such a climax that it strangled me and threatened to tear out my jugular vein.

I leap over an entanglement of uprooted, overturned young trees, and when my knee joint collapses, I am forced to somersault forward, almost sliding into the nearest pile of red and yellow leaves, and as the crunchy substances settled back in around me, I swear on my life that I hear a snicker from somewhere. Shaking my head to dislodge the maple leaves, I blink in surprise at the fact that Daniel is still alive, standing two feet from where I managed to fall, with a lifeless half-smile on his face and the barrel of the shotgun pointing down toward the ground, a tendril of smoke still unwinding from its opening. I have tripped right into the old target practise place we used to go to each summer when David and my dad were first teaching us how to handle weapons. Though the wooden stands attached to the trees have warped with age and the soda pop cans used as targets halfway to disintegration, there's enough left - including a large cardboard circle which had been painted to look like a target, the most recent abandoned item to be left here to rot - that Daniel has decided to make use of it.

Oh. He hadn't planned on killing himself after all. He just wanted to target practise to get out his anger. Because there's something about the kick back of a shotgun and the echo of the shot that helps him. Well. Guess who feels like a moron.

"What's up, Paul," he says easily. "Glad you finally joined me."

"DUDE.

WHAT.

THE.

HELL.

You can't just sprint off like that!"

"What'd you think I was going to do? *Kill* myself?" He scoffs a little bit before messing with the break-action and allowing the used shells to fall onto the ground. I wonder how many bullets litter this small clearing as I pick myself up and brush off the sticky leaves. "Sorry, man. Not even your sister is worth me taking my own life."

I'm not sure if I'm supposed to take offence to that or what, but I let it slide, much like I had just slid into the leaves, because holy mackerel, that is one of the easiest, most spirit-lifting things that I have ever done, and if I can apply that to the rest of the unfolding drama in my life, then I think I'll be home free. "Yeah, well, speak of the devil and she shall appear."

"I'm going to go out on a limb," and here, he motions to one of the hanging tree branches above him to imply that he made the pun on purpose, "and guess that you're talking about Ruth being the devil in this case."

I'm still a little bit peeved that he ran off like that, and even more so now, since he's acting like *nothing weird* happened. His sense of humour, therefore, irks me, and instead of letting him bring it up on his own terms, which is what originally I planned on doing, I instead choose to confront it without giving it time to fester.

"Yeah, *Ruth*. And she's not too happy that you don't

believe her, you idiot. What the hell was wrong with you back there, huh? You fly off the handle and storm around and look like you want to decapitate your head just to have something to throw at the wall."

"I lost it a little bit."

"You *lost it a little bit?* That's *more* than a *little bit.* You know, I realise that what Shane said can sound true, but she's Ruth. RUTH. And we know her better than he does!"

"Yeah, but do we *really?*" He inserts a shell into the shotgun, then another. "Do we *really* know her, Paul? So what that we've grown up with her? People can have complete personality changes. They can evolve into serial killers. Those quiet kids in the backs of the classrooms?" He takes aim at the Pepsi can. "Budding. Serial. Killers."

I don't have time to slap my hands over my ears before he pulls the trigger. But his words eerily remind me of the thoughts I had harboured toward Shane and his impending, or so I had hoped, demise.

"Look, Ruth isn't *those people,*" I say uneasily. It's clear, though, that he's unnerved me. "She hasn't changed since she was a toddler. And for you to believe the boyfriend who hit her across the face and beat her up - that's pretty shitty."

"I didn't say I *believed* him. I just said that he's *believable.* There's a difference." He unfastens the action and the shells plop out. "Do you want to take an aim or two?"

"No!" I shove the barrels into the dirt and I stare him in the eyes. "I want you to focus on the situation at hand here and realise that my sister is on her way home and that you better start thinking about who you're believing before she gets here. Wake the hell up, Daniel. I swear to God. Why are you being so dense about this? Who cares if he said believable things? You're actually going to put stock into things that a Curtis said?"

"I don't know what you want me to do or think, Paul. I told you, if your sister breaks my heart one more time, I'm not going to be able to handle it. I'm sorry that you thought it meant suicide, but actually it just means that I won't ever be able to speak to her or look at her ever again. Shane might be right; he might be wrong. That's not the point. The point is that he managed to vocalise everything that I have struggled with thinking for the past seven months, ever since she first started dating that sorry son of a bitch."

He attempts to yank the shotgun out of my grasp, but I keep it shoved down into the dirt, still glaring at him, not really giving a damn about gun conditions or control or rules or regulations; as long as he continues concentrating on me, he could throw this shotgun into the pond for all I care.

"He was like the voiceover for the devil on my shoulder," he continues, growing upset again. "And I think that's what makes me the maddest. Like, here I am, thinking these things, and all of a sudden, the worst person on the earth is saying them and I've been thinking them, and what kind of a person does that make me, Paul? The type of person that *shouldn't* be around Ruth, that's what. Because what if I end up treating her the same way? We both know I wouldn't *hit* her. But the words. The *needling*. The *this*. The *that*."

Relinquishing his hold on the shotgun, he clasps his hands and rests them on the top of his head, pacing away from me. He might not want to kill himself—but I'm still glad that he's letting me hold the gun. I remove the barrel from the moist soil and swipe it off.

"And if I'm capable of *thinking* like Shane, then I'm capable of *acting* like Shane."

"Come off it," I reply. "Seriously, dude. You're *nothing* like Shane. So what if you were thinking that Ruth was being indecisive? I'm pretty sure that we all thought that. She isn't the best about making decisions. Wasn't the whole thing last night enough proof for that?"

"Despite popular belief, and my act as a cocky bastard half the time, I'm not actually *that* confident, especially when it comes to her."

"You really have nothing to worry about." I hold my hand out. "Here, give me a couple new shells."

"Oh, so you *do* want to take an aim or two."

"Just one." He walks back over to me, rustling around in his front pocket, extracting two shells and dropping them into my palm.

"—You think I really have nothing to worry about?"

"I talked to her on the phone. You think I'm going to pull the wool over your eyes?" When I became the relationship counsellor to my childhood best friend, in relation to my twin sister, I'll never know for certain. "She was pretty torn up at the fact that you might have believed Shane over her." At least from what I could pick up through the three or four words she'd managed to insert through my initial panic. "So, you're going to have to apologise for that."

I take aim at the cardboard bull's-eye.

"I need to hear it all again."

The shotgun goes off; I've missed by about three thousand million feet. I think it even managed to ricochet off the trunk of the tree. I stare at him incredulously. "Excuse me?"

"Everything she said," he continues doggedly, snatching the shotgun away from me. "I need to hear it all again." His voice grows firmer. "What she said last night, what she supposedly said to Shane. I need to hear her tell me that she broke up with him. I need her to look me right in the eyes and say it all and not take a word of it back, and I just need that, Paul. I need that for my security."

"Is this some sort of "If' I hear it from the source, its true complex?"

"It's an insecurity complex, man. You wouldn't understand. You've never had a crush on a girl or wanted to be with her and maybe eventually marry her."

Not true. "Hearing this about my twin sister from my best friend is a little awkward, I'm not going to lie."

"Yeah, but didn't you always used to tell me how you'd prefer it if she dated me? Especially when it came to her being with Shane? And you can't deny it. You have said it. Several times over. Both drunk and sober, so don't try to pull that crap over on me, either."

Well, *shit*. He's got me. "Yeah, but I mean—"

"You never actually got around to thinking about it happening? Considering how much she and Shane were, you know, so in love."

"Quit putting words in my mouth. I just have a thousand other things to be worrying about, and my sister's dating life, as well as yours, aren't exactly top priorities when I've got Dad breathing down my neck like a thirsty hound dog."

"So you *were* planning on thinking about it seriously."

"Eventually. Once I managed to get a calm moment from his harping. Which could, at this rate, never happen. He always finds something else wrong to bring up."

He smiles at me a little bit, and I scowl.

"Don't get me off the subject."

"I'm not, Paul."

"Yeah, you are, you *minx*. This isn't a one-way street. You might know my tricks, but that also means I know yours; you're not going to steer me off-topic by letting me ramble on about how much Dad makes me want to throw myself headlong off the side of a cliff."

"You don't need any help from me."

"Are you *trying* to ask me for permission to date her?"

"M a y b e."

"Dude—"

"Want me to ask your dad instead?"

"Not unless you actually want to lose your head."

We're back to the bantering again, falling into the simple, old patterns which have been established ever since we can remember, and the more we talk in this manner, the more that the ominous portion of me, which threatened to overload the rest of which existed, fades. That part has been assuaged.

The conversation comes easier as we now take turns making shots at the dilapidated targets, screwing with one another and teasing one another about how our aim is off, and when we manage to hit something, how much we've improved. Back and forth, comfortable waffling, passing the time in the same types of ways that we used to do when we were kids. Avoiding the things which make us uncomfortable - in this instance, Ruth and dating.

I hand him back the gun, as I have just taken my shot, and he loads a couple of shells back into the barrels, when we hear one of the weirdest sounds. A high-pitched whine, as though an old vehicle is crawling to a stop and the brakes need oil. It lengthens into a spine-chilling bay, a wounded animal, and sooner rather than later, the culprit emerges from the bushes.

"Jesus," Daniel breathes, hesitating with his hand on the trigger.

It's a coyote, a relatively young one, perhaps six or seven months old, rail thin in the stomach, with long, gangly legs that didn't match proportions with the rest of his extended body, and a bushy tail matted with burrs, a soft sweet face that didn't belong on a proclaimed scavenger and relatively off-putting animal, ears pinned against his skull, eyes darker and more intelligent than, perhaps, even a human's; they were almost wolf-like in that yellowish-gold colour around the iris. His adult coat is just beginning to grow through that young tannish-red fur, and as he pulls back his teeth, baring them at us, baring them at the gun that Daniel holds, I can see that his baby teeth are just being pushed out by the adults sticking through the gums.

"What happened to it?" I ask no one in particular. Putting my hands out in front of me, I exhale slowly and begin to approach it as it crawls toward the pile of roots underneath the wooden shelf upon which the pop cans have been resting. It seems to be favouring its left frontal paw, and there's a bloodied, circular wound, deep and encased in ragged flesh, as though it had fallen directly into an animal trap and been set loose. "What did this?"

"Paul, what the *hell* are you doing?" Daniel hisses as I continue toward it. Its lip curls back a little bit more. "You don't just *waltz up* to wounded coyotes; what is *wrong* with you?"

I've never been the one, when we've gone hunting, who has been a fan of killing for the sake of killing. As long as I don't stare at the subject which will receive the bullet for too long and as long as I know it's for eating – I can do it. But Daniel and my father enjoy killing just for the purified sport of it. (I don't know if I've ever divulged this secret to you. And I'm telling you, it doesn't sit well with me. Not especially toward an animal with a face that looks kinda like Shawna's.)

The blood trickles out of the injuries and onto its scraggly stomach, and its lip starts to settle back into its original position, closing around its teeth, when it realises that I'm not going to kill it. I continue creeping toward it, and I extend my bandaged hand, just as slowly and tentatively as I had walked and it regards it with curiosity and seems about to accept the proposal.

CH-CH. —— CA - *B O O M.*

I startle back - and the coyote drops. Blood's splattered across my front. I'm not sure exactly where the aim was supposed to go, but it didn't matter; it had blown out the coyote's innards all over the place, against the tree, on me; I swallow as I notice a little bit of its stomach or its heart dropping from the middle of my shirt and onto the ground.

"Jesus, Daniel! What the hell?"

"It was dying anyway," Daniel says dryly. "Never knew you were such a wuss, Paul. Besides, it was just another mangy coyote that would've eaten your chickens as payback for saving it."

Just another mangy coyote.

"Right." Just another mangy coyote. Just another mangy coyote. Daniel. You've lost it. You've — LOST IT. You're *NUTS!* You're *crazy!* Stupid! Damn—it wasn't hurting anyone! Can we at least, like, bury it or something? — This is a mess."

"Vultures will come and get it."

I stare at him for a moment, and in that split second, just for the smallest amount of time, I think that perhaps he's right, in a way; that perhaps he has the capabilities within him to become just as coldhearted and cruel as Shane Curtis.

My disgust with this mustn't be obvious on my face. He shoulders the shotgun and stares at the carnage as though he isn't certain whether or not it's real.

"Thanks for getting blood all over me," I say flatly.

"Dude. *You're* the one who walked toward it! Like it was a poor sick helpless puppy or something. Calling for you."

"Okay, now you're just making it weirder than it actually was."

My frenzied heartbeat just calms down when there's a

rustle behind him. Of course, this is associated with the sudden wind, which has picked up and caused the outside temperature to plummet. "Damn. Let's get back to the house. Ruth's probably there waiting."

"Really?"

That hope in his eyes both sickens and relieves me.

"Yeah, *really*."

It would've been one of those faerie tale endings where the two heroes walk off into the sunset after a long, hard day's work. If the bushes next to us, as we had turned to head along the deer trail back toward the barn, and subsequently the house, hadn't rustled more violently than the wind could have conjured by itself.

I glance at it, but I think nothing of it. Perhaps if I had thought something of it, everything else could've not happened. But I digress.

"Do you smell something weird?"

Daniel is the one that asks the question as we walk along the deer path, one behind the other, me in the lead, considering him in front of me would have resulted in the double-barrels being constantly in my face. At the inquiry, I inhale deeply, and as I shove aside a branch from eye-level, as we break out into the clearing which holds the old deer stand that we all used in some consistency the summer before last, and my nose crinkles. Ugh. It smells like wet leaves and decay.

"Probably just my shirt," I remark, gesturing at it bitterly. "I mean, I do have dead coyote all over it."

"Shut up, man. Every time you say it like that, I feel worse."

But it isn't my shirt, and Daniel's little tendrils of guilt which reach up and bind around his ankles aren't enough. Because as we go to cross the clearing, another coyote appears.

One that isn't mangy, one that isn't injured in the back or the legs, one that has a more feral appearance to its eyes. It doesn't growl. It doesn't snarl. In fact, it doesn't do much of anything. It just stands there, blocking our pathway, and stares at us. Stares at me. Then at the gun. Then at Daniel. Leaving him for last.

"Another one?" Daniel says incredulously to me, coming to stand beside me, already fiddling around with shotgun shells, looking down at the action, focusing on his movements only. "Sheesh. It's like an infestation of dying coyotes."

"Daniel." My lips barely move.

"Why's it just staring at us? *Weird*."

"D a n i e l."

The word buzzes in my mouth as I swallow half of it.

"Look, Paul, I'm not going to listen to you on this. These bastards need to die. They're vermin."

"Daniel. Stop. Look."

He didn't see it, but I did. When he glances upward, he freezes, because then, he sees it, and I see it, and it will not be unseen. They have emerged from the shrubbery. They have dissolved to be in front of us, beside us, behind us. The fading sunlight glints off their irises and makes them more bestial, wilder, untameable, and merciless. All of them, the same as their fallen comrade. All of them with a strange tint to their eyes, that one that you only see reflected off the cameras as they film the interviews with serial killers on the television. A strange chill that runs through the spine, a shudder which wracks the limbs, and shamefully, I realise that my knees are quivering together, because they aren't saying anything. Not that coyotes should speak, but usually a pack of them would be yipping and yowling at one another, communicating between members, but these ones, they don't need to communicate, and that foreboding feeling comes back to me, comes back to me with more force than before, hits me squarely in the stomach, in the chest, swells within, a bloating corpse.

"And here I ask," Daniel says, whispering into the unsettling silence. "What the hell is going on?"

I attempt to step forward, but the coyotes lurking there quickly intersect my foot, swarming it, gnashing their teeth at it, though making no direct contact with the toe of the boot, nonetheless causing me to step backward. And as though this little intercession had started everything else, started it all to snowball, to avalanche, to accelerate at frightening speed in the progression of things, the rest of the pack took this as the necessary cue to begin closing in on us.

And the stupid thing about it: I know that we're going to die. Even as I extract my pocketknife. Even as Daniel swallows hard and presses his back against mine. Even as I inhale and hold my breath in my burning lungs, as he caresses the trigger and we dart our eyes every which way in order to take in the hoard, the numbers. There's no way we can escape this. Daniel can't reload fast enough. I can't swipe hard enough. We can't run quickly enough. There's no good end to this situation. And as the front lines of the army bare their teeth, rousing up a chorus of growls, it's a heady, harrowing feeling that fills me, and for a moment, I am floating in the sky, even as Daniel and I whisper to one another, our frantic voices interrupting the cacophony below us.

"Okay, I'm going to load the gun. You just start stabbing."

"Daniel, there's *no way* this is going to work.

There's too many of them."

"You want to just roll over and die?"

"Maybe we can take off running."

"Or the deer stand?"

All of it is folly. My pulse erratically quickens, and I can feel Daniel's uneven heartbeat through his shirt, so closely are we pressed together.

"Flight or fight, Paul. Take your pick."

"Okay. We fight through them, and we run. Screaming."

"Like the morons we are."

"You got it."

I'm still not certain entirely what happened next. But all of a sudden, as though the coyotes surrounding us eavesdropped, understood our hushed conversation to one another, our plan of attack against them, our plan on attempting to get out alive, they leap forward, through the air, propelling with those un-seemingly powerful hind legs, and I know that I strike out with the knife, and Daniel's back is against mine, and he lets out a strangled, wild yell as he shoots the nearest one in the chest, then rams another's skull into shattered bits with the butt of the shotgun, and we both move forward together, as one, connected through the vertebrae of our spine, two souls become one, and there's a chance that we make it, that we break through the furred swarm, the unruly enemies, that we emerge victorious on the battlefield.

B O O M !

But then he's gone. Disappeared. The warmth against my back is replaced by the bodies of dozens of fur-balls that I will never trust again, with their muscular jaws and their needle-like teeth, and the knife flies from my hand and is buried up to the hilt in leaves and forest grime

B O O M !

and I am smothered underneath their weights and breathing in their strands of loose hair and the decaying mange and the rashes on their skin, and I'm screaming

and I hear other screams, ones that don't belong to me, and I yell for Daniel, my hands flying this way and that.

And in the middle of it all, I realise they aren't harming

me. They aren't doing *anything* to me. They are merely making sure that I am unable to reach him. To reach Daniel. They pile up against me and they lay all of their masses over me and they threaten to smother me, but they don't, they don't at all, and their teeth are bared but they bite no flesh, and their claws dig into my skin and keep the back of my scalp against the ground, but there is no ripping and tearing.

But there is ripping and tearing elsewhere. Ripping and tearing and screaming. Noiseless, nameless screams. Ones that devour my soul. Ones that are interrupted by the last ricocheted bullet of the shotgun, and then, interrupted by nothing except the soft growls, the riotous yipping that begins, as the onlookers cheer on the bloodied gladiators in the last throes of the competition, as we in Rome do as the Romans do. And then it's my name that's called out, and though I continue struggling against the weights, hollering back at him, shoving and pushing against the immovable bundles, I get nowhere. Nowhere. I can't see. I can't feel. But oh, God help me, I can hear.

And as quickly, as devilishly, as it begins, it ends. They slither back into the shadows from whence they came, they disappear from my body and leave me with nothing more than a rumpled shirt and a little bit of askew hair, not that it wasn't already mussed to begin with. And I'm three feet away from where I originally began. A little bit further down the deer trail. Daniel is nowhere to be seen; of course, I haven't exactly made a move to get up and look, because I'm afraid. I'm afraid of the screams. I'm afraid of the screams which have now faded into silence. The silence, I will never be able to listen to it again.

Never.

"Daniel?" I ask the trees above me.

They give me nothing in return.

"Daniel?"

"DANIEL!"

There's no answer. Not from anywhere.

I skitter up from the ground and I look around, feverishly, looking for more of those tanned bodies, the devil themselves multiplied into several forms, and there are none, but I still look, under the brush, in the trees, not wiping the leaves or the soil or the mange from my clothing. And then, I sprint back down the deer path. And there's no erasure of that potent menace which drives my feet forward, back into the clearing I had been dragged from —

The shotgun lays at my feet. Broken into two. And then, Daniel is there, not even half a yard from it. Broken into more than two. Broken into thousands.

Not moving. Unresponsive. Unconscious?

A strangled sound comes from somewhere, and I am slightly confused as to where - but then, I realise with some chagrin, with some shock which settles into my bones, that it came from my own throat. I fall onto the ground next to him, and I crawl to him, on hands and knees, and as one hand gets closer to him than the others, I can feel the warmth, the ever-familiar crimson, and the blood which holds memories, which makes people more familiar than animals, which has regrets and filth, permeates my pores, and it's not corrupted, but pure, and it's unnecessary blood to be feeling, and I cannot believe I am feeling it and yet, there it is, sticky and warm, the same blood with which I made a pact so many years ago, in a copious amount. Irreparable. Unfathomable.

But not even the blood compares to what's been done to him. How many bite marks there are, in that same half-circle shape which had been implanted on the body of the dead coyote. All over his arms, his torso, his legs, his neck, his face. But they hadn't stopped. They hadn't stopped. They had rooted into his body, they had torn away the flesh, which now hung in ragged tatters alongside his clothing, and through the layers of the skin, through the torn muscular structures, I could see the glinting white of bones, and the glistening dark red of internal organs. His lungs - I can almost see them expanding and contracting, unless I am imagining things, and they are still, and I am merely wanting them to be moving, and one hand, one of my hands, now covered in his blood, but it doesn't matter, traces down the side of the ruined face, and though my eyes are dry, still there's a wordless sob that escapes.

I press my wrist against my mouth to stifle the rest, squeezing my eyes shut. This is nothing more than a proverbial nightmare. I'm going to be waking up from this soon, still in the bed, groggily wondering why the dog and why Daniel are both asleep on top of me. And then:

"Paul."

It's not a dream. Oh, Jesus, God, it's not a dream. His face is cool to the touch. My eyes whip back open, and there are tears now, and I'm unashamed of it. I'm unashamed that Daniel is the first and last person to ever see me cry. Those odd hazel eyes with the golden flecks are opened and they look back at me, still with life, but even I can see the way that they quickly are dimming, with exhaustion and shock. And death. He does that half-smile thing, though, and if I look at just his face, it makes me think that he's done nothing but taken a very bad fall and that he'll be all right.

But he won't be all right. Oh, that foreboding feeling, damn it to hell! It was for this all along. All along and I just *ignored it* —

"Yeah, I'm here." The words choke out from me. And I don't care that I'm sitting in an ever spreading puddle of blood, because they infuse me with memories, and lo, I remember all the small things I didn't think I would ever remember again and I am overwhelmed and unable to control the tears. I tuck an arm underneath the back of his neck, and his breath exhales sharply as I lift him up onto my lap. He doesn't even wince. "I'm here, Daniel."

"This—*sucks*."

"Don't make jokes, you son of a bitch." Even though I chuckle in spite of myself. Because it's stupid. It's stupid and senseless. "Don't make jokes."

And I should be dying with him. But I'm not. Despite this pale feeling on my insides, despite the raking of the claws which appear and travel down my sides, I am not dying. Not like he is.

"Wasn't a joke." He half-heartedly rolls his eyes, lips parting further. And a bead of blood appears at the corner of his mouth. I quickly swipe it away. I don't want anything on his face except the slices and the cuts and those eyes that look up at me. "This — *really sucks*."

He winces as he coughs — and only then.

"I can't — feel anything, Paul."

"It's okay."

I tell him this passionately.

"You don't have to feel any of this.

You don't have to feel anything at all. I promise."

"Shouldn't I—be feeling?" He half-smiles again. "That's what—live people do, I guess. And I'm not—alive. Not anymore."

"Yes, you are." I shake my head fervently. The tears make clean tracks through the grime on my cheeks. "Dead men don't run their mouths."

"Don't make jokes—" He rolls his eyes up toward me, and to my extreme pain, I see that he, too, has begun to cry. Just a single tear. Rolling from the corner of his left eye. The one that, in the old wives' tale, means pain and sadness if it falls first.

"We both—know I'm dead. The rest of me—just hasn't—caught up."

"You're not going to die."

He is.

"I'm going to go get help. You'll be put back together again."

"Afraid not. A-plus, though. For effort."

He coughs, and more blood trails down from his mouth. "Shouldn't - have shot—that—coyote. Now—I'll never—be able to— tell—Ruth that I love—her."

(—) "I'll tell her for you."

His hazel, wild, distant, feverish eyes glance up at me, and they capture me, freezing me, holding me there with all of the willpower which he has left. "P r o m i s e."

My lower lip quivers. I don't want to weep. Or sob. I don't want to break into a scream or a cry. The tears are enough. Aren't they? But the harder I clench my teeth, the more likely it seems to happen. And now he's looking at me. So full of hope. Because even now, with his head cradled in my lap and his blood seeping into my clothes and my hands and the death rattle filling his lungs, Ruth is his top priority.

"I promise, Daniel."

I lean down and I press my forehead against his.

"I promise."

He breathes out a quiet sigh of relief with the warmth and the physical contact that I give him, the heat that comes not from his life's blood leaving him. And though my spine cracks, aches, screams, I ignore it, because I love him, too. The brother I never had, as much of an idiot as he is sometimes. The best friend that's been there as Ruth and I learnt to walk, as we discovered trails and horses and cows and farming together, as we went over to one another's houses and listened to old records and sang along to radios and done everything and anything together and he's just a part of my life and a part of me and now it's being cut out with a knife, with such a jagged cut left that it'll never be filled completely.

And I love him, and if admitting that I love someone, in that unconditional way where no matter what they do, you can't leave them, and no matter what they say, it doesn't matter, and where it hurts to love them but hurts worse to not love them - if admitting this makes me any less of a man, then so be it.

"Don't—forget me."

He's afraid. I remove my forehead from his and I look at those eyes again. There's so little light left in them. But there's enough where he still is afraid of what's going to happen. And he doesn't know what's going to happen, or where he's going to go. And I can't imagine how it feels, though I know I'll know someday. And I know that I should be feeling it with him, but I'm not. I'm not, and I don't understand. I just understand that he's afraid, and he needs me still.

"Please. Paul. Don't. Don't—forget me. Don't let— Ruth."

I shake my head again. "Daniel. No one's going to forget you. Ever." I don't bother with telling him because you're going to live.

"Pro—mise me." His weak fingers come to the front of my undershirt and clasp at it. "Promis—"

"We're *not* going to forget you," I tell him, and another sob emerges, and I don't care about stifling it. "I won't. Ruth won't. I *promise*. You're a part of us, Daniel. You'll never leave."

But the last sentence doesn't reach his ears. Because the rest of what I have said is enough. And he relaxes, fully, into my lap, and that hand which clasps at me falls away from my shirt, slips down my chest and goes limp, and his eyes, they dim, and they blacken in a way and stare and from both eyes now his last tears fall, and I don't bother to wipe them away because it doesn't matter anymore.

"No." The word. It's there.

"No." … *"No."*

"Please don't leave."

"Oh, **God**, please don't leave."

I'm not screaming in pain as I expect; all of this comes out in a high, broken pitch, and my mouth and face crumple as I lean to his forehead, which grows colder in each passing second, and there is nothing beautiful about Death, not in the least.

My lips are feverish, beyond hot, compared to the temperature of his flesh. But I rest them there either way because it doesn't matter anymore.

"Please don't leave me."

You never realise how much you need someone until they're gone. You think you know. You think you understand. But until their absence is prolonged, stretched, until their absence is something that makes you twist and ache, until you realise that there is a permanence in their departure, that you'll never see them again, you don't know. And he's no different. And his name causes too much pain for me to say, and I don't know how long I sit there, rocking back and forth with what remains of him in my lap, struggling with the sobs, uncertain how to handle the emotions that overwhelm me expect to expound them, and he's the first and last person that will see me cry. That will hear me weep so openly.

"Please don't leave me."

I'm sure if he had any choice in the matter, he wouldn't have left. But it was too late. Because he already was gone.

I have to get help. I might not have the abilities to revive him, but there are people who can bring someone back. Right? I just have to hurry. I have to hurry. I have to run as fast as I can and I just, I stumble. I stumble and I sprint and I fling the tears out of my eyes and I pump my arms and I don't know how long it takes me to run, I just know that I have to run, and if I slow down, then I am going to fail, and if I fail in this, then everything in which I have ever succeeded will be for not, because this is the one place where I cannot afford to fail.

I should have made him stay in the truck. I should have put off the phone call. I should have stayed asleep. We shouldn't have gone out at all. We shouldn't have gone into the woods. We should've left the woods earlier. All of the should haves and the shouldn't haves fill my brain, overflow the edges, sting into the open wounds like saltwater. I run up the hill beside the driveway and all I can think about are the mistakes that were made, the things that could have been done in order to prevent any of this from happening, and the sky darkens rapidly and there's a peal of thunder, and the rain would wash the blood away but it wouldn't wash it away completely, because blood stays with you, remember? Blood stays with you and permeates your skin and brands you with that person's personality and memories and everything that made them what you know of them and what you didn't know.

I leave muddied, bloodied tracks on the concrete pad. My footsteps slow as I near the front door. The harrowing heartbeat echoes throughout my chest. The porch seems a thousand times larger than it is. My vision is blurred. My heart. My head. It all hurts. I swim through nothingness. The blackness starts to curdle, and I cling to my scalp, and mat my hair with Daniel's blood, and somehow, I continue to walk, though my feet want nothing more than to curl up underneath me. And I hear David across the street in the house opening and shutting the door, and he yells something indistinguishable and I know that he's coming but I can't tell him yet, even though I know he's going to follow me up the driveway and he's going to call out to me again and I am deafened by the roar of blood to the head, and blood on the head, and I am stained and I am matted and I am torn but not dead.

I push open the front door. A foreign car had been in the driveway. Ruth was home. There she is now. I stand there and I look down at the blood on my hands and I tremble and I don't know what to think. I think she's asking me something. I know she's staring at me incredulously. And I can hear David, and his deep, lumbering breaths, coming up the sidewalk, following after me, and he rounds the corner to the front door which is wide open, and the cat hisses at the sight of me and darts away, and I don't know what order this is happening in, but then Ruth touches me.

She touches me.

And I grab her. I'm alive again. Just for a moment. I'm not numb. The pain is too great. She tears herself away from me; I see her face, but it doesn't register, and I stare off into space again and my mouth quivers and there are more questions.

And all I manage to do is give them a name, no verb, no status. A name and a point, I think, and that's that. And I find myself swirling down the drain into a cesspit that I can't escape. And Ruth screams and it's like Daniel's screams but I'm deafened—

And I feel no more.

Part Three:

In Which We Crawl from Ashes

One Frayed Thread Only

October 13th
Sunman, Indiana

Aiden Kinsey

It's been a long-ass trip.

It's been Clunker's turn to drive, and besides me occasionally giving him directions, a quick *"Turn here"* or a *"Go straight"* or whatever else is relevant at the time, the car has been quiet. The van, actually. Considering we accidentally hijacked that nice lady's van. (Remember Kathleen? The one who gave us the sandwiches and the drinks? Yeah.)

Out of all the cars on that cliff we could've stolen, we just *had* to steal hers. And her dog. — And her money.

We'd found her cell phone number written on a slip of paper inside of the glove compartment, though, and we'd stopped briefly at a gas station, to fill up the tank, and since all of our cellphones had been lost in the ocean, I'd gotten out of the car, with the slip of paper in hand, and used some loose change from the cup-holders to dial the number on a public telephone.

"I knew you were supposed to take the van," she said to me when she answered after the second ring, after I had sputtered out a couple of apologies. "There are absolutely *no* coincidences, Aiden. None. Nada. *Zilch.* God brought me there for a purpose, and I fulfilled it. Besides, it wasn't too hard to call my husband to come pick me up. No worries, honey. You just take care of yourselves, okay?"

Okay. (Weird.)

I'd hung up feeling disoriented and dazed. But also relieved that she wasn't angry at us for doing it. We hadn't done it on purpose. (The first hijacking *ever* that we hadn't done on purpose. Well, okay, I mean, we'd stolen the thing on purpose, but not *hers*.)

Then we'd piled back into the van, and Clunker had taken over driving. I'm sprawled in the front seat, shoes off and feet up on the dashboard. Asher sits behind the driver's seat, head leaning against the window, mouth half-open as he snores softly. Gearteeth has his arm around Jam, and they're both conked out as well.

And Cheyenne hasn't emerged from the back area. She's been there the whole time. Hasn't accepted a drink. Hasn't accepted an offering of food. Hasn't accepted my attempts at conversation when it was my turn to sit in the back seat. Three whole days of driving with very small breaks at rest stops and two-hour cat naps. Traffic has been backed up. And she's been unresponsive. All she does is look at me, with those haunted, electric-blue eyes and a perpetual dampness to her, as though the ocean would never leave her, and cling to the fur of the fluffy dog next to her, who has, seemingly, become quite taken with her. She says nothing when we let the dog out to go to the bathroom. She feeds it handfuls of puppy chow from a small bag that was left behind, and taps Gearteeth on the shoulder and points toward one of the water bottles whenever she feels as though the puppy is thirsty. I think she's named it. But I can't be sure. Because she isn't talking.

And I don't know what to do. I'm at such a loss. A *complete loss*. I'm in shock. (Everyone is in shock.) None of us can believe any of this even happened. And the stupid thing is: it's everywhere. It's on every single stupid news channel, and yet when we go into gas stations or grocery stores or stop too long at stoplights, and people look at us, they don't see survivors; they see a ragtag group of ratchet-ass of people or some shit (stereotypes are dumb.) Stupid. Only *we* know the truth. Only we will ever know the truth.

I just know that once we get to our grandparents' house, everything's going to turn out *fine*. We just have to — you know, *get there*. And Clunker's decided to poke-ass along.

"Dude, can't you hurry up?" I rag on Clunker.

"Can't. I think there's a funeral."

He points to the line of traffic in front of us, blocking most of the road. The hearse is parked next to a familiar white church.

"Wait a second. I know this church."

I know the cemetery across from it as well.

"Is there any way around this?" Clunker looks at me, waiting.

"I mean, yeah, but all the side roads are blocked off by the traffic too. And there's barely any room to turn around."

"Then I guess we'll just wait for it to be over."

He pulls into grass just before the church; the stark white building is situated directly next to the road, with only a small bit of asphalt and a shoulder on the main to separate it from traffic. Putting the van into park, he rolls down all of the windows, and turns off the ignition, shutting off the terrible nineties' music that he turns on while he drives. Whoever's in the driver's seat is in charge of the radio. And by God, I hate it when he's in charge of the radio.

"Damn. I really wanted to finish that Backstreet Boys song." Jam's sarcastic, sleepy voice floats from the backseat.

"Shut the *H E L L* up," is Clunker's cheerful response.

I close my eyes for a second, planning on settling back into the seat and sleeping for the remainder of the funeral, however long that would be. I'm about to tell the others to do the same; we might as well grab some well-deserved rest while we were granted the opportunity. But with the windows down, despite the hundred-foot (at least) distance from where we sit and where the pastor speaks, his words float towards me, preventing me from conking out like I want.

"Through the tender mercy of our God: whereby the day-spring from on high hath visited us; to give light to them that sit in darkness, and in the shadow of death: and to guide our feet into the way of peace."

The concluding rites, I guess (never been to funeral), are followed by the gentle thudding echo of a book shutting.

"David - would you like to say a few words in closing?"

David. My eyes flutter back open. *David*. That's — wait a second, that's my grandfather's first name. I sit back up in the seat, straining over Clunker, who groans as I crawl across him to peer through the open driver's side window. Many people have attended this funeral, more than likely the entire populations of the local small towns. Despite the thickness of the crowd and their swaths of black, I manage to make out three distinct figures.

"They're *here*."

I furrow my eyebrows, pointing at the elderly man, who grasps a sheet of paper in one hand and steps forward; his wife, who has a shock of grey curled hair atop her head; and their daughter, twelve years old, hair still platinum blonde, sniffling as she rubs her nose and the corners of her eyes raw.

"Shit." Clunker takes in the sight himself. The recognition has attracted the attention of the other residents in the van. Asher and Jam shake the sleep from their eyes, sliding over to the left side, and Gearteeth finds himself squashed underneath Jam as we all stare out the window, openly gawking at the funeral-goers. "Who's funeral is it?"

"I have no idea. They're the sorts of people who'll attend strangers' funerals. Just to make sure *someone's* there."

Despite the little quip, something doesn't sit well with me.

And my grandfather's speaking so softly, I can't hear what he's saying or who he's giving a speech about. It *can't* be a complete stranger — not if he's reciting something to the onlookers, powerful words which elicit a strong reaction, a wave of nods, a collective sighing of breaths.

"—I'm gonna take a closer look."

"You want us to come with you?"

I look at Gearteeth, who asked the question, and then at the rest of the guys, even Asher, who looks very serious at the concept of having to approach funeral grounds.

"Nah, I'll be fine. Just keep an eye on Cheyenne and that dog."

I extract myself from Clunker's lap, unlatching and kicking open the passenger's side door. Once my feet hit the grass, it's all I can do to keep my sound of relief as quiet as possible; as it were, I do stretch my arms high above my head, grunting a little as each aching muscle and cramped bone pops back into place. (Standing up has *never* felt so good to me.) The clothes Kathleen gave me are beyond wrinkled, and I smell like a combination of sweat, sea water, whatever detergent she uses, sunlight, and the worn cloth of the van's seats. It's a weird smell, one I'm not accustomed to wearing. But even as I stretch my shoulders once more, cracking them, rolling them as I make my way towards the cemetery, I still feel better than I have in years.

In *ten* years, to be exact. I know it's a little ironic that I'll be reunited with this part of my family at a funeral, but — stranger things have happened, I'm sure. (Like part of the West Coast collapsing into the ocean. That's pretty weird, too.)

I see one cousin, but not the other—

Wait.

One cousin and not the other? He always gets drug along to these sorts of things.

But I forget, momentarily, the strangeness of it. Because then, when someone else moves forward in the crowd — I see her.

The same *her* who coached me through the nightmare of reality.

The same *her* who appeared to me in the last dream segment.

The same *her* who had made me feel very alive - and very dead.   # Wait.

She is the *her* — but she isn't. Not even close. Her hair's different. She's taller. She's dressed in black, and she never wears black. Even to the saddest occasions, she'd be caught in something like a deep floral or maybe a dark green. She wears makeup now. She stands there, and she stares down at something in her hands. Her face - it's somber. Her body language - it tattles she's fragile. There are shadows on her face, poorly concealed by makeup; bags underneath her eyes, which can't look up as Grandpa speaks; shoulders curled forward, as though someone's broken her. As though she's been beaten and cowed.

This isn't the *her* I know. And it stops me dead in my tracks, right behind the majority of the crowd, staring at her over the shoulder of a man I'll never meet.

The realisation hits me head-on, as though I've returned to the messy highway, as though I'm slamming on the brakes to avoid the oncoming, immoveable wall of cars. But instead of making it, I become one of the metal corpses, gnashed and torn and busted open. I feel the strength of the impact roiling against me, pushing at the emotions I had just opened myself up to accepting, pushing them

down

down

down. (Remind me to never dream again.)

Two Unravelling Tapestries
October 13th
Sunman, Indiana

Cheyenne Kinsey

Everyone's staring out the windows, and no matter how strong the temptation is to join them, I refuse. I heard the word *David* be confirmed as my grandfather. I recognised Aiden needing to satiate his undying curiosity to see what was going on. (To *take a closer look.*) The car's stopped, and everyone's staring, and I just — I just don't stare.

I don't want to look, not with this terrible feeling roiling in my gut. I feel like I know already what I'm going to see. I feel like I know what's waiting for Aiden even as he exits the van, pauses to stretch out his arms and shoulders, then takes off towards the cemetery at a brisk walk. That's the only time I raise my head, press my nose against the glass — to follow his retreating form, muscles roiling as he continues extending them out delicately, like a stretching cat.

Then I sink back down. I knot my hands into the fur at the scruff of the dog's neck. I'm sickened. Not just with this entourage of familiar scenery, with the realisation that we really *are* here (and that I haven't been enduring a terrible nightmare for all this time).

But because of E V E R Y T H I N G.

I'm perpetually wet. I'm ruined. I still feel the sea on my skin, as though it's seeped down into all of the razor cuts and remains there, boiling, churning, submerging me. I've named the dog *Cherie* because it means "d e a r" and it's the only French word I know, and that singular French word is beautiful, *so* beautiful, *much* more beautiful than *I'll* ever be. I don't want to answer questions and I definitely don't want to try and make conversation. In fact, I don't want to do *or* say much of anything. There's nothing to do, and I have nothing to say.

Someone died in my arms. Millions of other people are dead before their time. (Unless we're talking to Kathleen; then she might try to make the argument of all those people being *meant* to die.) And then Gearteeth almost drowned. (We all almost did.) But I rescued him, which I still can't wrap my head around. I dove into the ocean, I found him in the current, I pulled him out, I pulled the water from him, I stopped him from drowning. But if I try to explain the logistics, no one will believe me. It's better to be passed off. Passed off as a **M I R A C L E**.

Whatever. As long as I'm left alone back here, left to mull things over in silence, they can say whatever they want.

I wonder, briefly, if that means *she's* here. You know, the girl he's been pining after. The girl behind the true reason for him deciding to come back here instead of taking us to start a new life in Georgia or something. The same one who never responded to any of his letters. (You think I didn't know about that?) She can go to hell for breaking his heart and never writing back. Even just like a three-sentence response would've been better than that perpetual, aching silence. The one we Kinseys seem cursed to receive, whether it's from our parents, our relatives, our friends — or those who we *thought* were friends.

Asher takes advantage of Aiden's absence and turns in his seat, watching me momentarily as I continue stroking Cherie's ear, putting her back into a sleepy stupour. I'm still unsure about whether I regret my decision to bring him along or not. (Translation: Should I ever have even started talking to this guy? I met him outside of a nightclub. I should've just kept walking.) Besides, he could've stayed back in Arizona once all of the turmoil had settled down. He could've stayed behind and probably put himself to better use than *babysitting* me. Why's he still sticking around? Does he feel *obligated* to since he saved me from getting shot by that other son of a bitch?

Either way — I hope he's suffering. I hope he's being torn to bits inside because of what he did at the base.

"Cheyenne."

I don't respond. It's better that way.

"Cheyenne, just — at least *look* at me."

(—)

After a moment's hesitation, I follow through with that much. I do look. But I don't look at him. I look *through* him. As though he isn't even there. (Right now, to me, he isn't. No one really is.) We're all ghosts wandering about in this endless purgatory, waiting for Death and his scythe to decapitate us and be done. Just get it over with. We're not even supposed to be alive. We shouldn't have survived all that. So why are we? *Why are we still alive?*

Asher gives up, sighing heavily and turning back to face the front, getting comfortable again. Cherie whines a little, tail wagging back and forth so voraciously, her hind end moves with it. She needs to go outside (and so do I, because I'm suffocating.) I think this to the other passengers in the van and hope they hear me. She needs to go outside and I'm going to be the one to take her. Don't follow.

(Do not follow)

I unlatch the rear door and lift it high into the air. Asher stirs, about to get out, but someone must stop him (do not follow) because I find that even after the minute or so that it takes for me to crawl out, I'm still void of human company joining me. Overwhelmed when I'm graced by the afternoon air and the crispness of autumn, the season when everything dies and makes all seem beautifully desolate. Someone else calls after me, but that's the extent of the attempts to attract my attention. I let Cherie hop out of the back before I start cooing at her, and it's the only time I've bothered to open my mouth for this entire trip. Once she squats, an insuperable pride fill me. She's a fast learner. An adaptable dog. We'll keep getting along well, I think.

Then, I hear something very strange.

"As we lay DANIEL STAMP into his final resting place."

DANIEL STAMP.

But DANIEL STAMP is my *cousin.*

(He's technically my uncle.

Actually, we're technically not even related.)

But he shouldn't be *final-resting* anywhere. He's just a lazy son of a bitch; at least, he was the last time I saw him a decade ago. He's more than likely at home, *resting* there.

What the hell are these people talking about?

Aiden's stopped dead in his tracks. I can see him from here. He has his hands clasped at the back of his head and - *she's* there, and that's who he's staring at. He's staring at *her.* But no one has noticed him. No one has glanced up and seen this strange creature from the underworld observing the happenings.

THUNK.

THUNK.

THUNK.

THUNK.

They're shovelling dirt down into an opening. But it can't be Daniel. It can't be DANIEL STAMP who's being lowered into his *final resting place.* As if; this is all some sort of massive joke. A prank being played on us. He can't be — dead. He can't be *dead.* We've driven two thousand miles for this family. We've braved hell and high water for this family. We came all the way out here for them.

He can't be

he simply isn't

DEAD—

I need to get a closer look.

As I think this, my heart lurches, and I cling to my chest as though it has stopped, completely, fully, and I am sent to the ground, and Cherie licks at my hand, and it's hard to breathe (I can't breathe.) Because what if this isn't a prank? What if it's — *true?*

I can't help myself. I jump up and sprint across the road, Cherie following after. (do not follow) So many people have attended this graveside burial, absolutely no traffic's even trying to push through. Except for us in our dilapidated van. My mouth goes dry. My hands - they tremble. I reach Aiden much more quickly than I anticipated, passing through iron gates halfway overturned. I stand beside him, and look up at him, and his face whitens, eyes flitting from person to person.

I join in the gawking. I see David, who steps back, paper in his hand, jaw working as he clenches and unclenches it. I see Marlene, who exhales a trembling breath, whose hand darts to her eyes. I see Penny, who openly weeps, who stuffs a fist against her mouth, who can't watch as soil is thrown into the gaping wound of a grave. I see them all crying; I see the crowd, upset in their grief, hands accompanied by wrinkled handkerchiefs, scattered sighs and sniffling. I see *him,* the guy I never thought I would see again, and something fills me that I can't understand, and it's relief, and hatred, and understanding — because there he is, but he isn't *there,* he's gone elsewhere, different, (changed.)

Through all these unknowns and knowns, one stark individual remains missing.

D A N I E L S T A M P.

(Laid into his final resting place)

D A N I E L S T A M P.

(beloved son, dearest friend)

Different.

Changed.

(Gone.)

So is, apparently, everything I grew up knowing.

Everything that I thought would be here

W A I T I N G   for me.

This is what I get for letting myself hope.

This is what I get.

Three Stories Ending Here

October 13th

Sunman, Indiana

Ruth Reagan

I hold a rose in the palm of my hand. A rose, blackening at the edges, water forsaken from its stem for over twenty-four hours. A sickly-sweet odour emits from the centre; not the gentle of the freshness, but the pungency of decay. This rose — it's nowhere as alive as it should be. But — that's all right.

(It isn't. But if I say it enough to myself,

Maybe it'll be all right eventually.)

The flower matches all other things which surround me: the burial mounds with their dilapidated bones, their jars of ash stored within wooden, elongated hexagons, cherry and mahogany, oak and ash. The headstones with their brief inscriptions of a life we, the living, will never fully grasp. The army of the passed.

D A N I E L S T A M P has gone to join their ranks.

This shouldn't have happened. This reality — it's far too cloying of a grip. I can't escape into dreams with colourful words. No colour can be found in this world of grey.

I went into his bedroom.

I sat on his bed.

I looked at the clothes still strewn on the floor.

I took the sweatshirt laying beside me from its place where he had thrown it two days prior.

I picked it up.

I wadded it between my fingers.

I pressed it against my nose and I smelled him.

I smelled it — and he was alive.

553

And by God — I cried. I cried as though I'd never cry again.

Yet I did cry. (feel)

Again — and again — and again —

And I cry now. Shamelessly. Without ceasing. But not even my pain of loss can compare to the pain of being a witness.

Paul stands next to me, a copper sentinel who watches all. He saw him die. (Paul saw Daniel die.) He was covered in the crimson life blood which had spilled from split veins (the same veins in the same wrists which had pressed themselves against my face hours earlier). He'd been screaming incoherently, brief words manifesting to give rise to the situation. Roaring, guttural cries from his stomach.

HES DEAD THEYVE KILLED HIM

I TRIED TO STOP IT DAVID

WHERE ARE YOU? DANIEL?

THEYVE KILLED HIM HES DEAD HES DEAD HES DEAD THEY KILLED HIM HES DEAD HES DEAD

GOD WHY WHY GOD NO GOD WHY

David sprinted out from the house across the street.

WHAT IN GODS NAME ARE YOU YELLING ABOUT PAUL REAGAN YOU TELL ME WHAT HAPPENED RIGHT NOW WHAT THE HELL IS GOING ON OUT HERE

Paul responded and pulled at him in the middle of the road. (The screaming had started after he had seen me in the foyer. We were screaming together. I clung to him. I had no one else.)

DANIELS DEAD HES DEAD HES DEAD HES DEAD THEYVE KILLED HIM I COULDNT STOP IT

Together, they went into the forest, and Julia, roused from the chaos, came to me, put her hand on my shoulder (as it was now.) Pulled me in. Face white with shock and her own internalised pain. She hadn't really known him. But she knew I did. She let me scream. Curled up on the floor. She let me (feel) she let me (die) she let me (scream).

The damage, the coroners told us, was far too great for an open casket ceremony. This was of no problem to any of us. That was the last thing we wanted to see. The — indescribable remnants. The plastic of the face. The pure white of the skin. The ghostliness of the eyes. The lack of - all things. The lack of sensation. Forever trapped beneath the glass. No, his mahogany lid had been placed even before visitation. He had been surrounded by photographs and flower wreaths and a collection of his favourite CDs. Things that forced us to remember him as he was supposed to be: alive.

Pastor Drew begins the closing rites after David finishes his speech, a short and too final of a goodbye to his only son. He'd lost his daughter Laura first; and now, his son. And I stare at the wood of the coffin as Pastor Drew holds his hand above it, to bless it, and there it is, the potency of the ache, the grip enclosed around the organ, twisting and tearing and pulling me down. Anything wood —

It reminds me of his love of carving. God, it hurts me. It hurts me more than I can ever hope to put in the words. And I feel so guilty.

Julia had tried to stop me from feeling the potent G U I L T, but it had stretched around my shoulders and stayed, even warmer to feel than the human touch. It wasn't your fault, she insisted.

It wasn't your fault.

But it W A S my fault because — if I'd just answered my phone earlier, then this wouldn't have happened. If I hadn't caught a ride with Shane, this wouldn't have happened. He wouldn't have gotten mad. He wouldn't have run off into the woods. Paul wouldn't have gone after him. No damage would have been done. No lives would've been lost.

The coffin begins to lower. Inch by inch.

Tell Ruth I love her.

"He loves you."

That was all Paul had given me about the last moments. And I dared not press. I dared not beg for details. To plead for such things from an armoured automaton is to ask for further ruination. He knows I want to know; he knows I need the information to feel closer, to feel as though I've gained some closure. But

"h e l o v e s y o u"

is all he can give me right now.

Inch by inch.

Paul remains steely-faced. (I'm doing enough crying for the both of us.) Julia presses closer to my side, tall and strong despite her weakness. Marlene clings to a wad of tissues, pushing them against her nose. David weeps more openly than I do. His face, further creased and lined than before, crumples. The helplessness of doing nothing but watching. It's amplified here. Tenfold.

"No parent — should be burying their child."

I swipe at the moisture on my face, smudging my eyeliner and brushing over the concealed bruises around my eye. (he loves you) I'd wanted to try and look my best, but I'm uncertain why. No one important will be seeing me like this. He's gone. He's — (gone).

For the fate of the sons of men
and the fate of beasts is the same.
As one dies so dies the other;
indeed, they all have the same breath and
there is no advantage for man over beast,

for all is vanity.

All go to the same place.

All came from the dust, and all

return to the dust.

With Pastor's conclusion, the crowd begins to disperse. Most who chose to depart immediately were those who didn't know Daniel as we did - yet still had been touched by his presence, how short it had been, nineteen years. (nineteen years) Some teachers from school shoot me piteous, compassionate looks, both because of the loss and the poor cosmetics covering my injuries. Others in attendance include his acquaintances, those he'd played sports with, helped on homework assignments. Their grief isn't personal. (it shouldn't be)

So many offering their condolences and weeping. As though they knew him. This isn't their grief. (possessiveness) This is mine. It's *ours*. The last thing Daniel needs now is friends. (though isn't that how it works) Soon only David, Marlene, Penny, myself and my parents, and David's best friend, Dan, remain.

With this, I have the courage to step forward. I peel the petals from the dying rose and drop them, one by one, into the open mouth of the grave. Each one represents a memory that could've been made; an hour of time wasted on petty arguing; another cultivating regret.

(i run out of petals before i can bury them all)

When I glance up, little more than just the stem in my hand, I meet a pair of feral eyes. Golden and orange. Like smouldering flames.

A pair of eyes I thought I would

N E V E R

see again—

Four Walls Demolished Hence

October 13th
Sunman, Indiana

Paul Reagan

Where one thing ends, another begins.

The sky weeps. The soil turns to mud. Hate the mud. Think of the blood. Watch your sister step forward, dissect a rose, throw it into the opening that shouldn't have been made. Hesitate. Grind your heel into the dirt. Don't give a damn about the state of your shoes. Plan on burning them when you're done here. Burn the suit. Burn the woods down as well. Watch. Be satisfied.

No thought.

No energy.

I'm legitimately nothing.

She's my top priority. He would've tried to make her his, but now he isn't here.

He's nameless

I can't put a name to him

Too much too soon

Won't do it

The gashes and cuts and bruises from the scuffle throb, and throb, and throb, but I let them, because I *like* pain. I'm feeling. I'm feeling the pain and I will feel,

feel,

feel,

until I don't feel anymore.

I will not let this happen again.

I will *not* let this happen again.

I will K I L L anyone who tries to make it happen again.

Shane. My dad. My friends. I don't care who it is.

I swear to God, the reason for this death, if anyone, if anything, if any animal or human or immovable Unknown tries to take anyone else away from me, I will kill them

I will kill them

I will kill them all.

The toxic delight of this darkness and malevolence energises me. It makes me stronger than I was before. It keeps me disconnected. It keeps me from crying (screaming) again. No one else deserves to see it. I meant it. I meant it when I said it. No one else will see it. Ever.

The only time the suppression of the feelings doesn't work is when I look at David. He shouldn't be going through this. For God's sake, he shouldn't have lost both a daughter *and* a son. Prematurely. Unnecessarily. Not supposed to happen. (freak accidents)

No, this wasn't an accident

It had been on purpose

and I know because I saw it

Ruth had asked me no questions and I had given her nothing except the final words asked to be given. *He loves you.* Because what if she didn't believe me? What if I went to explain myself, what happened and all of the details coming out in a bewildered rush, and she didn't believe me? I didn't need to fail again.

I'd already failed twice. I look at the grave and I look at the state of her swollen face and I can't fail for a T H I R D time in one day. I won't be failing again. I *w o n ' t.*

Just watch me.

The sky weeps for us all. The extracted dirt compresses, turns to mud. (Think of the blood.) *Don't* think of the blood anymore because there's no blood here, and yet you can't get it out of your mind. There are memories in that blood, memories that you've shared with them, and when it runs into your fingertips, you start to remember the things you think you've forgotten, the moments that didn't seem so important but now are the things that stick out most. Don't think about the memories (but you can't help it.)

You can know a human's blood. You can make a pact, a promise, with it. It holds the secrets and the dirt that you don't share. It holds the good things and the bad. It holds the friendships, the broken hearts, the things you lost, and the things you found. When it flows onto your skin and into the small pores there, it brands you in a way that makes it not matter how much you wash with soap to remove that copper smell and that sweet tang if you accidentally get it in your mouth.

(i need to stop thinking

i need to remain disconnected
i need to not indulge in the cold prickling of the rain which reminds
me that i am not in the grave that i am alive that i have a life to live
that i need to carry on
that people need me
that i am unable to cope
that i am unable to continue on that i saw him die
i saw him i heard the shots i heard the boom the boom boom ca-
chink the boom the gun broken in two his body ripped apart
i saw the coyote he shot it they attacked him it was on purpose it
wasn't a freak accident but i cant tell anyone i just)

This facade isn't going to be able to last for much longer.

I break out in a sweat despite the rain flowing into my eyes and across my scalp. I swipe at the droplets briefly with the sleeve of the collared shirt underneath the suit jacket.

(theres no point but i have to do something cause i didnt do enough and someone died)

As much as I want this to remain like a protective barrier

around me, a mask which conceals my true features, I know it'll crack, and break, and crumble.

   We're almost completely alone. The Stamps (whats left of them) turn, preparing to depart from the gravesite. The rest of the cars have cleared out and stopped their blockage of the main road. It's over. The dirt will be filled in later. My dad straightens the lips of his coat and tucks an arm around my mother's shoulders. She's staring at the open grave, at the casket still slightly hovering above it. Just staring.

   I wonder what she's thinking
   if she's imagining one of us
   being buried instead of him.

   Julia remains next to Ruth (and at least I won't be alone in watching over her like I thought) and — it's over, it's just over.

                 (where one thing ends another begins)

   We all turn, a collective unit of grief, and we are met with an odd sight. A tall man, older than me, with feral eyes and black hair, hands clenched into fists. A girl, much shorter, who looks like him, but doesn't at all, with multi-coloured hair, a dog sitting by her side, a dog who whines the minute she stops rubbing its ears. They're staring at the grave. (they're staring at us) I know them —

         I know them
                  but I don't.
         I recognise those faces
                  but I don't.
         I can internally sense who these two are
                  but I don't want to.

                     (this is the last thing we need right now

      whats going on i swear gods playing tricks on us he thinks this is
   funny

      he just wants me to lose control never gain it back how did they
   hear

about **daniels death**

they look like death themselves who are they

i know them

i dont want to know them they hate us we hate

them

we separated our dad hates them

he still hates them

look at him look at them

this is madness)

David chokes out a "God help me."

(the guy looks a little like daniel they have the same colour eyes)

Marlene presses her wad of tissues against her mouth to hold in a sob; Penny screeches into her sleeve, halfway to despair.

The rest of us can't even speak.

(what is there to say

hey there

hows it going

what the)

T H U M P - T H U M P.

My heartbeat.

T H U M P - THUMP.

It sputters and accelerates.

THUMP-THUMP. —— THUMP-THUMP.

An echoing tribal drum.

(i have to speak over it

we are all staring

no one is going to talk

i have to do something

but what is there to say i)

T H U M P - T H U M P.

I speak over the drums of war.

"Well, *well*. — I'll be **damned**."

ACKNOWLEDGMENTS

They say it takes a village to raise a child. After this long of a haul, I believe it. It's taken an army to write this book. Seriously. My heart's all whacked out and I'm shaking and — I can't believe it. This thing has my heart, soul, pain, blood, tears, and sweat in it.

Right, here we go.

THE FAMILY:

God; You're the main reason I even made it through these past three years. I'm a hundred percent positive without your influence and guidance, I wouldn't have even obtained the courage to put this down on paper. It's been a rough road and You've seen every nook of it.

Mum; You're the second main reason I've made it through. Remember how we got this idea just randomly in the car one day? You always make sure to remind me how you knew I'd end up doing something like ever since, what, a decade ago now? You bring me gallons of sweet tea and remind me that school will come later and always have encouraged me to follow my dreams. You're the vocalisation of the encouragement I sometimes can't hear from the man upstairs. You'll be the reason I get through any of my other books, I know it.

Dad; I know you weren't on board at first, but — man, these last few weeks, and especially the frantic three days straight I did of editing, you've been rooting me on, saying you'd read it (and you aren't the sort of guy who sits down and reads a book; your leg always starts jiggling.) You approved and helped with the cover art, you work your ass off to make sure that I can even do this in the first place. I kept my promise. I'm paying back.

Grandma; You told Mum how it really is when it comes to me writing. You agreed that I'd choose the writing. You prepared her for it. You listen to us read you excerpts over the phone and you give us your valuable input. (You're eighty; you can say what you want.) You gave me the idea of the formatting, which I listened to. You approved of the synopsis on the back and the book jacket. You're one of my greatest role models *ever.*

Grandpa; You and Mum are the reasons I even have this talent for writing in the first place. I know you'll be in denial when you read this, but you have a damn talent, too. You've given me your writings and all of your detailed notes; don't think I haven't seen it. I'm going to make sure your books are written and published with justice.
I also want to acknowledge my sister, **Katie,** my brother-in-law, **Tyler,** since they both influenced some of the characters' backgrounds and attitudes. (But which characters? Find me and ask me if you really want to know.) I love you all.

I would like to mention **Lilly, Dewey, Sydney, Hershey,** and **Harley** for directly influencing the pets in this trilogy. Best cats and dog and horses ever.

THE FRIENDBASE

Julia; You are *in* this book. You were taken from this earth far too soon; you deserve to have and live out a life. This is my gift I'm giving to you. Even though you never got to read the whole thing, I sent you (your) excerpt and you heavily approved of my frequent usage of "babes" and "boo." Which, by the way, only you can still call me those things. I miss you dearly.

Erica; One of the first people I ever met in a special world where we all gather and write together. You were my first OTP and my first online friendship and a lot of my firsts. It's ended up becoming a countless number of Skype calls and unadulterated excitement. Plus you've been so supportive of this. (I still have that video you sent me one Christmas. "Go, Natlee.") Only you can ever call me by that wretched nickname. I can't ever state how much I appreciate you.

Roni; I pronounced your name like the latter part of "macaroni" because I'm kind of an idiot. But that doesn't change the fact that you're damn special to me. You get extensive thanks for spending four hours rewriting the synopsis on the back of the book and spending up *other* nights with me and constantly cheering me on with those blasted pom-poms. Without you, I wouldn't have even remotely gotten *anywhere* near finished. We still write and create magic together and you have forced me to grow so much.

Taryn; You're going to insist you haven't done anything to be put in here, but I *beg to differ*. I don't think you realise how much you HAVE done. You're partly responsible for the reason I go so deeply into characters, why I choose to make them so real (all the way down to who decorates for Christmas on November 1st and who just is the grumpy one in the corner.) You needled me about cliché language and were one of the first people to read the synopsis and critique it. Writing and talking with you has beyond improved my life. (We are, after all, on the same word.)

Vanessa; Bish. You and I legitimately don't sleep ever. I still can't remember even what made us start talking in the first place. But it doesn't matter. We have been through *so* much **** together, it isn't even funny. (and we go through similar situations at the same time; still not really over it.) You're the one constantly peppering me with questions about when it's going to be done, out, that you want a signed copy and you're going to get all you ask for and *more*. We're three years apart, have basically the same birthday. You've also inspired some character actions in here; have fun trying to figure out who and what. I love you.

-

I also need to mention all of the following for being absolutely a hundred percent supportive every step of the way. If I was to write a paragraph about each and every one of these special people, these would thunder on for ages:

Trish and **Bay** (the other two precious Halliwell sisters); **Lottie** (the legitimate twin across the pond); **Lena** (the Croatian shard of my soul); **Tati** (I found you again); **Claire** (the high school best friend and budding chef); **Alexa** (the other high school best friend who's an actual star); **Katie** (the wave of positivity); **Mark** Phillips (my IU bff); **Andrew and Koralyssa** (my best fellow English AP mates); **Jessica B.** (the fellow perfectionist); and **Olivia** (the "there it is" girl who makes me wonder why we weren't friends earlier).

THE MUSIC

I would like to give a nod to each of the following bands and composers for their music influencing scenes of this novel: **Evanescence, Falling in Reverse, My Chemical Romance, Bastille, Imagine Dragons, Taylor Swift, Saosin, 30 Seconds to Mars, Three Days Grace, Crown the Empire, Sleeping for Sirens, Pierce the Veil, Lana Del Rey, Lady Gaga, Armor for Sleep, Hans Zimmer, Natalia Kills, IAMX, Thousand Foot Krutch.**

ALL OTHERS

I would like to thank **Joan** for her input and **Alyssa** for being the first person to read through it. I would like to thank **Mrs. Pridonoff** for making me remember how to love my instrument again (I'm still playing, Mrs. P!) I would like to thank my high school teachers **Mrs. Stephens, Mrs. Whitehair,** and **Mrs. Miller** for influencing me, encouraging me, and telling me I can do anything I want to. I want to thank **Professor Miller** for influencing my writing style and the little tidbits in the text about the retrospective and the optative. (And I'm going to add: I'm very glad that your class doesn't fall into the category of: the class *not* taken. The material you taught haunts me and my characters to this day.)

I would also like to thank all of those people in my life who are no longer in it; it's situations with you that have also influenced my writing and make me a stronger person. Some I regret; others, not at all. However, I do hope you all have found some semblance of happiness and success. (If you see yourselves in certain characters in this book — well. You can always find me and ask me about it.) Last but not least - I would like to thank **myself.** Because after all this - I think I deserve it.

If you're not in this one — never fear, you might be in the next. There's a lot more to come.
xx Natalie

ABOUT THE AUTHOR

Natalie has immersed herself into the other worlds of books ever since she first was taught to read by her mother. It was only natural she eventually try her own hand at creation. She started dabbling in writing at the age of eleven, but she never thought it would go beyond short stories and random poetry. Then, at age eighteen, she began a project which would grow and expand to be her debut novel, *From Whence They Came.* Now, at the age of twenty-one, Natalie plans on graduating from Indiana University in May of 2015 and devoting her free time to doing what she loves best. Natalie also has played the piano since she was four, loves the solitude of country life, and has too many pets to count.

www.ingramcontent.com/pod-product-compliance
Lightning Source LLC
Chambersburg PA
CBHW072008020726
47501CB00006B/1729